Man Possessed

Salvatore Brotherhood MC Book Five

Haley Tyler

Photographer: Wander Aguiar

Cover Model: Drew Leighty

❀ Created with Vellum

For every Kennedy out there,
I hope you find your Kiwi.

Man Possessed Playlist

LISTEN TO THE FULL PLAYLIST HERE

You Know I'm No Good - Amy Winehouse
Nasty - Bryce Fox
Psycho Bitch - Cami Petyn
Feral Love - Chelsea Wolfe
Butterfly - Crazy Town
Coming Undone - Korn
Stupid Boys - Maddie Zahn
Bitch - Meredith Brooks
Closer - Nine Inch Nails
Psycho - Puddle of Mudd
Nobody Praying For Me - Seether
We Live in A Strange World - Spiritbox
Lonely Day - System Of A Down
Villain Mode - Witchz

Stay Connected!

Join My Newsletter!

Stay up to date on cover reveals, preorder announcements, merch drops, giveaways, ARC sign-ups, newsletters, and more!!

Join My Facebook Reader Group!

Author's Note

Hi, reader!

Thank you for picking up **Man Possessed**, book five in the **Salvatore Brotherhood MC** series. This one is all about our favorite New Zealander, Kiwi, and his take-no-shit girl, Kennedy.

I wanted to give you a heads up about these characters and their relationship dynamic.

They are toxic.

There isn't another way to say it—they're toxic. *Sometimes.*

They're two broken people coming together, and with that, things can get messy. They know what to say to hurt you and have no problem doing it.

Kiwi is unapologetically an asshole at times. He says and does things you might hate, but that's who he is. I wanted to stay true to his character and leave him as the unhinged man we all know and love.

Kennedy, while being a single mother who works two jobs and is known for being a bitch, she struggles with her self worth and identity. She will say and do things that will make you upset. Shit, some of the things she did made me upset, but again, I had to stay true to who she is.

And finally, Ian. Sweet Ian.

He's Kennedy's fifteen-year-old son and is dealing with his own struggles. You'll get his POV in this book and watch him navigate life as a teenage boy falling in love for the first time, while watching his mother fall in love with a biker—someone she told him to always stay away from.

Again. He might do things you won't agree with, and that's okay, but it's who he is.

I hope despite the slight toxicity of this couple, you can still love and enjoy this book. Their story is one of my favorites and holds a special place in my heart. I hope you love it as much as I do.

One more thing...

Man Possessed takes place at the same time as Safe House so you'll see some overlap in Kiwi and Ryder's stories.

xoxo,

Haley Tyler

Author's Note

This is a **DARK ROMANCE** and contains potentially upsetting
events.
Please read with caution.

Child abuse & neglect, physical abuse, implied assault,
LGBTQ+/coming out, degradation, some praise, spicy movie making,
bondage, knife & blood play, branding/scarification, some torture,
murder, talk of trafficking, violence, swearing, and gore.

SBMC Character Bible

Main Characters

Sebastian Salvatore aka "Bash" - SBMC President (Book, Killing Calm)

    Axel Salvatore - SBMC Vice President (Book, Little Bear)

    Reid Salvatore - SBMC Treasurer (Book, Lost and Found)

    Ryder Hutchins - Enforcer (Book, Safe House)

    Ezra King aka "Kiwi" - Road Captain (Book, Man Possessed)

    Tazman Jones aka "Taz" - Sgt. In Arms

Adelaide Amare/Salvatore aka "Addie" - Bash's wife (Book, Killing Calm)

    Takoda Beck/Salvatore aka "Koda" - Axel's wife (Book, Little Bear)

    Heather Graves-Salvatore - Reid's wife/partner (Book, Lost and Found)

Madison Hutchins aka "Madi" - Ryder's wife (Book, Safe House)

Kennedy Williams aka "Kenny or Kens" - Kiwi's partner (Book, Man Possessed)

Arden Halifax - Taz's partner

SBMC Kids

Skye Salvatore - Axel's daughter, Koda's stepdaughter

Isabella Hutchins - Ryder & Madi's adopted daughter

Ian Williams - Kennedy's son, Kiwi's stepson

SBMC Nomads

Cyrus

Gage

August

Zee

Side Characters

Mom & Pop - Madi's parents

Ginger - Slimeball & rat (& head trafficker's son)

John Oliver Charmichael - Head trafficker and biggest asshole of them all

Carter Marshal - The Horsemen President and general asshole

Jackson Mathers - The Horsemen Vice President, also general asshole

Ethan Montgomery - Trafficker

Logan Montgomery - Son of trafficker

Luka Crowe - Koda's ex-boyfriend

Berserkers MC

Spencer Halifax - BMC President
    Otis - BMC Vice President
    Blade - Enforcer and Medic
    Belfast - Tech guy
    Archer - Road Captain
    Maddox - Sgt. At Arms
    Arden Halifax - Spencer's sister
    Vanessa Gonzalez aka "Nessa" - Spencer's fianceé
    Riot - Assassin for hire

Prologue
Kiwi

Their conversation looks tense as I jog toward them. Bash and Addie are on top of each other as usual, but it's Axel and Koda I'm surprised are feet apart. Koda is mostly hidden behind the most terrifyingly gorgeous woman I've ever seen.

"Call 'em," Axel says smugly. "Wouldn't be the first time I've kicked their asses." Irritation flashes over the dark-haired beauty's face. I glance at him, my brow raised. He's not usually cocky, but right now he's the cockiest fucker I've ever seen.

"Spence is ready for us," I say, interrupting their stare-off. Her glare slides to me, and I grin. Broadly. I drop my eyes to her feet and slowly lift them, scanning her perfect, tattooed body. When I get to her scowling face, I can't help but wink at her.

There's something about intimidating women I love.

Heather, one of the most brutally beautiful women I've ever met, has my dick in a chokehold. But this woman, this too-gorgeous-for-her-own-good woman, could make me forget Heather ever fucking existed if she keeps glaring at me like this.

"Koda, you wanna come, baby?" Axel's voice is soft, softer than

1

I've ever heard. He doesn't even talk to his seven-year-old daughter that softly, and no one seems to care or even notice.

I'll admit, I think it's fucking annoying. But a part of me—a teensy, tiny, itty-bitty part I'll never admit to anyone—is jealous he has someone to take care of like that.

I wink at the tattooed babe before turning and strolling back to Taz and Ryder. It's probably best I get away from her before I do something stupid—like bend her over the closest table and fuck her stupid.

"Who the fuck is that girl?" I throw my thumb over my shoulder, and Taz's gaze follows. He gives me a wary look before glancing at Ryder.

"Kennedy," he says slowly. "She's been a bartender here forever. You've never met her?" I shake my head, shrugging slightly before I look over my shoulder. She reluctantly lets Koda go, and if looks could kill, Axel would be a pile of ash. "Oh shit. I know that look." I snap my head back to Taz, finding him pointing an accusatory finger at me.

"What?"

"Fuck," Ryder groans. "Leave the poor woman alone, Kiwi."

"I haven't done anything," I say, throwing my hands up. "Both of you can fuck right off." Ry scrubs his hand over his face.

"This won't end well," he says, and Taz nods in agreement. "You remember what happened with—"

"That was a one time thing," I snap.

"You always go way off the deep end when you get that look in your eye," he says. Rolling my eyes, I look over my shoulder again. Axel and Kennedy are in a hushed argument, Koda, Bash, and Addie nowhere to be seen.

"I'm gonna talk to her," I say.

"Don't do it, man," Taz says. "Please don't fuckin' do it. You don't need another restraining order." My hands tighten into fists at my sides, and it takes all I have not to punch him.

"Get one restraining order and suddenly everyone thinks I'm a fucking psycho," I mutter. "Worry about yourself, hey?" I jerk my chin at him and his jaw flexes. "I won't go crazy. You both can relax. I just wanna say hi. Fuck."

"Yeah, right," Taz snorts. "We don't have time. The meeting is about to start."

"Spence isn't my Prez," I say. "I'll be there when I get there." I look back at Kennedy again. Axel is gone, and she's behind the bar wiping down glasses. I can't take my eyes off her—the way she moves, the deep crease between her dark brows, the frown on her full lips.

Fuck.

What a woman.

Taz claps me on the shoulder as he passes, giving me a long look.

"Be careful, man. Pretty sure she's stabbed a guy for feelin' her up." My dick jerks to attention at that and I grin at him. "You crazy motherfucker." He shakes his head, huffing out a laugh. He and Ryder pass without another word or backward glance and disappear down the hall toward Spencer's office.

I don't give myself a chance to second guess myself. Whether this is a good idea, I don't know or care.

I stalk across the room, and our eyes clash. Her dark, arched brow rises higher as she narrows her eyes. I smirk as I lean on the bar, resting my forearms against it.

"Hey, love."

"Don't call me that," she snarls.

Fucking hell. I think I've found the love of my life.

Setting the glass down, she rests her hands on the bar and leans forward, bringing her face closer to mine. I get a soft whiff of her perfume, and the sweet and spicy scent imbeds itself in my soul.

"Get the fuck away from my bar."

"Is that any way to talk to a paying customer?" I ask tauntingly. Her lips curl away from her teeth.

"What do you want?" She scans the room behind me, but it's mostly empty except for a few of the Berserkers Old-Timers and the

3

bouncer. Finally, her gaze meets mine again, and I run my lip through my teeth.

Tattoos cover her arms and chest, flowing up her neck and stopping under her jaw. Her black hair is pin-straight down her back, but it's her fiery eyes that have me falling.

"You're beautiful," I breathe. She rolls her eyes as she straightens, folding her arms over her chest.

"Not interested." She eyes me like I'm worthless, but it only turns me on more.

"Didn't ask if you were interested, did I, love? Just said you're beautiful." She runs her tongue along her top teeth, then tenses her jaw.

"What do you want?" She huffs out an irritated breath. "Don't you have a meeting to get to?" I shrug and lean my whole body against the bar, bringing us closer.

"I'd rather talk to you."

"I'd rather you didn't." My smirk broadens until my teeth flash. She twists her lips to the side as she shifts, her eyes scanning the room again.

She can't meet my gaze, and if I was a betting man, which I usually am, I'd say she thinks I'm as hot as I think she is.

"You wanna get out of here when I'm done with this?" I ask, jerking my head toward the hallway. She lets out a bark of humorless laughter.

"Not if you were the last man on the fucking planet."

"You wound me, babe."

"Good." I throw my head back and laugh. This tough bitch act she has going is making my dick harder than a diamond and is solidifying that she's my fucking soulmate. Yeah, some might say it's too soon to know, but I know. I knew the second our eyes met that this woman was mine.

"I'm Kiwi," I say, and she scrunches her face, giving me a what the fuck look.

"You're named after a fruit?" she scoffs. "Why?" I gesture to myself.

"The accent doesn't give it away?" She tilts her head to the side, letting her hair spill over her shoulder. "New Zealand, love." She nods in understanding and taps her fingers against her arm.

"Right, well, as interesting as that is, Kiwi, I'd like you to fuck off now, 'kay?"

"You know," I say as I push myself up. "I like you, Kennedy." She stiffens, her face dropping all humor.

"How do you know—"

"Oh, I know everything," I whisper. I wink at her as I step away from the bar, tapping my knuckles against it. "Remember that, love."

"Stop calling me that," she growls.

"Nah." I walk backward, away from her, toward the hallway. Our gaze never drops. She stares at me the entire way, and I smile at her. "Don't think I will." Before I disappear, I throw a quick, "Love," out, just because I like the way she looks when she wants to kill me.

Kennedy
Two and a Half Months Later

I run my fingers through Ian's soft black hair. There isn't a lot of his father in him, which I'm thankful for. He's all me, all the way.

"It's time to get up, bud."

"Five more minutes," he grumbles, pressing his face into the pillow.

"You said that twenty minutes ago," I laugh. "Come on. I made breakfast. Waffles, your favorite. The bus will be here soon."

"Not hungry."

"How late did you stay up?" I ask, nudging him. He huffs out a breath and barely scoots over enough for me to lie down beside him.

He's big for fifteen, already six feet and pushing it. Between his father and me, he's going to be huge. It's one thing he can thank him for, I suppose.

"Ian." I jab my finger into his ribs, making him growl before turning his head away and slamming it back down on the pillow.

Yep.

He definitely got my temper.

"I don't know," he groans. "Please, Mom. Please. I'm begging you. Just let me sleep."

"You need to eat something," I say, and he groans again. "Fine. Five minutes, then I'm getting the ice."

He probably wants me to get up and leave him alone, but I don't. We don't see each other much right now, not with me working at the café during the day and the bar at night, and him working at the supermarket on the weekends. We're just too busy. Our mornings are our only time together, so I cherish them.

Sometimes I crawl into bed with him when I get home from the bar, just like I did when he was a kid so I can be close to him for a while. Now that he's older he doesn't love waking up with me beside him. Which I understand. It doesn't mean I'll stop doing it, though.

He is my entire world. He owns my heart and soul, so if I want to sleep next to him for a few hours, I'll do it. He'll understand if he ever has a kid one day.

Or he won't and he'll still think I'm a fucking weirdo.

Ian shifts his head back toward me, his thick dark brows bunched tightly together. I lightly trace my fingertips over his lips and smile to myself when he makes the face he did as a baby. He scrunches his face tightly together, pressing his lips out before relaxing with a soft sigh.

I could do this all day, just stare at him. He's fucking amazing. He doesn't do stupid shit like I did at his age. We hardly fight. He's respectful and responsible and turning into a good man. He's every-thing a mother could ask for and more.

"Okay, bud. Time to get up." I hate waking him up, but it's getting late. "I'll pack your breakfast to-go. You think Enzo wants some, too?" I slide out of bed and press a kiss to his forehead.

"Probably," he groans as he rolls onto his back. Cracking one eye open, he glares at me. "Why can't I just do online classes?"

"You need to socialize," I sigh. Not that he actually socializes while he's at school. He hangs out with Enzo, but that's it.

"I hate socializing." He throws his arm over his eyes as he huffs out a breath. "I really hate school, Mom."

"I know," I breathe, my stomach twisting with guilt.

I was always outgoing when I was his age. I had a lot of friends—until I got pregnant—and always wanted to go out and do things. But he's content reading a book, or playing his video games, or watching TV. He has no interest in hanging out with anyone other than his online friends and, again, Enzo.

Which is fine, but I want him to touch some grass every once in a while too.

"The school year is almost over," I say. "We can figure something out this summer. Maybe we can find a new school or something." He pulls his arm away to stare up at me.

"Really?" I chew my lip and shrug.

"Sure." I back toward the door. "You won't miss Enzo?" He groans as he pushes himself up and sits on the edge of his bed.

"Yeah, about that," he says as he rubs his hands over his face. "He's having a hard time with his dad again." I rest my forehead against the doorframe. "Can he stay here for a while again?"

"You know he can," I say. "I'll borrow one of the guy's cars and we'll go pick his stuff up this afternoon." He shakes his head as I speak and pushes to his feet, stretching his arms above his head and resting his hands flat against the ceiling.

"Nah," he yawns. "I'll tell him to take his shit to school."

"Ian," I groan. "He can't take his stuff to school. The kids will make fun of him." He shrugs and I roll my eyes.

"It'll be easier," he says, then his face grows serious. Too serious for a fifteen-year-old. "I don't want you near his dad." I snort.

"You know, it's supposed to be me protecting you, right?" He shrugs as he grabs a pair of jeans from the floor.

"We protect each other." I shake my head.

"That's not how it works, bud."

"It's safer for everyone if we don't have to go to his place," he says as he stands at his full height. He grabs his phone and taps out a quick text, probably to Enzo, then tosses it on his bed. "Thanks for letting him stay."

I shrug like it's not a big deal, but it is. I can barely afford to feed Ian, I don't know how I'll feed his friend, too. Not to mention our apartment is way too fucking small to have two teenage boys living in it.

Last time Enzo just camped out on the couch, which worked fine until it came to sharing a bathroom with them. Disgusting doesn't cut it. And I will lose my shit if I come home and find him with a girl again.

Okay, I lost my shit that time, too. But I'll really fucking lose it this time.

"No girls," I say, giving him a hard look. Ian had a girlfriend about a year ago, but otherwise he hasn't shown much interest in anyone. So, I really only have to worry about girls being here when Enzo is. I love that kid like he's my own, but sometimes I want to fucking throttle him.

"I know," he says as he slides a shirt on. "He thought you were gonna cut his dick off last time." I squeeze my eyes shut as he laughs.

"Can you maybe not talk about your friend's dick with your mom?" He smiles as he sprays way too much cologne over his body. "Does he want lunch too?" He gives me an apologetic look, but I just nod and turn down the hall. "Hurry or you'll be late!"

I ROUGHLY YANK my hair into a messy bun as I stalk out of the café. It was a shitty day. I hired a couple of new girls to take Addie and Koda's places while they're out—which will likely be forever since I doubt they're ever coming back.

The new girls are fucking morons.

There hasn't been an order they haven't fucked up, and guess who gets bitched at by customers? Not them. I spent most of the day

Man Possessed

getting yelled at by people for my barista's using the wrong fucking milk.

I down the rest of my triple espresso and try to force myself to calm down. I can't have an anger-hazed head when I go to the bar tonight. I need to prove to Spencer he can trust me to look over it while he's in LA with Taz. If I go in pissed off, I'll rip everyone's heads off—which is the worst way to show he can trust me.

It's nearly four in the afternoon and I start my shift at ten but need to get there at least an hour early. I might be able to squeeze in a nap when I get home, but I really need to get groceries and take a shower. And if Enzo is there, I need to lay down the rules for him again.

Just thinking about everything makes me even more exhausted.

A loud rumble breaks through the street, and I glance over my shoulder. A blond-haired asshole with a shit-eating grin is heading straight for me.

Fucking Kiwi.

I swear to God I'm going to kill him.

"Hey, love," he says when he stops beside me, his booted feet landing roughly on the asphalt.

"What the fuck are you doing here?" I snap, whirling toward him.

"You're such a sweet and gentle soul. Anyone ever tell you that?" That stupid grin never leaves his stupid face. I grind my teeth together as I fold my arms over my chest. His eyes drop to my tits, and I let out a hard breath. "I'm Spencer's messenger boy." He reluctantly tears his eyes from my cleavage.

"Well," I say, waving my hand at him. "I have shit to do, Kiwi. Come on."

"He said he needs you to come in at seven so Nessa can show you some shit." I groan and drop my head back.

"Fuck," I breathe, squeezing my eyes shut. "Anything else?"

"Yeah," he says, and I lift my head enough to glare at him. "He said to be nice to me. Maybe give me a kiss or two—" I throw my empty cup at him, and he easily catches it. Asshole. "You have a ride?"

"I'm fine." I start walking again, and he walks his bike beside me, his hands resting casually on the handlebars.

"Hop on, love. I'll give you a ride." I glare at him from the corner of my eye.

"Don't call me that."

"Why?"

"I don't like it." He shrugs.

"What would you rather me call you? My Queen?"

"Kiwi," I groan, stopping again. "I'm tired and want to sleep before my shift." I glance at my watch again. "Shit." I won't have time to get groceries.

"What?" I look at him but keep my mouth shut. I don't have a car, so I usually walk or take the bus. Or sometimes one of the guys will let me borrow their car if I really need it.

I stare at him, my bottom lip between my teeth.

"Kens, babe. Hop on."

If I accept this ride from him, he's going to look too much into it and expect something from me. And owing Kiwi anything sounds like a literal nightmare. But beggars can't be choosers, right?

"Fuck, you're gonna wear a hole through your skull if you keep thinking that hard," he laughs, and I roll my eyes.

"You got a helmet or something?" I ask, scanning his bike. He smiles and opens his saddlebag, pulling one out.

"Here you are, my Queen."

"Fuck off," I grumble as I grab and strap it on over my head.

"That's a good look for you," he says, and I flip him off before sliding on behind him. "Oh, I like this." He wiggles around, pressing his back and ass against me.

"Fuck off, Kiwi." I jab my fist into his stomach, and he grunts out a breath, then laughs.

"Keep doing shit like that and I'm gonna fall in love with you."

Kiwi

I step into the apartment behind Kennedy. It's small, and the place from the outside is a fucking dump, but inside, she's made it homey. Everything is spotless and even though most of her décor is as dark and terrifying as her, it doesn't feel small or closed in.

I like it.

I could get comfy here.

"Kitchen's that way." She waves her hand to the right and slides her leather jacket off, exposing her tattooed arms and back. Her black tank top is thin and shows every bit of ink she has on her body—which is a fuckton. "Bathroom is in the back. Ignore the dirty clothes. Ian never cleans up after himself, so I have no fucking clue what kind of mess he's left."

Ian.

My blood heats as I look around the place again. I didn't know she was with anyone, let alone a guy named fucking Ian. Really? Ian? With a girl like Kennedy? Absolutely not. He sounds like a bitch.

"I'm home!" she calls as she steps around me to lock the door, giving me an irritated look. I move to the center of the room and step

13

my feet apart, crossing my arms over my chest as I glare at the hall-way, waiting for this Ian prick to show himself.

I already decided I like Kennedy. I decided I want her. I decided she's mine.

I'm ready to claim her in front of everyone. All I have to do is convince her she likes me, then boom—I can hear the wedding bells already.

A little black pug trots into the room before a tall, lanky kid with barely-there stubble saunters in. He pauses when he sees me, our eyes locking. He's young, way too young for her. And could she have chosen a guy who looks more like her? They could be twins.

He has black hair and pale skin, like her, but his eyes aren't hazel. Instead, his are blue, but one is half brown, half blue.

That's the only fucking cool thing about the little prick.

"Ian, this is Kiwi," Kennedy says, awkwardly shifting on her feet. The dog runs to her and jumps on its hind legs, pawing at her thigh. "Hey, little guy." She scratches behind the dog's ear.

"He's a biker," Ian says slowly, narrowing his eyes as he scans me head to toe. I snort.

"You're an observant one there, mate," I say. Kennedy shoots me a look that could kill, and fuck if it doesn't make my dick stir.

"Kiwi," she grits out, "this is my son." Everything in my body freezes.

Son.

Son.

He's her son.

My body immediately cools, and I don't feel as ready to kill him. Son, I can deal with. Boyfriend or husband? I'd have to kill.

"Oh, hey man." I take a step forward and hold my hand out. He looks at it like it's a live snake, then glances at Kennedy. Hesitantly, he takes my hand and gives me a bitch shake. "Oh, you can do better than that. Really grab it—" I grip his hand tighter, and his eyes widen. "Do it." His hand tightens around mine, and I nod a few times, then shrug. "Better, but still needs work."

"Leave my kid alone, asshole," Kennedy growls, shoving my shoulder. She glares at me until I take a step away from him. Her face softens when she looks toward the kid. "Gotta go in early tonight. Is Enzo here?" She looks around his shoulder, frowning when she finds no one there.

"In my room," he says, tilting his head back. "He's not staying. Says he can deal with his old man." She nods a few times, then glances at me, fire in her pretty eyes.

"Enzo?" I ask, flicking my eyes between them. It's seriously eerie how much they look alike.

"My other son," she says. My head rears back in surprise. She doesn't look old enough for one, let alone two kids. She lets out a breathy laugh, the sound going to my fucking dick again. Fuck. This woman. "Ian's best friend."

"Speaking of the asshole," Ian says. I glance over, finding a shorter kid swaggering into the room with an arrogant grin on his face. It doesn't falter when our eyes meet. If anything, it just broadens.

Hm.

"Hey, Ms. K," he says, jerking his head at her. She lifts her brows at him, but a smile she can't hide spreads across her face.

"Hey, kid." Her smile falls as she searches his face. "You sure you don't wanna stay?" I can't help but stare at her. When she's not scowling, she looks softer. Younger. Not more beautiful, because that's fucking impossible, just...different.

"All good." He shrugs as he slides his hands into his pockets. There's a bruise on his cheek, he has a busted lip, and his eye is swollen. His dad did that to him?

"You're sure?" she asks as she chews on her lip. She grabs his arm, giving it a gentle squeeze. "You know you can stay here. Our home is yours." He glances at me, looking uncomfortable. She must pick up on it because she drops his arm, her bitch-mask slipping back into place.

"What's up? I'm Kiwi." He looks at me again, and honestly, he

15

looks unimpressed. He turns the look to Ian, and they share a silent conversation.

"Didn't know you were dating anyone, Ma," he says to Kennedy, ignoring me completely. "You know I'm turning eighteen in a few years. You couldn't wait for me?" She rolls her eyes.

My smile falls as I glare at him. Joke or not, kid or not, I don't like it—I don't like him. Maybe I'm a territorial prick, but I don't care. Kennedy is mine, and no one, not even some dumb fucking kid is going to flirt with her in front of me.

"Why would she ever want to get with some kid when she has a man?" My voice comes out harsh, and all eyes turn to me.

"Who's the man?" she asks, lifting her brows, a taunting smirk on her face. Ian and Enzo choke on a laugh, and I clench my jaw as we stare at each other. Not because I'm pissed, but because I'm seconds away from kissing her.

"We both know who the man is, love," I say, my voice low. I step toward her, and her brows lift higher.

"Wait," Ian said, his face growing serious as he scans me again. "You're seriously dating this guy?" His lip curls back, and I let out another laugh.

"Really, Ian?" Kennedy says, giving him an exasperated look. "No, I'm not dating him."

"Not yet, at least," I say, and she rolls her eyes.

"Not ever."

"We'll see."

Ian and Enzo flick their eyes between us, then look at each other again. Ian shrugs, and Enzo clears his throat before looking at me again.

"Anyway, I gotta go to work," he announces. "Sorry to run as soon as you get here." She pulls him in for a quick hug.

"You have a ride?" she asks when she pulls away, and he waves her off.

"Don't worry about me, Ma." He presses a quick kiss to her cheek. "Nice to meet you, man." He jerks his chin at me, and I nod back as he passes. He slips outside, leaving Kennedy, Ian, and I standing in the living room.

The dog runs in a circle around us, trying to get our attention, but all I can focus on is her. The way she's having a full conversation with her son with just her eyes. Finally, she sighs and rubs her forehead.

"I'll cook you something before I leave," she says tiredly.

"I'll just order a pizza." I swallow down my irritation. It wouldn't have bothered me if she didn't look instantly defeated.

"Let her cook for you," I say, and they both look at me with the same expression. "What?"

"Don't tell him what to do," she snaps.

"Why not?" I look at him again and scan him slowly. "How old are you, anyway?"

"Fifteen," he says slowly, then glances at Kennedy. "Why?"

"Are you old enough to be left alone?" His eyes widen comically at my question.

"He's fine," she growls. "Just because you can't be left alone without adult supervision doesn't mean everyone's like that. Some of us, even fifteen-year-old boys, are more mature than you."

"Never doubted his maturity, babe. Just asked if he could be left alone." I take a few steps back, holding my hands up placatingly. "I'll stay out of it. Please," I jerk my hand at him, "mother your son." She glares harder at me, but I just smile.

The hold this woman has on my heart already.

Kiwi

Kennedy spends the next hour and a half running around the apartment getting dressed. She's told me to leave, but I've ignored her and camped out on the couch instead. The dog, Rasputin, has been curled in my lap the entire time. I'm giving Kennedy a ride to the bar, if for no other reason than I like the way it feels to have her tits pressed against me.

"Kiwi!" she shouts from the bathroom. My heart lurches at the sound of my name from her lips. I groan as I stand, my knees popping. I'm not all that old, but I was a fucking idiot when I was younger and now my knees are fucked. So is my back. And my left hip. And right shoulder. Probably a lot of other shit, too.

"Yes, my Queen?" I ask as I rest my hands on the top of the doorframe and lean into the room. She glares at me through the mirror as she puts her lipstick on.

"Can you put a pot of water on the stove?" she asks, sliding her eyes back to her reflection.

"Oh, I'm mature enough to boil water now?" I smirk when her jaw tightens.

"Kiwi," she sighs, her eyes finding mine again.

18

"I like the way you say my name."

"Fuck off," she laughs. I want to move up behind her and wrap my arms around her. Maybe kiss on her neck...then bend her over the counter and fuck her until her throat is raw from screaming my name. "And take some pasta out of the pantry?" She bats her lashes at me, and I shake my head, a grin still on my face.

"Anything else, Your Majesty?" I bow, and when I stand up, she's flipping me off.

"No, just the water and noodles," she says. "Oh, and peasant?" she calls when I turn my back. I can't help the giant, goofy smile I have on my face when I look at her again. "The curly noodles, not the spaghetti."

"The curly noodles?" I lift my brow and she shrugs.

"Kid likes what he likes."

"He wants you to cook for him now?" I ask and she looks back at herself, her face falling.

"I figured I'd make him something, anyway. Just in case he gets hungry later, or if Enzo comes back."

I stare at her for another moment. She swallows a few times, her throat bobbing as she swipes blood-red lipstick on her lips. She's fucking terrifying. Gorgeous. So fucking pretty it's like looking at the sun, but terrifying.

After putting the water on the stove and taking out the curly noodles, as instructed, I decide to look around a bit. If things go as I plan, this will be my place soon enough. I need to know where to put all my shit. Or maybe we can buy our own place instead. We'll need the extra space.

There's not much to explore. It's a small, outdated place with brown carpet and popcorn ceilings. She has mostly dark-colored décor, and a lot of pictures of her kid. Some of them together, but it's mostly him over the years. She must've been a kid herself when she had him, judging by how young she looks in his newborn photos.

If he's fifteen, she had to have been his age when she had him. There's no way she's older than me.

Moving down the hall, I rush past the open bathroom door and pray she doesn't see me. When she doesn't tell me to go fuck myself, I know I went by unnoticed.

There are two doors at the end of the hall—one is for her room, the other is Ian's. I have a fifty-fifty shot of choosing hers. I think I value my life, though, so I probably shouldn't go in hers.

Oh, fuck it.

I will anyway. Maybe she'll let me fuck her while she holds a knife to my throat.

Slowly, I open the door. It creaks quietly, and I pause, waiting for Kennedy to pounce. When she doesn't, I open it further. I immediately know I'm in Ian's room from the overwhelming stench of adolescent cologne. It's probably the same shit I wore when I was his age, and it doesn't smell any better now than it did then.

Stepping all the way inside, I find him sitting at a desk with two monitors set on it. He's wearing a giant set of headphones with a mic attached, and is hunched forward slightly, staring intently at whatever game he's playing. There's a guy running through an abandoned place, a gun waving in front of his face.

"He's over there!" Ian shouts as he scoots to the edge of his chair, moving his face closer to the screen. "Shit. My health. I need a healer —fuck!" He bangs his fist on the table, and I jerk back, not expecting it. "Fucker killed me. Stupid prick."

Chatter erupts through the headset loud enough for me to hear, and I crack a small smile. Folding my arms over my chest, I just watch him.

"He's just pissed I fucked his mom last night," he says, chuckling to himself. "Then his sister." I can't hold in my bark of laughter, and he whirls around, his eyes wide as he stares up at me.

"You're funny, kid," I say as he slides the headset off. "Way funnier than I thought you'd be. Whose mom did you fuck?"

"No one's," he blurts, then glances at his screen. "Shit." He looks at me again, then back at his screen, looking torn.

"Go on." I jerk my chin at him. "Don't let me stop you."

I step my feet apart and sway back and forth, grinning at him. Hesitating, he turns back around and slides the headset back on. His shoulders stay stiff as he falls onto a new map. There's a mini war playing out before me, and I keep laughing at the stupid shit coming from his mouth. I have no fucking idea what's going on, but it's intense and has me on the edge of my seat.

"Fuck yeah!" I clap when the final guy on the other team dies. Ian glances at me over his shoulder, his dark brows quirked. "That was good, yeah?"

"Yeah," he agrees, then looks back at his screen. "Guys, hold on. I'll be right back—fuck you." I laugh again as he spins the chair around to look at me. "Why are you in here?"

"I thought it was your mom's room—"

"Why the fuck were you going to my mom's room?" he growls as he gets to his feet.

He's not a short kid, but he's a stick. But, judging by his size now and how he hasn't fully filled out yet, he's going to be a huge moth-erfucker in a few years, and he needs to learn he can't do this shit. If he bucks up to someone, he needs to be ready for a fight—and he's not.

"I suggest you sit back down before I knock you the fuck out." I keep my voice level, but the threat is clear. It's not a bluff, and he knows it. "If you wanna play with the big boys, you gotta hold your own or you'll get hurt. Can you back your shit up, kid?" He blinks at me, his mouth opening and closing. I drop the bullshit and smile, clapping him on the shoulder and making him wince. "It's good advice and something you should remember. If you're not willing to fight, sit down."

"I wasn't—I wasn't trying to fight you."

"I know," I say. He looks even more confused but gives me a hesi-tant nod and slowly steps back, the backs of his knees hitting his chair.

Yeah, I know my reaction isn't great, but I don't give a shit. I couldn't hold my own when I was his age and it got people hurt—it got them killed. He needs to know he can't do this shit without conse-quences.

"Ian!" Kennedy calls from somewhere in the apartment. I lift my brows at him, expecting him to rat me out. He clears his throat, his eyes locked with mine.

"Coming!" he calls back, his voice hoarse. "I'm not trying to cause trouble." He looks scared, so I drop my shoulders and let out a long breath, flashing him a grin.

"I know," I say. "I just can't have you thinking I'm a bitch." He barks out a laugh, making me grin wider.

"Trust me, no one would ever think you're a bitch."

"Your mom does."

"Yeah, but she thinks everyone is," he says, and I nod in agreement.

"She's a bit terrifying, isn't she?" I ask conspiratorially.

"Oh yeah," he says. "She threatened my history teacher when she found out he was failing me because she turned him down for a date. She really reamed his ass. In front of the entire class, too."

"Ian! Come on!" I laugh as we walk from his room. We're too broad to walk side by side in the hall, so I let him go first.

"She do that a lot?" I ask, and he pushes his brows together. "Yell at your teachers, I mean."

"Not just the teachers. She's jumped some parents and kids, too," he says as we walk through the living room. "She threatened to cut this one kid's balls off once because he was bullying me."

"Shit." I choke out a laugh.

"Yeah, so, where are you from anyway? England?" he asks. I blink at him, then bark out another laugh.

"Nah, mate. I'm from New Zealand. That's why they call me Kiwi." He makes an O with his mouth, nodding in understanding. We pause when we get to the kitchen, finding Kennedy with her hands on her hips and her brows raised. I smile at her, and her scowl deepens.

"What's going on here?" She waves her finger between us. "You're not to be friends with this asshole."

"Kinda fucked to call your kid an asshole, babe," I say, and she growls at me.

"Shut it, prick," she snaps. Her face softens when she looks back at Ian. "I made you pasta if you get hungry later. And you know the rules—no girls, no drugs, no leaving the apartment."

"Shit. What can he do then?" I scoff, and they both turn to me. "You just listed the three funnest things a boy can do." I didn't know it was possible, but she glares harder at me, her jaw tensing so tightly it hurts my teeth.

"I told you to shut it," she says, pointing at me. I zip my lips and toss her the key, which she doesn't catch, and looks back at Ian. "Call me if you need anything and I'll be on my way."

"I'll be fine," he says, shifting uncomfortably. "I always am." She takes a deep breath.

"Lock the door after us," she says as she grabs her leather jacket from the couch. "And don't forget to feed Raspy. And take a shower."

"I know, Mom," he groans.

"See you later, kid," I chuckle as I step onto the porch.

"Love you, bud." She gives him a quick hug, and he squeezes her before shutting the door. We wait until the lock clicks into place, then she lets out a heavy breath and glances at me before we head down the steps.

Kennedy

W alking into The Crossroads is pure chaos.

Bikers are running around, strapping weapons to their bodies, and yelling at each other. Some of them are arguing, while the Old-Timers sit at tables, ignoring everything happening around them. My heart aches at the sight. My dad should be one of those men, kicking back while the younger men go off to do whatever they're gearing up for.

Immediately, Kiwi wraps his arm around my waist and pulls me to his side.

"What's going on?" I ask quietly.

"Don't know," he says, his eyes scanning the room. He tightens his hold, and I find myself shuffling closer to him. "Stay by my side."

All his usual good-natured humor has left his body and voice. I don't even recognize him. His eyes take everything in as he pulls his gun from his waistband and half drags me across the floor toward Spencer's office in the back.

I feel myself pressing into his side, feeling safer beside him than with any of the men I've known my entire life. And how fucked is that? I trust this cocky asshole more than the men who were Brothers with my dad.

But the way he's so sure of himself, the tight, secure hold he has on me, the fierce way he's looking around the room like one wrong move and he'll kill everyone, makes me feel safe.

Call me crazy.

Kiwi doesn't hesitate as he shoves the door open and pulls me inside, acting like he owns the fucking place. Archer, Otis, and Maddox are standing in the middle of the office while Spencer sits behind his desk. Nessa and Arden are standing behind him, looking pale.

"What's going on?" Kiwi demands, interrupting their conversation.

He pushes me in front of him, keeping my back pressed against his chest and arm protectively around my waist. It takes my mind a moment to catch up.

I'm in Spence's office.

I'm with Spence and his Inner Circle.

I'm with The Berserkers.

I'm safe.

I side-step Kiwi and move toward Archer. Kiwi glares daggers at him and I momentarily second guess my decision to move to Archer when Kiwi has his gun in his hand.

Surely, he wouldn't shoot someone in a room full of people...right?

"You don't know?" Spencer asks, lifting his brow.

"Obviously not," Kiwi snarls. His eyes keep finding mine, and I force myself to stay put and not move to him again, but his eyes are beckoning me. He's magnetic. And it's fucking annoying.

"The Horsemen graced us with a fucking drive by about ten minutes ago," Spencer says as he runs his fingers through his short hair.

"Was anyone hurt?" I ask. It's not our first drive by. They don't happen often, but they're always scary. Archer rests his hand on my lower back, a gesture to comfort me, and Kiwi growls.

"Don't touch her." He grabs my wrist and yanks me forward. I trip on my feet and land against his chest, but he doesn't care. He just wraps his arm around my waist possessively, holding me tighter to his body.

"What the fuck?" Archer says, sounding genuinely confused. "Ken—"

"We don't have time for this," Spencer snaps. I give him an apologetic look as I push Kiwi's firm chest, but he doesn't budge.

"Let me go," I hiss.

"Not gonna happen, love," he says, not looking at me. He's still glaring at Arch over my head. "Do not ever touch her again." His voice is calm, but it's low and deadly. "If you do, I'll cut your hands off and fuck your ass with them. You understand?"

I let out a manic sounding laugh, mostly from shock. Who the fuck says that? When no one else laughs, I force myself to stop. What the fuck.

"Excuse me?" Archer says, his voice dropping.

For as confused as he can be, he's still a deadly motherfucker.

"You heard me," Kiwi growls. "Touch her again, I'll mutilate your fucking body." I bite my lip to keep from laughing again.

What's wrong with me? This isn't funny—not in the slightest. It's just so outrageous that he's threatening Archer for touching me. And the way he's threatening him, the shit he's saying? It's ridiculous.

"You're fucking crazy," Archer scoffs. Kiwi's hold on me tightens until I can't breathe.

"Oh, I'll show you fucking crazy," he says quietly.

I blink up at him. His eyes are darker, his face like stone, his body rigid—he's not the same man I walked in with.

"I'm doing a favor for Bash by having you here. If you keep threatening my guys, I'm sending you back to him black and blue," Spencer says as he stands. "Keep your shit under control, Kiwi, or I'll get it under control."

"Kiwi," I whisper as I place my hand on his chest. He's vibrating, his eyes still locked on Archer. "It's okay. Archer is my friend. He can touch me."

I don't even know why he's acting like this. We've met all of a handful of times and each time made me more annoyed than the last. I shouldn't have to calm him down for someone touching me. There's no reason for him to be acting like this, but more than that, there's no reason for me to act like this.

"No." He looks down at me, that deadly hunger still in them. "He can't. No one can. Only me."

"Ian?"

He rolls his eyes before adding, "Fine. And Ian."

I can't help the small smile that spreads across my face, and I drop my head to hide it. Seriously, what the fuck is wrong with me?

"I'll take half the guys' and ride out," Otis says, drawing everyone's attention. He's as serious as they come and has no patience for shit like this.

"I'll take the other half," Maddox sighs. "Fuck this shit, man."

"What can I do?" Kiwi asks. I try to wiggle out of his hold, but he doesn't let me. I work on prying his fingers off my waist, but they just snap back into place.

"Ride around for a bit, see if you can find anything," Spencer says, sounding tired.

"Can do." Kiwi gives him a firm nod.

"And me?" Archer asks, sounding reluctant. He shifts on his feet, and I glance at him. He's giving me a weird look, and I stop trying to pluck Kiwi's fingers off. My eyes snap down to them, and I stare shocked at what I was just doing.

I've never acted like this before. I've never acted so immature in front of my boss or my guys. I glance at Arch again, finding him staring at me with furrowed brows, like he's thinking the same fucking thing.

"Ride with Kiwi."

We snap our heads to Spencer. He did not just say that. He folds his arms over his chest, his dark brows low over his eyes. He's not giving them an option—it's a direct order.

"And Kens, I need you at the bar. You need to hold this place down. Can you do it?" He eyes Kiwi's hand digging into my side and his jaw clenches before his eyes meet mine. "Belfast will be here soon. But the place should be quiet, since most of the guys will be riding out."

"Don't worry about me," I say, waving him off.

"I wasn't," he says dryly. "Just don't want anything to happen to my bar." Kiwi's hold tightens until I'm positive I'll have bruises.

"I don't like her staying here alone," he says.

"She'll be fine." Spencer ignores him as he sits back in his chair.

"I don't like—"

"I don't give a shit." Spencer calmly stares at him, but his jaw is tight. "I don't give a shit what you do or don't like about the way I run my club or bar. You're a fucking guest here. You have no say." My breath hitches at his tone, and I slowly swivel my eyes to Kiwi. He's glaring at Spencer like he's seconds away from jumping over the desk and murdering him.

"I'll be fine," I say quickly, then glance at Spencer. "I mean, your bar will be fine. Everything will be fine." He stares at me for a moment, then sighs as he turns his attention to Otis.

"I don't know if I should leave," he says. Otis shrugs as he slides his hands into his pockets.

"It's not a problem, Prez," he says. "I can keep the club afloat while you're gone."

"We won't run it into the ground," Maddox says.

"Not too much, at least," Archer adds, grinning. I glance up at Kiwi, finding his glare turned back on Archer. It makes me uneasy knowing they're going to be alone together.

"Please don't hurt him," I whisper. He slowly lowers his eyes to mine. The guys talk around us, but I drown them out and focus only on Kiwi. "Please, Kiwi."

"You two—" He looks back at Archer, murder burning brightly in his eyes. "Are you two together?"

"No," I say, shaking my head. "We're just friends." He lets out a relieved breath and his arm loosens. "Don't kill or hurt him. I mean it."

"One condition," he says. I flick my eyes between his, then take a deep breath. There's no telling what this condition could be. Kiwi is unpredictable, so it could literally be anything.

"What?" I ask hesitantly.

"You need to stop calling me Kiwi," he says in a low voice so only I can hear him. "Call me by my real name." I scrunch my brows.

"What?" I ask again. "You want me to—what?" I give him a bewildered look, not believing that this was his condition.

"Call me Ezra," he whispers. "Please. I don't want to be Kiwi to you." I blink a few times and glance around at the guys. Archer is watching us, not even pretending to listen to Maddox and Otis. Spencer has moved on to talking to Nessa and Arden in a low voice.

"Why?" I look back at him and his throat bobs.

"I'm Kiwi to everyone," he mutters, "and Ezra to no one." I bite my bottom lip as his words roll around in my head. They don't make sense. Kiwi is just his road name—he's the same person regardless of a name.

"Aright," I finally breathe. "Fine...Ezra." He goes completely still, his entire body freezing against mine. I don't think he's even breathing. "Ki—Ezra?" His breath hitches and he blinks a few times before his expression shifts into one I can't read. But there's something about it that makes me feel relieved. And a multitude of other things I don't want to think about.

He gives me a slight squeeze before he drops his arm and takes a small step back. Not far enough to be separated from me, but far enough away, so he's not on top of me anymore.

"You ready?" he asks Archer. Archer looks between us, then jerks his chin at Kiwi—Ezra. Fuck, it's going to be hard remembering to call him by his real name.

"In a sec," he says, taking a step toward me. They tower above me and I hold my breath, anticipating the worst. Then Archer reaches for me and Ezra clears his throat pointedly. A warning.

Archer's hand immediately falls away, and my brows lift. What the fuck? I glance at Ezra, but he stays glaring at Archer. How the fuck did he do that?

"What?" I ask when I look back at Archer.

"Is there something going on between you two?" Archer demands, not dropping his voice. The others in the room cut their conversations off to turn toward us.

"No," I say, then let out an irritated sigh as I step away from both men. "Are we really playing this game?" I look between them, my brows raised. "We're in our thirties. We're not in middle school. Come on, guys. Grow up."

"I can assure you I'm plenty grown, love," Ezra says. He folds his arms over his chest and steps his feet apart, looking ridiculously arrogant.

"You already know how grown I am, babe," Archer retorts just as smugly.

That was the wrong fucking thing to say. I barely move out of the way before Ezra's fist connects with Archer's face.

Kiwi

.

After all these years of wanting to escape this fucking world, of being alive and alone, I'm finally going to die and be with Elaine again. I can already see her long blonde hair and sparkling blue eyes.

Instead of sending me to the other side, he lets go and I fall to the floor, the dark bar shrouding me and dimming Elaine's memory. I rub my throat as I take ragged breaths and lean back against the wall. Still sitting on my ass, I look up at him and grin again.

"You ever worry you're gonna rip your dick off from how tight your grip is?" He blinks at me but keeps his face blank. "Your poor little willy." He takes a step forward, growling low in his chest. My teeth flash as his hands tighten into fists, then the door swings open, and Spencer storms out.

"Get up!" I must move too slowly because he doesn't give me a fucking chance before his hand wraps around my shirt and he yanks me to my feet. "Did I not just warn you I was gonna beat the shit out of you? I can't have you beating up my guys, Kiwi."

I shove at his chest, but he doesn't budge. "Fuck off, Spence. We both know that cocky fucker deserves way more."

"He's my Road Captain, same rank as you," he says as he shoves me against the wall. "I need you two to get along."

"Can't."

"Can't?" he repeats. "Just like that?"

"Yeah." He lets go of my shirt and I smooth my hand over it a few times. "He fucked Kens." Otis and Spencer glance at each other, then look at me.

"Seriously?" Spencer says, then shakes his head. "You know what—I don't care. Work this shit out right fucking now, because you two are riding out in five minutes."

"You're kidding," I scoff. "After that—"

"After that," he shouts as he points at the office door, "you're lucky you're still fucking breathing!" The fury in his eyes makes me swallow my tongue.

I might be crazy, but I'm not an idiot.

"Fine," I grit out. "Tell him if he mentions her name, looks at her, touches her—if he has anything to do with her, he's dead."

"Not telling him that, and neither are you." He jabs his finger into the center of my chest. "Do you understand me?" I narrow my eyes, but don't give him the confirmation he wants. He's not my Prez. I don't owe him shit. He must realize that too because he sighs, then shouts for Kennedy over his shoulder. She hesitantly makes her way toward us, her eyes finding mine, then dropping. She steps beside me but stays as far away as she can. "I don't want this bullshit in my club." He waves his finger between us.

"Spence—"

"I should fucking fire you for this." Guilt twists my stomach. It's not an emotion I feel often, so when it's there, I know I've really fucked up.

"I'm sorry," she says quickly, her voice bordering on hysterical. "Please don't fire me. Please. I need this job—Ian—please, Spence." Her chin trembles, and that's what does me in.

"It's my fault," I say, and they both snap their heads to me, looking shocked. What? Can't a guy take the blame without everyone freaking out? "She did nothing wrong. Don't fire her." Her throat bobs and she quickly averts her eyes, looking at the floor.

"I'm sorry, Spence," she croaks, her voice thick. There's a beat of silence. If he's about to fire her for this, I will fucking kill him. But he clears his throat and glances at me before putting his hand on her shoulder. My eyes zero in on it, but I force myself not to react.

Punching Archer was one thing...punching Spencer would definitely get me killed.

But if he doesn't take his hand away soon, I might just fucking risk it.

"I'm trusting you, Kennedy," he says. "Please don't make me regret this." She lifts her teary eyes to him, then nods.

"You won't," she blurts. "Thank you–" He doesn't let her finish groveling. He turns on his heel mid-sentence and walks back into the office, telling everyone but Nessa to fuck off.

"Kenny," I say as I turn toward her. She holds her hand up.

"Don't," she says. "That was fucked up and you know it. I don't know what your deal is, but you can't go around punching people in the face–"

"I won't go around punching people in the face," I say. "Just him." She takes a deep breath.

"Why? What has he ever done to you? You haven't said two words to each other." She gives me an exasperated look—it's one I've seen a lot, but it hurts coming from her.

"You've slept together," I say. Her mouth opens, then closes. "He's touched you. Kissed you. Been inside you." My body vibrates more with each word.

I really should've just shot him.

"How do you know that?" she breathes, her eyes wide.

I didn't know for sure, but she just confirmed it. It makes my heart dip.

"Doesn't take a rocket scientist, babe," I say as I side-step her. "Gotta ride out with your boyfriend. Unless you need to ride him first?" Her face falls, her shoulders slumping with it, and I immediately wish I could take the words back.

Elaine always said I hurt people when I'm hurting. When my heart hurts, I use words to hurt people. When my body hurts, I use my fists. But no matter what, I want them to hurt worse than I am.

That's where she was wrong, though.

No amount of pain I could ever inflict on anyone could let them feel what I feel every day. The moment she died was the moment a piece of me died too, and I'll never get it back. It was the sane part of my mind that died, and until Kennedy said my real name, I thought Elaine had killed my heart, too.

It was still in there, beating silently and painfully. But when Kennedy said my name, it started to beat for her.

I hope Elaine can forgive me for that.

Kiwi

I glance at Archer riding beside me. I fucking hate him. I haven't said more than a few words to the prick, but I fucking despise him. If he was dangling off the edge of a cliff with sharks swimming below, I'd dance on his fucking fingers.

I. Hate. Him.

He pulls off to the side of the road and parks. I pull up behind him, cut my engine, and take a deep breath.

I promised Kennedy I wouldn't hurt him. If she was anyone else —and I literally mean anyone else—I would break that promise in a fucking heartbeat. But I can't and won't do that to her. So, I stare at the tall, tattooed fuck as he swings his leg off his bike and rests his helmet on the seat.

"Think anyone's home?" he asks, jerking his chin toward one of The Horsemen's latest hangouts. It's a dilapidated trailer in a deserted part of town. The perfect spot for them to cook meth and store girls and guns until they needed to be moved.

I shrug as I slide off my bike. "You go first," I say, and he snorts.

"Yeah, no." He sweeps his arm out, his gaze meeting mine. "After you."

"Puss." I walk past him, hitting his shoulder with mine, and trudge up the creaky steps. He laughs under his breath as I cup my hands around the dusty window to peer inside.

The trailer is abandoned.

It looks like everyone just up and left without a moment's notice. Clothes, food wrappers and takeout containers, blankets, even children's toys litter the floor.

"No one's here," I say as I pull my face from the window. "Everyone–"

"Shh." His brows pinch together as he tilts his head to the side. His eyes meet mine momentarily before he jerks his chin for me to follow. Quietly, we move around the trailer, our feet digging into the loose sand.

A few paces from the back, we hear them.

It's getting dark so we can easily sneak up on them. I'm not sure how many there are, but I know I can take them out. My blood hums with anticipation and my hands itch to kill.

I was never hungry to kill. Never. But now, as I've gotten older and the more I've killed, the more I crave it. The more I need it to stay sane. I need to kill to survive.

"Fuck," I mutter, and he barely nods.

Pressing our backs against the dirty siding, we silently shuffle along the wall. He peeks around the corner quickly, then moves back and looks at me.

"Two," he breathes, and I grin.

"One for each of us," I say. "But if you take too long, I'm taking your kill. Don't fuck it up."

"Anyone ever tell you you're not as hot shit as you think you are?" I tilt my head to the side and grin wider.

"Once or twice," I admit. "They're not alive anymore."

He falters for a moment, unsure if I'm joking or not—I'm not. If we didn't need the element of surprise, I'd lose my shit and laugh in his dumb face. But I just elbow him in the ribs, making him swallow his grunt, and round the corner.

It's two low ranking Horsemen. I'm not positive they're low rank-ing, but why else would they have been left behind? Important people are the first to leave. You leave the grunts to do the shit no one else wants to do.

Something whizzes past my head, and I curse as I dive to the side. One guy lets out an agonized scream and falls to his knees. I turn in time to find him reaching for a knife protruding from his thigh with shaky hands. The other guy scrambles for his discarded gun behind him.

"Wouldn't do that," I say, pulling my gun from my waistband and taking a step forward. "What's going on here?" I jerk my gun at the trailer, my eyes trained on him.

The kid can't be more than eighteen. He looks like he's about to shit himself. In other circumstances, maybe I would've felt bad for him or found his expression hilarious. But he's a Horsemen, and Horsemen have to die.

"Don't kn-know," he stammers. His friend groans on the ground, clutching his leg. It's not that fucking bad. I've been stabbed a million times and have never made the noises he's making. He's just being a little bitch.

Archer steps beside me, his gun out and aimed at the guy he stabbed. I crouch down, getting eye-level with the non-stabbed guy.

"Oh, come on, mate. You know what's going on. Big smart guy like you? Someone's told you something." He and his friend share a look and I glance up at Archer. He's still glaring at his guy.

Gotta give it to him. He set his sights on the kid and hasn't taken them off.

"Someone coming back here?" I ask. "I don't wanna kill you, but if you don't know anything, then I won't have a choice." I try to give him a sympathetic face.

"They said to get the rest of the stuff and leave," he says, his voice shaky. "That's it."

"The drive-by at The Crossroads earlier," I say. "Know anything about that?" He violently shakes his head, his eyes widening. I sigh. "I thought I was gonna like you." I shake my head disappointingly. "You just lied to me, man." I aim at his foot and shoot my gun. His head falls back as he howls and clutches his ankle.

"Shit," Archer breathes.

"You know about the drive-by?" I ask again, conversationally.

"Fuck!" he screams, rocking side to side. "No!"

I shoot his other foot and he screams again, his voice cracking. Tears stream down his face and his blood mixes with the sand. I stand, my gun still casually aimed at him.

"You know anything?" I ask Archer's guy. He shakes his head, his eyes wide and injury forgotten. I slide my gun toward him and he screams.

"Wait!" he shouts as he lifts his hand. "Wait! Please! Wait!" I lift my brows impatiently.

"Waiting," I drawl. Archer gives me a look I choose to ignore.

"Heard some guys talking about it. They said they're trying to take out The Brotherhood and—"

"And?" I crouch again and rest my forearms on my knees. Even though his face has gone deathly pale, his eyes stay alert as they track me.

"They're trying to lure them out by attacking The Berserkers," he mumbles. I look up at Archer, and he takes a deep breath as he shoves his fingers through his hair, looking distressed.

"Anything else?" I ask, looking back at him.

"No," he says, sounding resigned. "I swear that's all I know." Groaning softly, I push to my feet again, my gun still aimed at him.

"Wait." Archer puts his hand on my forearm and I glance at him, my brow lifting. "We can't just kill them."

"Why not?" I scoff. "They're Horsemen."

"They're just kids, man," he says, exasperated.

"They're Horsemen," I say again. He gives me a firm look and tightens his hold on my arm. With a long, drawn-out sigh, I tip my head back. "Call Otis and tell him we're bringing in some strays."

"You're not gonna kill us?" the one I shot asks, sounding hopeful. I drop my head to look at him.

"Not yet, apparently," I sigh as I rub my forehead with the hand holding my gun. "Maybe later."

Kiwi

Spencer shoves my feet off his desk, and they fall heavily to the floor. I huff out a sarcastic laugh as I slouch further down in the chair.

"Are you even listening to me?" Spencer asks, glaring at me. I shrug and glance at Taz. He gives me a pointed look, barely shaking his head.

Don't antagonize them—that's what he'd told me before this meeting.

Like I'd ever antagonize anyone. It's like he doesn't even know me.

Archer clears his throat, and my grin falls. Fucker. The only reason I'm in here having to talk to Spencer is because of him. Because he couldn't kill those Horsemen like a fucking man. *We had to do the right thing.*

The *right thing* would've been killing them and ridding the world of two more Horsemen.

"Of course, I'm listening," I say. He pinches between his eyes, sighing loudly. Nessa and Arden glance at each other, a hidden smile on their faces. When Nessa looks back at me, I wink at her, making

40

her face turn tomato-red. "The Horsemen fucks are in your kill room."

"Did you get any information from them at all?" He lifts his eyes over my shoulder to look at Archer. He clears his throat again, and his boots grind against the old wood floor as he takes a step forward.

"Not really," he admits. I tighten my arms over my chest, trying to hide a smug grin. We could've gotten information if he would've let me ride in the back of the van with them. I could've had fun the whole drive back to their compound, but *no*.

"You don't have to come," Taz says. Spencer's eyes shift to him.

"And leave my sister alone with you?"

"She doesn't have to come either." He shrugs like it doesn't matter either way, but his shoulders tense. He's had a thing for Arden for years. She's a cute girl, but quiet. I don't know why he's so hung up on her, honestly. Apart from being able to drink any man under the table, she stays mostly to herself.

I know they've had their moments, but no matter how often I tell him to just move on, he can't. I've been punched in the face one too many times to continue suggesting it.

"We're going," Spencer says, his tone final. "You need the help, and the girls will make things...easier." He grits the word out, and I know it's because he doesn't want his girl or sister involved in this shit. And I understand it. I fucking agree with it.

If it wasn't for Addie and Heather, the women would be totally out of this, as usual. At first, I was all for it. I thought we needed to change things up, but after knowing what those fucks did to them, I regret ever voting in their favor.

They should be protected, not put in the middle of this shit.

I'd never let Kennedy be involved in this.

Not that she'd fucking listen to me.

I scrub my hand over my face, trying to ignore the way my heart dips at the thought of her. When we got back to The Crossroads, she wouldn't look at me. She wouldn't look at Archer either, though, which gave me the sickest sense of triumph.

"The Horsemen are targeting your club," I say, drawing Spencer's attention back to me. "They're using you to get to us. We need–"

The door bangs open and Bash stalks in, kicking it shut behind him. I don't have to look at him to feel the fury rippling off him in waves. He's suffocating the room with it.

"What the fuck is going on?" he demands, ignoring Taz and I completely, and resting his fists on Spence's desk. He leans forward, bringing them closer. The two presidents stare at each other for a long moment, the room growing even thicker with tension.

Taz and I glance at each other, ready to pull Bash away and protect him. It's our duty. He's our Prez—we protect him and Addie, and their future child, with our lives.

"That's what I'm trying to figure out," Spencer grinds out. "Could you please sit–"

"No," Bash barks. "Fuck." He shoves his fingers through his grown-out hair as he pushes off the desk. He begins pacing, his fist in front of his mouth, a deep crease between his brows.

"They're targeting The Berserkers," I say, and he slides his eyes to me.

"Did you take them out?" he asks. I don't respond. I just stare back, and he huffs out a hard breath before turning toward Spence. "Did you give him the order to not kill Horsemen?" He sounds tired. The man needs a vacation.

"No," Spencer grits. He doesn't like to be questioned, and it's obvious he doesn't play well with others. To be fair, neither does Bash. "It was a call made by my Road Captain, and I support it completely."

I snort and all eyes turn to me.

"He was too scared to kill them," I say. Bash's shoulders rise and fall with another deep breath.

"I'm not too scared to kill you," Archer says darkly.

I feel him looming over my shoulder, but if he thinks he has the upper hand, he's wrong. I barely turn my head to look at him before laughing.

"Sure, okay. Whatever, fuckface."

"Kiwi," Taz hisses.

Right.

Don't antagonize them.

"Anyway, we didn't learn much," I say, trying to hurry this along. "That's about it. I'm sure they'll target you again. Be prepared." Spencer stares at me, the muscle in his jaw feathering.

"I can tell my guys to hang out here," Bash says. Spencer waves him off.

"My guys can handle their own," he says.

"Can they protect the bar and the people in it?" I ask. Both presidents look at me. "What?"

"The people in it are Brothers," Spencer says slowly.

"Kennedy?"

Her name is like a bomb in the room.

I wait for him to answer, and when he doesn't, I look at Archer. Surely he's not fine with her being here alone. But he doesn't say anything.

"So, what? She's just supposed to protect herself?"

"We've had to deal with drive-bys for years," Spencer says. "She's used to it."

"And if they break in?"

"They won't."

"Kiwi," Bash says under his breath. "Drop it."

I glare at him. I know it's not the right thing to do, show any sign of friction with him in front of another club, but fuck. What does he expect?

"Belfast will keep digging to find their hideouts," Spencer says.

"I'll work with him," I say, and again, everyone looks at me. I don't want to leave Kennedy alone, and if I'm working closely with Belfast, I'll have a real excuse to be here all the time.

Even if she doesn't want me around, I'm not going anywhere.

43

"He works alone," Spence says, and I shrug.

"We go back," I say. It's semi-truthful. We don't go way way back. But we go back far enough for us to be...*friends*? Does Belfast even have friends? He's even more unhinged than I am, and a loner. But we get along enough for him to be fine with me tagging along.

"Right." Spence and Bash exchange a look, then Bash nods. "Fine." Spencer glares at me. "Don't fuck up my club. I mean it."

"I wouldn't dream of it," I grin. Bash sighs again, pinching the bridge of his nose. I push to my feet, rubbing my hands along my thighs as I stand. "Are we done?"

Spencer looks ready to say no, but he pauses and looks around the room. "They're still in the kill room?" he asks Archer. Archer nods, and gives me a sidelong look. "We'll question them, then kill them." He gives another nod, but keeps his mouth shut.

I've never understood people's reluctance to kill bad people. It's not hard to understand.

Someone does something bad, that means they need to die. Simple as that. It's why I have no problem with the blood on my hands. Even if I am a monster, I can justify it.

"Then we're done," Spencer says. "Need to talk to you and Taz, though." That's my cue to leave, and I'm more than happy to.

Archer stalks from the office behind me, but I ignore him. We don't say a word to each other as we make it to the main floor. I search for Kennedy, not finding her anywhere. Panic bolts through my chest, but when I see her coming from the back with a crate of bottles, I let out a relieved breath.

"She can take care of herself," Archer mutters. "She won't like you hanging around." I glance at him. He really believes that, doesn't he?

"I don't care if she can take care of herself," I say. "She doesn't have to when I'm here." His throat bobs as he swallows, his eyes tracking her. I wait for him to say something, wait for him to give me a reason to deck him, but he doesn't.

He looks lost in thought while he walks across the room and out of the bar.

When I find Kennedy again, she's staring at the door like she's waiting for him to come back in. A few seconds pass, then she straightens her shoulders. I see her mask slip back on as she begins making her rounds and pouring drinks for the guys.

I don't know if she's noticed me or not, but I stalk to the back corner of the bar and sink into the chair. If her club can't promise to protect her, then I will.

I'll sit here every night for the rest of my life to protect her.

Kennedy

Walking into the apartment, I quietly shut the door and lean heavily against it. It's nearly four in the morning and I'm fucking exhausted. Spencer was reluctant to leave after the drive-by, and even more reluctant to leave me in charge after that bullshit with Kiwi—Ezra, fuck.

I got busy after Archer and Ezra left; too busy to worry about if he killed Archer or not. But now that I'm off work and my mind has ample time to worry, the only thing I'm wondering is if Archer is still alive.

It's too late to call him. If he's alive, he's probably shacked up with some girl, anyway.

Pushing off the door, I make my way to the kitchen. I pull a beer from the fridge and crouch to scan the contents. It's bare. I really need to get groceries, but between the café and the bar, I have no time. And it seems Ian ate the pasta I made. All of it.

Looks like I'm drinking my dinner tonight.

Alright.

That's fine.

With a small sigh, I push my feet and lean against the counter, sipping my beer. The kitchen is dark—the entire apartment is dark. I can't hear anything from Ian's room, which means he's asleep and not on his game.

Good.

He needs to sleep.

As I finish the beer and set it in the sink to recycle tomorrow, I hear someone stomp up the wooden steps outside. My neighbors are usually quiet and don't have guests over this late, but there's a girl who lives above me that has friends over all the time. Maybe one of them is leaving.

I pause by the front door, making sure it's locked and lean on it, listening to the person on the other side. Instead of their footsteps retreating, they're getting closer and closer.

Bang!

I jolt and jump away from the door. Rasputin sprints into the room, barking ferociously. Or as ferocious as a pug can.

"Hush, dog. It's me." Ezra's voice is muffled through the door and I let out a harsh breath. Fucking man nearly gave me a heart attack. My hand presses into my chest, my heart pounding beneath as I move toward the door.

"Mom?" Ian rushes into the room as he yanks a shirt over his head. His black hair sticks up in fifty directions and he has lines creasing his cheek from sleep. "Get back." He pushes his way in front of me, puffing his chest out as he moves toward the door.

"Ian." I reach for him, but he easily shakes me off.

He grabs the baseball bat we keep by the front door. It shakes in his hand, but he brings it up, resting it on his shoulder as he slowly walks forward. Ezra knocks on the door again, and Ian jumps, then glances at me over his shoulder.

"It's just—"

"Go to your room," he says. "I can take care of this."

"Ian—"

"Mom, please—"

Bang! Bang!

47

"It's Ez—"

Ian yanks the door open and swings the bat in one fluid motion.

The metal makes a hollow dinging sound when it connects with some part of Ezra's body. He grunts, then stumbles back a step.

"Ian!" I rush forward and grab his arm when he pulls the bat back, ready to attack again. "It's Ezra!"

"Who?"

"Kiwi!" I shout. "Ezra is Kiwi!" I move past Ian, finding Ezra clutching the side of his head.

"Fuck," he groans.

"Shit." I wrap my arm around his broad shoulders and usher him inside. "Grab the First-Aid kit, please."

I flip the overhead light on, making everyone hiss at the sudden brightness. I push Ezra onto the couch, his face scrunched. He's still clutching his head, but there's no blood, so that's probably good?

I hope.

Fuck, I don't know. I'm not a fucking doctor.

"Please tell me that kid is in baseball," he grumbles as I kneel in front of him.

"He doesn't like sports," I say. He cracks an eye open and stares at me.

"With an arm like that, he'd hit the ball outta the fucking park every time." His accent is thicker, and I laugh softly.

"I've been telling him that for years."

Ian rushes back into the room, looking pale and terrified. His eyes are wide and his hands are trembling.

"It's okay, bud," I say gently. "Sit." I jerk my chin at the spot beside Ezra, but Ian just stares at him, shocked.

"Sit," Ezra says more firmly and Ian's feet automatically move. "I'm fine, kid. I blocked most of the hit." He leans into Ian, resting his shoulder against him. "Got a hell of an arm on you."

"Are you okay?" Ian asks, his voice higher than usual. "Oh my God. Are you going to die? Will I go to jail?" Ezra and I blink at him, then he glances at me before clearing his throat.

"No, bud. He's not going to die," I say.

"I'll just have a headache for a bit, that's all," Ezra says with a small shrug. "I've had worse." We stare at him and I know Ian wants to know the same thing I do.

What?

What's been worse than a baseball bat to the head?

He must see it on our faces because he huffs out a laugh, wincing slightly. Dropping his arm, he rests it on his knee and squeezes his eyes shut. He leans back and grabs the bottom of his shirt, pulling it up.

His abs are on full display a few inches from my face and I suddenly realize I'm on my knees between his legs with my kid beside us. Not great. I scoot to the side and drop my eyes to the First-Aid kit to keep myself busy.

"See this?" I glance up, finding him running his finger along a long scar from the bottom of his sternum to his navel.

Ian nods, his eyes wide. I can't miss the excitement burning in them, and it makes me fucking anxious. He hasn't done anything stupid in his life...*yet*. But he's a boy, and the day will come that he wants to do something to impress a girl or show off for his friends. I know he'll end up with a few scars, but I don't want Ezra encouraging it. Rasputin jumps onto the couch and snuggles into Ezra's other side. He rests his hand on my dog like he's done it a million times, like Raspy is his dog.

It shouldn't make my heart feel as warm as it does.

"Got it when I was twenty-one. Some guy was running his mouth all night. He wasn't bothering me until he groped the waitress. So I broke my beer bottle and stabbed him."

Ian's mouth falls open.

"Ez," I hiss. "You can't tell my kid shit like that." I slide my eyes to Ian, but he's still staring at him in wonder, in excitement. There's no trace of fear. He's looking at Ezra like he holds all the secrets to the universe.

"Why?" he asks. "He's not a kid."

49

"Yes, he is."

"No." He shakes his head. "He's not. He's a man." We glare at each other. Ian shifts beside us, drawing our attention.

"What happened next?" he asks.

"Oh, his buddy stabbed me back," Ezra says casually. "Taz took me to the hospital, but I was fine."

"They clearly didn't do a mental evaluation," I say dryly, and he laughs. "Maybe you should go tonight." I inspect his head, cringing at the giant lump forming.

"I'm fine, love," he says, waving me off. "This one–" He shows Ian another scar, "I got when I was surfing. Fell off my board and some coral scratched the shit out of me."

Ian looks enthralled, hanging on every one of Ezra's words.

"You know how to surf?" he asks, then glances at me, his face falling. "She won't teach me."

"Why's that?" Ezra shifts his eyes to me, a lazy grin spreading across his face.

"It's not safe." I give a small, unapologetic shrug. He snorts, then rolls his eyes and looks back at Ian.

"I'll take you some time," he says. "I'll teach you."

"Really?" Ian's eyes sparkle with excitement. "Can we go this weekend?"

"Sure," Ezra laughs. "We can go whenever you want. You can even come with us, love." I roll my eyes.

"What part of it's not safe did you not understand?" I grumble. "I don't want him doing it."

"What part of it's perfectly fine and I'll protect him with my life don't you understand?" He gives me a firm look and I falter.

"You don't mean that."

"I do," he says. "Wholeheartedly."

"Not when it comes down to it," I say quietly. "They're pretty words, Ez. But that's all they are." He stares at me for a moment, his jaw flexing. "Do you need the hospital?"

"No," he says again, and I nod as I push to my feet.

"Then you can go home." I turn to move toward the bathroom. His manic laugh makes my spine stiffen, and I freeze.

"I am home."

"What?" I whirl to face him, finding him with his arm resting along the back of the couch, his legs still spread wide.

"I said, I am home."

"No," I say, drawing the word out. "You're in my home. Go to yours."

"This is my home."

"Ian, go to your room," I say in a low voice.

I glare at Ezra. Whatever tension is building between us, even Rasputin can feel because he jumps off the couch and follows Ian. I give him the First-Aid kit as he passes, then move slowly back to Ezra. Standing in the middle of the room, I put my hands on my hips.

"You need to get the fuck out of my house before I call the police," I say. He settles deeper into the couch, giving me his cocky grin.

I want to fucking throttle him.

And to think, I was just feeling bad about Ian hitting him with the bat. Now I wish he would've hit him harder.

"Get out, Kiwi. I mean it."

"That's not my name," he drawls.

"It's the nicest thing I can call you right now." I pinch between my eyes.

"Please get out. I'm tired and have to go into the café in a few hours."

"Go to bed," he says, jerking his chin toward the hall. "I'll camp out here." He scoots further down, making himself comfortable.

"Go. Home."

"I am home," he says again. He pushes to his feet, and I tip my head back to glare at him. I'm tall, but he's still taller and I hate it. "One day, you'll see this place as my home, too."

"You're not some fucking stray cat I'm bringing home!" I shout. "Get out!" I shove at his chest, trying to push him toward the door.

51

He chuckles, as if it's hilarious he's refusing to leave my fucking house when I'm asking him to. Irritation fills me and I drop my hands away, letting out a frustrated growl. "God, you're such a fucking freak. Get the fuck out!"

His face loses all humor and his eyes darken in a way I've never seen before. The hair rises on my arms, and goosebumps ripple across my skin. I take a hesitant step back, feeling his mood shift instantly.

"I'm not a freak," he says in a low, lethal voice.

"I—I just meant—" I take another step back when he steps toward me. "Ez?"

"Get back!" Ian shouts and we both turn our heads toward him. I don't know if he ever went to his room, or if he's stayed standing in the hallway the entire time. Either way, he shouldn't be here right now.

He rushes forward and pushes his way between us. His back presses against me, pinning me to the wall.

"Get out and stay away from my mom." I peek around him and up at Ezra. He's glaring at Ian, and a part of me is terrified he's about to lose his shit.

"Do you remember what I told you earlier?" he asks in that same low voice.

"I'll do it," Ian says, his voice rising with each word. "I'm not bluffing this time."

"What's he talking about?" I ask, but they ignore me. Kiwi gives him a slow grin as he tips his head down, looking at him through his brows. Fear rips through my body. That look—that look is all Kiwi, no sign of the man, Ezra, in it. "Ian, move." He pushes me harder against the wall, not letting me get out from behind him.

"Good," Kiwi says. Ian's hands ball into fists. They tremble as he brings them up.

"Wait!" I shout. "What the fuck is happening?" They still ignore me, so I shove Ian's back, but he presses against me again. "You're not fighting my fucking kid, Kiwi! If you touch him, I'll fucking kill you!"

His eyes slide to me, and when our gazes lock, he takes a deep breath. He steps back and lets his grin fall.

"Get off your mom," he says tiredly.

Ian doesn't budge.

"Get off me, Ian." I shove him again, but he doesn't move. "Ian!"

"Get out of our house," he sneers at Ezra. "Never come back. Leave my mom alone."

"Ian," I say again. I finally slide out from behind him and shove myself between them. They tower over me, but I press my hands against their chests, pushing them apart. "Get away from each other. You, go to your room." I point to the hallway. "And you," I turn toward Ezra, "get the fuck out."

"I can't," he sighs. "It's not safe."

"What do you mean?" I ask. "For you, or me?" He drops his head forward and lets out another sigh.

"A couple Horsemen said they're targeting The Berserkers to lure The Brotherhood out. I've already told Bash and Spencer, so they know what's happening. I don't know if anyone has seen you at the bar, and I'm not leaving you here unprotected. I'm not risking you."

"I'm here," Ian snaps. "I protect her." My heart squeezes at the fireceness in his tone.

"I know you do, bud," I whisper. But if Ezra is right, then they might've seen me there and they could have followed me home. I can't risk anything happening to Ian. "If they come here, you save him first." I stare up at Ezra, finding his lips tight.

"Kens," he sighs, giving me a look that tells me he won't.

"Please," I say. "Please promise me you'll save my son first." I press my fingers harder into his chest, and watch his throat bob as he swallows.

"We don't need him here," Ian says. "I can protect you, Mom." Ian side-steps me and tries to get between us again, but I don't let him.

"How long will you be here?" I ask and Ezra shrugs.

"Few days, maybe a week. Just until I'm positive they're not targeting you."

"And that shit about this being your home?"

"It was a joke," he says, his voice tight.

"I don't want him here," Ian says. "I don't like you." He shoves Ezra's shoulder. "I don't want you around my mom."

"Tough shit, mate."

I pinch between my eyes again, letting out a long breath. I feel a migraine coming on and could use a long bath and a few tequila shots. Ian shoves Ezra again and he huffs out a laugh.

"Do it again, kid, and I'll fuck you up."

"Okay, enough," I snap. "Ian, go to bed. I'm serious. Right now." He doesn't move and I sigh. Whatever, I'll deal with him in a minute. "You can have my bed, Ez. I'll sleep on the couch." He stares at me like I have six heads.

"I'll sleep right here," he says, taking a step back. When I open my mouth to protest, he shakes his head. "If anyone tries to come in here, they'll have to go through me to get to you. Trust me, no one wants to meet me when they break into my house."

"Whatever," I sigh. "I'm going to take a shower and go to bed. Ian, leave him alone. Ez, leave my kid alone."

"I'll leave him alone when he stops looking at you like that," Ian snarls.

"Just go to bed," I say.

"When you grow up, you'll learn that men like looking at beautiful women. Sometimes, they even like to fu—"

"Ez, shut the fuck up," I growl as I push Ian down the hallway.

Fuck.

This is going to be a nightmare.

Ian

I stand in the doorway, waiting for Mom to walk toward her bedroom. I thought I liked Kiwi, but now I'm not so sure. He seemed cool, but I don't like the way he was looking at Mom, and I don't like that he's trying to make this place his home.

It's not.

She turns down the hall, her usual deep scowl on her face. When her eyes meet mine, she rolls her eyes.

"Go to bed, Ian," she says. She looks exhausted. Dark marks are under her eyes, and her usually slim frame is thinner. I hate that she works two jobs. I told her I would take more hours at the store, but she refused to let me.

She wants me to be a kid and not worry about money and bills until I'm older. But how can I not worry about it when that's all she worries about? I can see the strain and stress on her face every day and if I can do something to help, I don't know why she refuses to let me.

"Why is he here?" I ask, following her into her bedroom. She lets out a sharp breath as she moves to her dresser, taking her earrings off as she goes. "I don't like him."

"You liked him fine earlier," she says, her back to me. I plop onto her bed like it's my own, and watch her flit around the room. "He'll just be here for a few days. Play nice." She gives me a hard look over her shoulder and I roll my eyes.

"I will if he does," I mumble. "But if he keeps looking at you like that, I'm going to punch him in the face." She snorts a laugh as she flips her head down, gathering all her hair into a bun at the top of her head.

"No punching anyone in the face," she says as she stands. She puts her hands on her hips as she stares at me. "How's Enzo?" My stomach twists, but I force myself to shrug.

"Fine," I say, and her eye twitches. She always knows when I'm lying, or holding back. I hate it. Just once I'd like to not be transparent.

"Is he home again?" I nod as she speaks. She sits at the end of the bed, propping herself up with one hand. "You okay?" She rests her other hand on my knee, squeezing slightly.

"Fine," I say again, but she still doesn't look convinced. "I just have a big algebra test today."

"You know you come first," she murmurs, her hand tightening on my knee. "If you don't want him here, I don't give a shit what he says or how crazy he is, I'll kick him out." My mouth tucks up at the corner as I shrug.

"As long as he doesn't get in my way, it'll be fine." She laughs as she pushes to her feet. She presses a kiss to the top of my head, then runs her fingers through my hair.

"You can sleep in here if you want," she says hesitantly. "It'll be like the sleepovers we did when you were a kid." My face heats. Sometimes I think she forgets I'm fifteen.

"I'm good," I say, rolling off the bed to my feet. "That would be weird." She rolls her eyes.

"I'm your mother, it's not weird."

"It's weird because you're my mother," I retort, and she huffs out a laugh.

"So, it's not weird to sleep with Enzo, but it's weird to sleep with me?" She lifts her brows, and my stomach drops with anxiety.

"I don't sleep with Enzo," I say seriously. "He sleeps on the floor or couch. Not in my bed." Her smile slowly falls as she flicks her eyes between mine.

"You know what I meant," she says. I nod as I move toward the door, not trusting myself to say anything else.

"Will you wake me up for school?" I ask, forcing myself to keep my voice light. I glance at her over my shoulder, and she nods.

"Of course," she says. She moves from the room, squeezing my arm on the way out. "You'd tell me if anything was going on, right? If you didn't want Kiwi here?"

"Yep." I open my door, bending to scratch Rasputin's head. "If you want me to get rid of him, I can." She's halfway to the bathroom when she laughs softly.

"I know you can, bud," she says, her hand on the doorframe. "But let me take care of him, alright?" I let out a long sigh, making her laugh. That was my goal, and it makes me feel lighter.

She's always so worried about everything and never lets anyone shoulder any of the burden. I'm old enough to take care of her, so I don't know why she won't let me. We stare at each other for a moment longer. She looks like she wants to say something more, but she just presses her lips into a tight smile.

"I'll get you up in a bit," she says. "Rest." I nod again and turn toward my room, ready to disappear into the darkness. "He won't be here forever." I pause and turn back toward her.

"I know," I say. Again, she hesitates, like she's holding back her words. "Don't worry about me." I smile tightly, and she twists her lips to the side. "I stay in my room most of the time, anyway. It's not like I'll have to talk to him." She still doesn't look convinced, but she nods nonetheless.

"Goodnight, bud," she murmurs. I knock softly on the doorframe as I walk through it.

"Night, Mom."

Kennedy

I 'm forcing Spencer to hire more people when he gets back. I don't care if my pay takes a cut, I can't do this alone anymore. I'm the only bartender and waitress while Arden and Nessa are gone, so I'm running around like a fucking lunatic trying to make sure everyone is covered.

The guys know me and know I'm trying my best, but they're all drunk bikers and their patience only goes so far.

"Come on, Kens!" one of the guys shouts. "I need my fuckin' beer!"

"I'm coming!" I shout back. "Fuck." I hurry past a table and someone pinches my ass. I swat blindly at them, but with how crowded and dark it is, it's impossible to know who it was.

I haven't seen Ezra all night. Come to think of it, I haven't seen anyone in the Inner Circle all night, either. That thought sends a chill down my spine. There's usually at least one of them around to make sure the girls are protected. But Milo, the bouncer, is the only friendly and safe face I see.

Friday nights are our busiest and craziest nights. So even though

I'm the only girl Milo has to keep an eye on, he still has his hands full with drunk men starting fights.

It's nights like these I ask myself why I'm still doing this. Why I haven't just found some stuffy office job and work a nine-to-five. It would be safer, I'd have a steady income, and I could see Ian more.

But I know it would kill me.

"Excuse me," someone snaps.

"Just a sec," I say, my back to them. "I'll help you after I run this to–"

"I just need a fucking beer. I've been standing here for twenty minutes." I whirl toward the man, now just as irritated as he is.

I don't recognize him or the other man he's with. On busy nights, we have a lot of outsiders come through. These two look especially out of place, though. They don't look like bikers. They look like tweakers.

"I said I'll get to you in a sec," I grit out.

"And I said I want a fucking beer," he says. "Where are they? I'll get it myself." He pushes off his barstool and I hold my hand up.

"You're not allowed back here." He scoffs as he approaches. "Milo!" I shout and hope he can hear me over the music and men yelling. "Milo!"

His blond head turns my direction, and the giant bastard makes his way toward me, shoving people out of his way. He's massive and built like a fucking wall, but has a baby face and is more loveable than a golden retriever.

He can fuck someone up, though.

"What's up?" he says, eyeing the man standing in front of the bar.

"He's trying to come back here," I say. "Get him and his friend out of here."

"What?" the man shouts, his face turning red. "I just–"

"You heard her," Milo says, waving his arm toward the door. "Get out."

"This is fucking bullshit," the man scoffs. "You've been waiting on everyone else but us."

"For good reason, too, apparently," I say as I fold my arms over my chest. "You're a fucking prick. Get the fuck away from my bar."

"You fucking bitch!"

"Yeah, I know. Been called a lot worse. Get out." Milo covers his laugh with a cough, and I shoot him a wink.

"I want a beer!" the man shouts, drawing my attention.

"Get it somewhere else." I rest my hands on the bar and lean forward. "Get out before I have Milo throw you out. And trust me, you don't want that." The man's eyes bulge as he glares at me, the veins in his neck popping. I grin at him, knowing I've won.

"You're gonna get yours, bitch," he snarls.

"Sure am," I agree.

He stumbles back a step and his friend grabs him. I tilt my head to the side and watch as one drunkard tries to converse with the other. Milo and I exchange a look, then turn our attention back to the men. A third stumbles from the hallway, looking more drunk than the mouthy one.

The mostly-sober one quickly catches him up, and the three of them make their way out. Once they're gone, I let out a long breath and glance at Milo, giving him an appreciative smile.

"Thanks, man," I say. "I hate guys like that."

"Me too," he snorts. A few men start shouting by the pool tables in the back and he swears under his breath. "You good?" He doesn't look at me as he asks it, instead keeping his attention on the crowd.

"All good," I say. He barely lets me get the words out before he starts pushing his way through the crowd.

"Get back!" he shouts, shoving people away from him. I wait for it to die down before returning to the floor.

It was the wrong night to wear a skirt. The drunker they get, the bolder they get, and the higher their hands get. I want to fucking slice them off their bodies, but I keep a smile on my face. If I don't, I won't get tips and all this will be for nothing.

But when Spencer gets back, we're having a serious talk about this. Everyone knows not to touch Nessa or Arden, since they belong to him. But I'm fair game.

By two, the bar is rowdier and everyone is demanding more drinks. Bar close is at three, so I only need to survive until then. As I round the bar, my eyes lock with Kiwi's and I groan.

"What are you doing here?" I move past him as I grab liquor bottles off the shelf and begin pouring them into glasses.

"Came to take you home," he says. I glance at him, finding him resting his forearms on the bar. He's watching me carefully, his face uncharacteristically humorless.

"I don't leave until four," I say.

"Kenny, baby, we need another round!" someone shouts, and I take a deep breath to calm myself. Kiwi's jaw tenses and his hands tighten into shaky fists.

"Got you!" I call back and slide the bottle back onto the shelf, then grab a few bottles of beer. Piling them all on the tray, I sigh when I look back at Kiwi.

"Why do you work here?" he asks.

"I don't have time for this," I huff. "I can take the bus home. You don't need to stay here."

"Kenny!"

"Oh, no. I'm staying right here," he says as he turns around. He rests his elbows on the bar and stares out at the sea of men. He glares at them all, and, for a moment, I'm worried he's about to lose his shit. But he doesn't say another word. He just watches them.

I try to ignore him as I make the last of my rounds. He gets antsier every time I come back to get more drinks, but I told him he could leave. He doesn't have to stay.

If he's tired or annoyed, he can go home.

To *his* home.

Kiwi

"You really don't need to help," Kennedy says for the millionth time. "You don't work here."

"The faster we get this shit done, the faster we can go home," I grumble.

I grab a few beer bottles by the necks and trudge them to the bin at the back of the room. I'm helping Kennedy and Milo clean up after kicking everyone out. It took nearly an hour, and instead of her leaving at four like she'd said, it's closer to five now.

I'm fucking exhausted.

I rode around with Belfast all fucking day trying to find where Montgomery is holding his girls. We found a few places, but most of them were dead ends. I'm sweaty and tired, and just want a shower, a beer, some greasy ass food, and to sleep for a week.

Instead, I came here to pick up Kennedy and ended up nearly slaughtering everyone in the bar. Every man in this fucking building grabbed her at some point in the night. And she didn't even fucking care.

She laughed and swatted at them, or told them to fuck off, but still batted her lashes at them. She flirted with guys left and right.

One guy even grabbed her tit and, instead of knocking him the fuck out like I expected her to, she just laughed.

That's it.

Just laughed.

It makes me wonder how many other guys she's fucked in the club. I know about her and Archer, but who else?

Before Bash took over as Prez of The Brotherhood, we had a lot of hang arounds—club sluts, the Old-Timers called them. They were there to become someone's Old Lady, but none of us ever wanted them for anything more than pussy.

I never fucked them. I fuck outsiders, not girls associated with the club. That shit gets messy fast.

Bash got rid of them all. He didn't want women whoring themselves out on the off chance one of the guys would want to wife them up. He thought if a guy wanted her badly enough, he'd chase her.

None of the guys did that.

What I'm getting at, is Kennedy just The Berserkers club slut? Does she fuck any and all members because she wants to be an Old Lady?

She didn't seem like the type when I first met her. Shit, she still doesn't seem like the type. But after tonight, after seeing her not care about being groped and fondled by everyone, maybe I've been wrong about her the whole time.

But if she's just another club slut...why won't she look my way at all? Is it just a Berserker she wants? Does she not want to be a part of The Brotherhood and that's why she won't acknowledge me?

It can't be me—I'm hotter and more of a catch than any of the fucks here tonight, but she won't give me the time of fucking day.

Maybe it's just my club.

That has to be it.

"Alright," Kennedy sighs as she leans on the bar, drawing my attention. Milo rests his hand on her upper back and pats her softly.

"Spence should give you a raise," he says, and she snorts.

"That'll be when Hell freezes over. You ready?" She looks at me and I swallow hard. It takes everything I have not to rip Milo's hand off her. I give her a tight nod and move toward the door.

I can't talk to her. I can't look at her. I can't look at either of them. I just fucking can't right now. Not without losing my shit.

Images of Elaine flash through my mind—of her running and laughing, of her smile and her blonde hair floating behind her.

"You always let your emotions rule you. Breathe through them, Ezzy. You're stronger than they are. You control them, they don't control you."

Her voice is so clear in my head it's like she's standing beside me. Tears sting my eyes and I wipe roughly at them, trying to force them to disappear. Trying to force *her* to disappear.

When I get outside, I ram my fist into the side of the building. It's brick and should hurt like fuck, but I can't feel it.

I can't feel a fucking thing.

All I feel is Elaine.

Rearing back, I slam my fist into it again, barely noticing when my knuckles split.

"Ezra!" Kennedy's arms wrap around mine as she pulls me away from the wall. It's then I realize the hot blood dripping from my hand. "What are you doing? Let me see your—fuck! Ez!" She grabs my hand and tilts it back and forth, inspecting it in the moonlight.

I stare blankly down at her, at my hand.

"Why would you do that?" she scolds. I pull my hand away and wipe the blood down the front of my shirt. Nothing feels broken. The skin is just busted open and things will be bruised for a while.

Nothing I haven't felt before. Nothing I won't feel again.

"Let's go," I say.

"Ez, wait." She grabs my arm, but I yank it from her. "What's wrong?"

"Let's go," I say again.

"Talk to me." She grabs my cut and I stop. Closing my eyes, I take a deep breath. But I can't fucking breathe through my emotions like Elaine always wanted me to. There are too many of them. "Please."

64

Kennedy's voice is small, and when I turn around, she looks...different.

Afraid.

She looks afraid.

Of me.

It makes me want to fucking kill myself.

I want to kill myself for making her think she should fear me.

"I won't hurt you," I rasp. "I never would."

"I know," she mutters, then wipes roughly at her cheek. "I know you wouldn't." She laughs and looks away as she wipes at her face again.

"Kens," I whisper, but she shakes her head.

"What's wrong?" She looks up at me, her eyes shadowed.

"Nothing," I sigh. "It's been a long day." She looks disappointed, but that's all I can give her. I can't outright ask her if she's a club slut. And I don't know if that's entirely why I'm pissed.

I don't really give a shit if she's fucked a million men; I'm not exactly a fucking saint. I've fucked more people than I can count, so I can't judge her for doing the same shit.

But maybe it *is* me.

Maybe she doesn't want me.

Maybe it's not my club or the fact that I'm not a Berserker. Maybe it's just that I'm me and she just doesn't fucking like me. Maybe her words last night were true. Maybe she really thinks I'm a fucking freak.

Freak.

Freak.

Freak.

That word has been screamed at me more than my own name has, and I can't blame anyone for it. It's true. I am a freak.

I'm not a protector like Axel is. I'm not a leader like Bash. I'm not a good, All-American boy like Reid.

I'm just a fucking freak.

People die because of me—whether I'm the one killing them or they're being killed, it's always because of me. Either way, it's always my fault they end up dead. I don't do the right thing because I don't care about the right thing. I'm not a good person and I'll never pretend to be.

I care only about myself and the few people around me who have proved themselves worthy of my time and loyalty.

Kennedy deserves someone better than me, I know that. But when she said my name—my *real* name—something inside me clicked into place. Elaine always told me I'd know when I found her—the one. My soulmate. And when Kennedy looked at me and said Ezra, I felt it. I felt it deep in my fucking soul.

She's the one.

She's *my* one.

So even if she deserves someone far better, I'm who she's getting.

Kennedy

I tiptoe out of my bedroom, trying to stay quiet so I won't wake Ezra. He slept on the couch again last night. There's no way that was comfortable for him. His legs dangle over the opposite end so his head can be flat on his pillow. I offered him my bed again, but he just said no, kicked his boots and cut off, and laid down.

I don't know what happened.

His mood was different last night—*he* was different last night. I'd never seen him like that, so upset, so opposite of him before. I wanted to joke with him, but he wouldn't say a word to me. His eyes were vacant in a way I've never seen in anyone before.

I hated it.

That wasn't him. Whoever that was outside the bar last night was not Kiwi. It wasn't Ezra. It just wasn't him.

I poke my head into the living room, surprised to find him awake. He's lying on his back with Rasputin sitting on his broad chest. His large hands dwarf Raspy, making him look a lot smaller than he is. It would be funny if Ezra's eyes weren't damp.

I freeze, unsure of what to do. Should I make myself known? Should I go to him and make sure he's okay? Maybe that would just embarrass him more to know that I've seen him crying. But if I don't do anything, this will eat me alive. I can't let him suffer alone.

"I know you're there," he says quietly, his voice raspy and deep from sleep. He slowly turns his head toward me, looking even more withdrawn.

"Good morning," I say as I walk into the room, wringing my hands together. "How'd you sleep?" He snorts and looks back at Rasputin. He wheezes, and his tongue flops out of his mouth as he pants. Ezra's brows pinch tightly together as he smooths his hand down Raspy's back.

"Should he breathe like that?"

"He's fine," I say, taking a step closer. "It's just his flat nose." I scratch behind his ear, and his breathing gets heavier, and Ezra chuckles. "He has asthma, too. But pugs usually have breathing problems." He nods mindlessly, his eyes trained on the dog.

"What time is it?" he asks. I clear my throat and glance at the clock by the front door.

"Nearly ten," I say, and he looks up at me.

"You don't have to go to the café today?"

"I'm off." I let out a long breath, feeling awkward. "Are you hungry? I can make–" I look toward the kitchen and groan when I remember the lack of food. "Well, I don't have any breakfast food. But I can make fried rice or pasta or something. I'm pretty sure we have instant rice and frozen veggies." He snorts again and shakes his head.

"I gotta get going." He lifts Raspy as he sits up and puts him on the floor. He trots down the hall, probably to jump into my bed or paw at Ian's door until he lets him in.

"Going where?" Ez stands and lifts his hands above his head, groaning as he stretches.

"The clubhouse," he says. "Need to talk to Bash about some shit."

"Oh." I look down at my feet. Why do I feel so awkward? "Ez?" I risk a glance up at him, finding him already staring at me.

"Yeah, love?" He smirks at me when I roll my eyes. I don't know why he started calling me that. It's just so fucking weird, but so fucking Kiwi.

"What happened last night? What was wrong?" His face falls immediately. The blue in his eyes dim and it's like all the light that was beginning to build, fades.

"Nothing," he says as he scrubs his hand over his face.

"Did something happen with Arch?" His head rears back like I slapped him.

"Archer? Why the fuck would anything happen with him?"

"Well, you hate him," I say hesitantly. "I just assumed you were in a bad mood because you had to see him again." He laughs humorlessly as he rolls his eyes.

"Nah, babe. I wasn't in a bad mood because I had to see your boyfriend again." He moves past me toward the hall, and my temper spikes. I grab the back of his shirt, stopping him.

"He's not my boyfriend," I snarl. "Stop saying that."

"So, you fuck guys who aren't your boyfriend often then?" He whirls around to face me, and I step closer to him, pressing my chest against his. I hate that he's taller than me. I want to be in his face. "Don't do that shit, Kens. Don't buck up to me."

"Or what?" I challenge. "What will you do, Kiwi?" His eyes darken and, if I were smart, I'd back off. But I'm not, so I shove his shoulder, taunting him.

Maybe I'm provoking him so I can have him back, the real him. Or maybe it's because I want him to unleash his crazy so I can see how deep it really goes. Maybe I'm a glutton for punishment and like men who can hurt me.

"If you're looking for me to hit you, you're looking at the wrong fucking man," he says in a low, calm voice. "But if you're looking for one to tie you to the bed and edge you until you cry, then I'm your guy." I blink at him, letting his words sink in.

"What?" I breathe. "Edge me? You'd fucking edge me?" He grins as he rests his hand on my waist, digging his thick fingers into my skin.

"Like the thought of that, do you?" I shove at his chest again, and his hold tightens.

"No, you fucking sadist." He throws his head back and laughs, his Adam's apple bobbing like it always does when it's a real laugh. I hadn't heard it in a day and I hadn't realized how much I'd really missed it.

Fuck, this man. He's getting under my skin.

He grabs the back of my neck suddenly, and I squeak. It's a sound I've never fucking made before, and when he lowers his eyes to mine, they're twinkling with hunger. He lowers his head closer to mine until I feel his warm breath along my neck. His lips brush against my ear and goosebumps ripple across my skin.

"I'll show you fucking sadist, baby." His hold on my neck barely tightens, and I suck in a sharp breath.

Bunching his shirt in my fists, I drag him closer. I don't know what I want from him. I don't know if I want him to fuck me or fight with me.

Our eyes stay locked as we glare at each other, his hold on me an anchor. His gaze drops to my mouth as he runs his tongue along his bottom lip, and I feel it–I feel myself melt into him.

My lips part on a silent plea, but just as fast as he'd grabbed me, he lets go and steps away. My head spins, and if it wasn't for his hand on my waist, I'd fall.

He's intoxicating. He's potent.

I blink a few times, ridding myself of the daze he caused, and glare up at him. He just stares back smugly. I want to slap that look off his face, but a bigger part of me wants to kiss it off.

What the fuck is wrong with me? Why is he the only man to make my head go fuzzy like this?

"Get away from me, asshole." I shove at his chest and storm past him, letting his laughter follow me down the hall. Walking back into my bedroom, I slam the door shut and begin to pace.

This isn't good.

Having his full attention is not good. I've learned that now. I can't poke him and expect him to back off like everyone else does. He'll take the fucking bait and switch it on me, giving me a bigger dose of my own medicine. He makes me go fucking crazy, in more ways than one.

And that can't happen.

I've been single my entire fucking life. It's just been my kid and me, and that's all I've ever needed—it's all I've ever wanted. And the guy I'm starting to fall for is fucking Kiwi? Absolutely not. *Nope.* No fucking way.

It wasn't until this exact moment that I even realized I was starting to *like* the fucking asshole!

He's the one my heart is choosing after all these years? After years and years of telling Ian to stay away from bikers because they're nuts and scary, I choose to fall for the nuttiest and scariest of them all?

Am I crazy?

I rub my forehead as I lean against the wall. This isn't happening —I'm refusing to let it. I'm not starting to develop feelings for him. I can't be. He's obnoxious and arrogant. He wouldn't know modesty if it hit him with a fucking truck. He's not my type at all. He makes me want to rage.

But...

But he's also so fucking hot it's unreal. And that crazy streak in him, the one I know runs deep and I haven't even touched the surface on? Yeah, that's the part calling to me. That's the part I'm falling for.

He's protective and overbearing. But he's possessive. I can't handle that. I'm independent. I can deal with protective, but not possessive. I need space. And him deciding my home is his is the opposite of space.

But I can't see myself waking up without seeing him on that stupid fucking couch.

He's been here two nights–that's it, two fucking nights, and already he's engrained himself into my fucking home. Into my life.

"Fuck," I mutter as I close my eyes. Resting my head against the wall, I breathe deeply. I can't be falling for him. He's no good for Ian or me. He'll be a terrible influence on Ian...or he might not be.

He's a good man. He's honorable...when he's not being a fucking basket case.

I stare at the door, anxiously waiting to see if he's going to come to me. But when a few minutes pass and he never knocks, I let out a breath and climb back into bed, deciding to sleep for a few more hours. Maybe I'm just sleep deprived.

That has to be it. Because there is absolutely *no* fucking way I'm falling for Ezra fucking King.

Kiwi

"**H**ey, Prez," I say as I stroll into the Chapel. Bash leans back in his chair, locking his fingers behind his head as he levels me with a look. He looks worn the fuck out. "You should ask Addie for a blowjob or something. You need to relax."

"Kiwi," he sighs as he closes his eyes. "I'm gonna pretend you didn't say that because I'm too fuckin' tired to get up and beat your ass right now."

I laugh as I slide into Axel's chair beside Bash. Rolling the chair away from the table, I kick my booted feet onto it and slump further into the chair as I fold my arms over my chest, grinning at him.

"You requested to see me?" I ask, and he lets out another long breath. "Really, man, you okay?" He shifts his eyes to me, looking shocked.

"What?"

"I asked if you're okay."

"No, I heard you," he says as he leans forward, resting his forearms on the table. "Are you sick? How much time do you have?"

"Fuck off," I laugh. "Can't I want my Prez to not keel over before you turn twenty-eight?" He rubs his forehead, sighing loudly before looking at me again.

"Right," he says. "There's a lot going on."

"Yep," I agree. "That's why I'm here. I'm your peasant. Put me to work." The word slips out before I can stop it and my stomach twists. Peasant. What Kennedy had called me.

I'm happily her peasant, or at least I was before I realized she was just another woman looking to be an Old Lady.

The thought doesn't sit right with me. She just doesn't seem like the type. She doesn't seem like she wants to get with any of the guys, but she's not stopping anyone from groping her, either.

It makes me fucking furious to think about, and I'm trying to force my crazy back but Bash sees through it. He always has.

"What's going on?" He narrows his eyes, scanning my face.

"Nothing," I say, and he lifts his brows. I scrub my hand over my face as I rest my head back against the chair. Staring at the ceiling, I let out a long breath. "I think Kennedy is The Berserkers club slut."

He's silent for a moment, then he clears his throat. "Why?" I shrug, not trusting myself to speak. "Kiwi." I roll my eyes at his warning-filled tone.

"I know, Prez," I say. "I'm not gonna kill anyone." I look down at him and smirk before adding, "Yet."

"They're our fucking allies, man," he groans.

"Someone touches my woman—"

"She's not your woman," he says sharply, and I shrug again.

"Sure she is."

"No, she's not."

"Yes." I drop my feet to the floor and lean forward, resting my forearms on the table as I glare at him.

"Does she know about this?"

"Doesn't matter," I say. "I say she's mine, so she's mine."

"That's not how it works," he laughs. "She has some say."

"Nope." I shake my head. "She'll come around."

"Kiwi." He runs his hand over his head. "Don't scare the woman. We don't need another—"

"That was bullshit and you know it." I point at him and he shakes his head.

"Look, all I'm saying is it wouldn't be the first time a girl has taken a restraining order out on you. Don't go all fuckin' nuts on Kennedy and make her go to the cops." He gives me a hard look and I roll my eyes. "They'll lock you up this time, man. And that's the last thing I fuckin' need right now."

"The charges were dropped as soon as a judge looked at the case," I say. "She was cheating on me and I wanted my shit back."

"You broke into her apartment and slept in her closet for three fucking nights," he says dryly. "And it's not cheating if she didn't know you were even together."

"The guy she was with was a known woman-beater," I say. "I couldn't let him hurt her."

"Kiwi," he says again, exasperated. "Man, come on."

"Like you would've done anything different," I scoff.

"I would have," he says. "I wouldn't have slept in her fucking closet, for one. And two, I would've—"

"Gone Reaper on his ass and killed him?" I snap, lifting my brows. "Why is it okay for you to go crazy and not me? Why is your crazy fine?"

"Because my crazy gets only one person hurt. I know when to stop. You don't."

He's not wrong, but he's not right either.

I know when to stop, it's just that I don't want to stop.

I want every evil motherfucker buried six feet under, and I don't want to stop until that deed is done. But I can't do it all at one time, and that's the thing I forget when I'm in the middle of it.

"What do you need from me?" I ask. He sighs again, knowing I'm done listening to him.

"Have you found anything with Belfast?" he asks. "You know where they're holding the girls?"

"We have a few leads, but nothing solid yet."

"You gonna give me more than that?" he asks, and I shake my head.

"Nah." I push to my feet and knock on the table a few times. "That's it for my status report, Prez. And don't worry about Kens. My crazy is locked up tight."

Kennedy

A knock comes from my door, and I quickly tie my robe before moving to my dresser.

"Come in," I call over my shoulder. I know it's not Ian, since he's at work, and Enzo is still refusing to stay here, so there's only one person it can be. I slide a gold hoop into my ear as the door opens.

"Hey, love." I glance at Ezra, finding him leaning into the room with his hands on top of the doorframe. I hate when he does that, he looks too fucking hot.

I quickly look forward again and ignore his cocky laugh behind me. "What do you want?"

"Thought you'd be dressed already. Don't you start work in a few minutes?"

"Not today," I say, turning to face him as I put the other hoop in. "I go in an hour later today." He nods as he looks around my room.

"I like it in here," he says as he stares at my bed. It's big, comfy, and overflowing with pillows.

"Me too," I say. "Which is why I don't want you in here. You'll fuck up the vibes." He throws his head back and laughs, and I can't

77

help but smile with him. His laugh is contagious. Everything about him is contagious. When he looks back at me, his ocean-colored eyes are twinkling.

"We both know that's not true," he says. "We know the real reason why you don't want me in here."

"Yeah? And what reason is that?" I ask as I fold my arms over my chest.

"Because you'd jump my bones if I came in here."

"Whatever," I laugh. He grins wolfishly as he saunters into the room, kicking the door closed behind him.

"Or maybe I'd jump you." My smile fades as I shift on my feet, uncomfortable under his full attention.

"Whatever," I say again. He prowls toward me, that stupid grin on his face. "I wouldn't let you."

"No?" He tilts his head to the side, a golden curl falling across his forehead. "Can I ask you something?" I scrunch my brows, then nod slowly. "Why haven't you looked my direction, but you've fucked half The Berserkers? Is it because I'm in The Brotherhood, or do you just not like me?"

His question shocks me into silence. My mouth opens and closes a few times, but nothing comes out. I shake my head and take a step away, pressing my back against the dresser.

"I haven't fucked any of The Berserkers," I say slowly. "I haven't—"

"Don't lie to me," he scoffs, his smile sarcastic. "Archer?"

"One time," I say, holding my finger up. "One fucking time, Kiwi. We were both drunk three years ago. It was my birthday, and I was lonely and sad, and he was there. It didn't mean a fucking thing."

"Why does he always touch you? Flirt with you? And you flirt back." He folds his arms over his chest, his eyes narrowing into slits.

"It's a stupid game we play," I say, throwing my arms out. "I don't know. What do you want me to say? That I'm sorry for fucking some guy before I ever knew you even existed?"

"I want you to tell me the truth," he says in that low, lethal voice.

"That is the truth!" I shout, my throat tightening. "What—what are you asking me?"

"I think I've been pretty clear about that, babe."

"Don't fucking call me that," I snarl. "I haven't slept with anyone else in the club. Only Archer."

"Whatever." He shakes his head, laughing mockingly. "I see the way the guys look at you, the way they grab your ass—"

"You think I want that?" I shout, my voice trembling. "You think I like being groped every night by men twice my size for a few bucks?" I close my eyes, willing the tears to stay inside. "You don't understand."

"Why do you let them?" he asks, and my eyes snap open. "You don't even try to stop them."

"I've tried," I say, my voice breaking. A tear finally slips down my cheek and his eyes latch onto it. "What they've done—I couldn't stop him." I wrap my arms around myself. He stiffens, and his face turns deadly.

"Are you saying one of them—"

"Like you give a shit," I laugh. "Like any of you give a shit. No one cares what's happened to me, Kiwi. No one cares about me." It's his turn to look stunned. Stepping forward, I shove his chest, making him step back. I'm mad. I'm pissed at him for blaming me for what they've done to me. How is it my fault? Why should I even have to stop them? They shouldn't be doing it in the first place. "What? Nothing to say now?"

"Kens—"

"What?" I say, shoving him again. "You thought you could come in here and I'd open my legs for you since, apparently, I've fucked everyone else?" He blinks at me, his lips parting. "Is that what you thought?"

"No, I—"

"Then what? You'd fuck me, then what? Add another notch to your belt? Earn bragging rights at the bar?" I shove him again. My tears blur his face, and I bang my fist against his chest. "What do you want?" I shove him again, and he catches my wrists, pinning my hands to his chest.

"I don't want to fuck you," he says, then squeezes his eyes shut and shakes his head firmly. "No, no. I *do* want to fuck you, but not because you're the club slut. Well, no. I thought you were, but—"

"Get out," I say as I try to pull my hands free. "Get the fuck out and never come back."

"No," he says again. "Stop. I'm trying to think." I jerk on my hands again, but he tightens his hold. "Stop it, Kennedy. Let me talk."

"I don't want to hear what you have to say!" I widen my stance to have a better chance at wrenching my hands free, but his grip is iron tight.

"Too bad. You're going to listen to me." His voice is hard, and it makes me pause. I look up at him and stop struggling. "I didn't think you were the club slut, not until last night when I saw everyone touching you. I thought you were trying to become someone's Old Lady—" I guffaw at the idea. That's not me. Not now, not ever. "I was pissed at you today because I thought you fucked everyone—"

"I haven't—"

"I know, baby. I believe you."

Him calling me *baby* takes me by surprise. It's the first time he's ever said it, and the way he did, the way his face looks, it makes me melt. And I hate that he has this effect on me. I shouldn't want to kill him and kiss him at the same time.

His face darkens, losing any softness and warmth he just had, and chills ripple across my skin. "Tonight, you're gonna point out who it was and I'm gonna kill him," he says, his voice deathly low. I blink, then laugh. It's a manic sounding laugh.

"You're not serious."

"I'm dead fucking serious," he growls. "I'm going to kill the fucker. And if it was more than one, they'll die, too. And if you say it was the entire club, then I'll kill every fucking Berserker. If anyone touches you tonight, they lose their fucking hand. They say anything to you, they lose their tongue. I don't give a shit, Kennedy, I will kill everyone for you."

My lips part as I stare into his deadly serious face. His blond brows are bunched, his eyes intense, his hands tight around mine.

He's serious.

It should terrify me. His threats should scare the shit out of me and make me want to call the cops. But they don't. They make me feel...*safe*. He makes me feel safe.

I don't give myself time to think, otherwise I would talk some sense into myself. Lifting up on my toes, I press my lips to his. I think it shocks him as much as it shocks me because he stays totally stiff for a moment.

Then he pounces.

His hands move from pinning mine to his chest to wrapping around me, pulling me to him. He devours me, his tongue sliding against mine, his teeth nipping at my lip. He slides his hand up my back and into my hair, gripping it tightly and yanking my head back. He licks the length of my throat, flicking it over my pulse before biting down.

"Ezra," I moan, my eyes closing.

"Fuck," he rasps against my skin. "I love hearing you say my name. You have no idea how much I've wanted this." He picks me up and I wrap my legs around his waist as he carries me to the bed.

He lays me on the edge and drapes his body over mine, rocking his hips against mine. I claw at his back as he bites my neck again, and the sound that comes out of me isn't one I've made before.

"I wanted to bend you over the bar and fuck you the first time I saw you. I wanted to make you mine, then and there."

I kiss him before he can say anything else. My fingers tangle in his curls and he groans. He stands above me and yanks his shirt off in a fluid motion, exposing the whirling black ink of his tattoo. A cocky grin spreads across his face and I laugh.

"Did you practice that?"

"In the mirror everyday for a year," he says, and I laugh again. "Was it impressive?"

"Not at all."

He dives back down and bites my neck harder, making me cry out. His hips slam against mine and my nails dig into his biceps.

"Was it impressive, Kennedy?" he growls as he grinds against me.

"Yes," I moan, arching my back.

"That's what I thought," he says smugly. "Don't lie to me again." His hands slide up my waist to my breasts, and he roughly cups them, pushing them together. "Fuck, your tits are nice."

He kneads and squeezes them before untying my robe and letting it fall open. It exposes my black bra and panties and his eyes roam over my body frantically, like he doesn't know where to look first. I run my fingers along his abs, feeling them flex under my touch.

"You're so fucking hot," he breathes as he rubs his thumbs over my peaked nipples. Gently, he tugs the cups of my bra down, exposing my breasts. He drops his head into my neck and groans. "Fuck." He pauses for a moment before he moves his mouth to my nipple and swirls his tongue around the piercing, then gently sucks on it. I arch my back more, pressing my breast into his mouth. "Are these real?" He lifts his head to look at me as he continues squeezing them.

"Yes," I laugh. "I can't tell if that's a compliment or not."

"It is," he says, nodding as he drops his eyes back to my tits. "Fuck, it is."

He presses his face between them, groaning as he kisses my sternum, the curve of one breast, then the other. His stubble is rough against my skin, but I love the way it feels.

"You smell so fucking good," he breathes as he trails kisses around my chest. I lift my hips, grinding against his cock through his jeans. Finally, he stands to his full height and stares down at me, his warm hands rubbing mindlessly up and down my sides.

"I love your tattoos," he says as he traces the one under my breasts with the tip of his finger. "One day, when we have more time, I'll kiss every single one of them. When we have the time, I'll worship your body the way it was meant to be worshiped."

I shudder at his words and tighten my legs around him. He grins as he slides his hands lower. He rests one on my hip, the other slides onto my lower stomach. He teasingly runs his thumb over my panties and smiles broader when he feels them wet.

"So wet for me, love," he says. "So eager. I like that." He presses on my clit and rubs his thumb back and forth, then pauses, his eyes widening. "Wait."

Roughly, he yanks my panties off and tosses them to the floor, then pushes my legs apart, pinning my knees to the bed. He drops to his knees and stares at my clit piercing in awe. Finally, he lifts his eyes to mine.

"Will you marry me?" he asks, and I swat at him. "I'm serious. I've never seen one in person. You're perfect." He hesitantly flicks the piercing with his tongue and I whimper softly. His eyes stay on my face as he slides his tongue back and forth, watching me writhe.

"Ez," I moan, "please." Something snaps inside him at my words. He pushes my legs up to my chest, forcing me open wider for him.

He flicks my clit faster with his tongue, turning me into a moaning mess under him. When he sucks it into his mouth, rolling the piercing between his lips, I lose it. It makes me see fucking stars. I drop my hand to his head, holding him tightly against my pussy.

"Hold your legs," he demands. I hook my arms behind my legs, pushing them back, practically folding myself in half. "Seriously," he says, his eyes widening comically, "we can go to the courthouse after this."

"Just eat my pussy," I say, and his brows flick up.

"I don't think you're the one in charge here," he says and I drop my legs. As soon as I let go, he slaps my pussy. Hard. I scream, my hips shooting off the bed.

"Kiwi! Ezra!" I sputter, my eyes wide with shock. He gets to his feet and towers above me. "Let's get this clear right now. I'm the one in charge. You do what I say, not the other way around. When I tell you to get on your knees and suck my cock, you'll get on your knees and open your mouth. When I eat your cunt and make you come, you'll thank me for it. And when I bury my cock inside you, you'll scream and beg me to let you come, and I might allow it. You'll open your legs wider and let me come inside you. You'll do whatever the fuck I say like a good little slut, or you will be punished. Are we clear?"

My breathing is harsh as I stare up at him. His face is less than an inch from mine, and the way he's looming over me, his body not touching mine but close enough for me to feel his heat, and the sternness in his voice...it makes me sick with desire. I nod slowly, feeling dazed.

"What do you say?" he growls.

"Yes sir," I immediately say, hoping it's the right thing. He grins slowly, his full lips tipping up mischievously.

"I've never been called sir," he says. "I like it. Good slut." He dips down and presses his lips firmly to mine before dropping back to his knees. "Now, do whatever yoga shit you were just doing and let me eat this sweet little pussy."

He drops his mouth back to my clit, and my hands tighten around the back of my knees. I squeeze my eyes shut as he rolls it between his lips, then sucks roughly on it. He shoves two fingers roughly inside me, and my eyes snap open.

"Ez." I stare down at him, panting hard as he flicks the tip of his tongue against the piercing, moving it back and forth, causing just enough friction to tease me. "Come on." He hooks his fingers up and presses them against my walls as he flattens his tongue against my clit.

"Have you ever squirted?" he asks, and I shake my head.

"No," I moan. "I don't think I can. If I could, I would've done it by now."

"A challenge," he says. "I'll get you to squirt all over me." He fucks me harder with his fingers. "I want to drink you down and absorb you into my blood."

"What the fuck," I breathe as my eyes roll back.

"I want you to become a part of me," he continues. "And I'll become a part of you. We'll be one."

"I don't even know what the fuck you're saying right now," I groan. My nails dig into my skin as I pull my legs back further. My toes touch the blanket above my head, and he swears under his breath.

"You don't need to understand right now. You'll understand soon enough." Maybe after I come, his words will terrify me, but right now, whatever the fuck he's doing feels too good for me to care.

"Just don't kill me," I say, and he laughs, the vibration shooting through me. I tighten around his thick fingers, feeling my orgasm build.

"I'd never do that," he says. "This world needs a dark gem like you in it." He moves his mouth back to my clit and licks faster, driving my pleasure up. Before I can reach the edge, he pulls his mouth away and I let out a frustrated growl. "Give yourself to me."

"What?"

"Tell me you're mine," he says.

"I'm not," I breathe. He stretches his fingers apart inside me, and I cry out. He fucks me harder, using the force of his entire arm.

"Say it." My back arches off the bed, my orgasm so fucking close.

"Fuck! Fuck, please," I cry out.

"Say it, slut. Say you belong to me." He sucks my clit into his mouth, then bites down until I scream. His movements are almost painful as he rams his fingers into me. He shoves a third finger inside, and I scream louder. "I'll stick my entire fucking fist inside you. Tell me you belong to me. Tell me I own you."

The words won't come.

My breath gets caught in my lungs as I open my mouth to scream. He reaches around with his other hand and spreads my pussy apart, exposing my clit more, and lightly taps it with the tip of his tongue.

"Say it," he growls. "Mine." He flicks it again, fucking me harder.

"Say. It. Mine." He says it over and over, punctuating his words with each hard thrust and lick.

My toes curl and my legs straighten as they shake. "Ezra!" I scream his name as I come, my pussy clamping down around his fingers until he can't move them. My entire body convulses until my orgasm passes, then I collapse.

He continues lapping at my clit, making me whimper with each lick, but he doesn't stop. His fingers begin moving inside me again, slower this time. He works a fourth finger in, and my eyes roll back. I can't come again. My body can't handle another one.

"Not again," I beg. He ignores me as he hooks his fingers again.

"Why didn't you say it?" he asks as he finger-fucks me at a casual pace.

"Because—" I pause as I stare down at him. "I'm not."

"Yes, you are."

"Can we have this conversation later? When you're not—"

"No," he snaps, and rams his fingers harder into me, making me gasp. "We'll talk about it now. I say you're mine, so you're mine. Now tell me."

"I can't just get into a relationship with you," I say. He reaches around with his other hand again and slowly strums my clit. "Fuck, can you not do that right now?"

"I want you to come again and we need to talk about this," he says, like it's the most reasonable and normal thing in the world. "Why can't you?"

"I have a kid, Ez. I can't just get with some guy I don't know."

"I'm not some guy," he growls. "I'm your soulmate."

I stare at him and wait for him to laugh or say he's just kidding. But when he never does, I push my brows together. Another orgasm builds if I want it to or not, and I have to try really fucking hard to focus on talking.

"You don't really think that," I pant. "Soulmates don't exist."

"They do. And you're mine." He strums his fingers faster and my eyes roll back.

"Ez, please," I moan, but he doesn't stop, not that I want him to. "I can't say it." He lets out a low growl, moving his fingers faster until I can't hold back anymore. I come again, not as hard as the first time, but it's still one of the best orgasms of my life.

When I come down, he pulls away and I drop my legs. He massages my hips, then leans over my body and kisses me before resting his forehead against mine.

"You will give yourself to me, Kennedy. One way or another, you'll be mine one day and I'll do everything I can to get you. I'll never stop chasing you. I'll never stop begging you." He looks into my eyes, the fierceness in them making me hold my breath. "You'll never get rid of me. You're stuck with me forever, whether you want me or not. Because even if you don't believe it, we're soulmates, baby."

Kennedy

"**Y**ou don't need to help," I say again.

"I know," Ezra says as he wipes the bar down. "You keep saying that."

"Because it's not your job." I toss the towel onto the table and turn toward him, my hands on my hips.

"Who else is gonna help you?" He rests his hands on the bar and leans forward. "I'm here. Use me. Tell me what to do." I smirk at him and lean my hip against the table.

"Now I can tell you what to do?"

"Only outside of the bedroom, love." He winks as he tosses his rag onto the bar. I laugh as I shake my head at him, grabbing my towel to continue wiping down the tables.

I don't know what to make of the whole *soulmates* thing. But after he said it, he kissed me again, then left me alone to let me finish getting dressed.

Maybe he just went a little crazy from the lust. Now he's back to normal—or as normal as Kiwi can be. I swear it's like dealing with Dr. Jekyll and Mr. Hyde.

"Can you grab the beers from the storeroom in the back, please?"

"Sure thing." He claps his hands, giving me a wicked grin. "Was that so hard?"

He's teasing, but it was hard.

Asking for help is fucking hard.

He swaggers to the back while I finish the tables and bar. Milo doesn't come in until we're about to open, but he stays late to help clean up. It works out, so I don't complain. Plus, I like setting up on my own. It lets me get in the right headspace to deal with these assholes.

"How do you work without music?" Ezra asks as he walks back into the room. He's carrying boxes of beer stacked on top of each other effortlessly, his biceps bulging deliciously. "You gonna stop eye fucking me?" I blink a few times as I lift my eyes to his. He grins as he sets the boxes on the bar.

I clear my throat and throw my thumb over my shoulder. "The jukebox is in the back. Knock yourself out."

"Oh, goody," he laughs as he wiggles his fingers. He taps my ass as he passes me and I swat his shoulder, but smile to myself. He shouldn't make me feel like this—*happy.*

Ian's going to fucking kill me when he finds out. Finds out what exactly, I don't know. I don't know what the fuck is even going on between us. I can't tell my son Ezra went down on me and now he thinks we're fucking soulmates and I need to give myself to him, whatever the fuck that means.

I roll my eyes when the opening notes to *Rock And Roll All Nite* by KISS comes on. I turn around, finding him dancing, if it can even be called dancing.

He's swinging his hips and jerking his thumbs over his shoulders, his head back and his golden hair swaying. He looks fucking ridiculous. Mesmerizing.

He starts screaming the words, startling me, and I laugh. Turning toward me, he slowly prowls forward, still singing totally off key. I grin and toss the rag down, then fold my arms over my chest.

"Come on, you know this one," he says. He grabs my waist, pulling me to him as I nod.

"Of course," I scoff.

"Sing with me then, love." He roughly pulls me to him, forcing my hips to move with his. I rest my hands on his shoulders, laughing to myself as I start singing with him.

He spins me around, then pulls me back and presses my ass against him, moving in time with the music. He's a terrible singer and an even worse dancer, but I can't stop laughing. His head rests against mine as the song begins to fade, and he wraps his arms around me.

We stay swaying in the middle of the empty bar, his chin resting on my shoulder, my hands over his arms. I want to stay like this forever. Just him and me, alone in the world, without a worry or care.

Just us.

A throat clears and the bubble bursts. My eyes snap open, and I try to bolt, but Ezra's arms tighten around me. I jerk my head toward the entrance, finding Archer standing there with his eyebrows low over his eyes and his hands in his pockets. I try to leave Ezra's arms again, but he doesn't let me.

Instead, he tightens his hold even more, then kisses my neck before biting it. I squeak, my eyes locked with Archer's. Ezra's teeth sink in further and he presses into my ass, grinding against me.

Surely he heard Archer?

Archer clears his throat again, shifting from foot to foot, looking uncomfortable. That's all it takes to clear my head and realize what the fuck is happening. I slap Ezra's wrist and he chuckles low in my ear before letting go. I wipe at my neck, but feel a mark already starting to bloom.

"Hey, Arch," I say breathlessly.

"Sorry to interrupt," he says awkwardly.

"You're not interrupting," I say.

"No, you are," Ezra says dryly. "What do you want?" I whirl toward him, finding him glaring at Archer. I stare at him, waiting for him to laugh or apologize for being rude, but he doesn't. He just lifts his brows impatiently. "Well?"

"Belfast called and said he's been trying to get ahold of you," he says, sounding irritated. "You know, I have better shit to do with my time than hunt you down."

"Yeah? Like what?" Ezra challenges. He folds his arms over his chest as he tilts his head back. "You have an appointment to get your asshole bleached?"

"Kiwi," I hiss.

"Why? You wanna see?" Archer retorts and I snap my head to him.

"Nah, I'm good, mate," he says. "But if you're down to show just anyone your ass, I'm sure the homeless guy out back would love a taste."

"Know that from personal experience, do you?"

"Nah, but your mom told me he's real talented with his tongue."

I drop my head back and squeeze my eyes shut. Men never really grow up from boys, do they? I hold my breath, waiting for one of them to take the first swing, but to my utter fucking surprise, Acher laughs.

I stare at him like he's lost his fucking mind.

Then Ezra laughs, and I stare at him like he's lost his mind too. Which, to be fair, he probably has.

"Gotta say, I haven't heard a *your mom* joke in at least a decade," Archer says.

"It's a classic." Ezra shrugs, still grinning.

"What the actual fuck," I mutter as I look between them. "You know what? As long as no one is getting killed, I don't give a shit." I throw my hands up. "Become best friends for all I care."

"Does that mean we can compare notes?" Ezra says, and I whirl to glare at him again. Archer stays silent behind me, but I can feel his gaze stabbing into the back of my head.

"Really?" I snap. "Are you fucking kidding me? It's been less than an hour—this is what I was talking about, Kiwi. You just wanted bragging rights." I shake my head. "I can't believe I was so fucking stupid."

I open and close my hands a few times before storming off to the back of the bar. Both men call out for me, but neither of them follow. I won't lie—it hurts that they don't. But I should've expected it.

Apart from some light flirting, I can't count on Archer for anything major. And emotions fall into the major category. And with Kiwi—I don't even know. I just thought he would be different.

I thought...

I don't know what I thought.

I slam the door to the storeroom and wipe roughly at my cheek, annoyed that he could make me cry. But I thought he was different. I thought he'd be the one guy I could count on to not make me feel cheap. But I should've known better. He doesn't care. He doesn't think about anyone but himself. He just does what he wants, and doesn't give a fuck who he hurts in the process.

Kiwi

"**W**hat the fuck?" I breathe as I watch Kennedy storm away. I glance at Archer, finding him staring after her, too. "What just happened?" He turns and glares at me, which makes me even more fucking confused. "What?"

"She's not the type to kiss and tell," he says. I scrunch my brows together.

"What does that have to do with anything?" I ask, and he sighs.

"Man, you just said we could compare notes. So, obviously, you've slept together—"

"We didn't, though," I say, cutting him off. "We just hooked up, but didn't fuck." He scrubs his hand over his face.

"She doesn't like people in her business."

"But I thought you two were close." I use air quotes around the word before folding my arms over my chest to glare at him. He shakes his head, then wraps his hand around the back of his neck.

"We're friends," he says. "We slept together years ago when we were both drunk. But we're friends first. I mean, I wanted to be with her, but she's not the relationship type, you know?" I stare down the hall, wanting to see through the walls and rooms to see if she's okay.

93

"She has a hard time here, you know, being a woman who's crazy fucking hot." I snap my head back to him.

"Don't." He grins, and I know he's just taunting me. "Fuck you." He grins broader, and I turn toward the hall, ready to chase her when my phone vibrates. I close my eyes and take a deep breath before pulling it from my back pocket. Without looking at who called, I answer and bark, "What?"

"Need you at the clubhouse," Bash says briskly.

"For what?" I grip my phone tighter, my eyes still trained on the door at the end of the hall.

"Belfast is here, but isn't fucking talking to anyone. Only you and Ry know how to communicate with him, and Ry isn't answering his fuckin' phone." He sounds more irritated than usual, and I sigh as I scrub my hand over my face.

"Give me thirty minutes," I grumble.

"Where are you?"

"The Crossroads," I say, huffing out a breath.

"Should only take you fifteen to get here," he says. "Ten if you hurry."

"Give me—"

"Now," he snaps, using his Prez voice. I drop my head back and let out a long breath.

"Fine. I can't stay long," I say, but he hung up as soon as I said fine. I want to throw my phone against the wall, but I don't. Honestly, I should get an award for that alone. Turning toward Archer, I study him. Do I really want to invite him? "Wanna go to the clubhouse?" His brows lift and he glances down the hall.

"What about—"

"I'll talk to her later," I sigh. My fingers tangle in my hair as I try to comb them through, so I yank roughly on it.

"I think you should—"

"You coming or not? I don't have time for this." I walk past him, hitting his shoulder with mine. He hesitates, but quickly follows after me as I shove the door open and step out into the balmy night.

"Can't fucking believe this." I slide onto my bike, immediately turning it on.

"What's going on?" Archer asks over the rumble of our bikes.

"Bash can't talk to Belfast, and apparently, I'm the only fucking one who can do it." I grip the handlebars tighter, then take off down the street before he can say anything.

As Bash predicted, it takes only fifteen minutes to get to the club-house. Archer is with me, keeping close to my side as we walk into the Chapel. Bash is glaring at Belfast while he sits calmly in Reid's usual chair, staring back at Bash. Addie shifts uncomfortably in her chair, then glances at me.

"Thank God you're here," she breathes, then immediately looks to Belfast. "I just meant—I haven't seen Kiwi in a while and—"

"It's fine, babe," I say. "He's pretty much a robot." Belfast grunts as he turns his eyes to the laptop. "See?" Addie gives me a pleading look, and I laugh. "What was so important that you needed me here?" Bash turns his attention to me, his eyes dark.

"Excuse me?" he says in a low voice.

"Come on," I say, rolling my eyes. Addie puts her hand on his forearm and squeezes gently. He glances at her and sighs, then leans back in his chair.

"I can't get him to tell me anything." He throws his hand toward Belfast, and I swear his lips fucking twitch. That's the closest thing to a smile I've ever seen from him.

"What is it?" I round the table, leaving Archer awkwardly standing at the door. Peering over Belfast's shoulder, I see the locations we've been scouting. "You couldn't have just told him this?" I mutter and he looks at me over his shoulder, his face as blank as ever. "Right. It's just a list of places we've checked out. We haven't had any luck. Still have two more places to scout."

Bash looks fucking exhausted when I look at him. Addie doesn't look much better. He nods and slouches down in his chair more.

"Figured, but—"

"Next time, will you just tell him what he wants to know?" I grumble, staring at the back of Bel's shaved head. He gives the slightest shrug.

"I can try," he says, his Irish accent thick. Bash's eyes bug out of his fucking head as he stares at Belfast. He looks seconds away from losing it.

"Is that it?" I ask. "I really need to take care—"

"One more thing," Bash says. "I want you to go check on Reid and Heather."

"Since when did I become an errand boy?" I snap, throwing my arms out. My rage is simmering and I'm trying really fucking hard to control it, but with every order Bash gives me, I feel it about to boil over.

"Kiwi," he says in that same low voice.

"I have shit to do, too, you know." I fold my arms over my chest and step my feet apart. Archer clears his throat from the door and we both turn to look at him. Immediately, he puts his hands up.

"I didn't say anything," he says quickly. Bash's eyes narrow and Archer takes a step back. "Not a word." He shakes his head, his hands still up. He's nearly backed into the hall when Bash sighs.

"Just check on them," Bash says, looking back at me. "Heather told Addie Reid's going stir crazy."

"He's been there a few days," I say, and he shrugs. "Fine. Whatever." I stomp toward the door and Bash clears his throat, making me pause.

"I know this is a stressful time," he says, and I stare at Archer, daring him to say something. "So I'm letting this attitude slide. But you need to lose it before I see you again. We clear?"

"Crystal," I grit out. Archer's lips tuck up in a smirk, and I storm out of the room, slamming the door behind me.

Kiwi

I bang on the door of Heather and Reid's place. They're in a safe house since he was beaten to shit by Montgomery's men, and Heather's name is still on the auction list. They're supposed to be lying low but apparently don't give a fuck because they've been begging Bash to let them leave.

Well, Reid has been begging Bash to let them leave. I don't know if Heather really cares.

"Open the fucking door!" I bang on it again, irritated that I'm here and not with Kennedy. I need to fix what I fucked up and I can't do that when I'm running around doing shit for everyone else. "Reid!" The door swings open and I meet Reid—a shirtless, sweaty Reid. I glance down, finding him adjusting himself, trying to hide his hard on. "Really?"

"I didn't know you were coming," he says, and I grin.

"Looks like you're not either, huh?" He rolls his eyes and pushes the door open further. I clap him on the shoulder as I pass. Archer left somewhere along the way, probably heading back to The Crossroads so he can play white knight and be the shoulder Kennedy cries on. "Nice place."

It's a small one-bedroom house that's more like a fucking studio apartment than anything else. It's one giant room with a bed and TV on one side, the kitchen on the other, a door that leads to the bathroom, and the front door.

Heather scrambles to lift the sheet up to her shoulders, giving Reid a look. "Nothing I haven't seen before, Heather-babes," I say, winking at her. She rolls her eyes, but grins.

"What are you doing here?" she asks.

"Bash told me to come check on you," I say, leaning against the kitchen counter, looking between them. Heather's hair is a wild mess, Reid's isn't much better, and the state of the place looks like a boy's dorm room during his first year of college—a fucking wreck. "What the fuck have you two been doing?"

"It's pretty obvious," she says, and I shake my head.

"This place is a mess." I kick a soda box with my foot and she shrugs.

"We're busy."

"Busy doing what? You're in a cardboard fucking box on lockdown. There's nothing else for you to do except clean."

"And fuck," she says slyly.

"Touche." She smiles triumphantly, then slides to the end of the bed and grabs Reid's discarded shirt. Sliding it on over her head, the sheet falls, exposing her breasts. She's still bruised and her cuts are still healing, but fuck. I remember those tits well.

Reid snaps his fingers in front of my face and when I look at him, he looks ready to kill me. I just grin and fold my arms over my chest.

"Clearly, we're fine," Reid snaps. "You can leave now." My eyes drift back to Heather as she bends over, showing off her perfect ass, as she searches for her bottoms. "Kiwi, I swear to fucking God–"

"I have a girl, I don't need yours." They both pause. Heather slowly slides her shorts on and turns toward me, looking stunned. "What?"

"You have a girl?" she asks. "Who?" Reid shoots her a look, but she stays staring at me.

"Kennedy." Reid throws his head back and laughs. "What?"

"I thought you were serious," he says, shaking his head. "She's not your girl."

"Yes, she is."

"Why isn't she?"

Heather and I say at the same time. Reid's smile never falls as he sits on the edge of the bed.

"She's such a hard ass she would never fucking date you," he says and I clench my hands into tight fists.

"Reid," Heather hisses. "That's fucked up."

"It's true," he shrugs. "If she hasn't ended up with one of The Berserkers, why would she end up with him?" He throws his arm toward me, and Heather winces.

"She's mine," I say, my voice low, Heather's eyes widening at my tone.

"Reid," she says again, still looking at me. "Apologize." He snorts, his face smug, and I see fucking red. "Apologize. Now." He just stares at me. We play a silent game of chicken, each waiting for the other to snap first.

"Maybe I should call her," he taunts, "ask her if she's yours?" Heather takes a few steps back, pressing her back against the wall as she looks between us.

"She is mine," I say again. "She is."

"Keep telling yourself that," he laughs. "Is this like Arianna?" I grit my teeth.

"Arianna?" Heather asks, her eyes still darting between us.

"You wanna tell her about that?" Reid reclines back on the bed, wincing slightly. "Or should I?"

"It was a misunderstanding," I ground out.

"Misunderstanding?" he laughs. "You stalked her."

"It wasn't stalking," I grumble, then turn toward Heather. "I thought we were something more than we were, and when I saw her with another guy, I got a little upset." Reid snorts again, and my hands tighten into fists.

"A little upset?" he prompts.

"I might've lived in her closet for a few days," I say under my breath.

"You lived in her closet?" Heather breathes.

"And?" Reid says. I huff out an irritated breath.

"And she took a restraining order out on me." Heather's eyes widen even more. "But the charges were fucking dropped!" I turn back toward Reid, my chest fiery. "I was only looking out for her. The guy she was with was a piece of shit and I just wanted to protect her."

"So, is that what you're doing with Kennedy?" Reid asks, lifting his brows. "Protecting her from something as a way to get close?" I open my mouth to deny it, but I pause.

That's exactly what I'm doing.

Fuck.

"Fuck you," I snarl and storm across the room. "Prez wanted me to check on you, and I did. You can fuck yourself now." I slam the door behind me and stomp toward my bike.

Bullshit.

This is different. Shit with Kennedy is different than it was with Ari. Things with her were complicated, and I was in a bad place. Yeah, I wanted to protect her, but I was in the right on that. And I'm in the right on this, too. I'm just trying to look out for Kennedy. And Ian.

I'm watching after them both.

Even if everyone thinks I'm a psychopath, I know I'm doing the right thing. I am. I know I am.

But why do I still feel so guilty about it?

Kennedy

I abruptly stop when I walk out of the bar and Milo runs into my back, making me stumble forward a few steps. His thick arm wraps around my waist before I can fall, and a feral-sounding growl rips from Ezra's chest.

"Don't touch her," he says as Milo helps me stand. His hands hover around my waist, ready to catch me if I trip again.

"You'd rather I fall?" I snap as I glare at him. He's still leaning against his stupid fucking bike, his face deadly as he stares at Milo. "What are you doing here? You leaving was a clear fucking message."

When I came out of hiding and found the bar empty except for Milo, it hurt. I won't lie. My chest ached. Even if he hadn't chased me, I'd at least expected him to stick around but when I realized he hadn't...I understood perfectly. I was just a girl to fuck before he moved onto the next one.

"Bash called and needed me," he says and I lift my brow, waiting for a better excuse. "I couldn't tell him no." I continue staring at him and he huffs out a breath. "He's my fucking Prez, Kens. I can't tell him to fuck off when he needs me."

"So, you can tell me to fuck off when I need you?" I hate the way my voice shakes. Milo clears his throat, then sidesteps me.

"You gonna be okay, Kenny?" he asks, glancing at Ezra. "You still need a ride?" He throws his thumb over his shoulder, looking uncomfortable as shit.

"She has one." Ezra and I stare at each other. I shouldn't give in. I should tell him to fuck himself and hop on the back of Milo's bike, but I find myself wanting to fight with him.

"I'm fine," I say, never taking my eyes off Ezra. "I'll see you tomorrow." Milo hesitates before he nods and heads toward his bike. We stay silent until he's ridden away, leaving us completely alone.

"You needed me?" he asks, taking a step forward.

"No." I keep my lips pressed tightly together. "I don't need anyone."

"Everyone needs someone," he says quietly.

"I have Ian." His jaw tenses as he takes another step forward. I don't back away, though. I want to push him, I want him to push me, until we've broken each other. "You don't need to lie to me, you know. If I'm too much—"

"You're not," he snaps. "I didn't understand what happened at first. But when I did, I was going to go to you, then Bash called and—"

"And he comes first," I say, nodding.

"No—"

"The club comes first," I continue. "It'll always come first."

"What do you want me to do?" he says, his voice rising. "Want me to cut my patch off? Give up my colors?" I work my jaw to the side, trying not to scream at him. "Answer me, is that what you want?" He takes another step closer, his voice frantic and loud. Tears swim in my eyes even though I don't want them to.

"Yes."

He lets out a breath like I gut-punched him. His eyes widen, like he can't believe I said it. But I did. And maybe it's a stupid fucking game to see if he'll choose me over his club, but I want to play it.

"You—" He's breathless, sounding like he's edging a panic attack.

"You want me to give it up. Leave The Brotherhood." I lift my chin, staring at him as I wait for him to process his emotions and figure out what he's really feeling. "I—Kennedy."

"If you weren't serious, why would you offer it?" I ask. "If you wouldn't really do it, why—" His phone rings and I roll my eyes, huffing out a humorless laugh. "Better get that."

I take off down the sidewalk, ignoring him shouting my name. But I don't hear him coming after me.

I know what I'm doing. I know I'm pushing him away. And I don't care. I don't care that I'm hurting us both in the process. I just— I can't be with someone like him.

Ian needs someone who isn't going to fucking die on him, like my dad did. He gave his life up for The Berserkers, and I won't let Ian go through that kind of pain. Even if Ezra wouldn't be his real father, he'd be like one to him, and him dying would destroy us both.

I swallow my emotions as I realize that's the real reason why I'm doing this. I can't have another man get taken from me because of club life. Everyone wants to be with a biker, every girl wants to rep their man's colors, until it comes down to it. Until they're on the outside looking in. Until they're left with nothing but a bloody cut to remember them by. Until they're nothing but another club widow.

Ezra's bike rumbles to life and I turn toward him, finding him riding toward me.

"Get the fuck on, right now." I pause at his tone. "Someone took Madi, and I need to take you home before I go to the clubhouse. I don't care that you're pissed. I'm not letting you walk home alone."

"Ez—"

"Just get on." He holds his helmet out to me, and I take it in my shaky hands. "Hold on tight. I'm not slowing down for anything." I nod as I slide onto the back of his bike and wrap my hands tightly around his waist.

He was serious. He soars through the streets, everything around us a blur. It feels like we're flying, like I'm weightless. I always understood the appeal of a bike, but the fear of them always kept me from getting my own. The fear always kept me from getting with a man who had one.

Too soon, he pulls right up to the stairs that lead to my apartment. "Do you need me to walk you up?" he asks, his body shaking.

"No," I say as I slip off. I turn, then take a deep breath, wondering if I'm a fucking idiot. Turning back, I grab his shirt and press my lips to his. "You better come back, Ez. We're not done."

His lips tip up, but his eyes are all wrong. They're not the same twinkling blue I'm used to. They're darker, and the crazy shimmering in them has my skin prickling.

"We're not done," he agrees before pressing his lips to mine again. "I'm coming back, love. Now, get your ass upstairs." I shove myself away from him, still glaring at his stupidly smug face. His brow lifts as I turn, and he smacks my ass. I growl at him over my shoulder and stomp up the steps. "Love you." His voice is barely a whisper, and I don't know if I heard him right. Surely he didn't say what I think he did.

But as I go through my night routine and slide into bed, they echo around my head. I had heard him correctly.

And I'll be fucking damned if I'm not starting to feel the same fucking way.

Kiwi

"**P**regnancy looks good on you," Jackson says to Addie. "Of course, you'd look better if my kid was in there." Bash slams his fist into Jackson's face until blood pours from his nose, down his shirt, and drips onto the stained concrete floor beneath.

I circle him, my eyes never leaving him as he groans in pain. His arms jerk with every punch, but he still has the audacity to stare at Addie.

When Ryder's gun went off at the slaughterhouse, I didn't hesitate to start taking the masked fucks out. They were dragging women, kicking and screaming, to unmarked vans. I knew if we let them get away, we'd never see those women again.

I was lost to the bloodlust, clouded by the killing that I was doing. Every slice of my blade through someone's throat, every time my gun went off, my soul calmed. It wasn't until I heard a final shot and saw Ryder hit the ground that fear, real fear for the first time in my fucking life, overshadowed everything else.

He raised his gun, but didn't shoot. Why didn't he just fucking shoot? I wouldn't have hesitated. I wouldn't have thought twice about it. But he did. And I couldn't fucking understand it.

"Talk," Addie says again, her voice hard and deadly. "Talk or I'm leaving. You have five seconds." I continue circling him—my prey.

He slumps forward, his bound arms straining against the chair we have him tied to. Blood spills from his mouth and nose. It makes me fucking giddy–the sight of all that blood, of the life spilling slowly from him.

"Alright," she says, waving her hand dismissively. "Do what you want with him." She walks toward the door, her steps never faltering.

"Wait," Jackson rasps. My eyes narrow as I close in, ready to slit his throat when Bash gives me the look. But I know I can't. I know this is Reid's kill and he'll never forgive me if I take it from him. But if Bash gives me an order—silent or not—I'll follow it. "I know who the rat is."

I halt, and Addie freezes, her hand on the doorknob. She barely turns and looks over her shoulder, her eyes locking with Bash's. I stare down at Jackson, my body vibrating with the need to ruin him.

"Who?" she says, her voice just as deadly as any of ours.

"I know where they take the girls," he says, and she lets go of the doorknob to take a step toward him.

"Where?"

"I know how to get their names off the list."

"How?" Addie moves in front of him and Bash and I flank her, ready to intervene any second. "Start talking." She's the only pregnant woman in the club right now, and we would all protect her with our lives. She's not only Bash's Old Lady, but she's his equal. It's never happened in this club before, but she's changing shit. She has my respect.

"The girls–your girls, they're not on a real auction list." Jackson slumps against the chair again. "It was a distraction."

"Why did they need us distracted?" she asks darkly.

"Think about it." He grins, his lips parting to reveal his bloody teeth. "If you're focused on this, what are you ignoring?" Bash and Addie look at each other, and I glance up, my eyes finding Reid's.

"I don't know," she breathes. "What are we missing?"

"The rat," Bash says. I lower my eyes back to Jackson, finding him still smiling. "Who is it?"

"Don't know his real name," he says. "But he's new around here."

"Fuck," Reid groans, and I find his eyes again. "There's five Prospects and three we just patched in. Could be any one of them."

My mind races through names and faces. Who the fuck could it be? I've had my suspicions about a few but haven't voiced them. I'll kill anyone, but I won't kill an innocent.

"What's he look like?" Bash asks.

"Never saw him, only heard his voice." Jackson spits blood onto the floor beside him.

"Where do they take the girls?" Ryder asks. My eyes stay on Reid's, and he gives me a small nod—one I don't understand. Then I lower my eyes to Jackson again, finding him staring at Ry. I take a small step forward, my hands clenching and releasing at my sides.

Who the fuck is the rat?

I bring my phone out and start scrolling through Prospect and patched members' photos. One of these fucks betrayed us. They have to die. There's no way around that. They put our women in danger, they put baby Skye in danger.

I'm going to fucking slaughter whoever it is.

"L.A," he says.

"We know that already," Ryder spits. "Where in L.A.?"

"Look for any buildings with the name Carmichael attached to them," he says.

"He's the real ringleader." The room gets eerily silent, the only sound my heavy breathing as I step forward.

"Any of these fucks look familiar?" I shove my phone in his face and scroll through the photos.

"I told you, I haven't seen him," he says. "Only heard him." I glance at Bash, and he shakes his head, telling me to stand down. But I don't want to fucking stand down. I want to fucking kill him. I want to kill the rat. I want to fucking murder anyone who has ever looked at my Brothers and their girls wrong. I want to take down the entire fucking ring.

"What are we missing?" Addie asks, drawing everyone's attention. "What are we ignoring?"

"Everything," Jackson says. "If you're focused on this, on trying to get their names off that list, you're not paying attention to the girls who are really on the list. How many of them have been taken since you started looking into this?" He looks to Bash, and I take a small step toward my Prez, ready to protect him. "How many of those girls' blood is on your hands, Bash? How many have you let die because you haven't focused on anything else?"

"Enough," Addie snarls, slicing her hand through the air. She tries to step forward, but I wrap my hand around her arm, holding her in place. "You can't blame him for the shit you've done." She easily pulls her wrist from my grasp and jams her finger into the center of Jackson's chest. "You can't blame him for the girls you've kidnapped, sold, or killed. You're the fucking monster here, not him. Stop speaking in circles and tell me what the fuck we're missing."

"Bash knows," he says, jerking his chin at Bash. He looks so fucking smug I want to slice his face off. "Don't you?" His words hit me a moment later and I turn my attention to Bash. He's pale as he stares back at Jackson, his eyes haunted.

"Bash? What's he talking about?" Addie steps toward him warily. "What do you know?"

We leave the room quickly and head to the Chapel. Reid stays by my side, his shoulder pressing against mine. "What the fuck is happening?" he whispers low enough for only me to hear. "You don't think Bash has betrayed us, do you?" I snap my eyes to him, finding him staring at his brother with a guarded look.

"No," I say flatly. "Bash wouldn't."

"You sure?"

It pisses me off that he's questioning our Prez. But it's pissing me off more that he's making me question him, too.

Kiwi

August, one of the Nomads, and I lean against the door, his arms folded over his chest. Everyone is in the room—Heather and Reid are at the table, Axel and Taz are on FaceTime, Addie is leaning against the wall, Ryder and his new family are huddled together. We're all staring at Bash, waiting.

"Sebastian," Addie says. She and Mom are the only ones who can call him that without getting hurt. "What's going on?"

He pauses and runs his hands through his hair before turning toward the table and looking at us. He looks fucking wrecked. But Reid's words bounce around in my head.

Could he have betrayed us?

"When I first got the Prez patch," he taps the patch on the front of his cut, "a guy named John Oliver Carmichael approached me. He wanted to hire me–well, he wanted to hire the club to be his muscle. He wanted us to work for him, but I told him we didn't do that shit and to fuck off. He didn't like that answer." Reid's eyes find mine again and narrow slightly.

"But what was Jackson talking about?" Addie asks. "What are we ignoring?"

"We're ignoring the bigger fish," Bash says. "We're ignoring Carmichael."

"Who is this guy?" Ryder asks. "We've never heard of him before."

"He's some rich fuckin' asshole in L.A.," he responds.

"What did he need muscle for?" Axel asks, his voice garbled through the phone. "What did he want us to do?"

"He wanted us to run guns and drugs and kill his competitors," Bash says. "Said he'd pay us a shit ton of money if we did it for him, but—" He shakes his head, and I let out a breath. The way this is going, it doesn't sound like he's turned on us. Honestly, I don't know what the fuck I'd do if he had. I don't know if I could kill my Prez. "That's not us. We don't do that shit. And I think if we would've gotten mixed up with it, we'd be running girls right now."

"What are we missing?" I ask.

"While you've been focusing on these auctions and keeping our girls safe, I've kept tabs on Carmichael. He owns Montgomery and every other fuckin' ringleader in California. He's recently expanded his business and has started buying and selling girls. He's buying, taking them to these brothels around the world, and selling them to the highest bidder. Sometimes he doesn't even sell them. He just sends them to the street to sell their bodies and collects the money they make at the end of the week." My mind is reeling trying to keep up with everything.

"So, why distract us from that?" Ryder asks. "That doesn't make sense."

"Because if he thinks we're distracted, he thinks our guard is down."

"You think he's gonna try to attack us here?" August asks. "Why does he want our guard down?"

"He's going to try to take over The Brotherhood," Bash says darkly. "He's trying to get me taken out and have the rat take the Prez patch so he can own us." My body recoils at that.

"Why not find a club who wants to work for him?" Ryder asks. "This doesn't make any fucking sense."

"Because we have chapters all over the country, we're well respected," Bash says. "If he owned The Brotherhood, imagine how much damage he could do."

"We need to figure out who the fuck the rat is," Reid says, saying exactly what I'm fucking thinking. Bash takes a deep breath and Addie rests her hand on his back.

"I know who it is."

The room goes deathly silent, the air thick as we all stare at him. As soon as he gives a name, I'm walking out and killing the motherfucker.

"I'm a fucking idiot. I'm the biggest fucking idiot and let his son into our ranks."

"Carmichael's son?" Addie asks, her voice breathless. "Who—"

"Ginger," Bash says. "Ginger is the rat." My breath gets lost and my body begins to vibrate. I don't hear anything else as I begin to pace.

I need to kill him. I need to kill him. I have to take out the threat. I have to protect my family. I have to kill him. I can't let him hurt anyone. I need to fucking kill him.

"We need to kill him," I say and turn toward the door. August steps in front of me, and I glare at him. "I'm gonna hang him from his fucking dick." I start pacing again. "Gonna kill him. Gonna fuckin' ruin him. Gonna—"

Someone calls my name, but I'm too far gone.

I need to kill the threat.

I need to protect my family.

Kill the threat.

Kill him.

"Gonna kill him. Gonna kill him." I slam my fist into my other hand, my vision turning black. I know I'm moments away from a blackout, from going fucking crazy and killing everyone. "Gonna kill him."

"Kiwi!" My name echoes off the wall and I stop to look at Bash. "Not gonna kill anyone yet." My blood hums.

"He's a rat, Prez," I growl. "He needs to die. Gotta kill him."

"He's gone," Bash says, and the news is like a bomb exploding in the room. Everyone holds their breath, even my blackout starts to fade. Then Reid erupts.

"What the fuck do you mean he's gone?!" he shouts. "He's been spying on us for weeks, and you've known it was him this whole time. And now you know he's gone? You're protecting him!" He shoves out of his chair, his face red and the veins in his neck popping.

"I'm not protecting him." Bash glares at his brother. "I went looking for him before we left to rescue Mads, and Bug said he was gone. Didn't know where he went or when he'd be back."

"You think he'll come back here?" Ryder asks.

"If he knows Jackson has been taken, he won't come back."

I figured as much.

I start pacing again.

"Gonna find him, then kill him," I say, my blood heating again.

"Alright," Bash says, shocking me enough to stop and stare at him. "Find him and bring him back here."

"Kill. Him." Every muscle in my body is coiled tightly. "Kill him."

"Yeah," Bash says. "You'll kill him."

And that's all I need to fucking know.

Kennedy

I haven't been able to sleep. The sun is rising and I still haven't heard from Ezra. I want to call him to make sure he's fine, but I don't want to distract him. But there's a sinking feeling in my gut telling me something is so fucking wrong.

A bang has me bolting out of bed and reaching for the bat I keep under my bed. Heavy footsteps stomp down the hall and I hold my breath as I press my back against the wall next to the door. It slowly opens, hiding me.

"Kens?"

Tears prick my eyes and I drop the bat as I shove at the door. Ezra lets it swing shut and I launch into his arms. He holds me tightly to his chest, his body vibrating.

"You're back," I say and his arms tighten. I pull away from him, needing to see him, needing to reassure myself that he's whole. My eyes widen. "Oh my God, are you hurt? Where are you hurt?" I step out of his embrace and take in the full state of him.

He's covered in blood.

It's caked in his curls, in his short stubble. It's smeared across his

114

face, and stained into his shirt and jeans. Flakes of dried blood fall from his boots onto the carpet.

"Ezra," I breathe, and he takes a deep breath.

"I killed a lot of people tonight," he admits. "But we got her back." I nod a few times. I don't know who Madi is, but she's apparently important to him. To the club. "She's safe. Her girl is safe."

"Her girl?" I ask as I grab his hand. He tells me the heartbreaking story as I lead him to the bathroom. I ache for her, for the girl and her mother, for Ryder. For Kiwi. "Take your shirt off." I turn the shower on and hold my hand under the water, testing the temperature.

"Why?"

"Baby, take your clothes off. You need a shower."

"You called me baby," he says, his voice thick. I turn toward him and feel like I'm seeing him for the first time.

"Yeah, I guess I did," I say, smiling softly. "Please? Let me take care of you." I hold my breath, readying myself for him to reject me. But he doesn't. Without a word, he peels his clothes off as I turn the shower on. I hesitate before sliding my shirt and panties off and tossing them to the floor.

"What are you doing?"

"I don't want my clothes to get wet," I say as I pull the shower curtain back. "Get in." We stare at each other, the steam from the hot water filling the room. He climbs into the tub and holds my hand, steadying me as I follow in after him. "You might have to crouch so I can wash your hair." I turn him toward the water and watch the red liquid leave his hair.

"I can do this," he says, but I ignore him as I grab the shampoo. When I look back at him, he's staring at me with guarded eyes. "Why are you doing this?"

"Crouch down," I murmur. He stays staring at me for a long time, then he sits on the edge of the tub, bringing his head level with my chest. I pour the shampoo into his hair and massage his scalp as I wash all the blood out. He lets out a long, tired sigh, and I dig my fingers in more, wanting him to relax. When I finish, he stands and rinses the soap out, his eyes on mine the whole time.

I make him add conditioner to his hair as I grab Ian's body wash. As I lather the soap over his body, washing the blood away, more of his scars, fresh cuts, and bruises reveal themselves.

"I thought you said you weren't hurt," I say, gently probing at one of the bruises. He hisses and grabs my hand.

"It doesn't hurt unless you touch it," he says. "Kens—" I kneel in front of him, not letting him say anything else. I lather the soap on my hands and start washing his legs. When I look up at him, his cock is standing straight up. It's long and thick with a vein throbbing underneath. My mouth waters as I stare at it. "Sorry." He roughly clears his throat, but never takes his eyes off me.

I hesitate before reaching up and lightly gripping his cock. He rests his hand on the wall, bracing himself. Slowly, I slide my hand up and down, squeezing gently.

"Is this okay?" I murmur, and he nods. I keep my eyes on his as I pump my hand over him, his thighs flexing with each stroke.

"Your mouth," he grits out. "Put it in your mouth, baby. Please."

Leaning up, I wrap my lips around him and slowly take him deep into my mouth. He groans and leans his head back, letting some of the water spray down his body and into my face. His other hand moves to the back of my head, gripping my ponytail tightly.

"Let me fuck your throat," he groans. I open my mouth wider and he tips his head down to look at me, his eyes hooded. He pushes his hips forward, his cock sliding into my throat. He hesitates before pushing further. My eyes water, but I keep them open and on his. "Fuck, you look good with my dick in your mouth. Stand up, I need to fuck you."

"Not yet," I breathe as I slide off his dick. "I–I'm not there yet." His jaw tenses, but he doesn't argue.

"Play with your pussy then," he says as he pushes his cock back into my mouth. "I want you to come." I slide my hand between my legs, whimpering when my fingers connect with my swollen clit. "That's right. Don't take your eyes off mine." I barely nod before he thrusts forward, making me gag. I move my fingers faster, feeling my thighs tremble as he uses my mouth the way he wants. "Take it. Fucking take it, Kennedy." His voice is guttural and it makes my body tighten.

His movements become faster and rougher, making me gag with each thrust. He wraps my hair around his hand like a rope and forces my head back so he can slide his dick deeper.

"Are you close?" he grits out. I nod as much as I can. He starts thrusting harder and I feel his cock thicken. "I'm about to come. Swallow it all, love."

My heart squeezes.

It's the first time I haven't felt repulsed by him calling me love.

I move my fingers faster and feel my orgasm rise. "Fuck, I can't hold back. Shit." His thighs tense as he thrusts faster. "Fuck, fuck, fuck." My eyes roll back as I come, whimpering around his cock. "Oh, fucking God." He pushes deep inside my mouth as he comes, his hand in my hair tightening to the point of pain.

My body convulses as I come, and I have to force myself to focus on swallowing. Finally, we relax, but instead of taking his cock from my mouth, he starts thrusting again. It's softening, but still fills my mouth completely.

"I'm not ready to take it out," he murmurs, gently stroking my head. "Suck on me some more, baby." I run my tongue over his sensitive head, making him groan and lean against the wall. His eyes are heavy as he stares down at me gently sucking him until he's fully soft. But still, he doesn't pull out. I keep sucking until he leans his head against the wall and closes his eyes.

"Ez?" I ask when I slide off.

"Hmm?" His eyes barely flutter open. He looks so tired, so vulnerable and so unlike Kiwi that my heart melts for him.

"You want some food, then you can get some sleep?" He nods and helps me stand, then dips down to kiss me gently.

"Thanks for that," he murmurs against my lips. "I—I needed you." His eyes stay closed, like he doesn't want to see my reaction.

"I needed you, too, Ez." I rest my hand against his firm jaw, feeling him flex under my touch. He rests his forehead against mine and takes a deep breath.

"I'm going to kill someone," he whispers, his eyes still closed. "And I'm going to enjoy it, Kens." Finally, he opens them and stares deep into my soul. "I'm going to fucking *enjoy* it." I swallow hard at the promise in his voice.

"What did they do?" I ask, unsure if I want to know.

"Does it matter?"

"Do they deserve it?" His eyes search mine before he nods, his forehead slick against mine.

"We had a rat in The Brotherhood. We think he wants to buy my VP's seven-year-old daughter." My heart stops and I jerk away from him.

"What the fuck?" His face darkens, and any amount of softness he just had disappears. "What exactly are you involved in?"

"We're not involved in anything," he grits out. "We're trying to save girls that are being trafficked."

"Is this why The Berserkers are helping you?" His throat bobs before he nods.

"There's a lot to explain," he mutters. "But we're the good guys here. We're trying to help them." My stomach twists.

I don't know why I thought things could be different. I can't let The Brotherhood or The Berserkers get close to Ian if this is the shit they're involved in. When my dad was a Berserker, he just dealt with rivalries and ran drugs. They never got involved with girls or trafficking. Never.

And if that's what Kiwi's club is into, I can't let him around Ian. His enemies might be hunting him. They might follow him here and see Ian. They might take him away from me, and my son's safety has to come first.

"We're trying to save them," he says again, his voice harder. "You didn't know any of this?"

"I'm not a part of the club," I say. "I–I know some things from hearing the guys talk, but not the full extent...is that why Spence went to L.A.?" He nods, his eyes carefully tracking me.

"He's helping Taz find where the girls are being held before they're sent somewhere else." I feel like I'm going to be sick. "Stop looking at me like that."

"Like what?" I breathe.

"Like you're scared of me. Like I'm a monster."

"I know you're not," I murmur. "But—"

"But." He pulls away from me, standing at his full height. "I don't need to hear whatever else you're going to say. *But* says it all for you." He yanks the shower curtain back and stares at me. "Get out." I blink at him, my heart racing.

"What?"

"Get out. I had you on your knees. You made me come. I don't need anything else from you. Out."

Tears fill my eyes and my chin wobbles. "You're a bastard," I say, trying to keep my voice level, but it comes out broken. "You're such a fucking bastard, Kiwi. You get out." I shove his chest, making him slip and land heavily against the wall. "This is my fucking house. You get out and never come back. I never want to see you again. Get out!" I bang my fists against his chest, then rear my hand back to slap him. He catches my wrist before it connects and glares at me.

"Don't do that."

"Or what?" I shout. "What the fuck will you do?" His hand tightens around my wrist until pain shoots up my arm.

"You don't want to test me right now, Kennedy."

"Fuck you, you psycho fucking freak." His hand tightens more, and it feels like my bones are grinding together.

"I've told you not to call me that," he says darkly.

"Freak," I spit the word at him. His jaw works to either side as his chest heaves. "Fuck. You."

119

Suddenly, he shoves me back and my feet slip on the water. He barely catches me before I fall, but he doesn't help me stand. Instead, he just drops me. I land on my ass and stare up at him, shocked.

"Fuck you, too." He rips the curtain back and steps out. "I came here because you were the only person I wanted after tonight." He grabs his bloody jeans and slides them up his legs, not bothering to dry off. "I was stupid enough to think I fucking loved you. Even though I didn't know you, I thought you were mine." He roughly buttons and zips them up, laughing humorlessly as he shakes his head. "I thought you were something special. But I was wrong." I stare at him, the water spraying the side of my face. "You're just another fucking bitch, huh? Just fucking here to taunt me, remind me of what I'll never have, what I'll never be. Yeah," he turns toward me, his chest heaving as he bangs his fist against it, "I know I'm a fucking freak, Kennedy. You don't need to remind me. I know."

"Ez—"

"Don't," he snarls. "Don't say my name. Don't ever say my name again." We stare at each other, the tension filling the space between us. "When I walk out that door," he points at it, "you'll never see me again." It's silent except for the running water and our harsh breathing. But I steel my spine as I glare at him.

"Fine," I say. "Leave." He continues staring at me, like he's waiting for me to change my mind. "Go."

"Bitch."

"Freak."

He shoves his boots on and dips to grab his bloody t-shirt. He slides it on over his head as he storms to the door. Yanking it open, he stops and looks back at me.

"Never coming back," he says. "That's what you want?"

No.

It's not what I want.

And honestly, I don't know how this all went so wrong so fucking fast. But it did. And there's no going back. There's no repairing it.

"Yes," I finally say. "Leave, Kiwi. Go. Go back to your fucking club and leave me alone. I was fine before you, I'll be fine without you." He scoffs, rolling his eyes.

"Whatever."

He slams the door shut behind him, and when I hear the front door slam, rattling the walls, I clutch my knees to my chest. Faintly, I hear the rumble of his bike and a sob works its way up.

The water sprays on me, some of it getting on the floor outside the tub as I cry into my knees. My hot tears slide down my face, mixing with the water. Each sob is harder than the last, every emotion I've never let out barreling through me.

There's a faint knock on the door and I clear my throat as I pull the shower curtain shut. "Yeah?" I call, my voice shaky.

"Is everything okay?" Ian asks warily.

"Fine," I say. "I'll be out in a second, alright?" I let the water hit my face, washing away the tears, then turn it off and grab a towel.

I don't know why I feel so worked up about this. He was only in my life for a few days. He shouldn't mean anything to me. It doesn't matter that he's gone. And I meant what I said—I was fine before him, and I'll be fine now. All I need is my son, and we can get through anything.

Kiwi

Someone knocks on my door, but I ignore it and pull the pillow over my head. I came back to the compound last night. I'm still in my blood-stained clothes. I still smell like her. I still feel her.

My heart fucking hurts.

"Kiwi!" Bash bangs on the door again. Still, I ignore him.

I'm not in the mood to see anyone. I'm not in the right fucking headspace for it. If he walks into this room, I'm going to beat the shit out of him.

I think I broke my hand. I've never punched a wall as hard as I had last night. She didn't know how badly those words tore at me; she didn't understand it. To her, it was just an insult. It wasn't something that was carved into her skin, into her soul. It wasn't said to her every day of her fucking life, engrained into her very being.

Mindlessly, I run my hand over my stomach. It wasn't deep enough to scar, but I still feel it. I feel it embedded in my skin forever.

"Kiwi!" he shouts again. I roll onto my back and stare at the ceiling. It's weird how much I miss that old popcorn ceiling at Kennedy's

122

place. I miss hearing Ian yell at his game. I miss the way she ran around, a scowl on her face no matter what she was doing. Cooking, cleaning, doing her hair and makeup, coming...it didn't matter. She always had the most beautiful scowl on her face.

He knocks again and I finally fling myself out of bed and storm across the room in a few large strides. I grab the door and let it fly open, crashing into the wall behind it.

"What?" I snap. His brows lift, shocked. We stare at each other and I wait for him to do something, give me a reason to knock him out. But he doesn't.

"Belfast is in the Chapel," he says, narrowing his eyes. "What's wrong with you?"

"Nothing." I step back and grab my cut that's hanging on the back of a chair.

"Your hand," he says, but I ignore it as I push past him into the hallway, slamming my door behind me. "Kiwi." Still, I ignore him, ignore the way his gaze burns into the back of my head. "Ezra King!"

I halt, my heels digging into the wood. My chest heaves as I stare down the hall into the empty common room. Finally, I turn toward him, and he lifts his chin, readying himself.

I know the look well. It's his "I'm ready to kick ass" look, and instead of firing me up, it just makes me exhausted.

I'm so tired of fighting.

I'm tired of coming home to a cold bed.

I'm tired of not having someone to rely on. Of having them rely on me.

I'm tired of having nothing and no one.

If only Elaine could see me now, not fighting or giving into my emotions like she always said I did.

"What?" I say again, tiredly. He looks even more shocked as he lowers his guard and takes a step toward me.

"What's going on?"

"Nothing," I say again.

"Kiwi, talk to me." It comes out as an order, and I don't know if he really thinks he can Prez his way into me telling him what's wrong. I just stare blankly back at him until he grits his teeth and says, "Please." I snort and turn around again.

"Just ready for this shit to be over," I mutter.

He's silent as he falls into step beside me, and doesn't say another word until we get into the Chapel. I sink into the closest chair and fold my arms over my chest, my eyes trained on the scuffed table. Bash sighs as he walks past me to his seat at the other end of the table.

"Can you talk to him?" Bash says, and I look at Belfast, lifting my brows expectantly.

"What?" he says and Bash slumps into his seat.

"He speaks," Bash mumbles.

"I found Ginger," he says, ignoring Bash. I sit straighter, my body jolting with excitement.

"Where is he?" My voice is low and even.

"He's in Oregon."

"Oregon?" I repeat. Belfast nods, his face blank. "Why the fuck is he there?" I look at Bash and he shrugs.

"His father has a house there. Lots of protection," Belfast says.

"What else do we know about him? His father?" My hands tighten into fists as I stare at Belfast, waiting. He's slow to respond, and it pisses me the fuck off. Finally, he lifts his eyes to me.

"Carmichael had three kids, two sons and a daughter, one son is dead, the other is Ginger, and the daughter." He shrugs as he looks back at his computer. "She's the youngest of the three, around seventeen. She could be dead, or she could be hidden away. No one has seen her in almost five years." My stomach rolls at the thoughts shooting through my mind.

"Think he sold her?" I ask, glancing at Bash. He looks like he was thinking the same thing. Belfast shrugs again.

"It's possible. I don't know her real name, so it took me a while to hunt down that he even had a third kid," he says. "Since she's been missing, it's possible she could've been sold. Or maybe her father knows he has a lot of enemies and is keeping her hidden to protect her."

"I don't think a man like Carmichael would give a shit if anything happened to his family," Bash says. "I think he cares about himself and how much money he can make. That's it." I nod my agreement. He turns his attention to me, disgust and fury on his face. "You gonna go after Ginger?"

I need to go after him. I need to bring him back here so I can have my fun before Axel kills him. But the thought of being that far away from Kennedy makes me itchy.

But she made it clear she doesn't want me.

She made it clear what she thinks of me.

"Yeah," I say, nodding as I slid my eyes back to Belfast. "Can you get me an exact location?" He nods as he types on his laptop.

"Spence is sending one of his guys with you," he says and I stop breathing. "One of his...investments." My eyes narrow.

"Who?" I ask darkly. I go through the lists of men associated with Spencer and The Berserkers, and everyone is accounted for. Everyone except—

"Riot," Bash says. I groan and press my back against the chair.

"He's a fucking asshole," I say.

"He's good at what he does. He's stealthy and can kill a man before they even realize he's there. You need backup and all our guys can't fucking do it. You know Riot will cover you."

"Riot doesn't give a shit about anyone but himself," I retort. "If shit goes down, he'll get himself out first."

"He's not that much of a bastard," Bash laughs. "He's got a code. He'll have your back."

I know that Riot is good, he's better than good, but still. I don't like sharing. I want to do this on my own. But I can't argue my way out of this one.

"Fine," I grit out.

"Remember, this is Ax's kill," Bash says. I roll my eyes as I push to my feet.

"Yep, I remember, Prez." I knock on the table and Belfast lifts his eyes to mine. "Just text it to me. I gotta handle some shit."

"What—"

"I just gotta go," I say, waving dismissively as I walk toward the door.

I HESITATE before lifting my fist and knocking on the door. I'm not sure if she's even home, and a weird mixture of wanting to see her and never wanting to see her wars inside my chest. But even if she doesn't want to see me, I want her to know I won't be here.

I asked myself why I even cared if she knew I would be in town or not. It's not like she'll give a fuck either way. But...if she needs me, I want her to know I'll still get to her as fast as I can. I want her to know she can call my club and they'll protect her. She's still mine, even if she hates me.

Even if a small part of me hates her.

The door slowly opens before I can knock again and Ian glares at me. I shift uncomfortably on my feet, clearing my throat.

"Hey, kid. Your mom home?" He folds his arms over his chest as he narrows his eyes, glaring harder.

Fuck. He looks like Kennedy.

"Nope," he says. "And even if she was, I wouldn't let you see her." I nod a few times.

"She told you what happened, then?" He shrugs, feigning nonchalance, and I grin at him. "She didn't." His throat bobs as he swallows. Leaning against the doorframe, I cross my arms and smile broader. "So, you're pissed at me...why?"

"Because she is," he says plainly. "And I don't like you."

"You liked me fine the other day."

"That was before you came into our house and wouldn't leave," he snaps. "You scared her. I should've beaten you with the bat 'till you left." I shrug and look down at my feet.

"Yeah, probably should've." He's silent, like he was expecting me to argue with him. "Just let her know I won't be in town for a few days."

"Why?" I look up at him. His glare has morphed into something cautious, unsure. Curious. "Where are you going?"

"Gotta go to Oregon." His brows lift, and I huff out a laugh. "I'm hunting."

"Hunting?"

"Hunting a guy who betrayed my club."

"You're going to kill him?" His voice comes out quiet, and his eyes widen.

"Nah, just bringing him back so my VP can." I don't know why I'm telling him all this shit. Maybe so he can relay it to Kens, but I think it's mostly because I just need to talk to someone and he's here.

"Your club really kills people?" he whisper-shouts, and I laugh again.

"We do a lot of things, kid." I rest my head against the doorframe, suddenly feeling how tired I really am. "You ever thought about getting a bike? Maybe joining a club when you're older?" He bites his lips and drops his eyes. "I'll take that as a yes."

"Mom doesn't like it," he mumbles. He steps his foot to the side, blocking Rasputin from running outside.

"She'll come around," I say as I crouch to pet the dog. "If you told her you murdered someone, she'd help you hide the body." He snorts.

"Yeah, after she yelled at me for it." I grin as I scratch behind Rasputin's ear. It slowly falls as I remember her words. Sighing, I push myself up and wipe my hands on my jeans.

"I gotta go, but just let your mom know I won't be around, okay?" His eyes meet mine, and a lot of that hatred he had is gone. "If she needs anything, tell her to call Bash. He'll help her."

"What happened between you?" he asks quietly, and I sigh again.

"We said some shit to each other we shouldn't have. Even if I didn't mean it all, I think she meant what she said."

"Then why are you here?" he asks, not unkindly. "If you fought, and she said shit to make you think she doesn't want you around, why did you come back?" I stare at him, at a complete loss for words.

"I don't know," I admit. "I just–I wanted her to know she can still call me for anything. That goes for you, too, Ian." His eyes widen, but I can't stop the words. "I know I'm a...freak." I bite the word out, feeling that sharp knife carving into my skin. "But I care about your mom. I care about you. So if you need anything, ever, no matter what's going on with Kens and me, just call, yeah?"

"You mean that?" he asks quietly, and I nod.

"Of course," I say. "When I claimed your mom, I claimed you, too."

"Claimed...her?" His eyes narrow into a glare again and I laugh.

"I don't think she knows that," I say, grinning. "You can't help who you fall for, and even if we're pissed at each other, it doesn't mean she's not still mine."

"You sound like a caveman," he says, and I snort.

"Not the first time I've heard that." I take a step back. "Just watch out for your mom for me?" He straightens to his full height and throws his shoulders back as he nods.

"I will."

"And you'll let me know if anyone fucks with her?" I take another step back and he nods again.

"What will you do to them?"

"Don't worry about it, kid." I smile as I step onto the first stair. "You'll let me know if anyone fucks with you?" He nods again. "See you around."

"See you around, Kiwi."

As I walk back to my bike, I realize he said my name for the first time. I said his name for the first time, too.

If I can get through to him, maybe I can get through to Kennedy, too.

Kennedy

Someone knocks on the bar to get my attention, and I grit my teeth before turning toward them. Archer leans against it, his face uncharacteristically guarded.

"What?" I snarl, tightening my hold on the damp rag in my hand. His dark blond brows lift, but that's the only shift of his features.

"What's up with you?" He jerks his chin to me and I roll my eyes as I turn back toward the glasses on the other side of the bar.

"Nothing."

"Something's wrong," he says. I ignore him, forcing my hands to move to the glass I'd been wiping down. "Kiwi left this morning." My back stiffens, and I know he's just prodding at me until he figures out what's going on.

"Okay." I swallow hard. He left? Where the fuck did he go? Why?

"To Oregon." My brows pinch together, but I still don't give him the satisfaction of asking why.

"Good for him." He huffs out a laugh and I grip the glass tighter.

"You're the most stubborn person I've ever met," he says. My lips

129

barely twitch, but I force them back to neutrality before turning back to him. I lean against the counter, my eyes narrowed as I stare at him.

"Why are you here?" I ask, my voice level. He shrugs as he slides onto a barstool, his forearms still resting against the bar.

"Can I get a whiskey?" He tilts his chin to the bottles behind me and I let out a hard breath before turning and grabbing the first bottle of whiskey I see and pouring some into the glass I'd been cleaning. Sliding it across the wood to him, he downs it in one gulp, his face not even twitching from the amount of alcohol he'd just drunk. "Spence is back in town." I nod a few times and set the bottle back on the shelf.

"Yeah, I know. I saw him when I got here." I toss the rag onto the counter and fold my arms over my chest, studying him. "Why are you here, Arch?" He shrugs again.

"Just wanted to check in with you."

"Why?" He shrugs again and it pisses me off. "Whatever. I'm fine. You can leave me alone now."

"Yeah, you seem fine," he deadpans. "Life with Kiwi not everything you thought it would be?"

"Fuck off," I snap. "My life is just fucking fine without that asshole in it." He grins like he won and it takes all I have not to slam my fist into the center of his face. "Did you just come here to bother me?" His face falls, and so does my stomach.

"What all do you know?" he asks. "About what's going on?"

"Enough to know I want nothing to do with it." I lift my brows in a challenge, waiting for him to argue with me. But he doesn't. He just nods again.

"Good," he says, his head still bobbing. "Good. Stay away from this shit."

"Yeah, obviously. I have a kid to think about." His eyes narrow slightly.

"And if you didn't?" I blink at him. What the fuck does that even mean?

I try to calm my whirling thoughts, but they just get more

jumbled. If I didn't have to worry about Ian, would I care? Would I have still reacted the way I had? Would I have tried to help instead?

My first instinct was to protect my son—it'll always be my first instinct. But the second one...the second feeling that bubbled up my chest was pride. Pride to know that Kiwi was one of the good guys. I didn't want to acknowledge it.

But it was there, and it's been there since he told me.

And a part of me feels like if I only had myself to worry about, I would've asked him to bring me in on it. I would've helped. I would've...

"It doesn't matter," I say. "It's a stupid question. I have Ian, and no amount of thinking about what if's will change that." He assesses me in a way that makes me squirm.

Everyone looks over Archer, only seeing his good looks. They don't see that cunning mind of his, or the way he's scary observant. He's always watching, always aware of everything. No one notices what he's capable of, but I never miss it. I've always seen it.

And I hate to admit that I see a lot of Kiwi in him, too. Kiwi is just as observant and cunning and brilliant. They're so alike in so many ways, but also so fucking different. So, so different.

Archer isn't a settle down kind of man. But Kiwi? I don't know if he is, but I think he could be. I think the possibility is there.

I can see him being a father, and fuck me for even thinking he'd be a good one, but I know he would be. I think he'd be the perfect husband too...when he isn't being a fucking psychopath.

But I know I'd always come second to the club. I know I'd never be his first priority—Ian would never be his first priority. It would always be the club. Always.

And I can't live that life.

I'd seen my mother and stepmother live it, and I always promised myself that I'd never be them. I'd never make the same mistakes they had. I'd never get involved with a biker.

But maybe a part of me always wanted to. Why else would I always come back to working at The Crossroads? It wasn't because these guys were like family. I was just another bartender to most of them. I wasn't in the club, not like I had been when my dad was in it.

Maybe I always knew the only man who could ever put up with me would be a biker, someone dominant and comfortable enough with himself that he could see through my bullshit. A man like that would love me no matter how hard I was to deal with. A man like that...

A man like that walked out of my fucking life yesterday.

Tears fill my eyes and I hate myself for it. Archer's face shifts into momentary panic before he forces his features to relax again. "You wanna talk about it?" I nod a few times, wiping roughly at my face, probably smearing mascara down my cheeks, and grab the bottle of whiskey. "That bad?"

"I fucked up," I say as I round the bar. I pour some liquor into his glass, then pour some down my throat. He watches me swallow it down, grimacing at the burn, his eyes wide.

"You must've fucked up. I've never seen you drink like that." He takes a sip of his drink and sets his glass back down. I take another long pull, then set the bottle down in front of me.

I have an empty stomach, and the warmth of the liquor affects me immediately. The room barely spins as I shift my head toward Archer. More tears fill my eyes as I stare at him.

I can't say it out loud. I can't tell someone what I'd said, what he'd said. I can't. If I do, it's real. It's real, and he's in a different state, and I'm fucking sad, and—a sob spills from me.

"Shit," Archer swears, then scoots closer to me. "Talk to me, babe."

So I do. I tell him everything. I tell him every fucking thought I've had about Kiwi, about the fight, and how bad it was, how guilty I feel. As I do, I take long pulls from the bottle. Before I know it, half of it's gone and I'm slurring and the room is fully spinning.

I get to my feet, swaying. Nausea hits me and I put my hand to my mouth. Archer swears again, then scoops me into his arms and runs across the floor toward the bathrooms in the back.

"Do not fucking puke on me, Kenny," he says. The jostling from him running makes my nausea worse and I feel bile rise in my throat. "I swear to God. If you puke on me, I'm going to puke, and it's going to be so fucking gross—" He gags when he hears me do it, and kicks the bathroom door open.

Suddenly, I'm dropped on the dirty floor in front of a toilet and Archer runs to the one in the stall next to mine. The sound of him dry heaving makes me dry heave. The more we listen to each other, the worse it gets, but we can't stop. It's a vicious cycle that would be comical if it was happening to anyone else but us.

Somewhere behind me, the door opens. "What the fuck—fuck." Resting my arm on the toilet, I drop my forehead to it, feeling exhausted and too drunk to keep my head up. "Kennedy, are you drunk?"

"Mmm." It's all I can manage.

"Fuck." Finally, I turn my head enough to find Spencer standing in the doorway, his brows low.

"You're mad," I slur and he folds his arms over his chest.

"A little bit," he says. I close my eyes, dry heaving again when I hear Archer do it. "Go home."

"I can work." I try to push myself up, but slide back down to my ass. "Help." I hold my hands out to Spencer and he looks thoroughly shocked. So shocked, I start laughing. I can't help it. I make grabby hands at him and he takes a hesitant step forward.

Slowly, he helps me to my feet, dropping his hands to my waist to steady me when I start swaying. I bang my fist on the stall wall, laughing when Archer groans.

"You okay in there, buddy?" I laugh again, then my head falls back, nearly toppling me off balance. Spencer's hands tighten and I give him a big smile. "Thanks, bossy boss man." I pat his chest, then laugh at his expression again.

"Arch, come on. I'm taking you both home," he sighs.

"I can work," I say, remembering I need to do that. Spencer shakes his head, his big hands still on my waist. I pluck one of his fingers, giggling to myself. "Kiwi's gonna cut your hands off." My voice comes out light, like a song, and I laugh again before singing, "Cut your hands off. Cut your hands off."

Suddenly, my heart dips as I remember he hates me. I don't blame him. I hate me, too. I should apologize to him. Maybe I'll call him. Yeah, after I'm done with my shift, I'll call him and tell him how sorry I am.

Archer comes out of the stall looking green. "I'm not drunk," he says, resting his forehead against the stall door. "I just don't handle puke–" He holds his fist in front of his mouth as he gags and rushes back into the stall. Spencer grimaces while we listen to Archer.

"Come on," Spencer grumbles. "You sure you're not drunk?"

"All good, Prez," Archer groans. Spencer shakes his head as he wraps his arm around my waist, helping me walk toward the door.

"I'll get you home," he sighs. "I guess I'll be on bartender duty tonight."

"I can—"

"If you say you can work again, I'm going to fire you." My mouth snaps shut, and when my chin wobbles, he sighs again. "I won't really fire you, Kenny. You know that." I rest my too-heavy head against his big arm as he ushers me down the hall toward the back door.

"My purse." I try to turn, but he holds me in place.

"I'll get it after I put you in the truck," he grumbles as he shoves the door open. The balmy night air helps sober me some, but everything is a blur as he opens the truck door and shoves me in. "Stay there." He points at me and I salute him, then laugh as I rest my head back against the seat.

I don't remember him driving me home or helping me to bed. I just know I'm in bed and Ian is standing in the doorway, staring worriedly at me.

"I'm fine," I say, waving at him. "Don't worry so much. You'll give yourself gray hair." He doesn't laugh. He doesn't react. He just stares. I scoot further under my blankets, smiling at him reassuringly.

"Call if you need anything," he says warily. "I won't have my headset on—"

"I'm fine," I say again. He hesitates before he steps out of the room, shutting the door firmly behind him.

My eyelids are too heavy to stay open, but when I close them the room spins. I don't know why I let myself get drunk tonight, I never do this. The last time I drank with Archer, it ended with us waking up next to each other.

At least that didn't happen tonight.

Kiwi

It's been a long time since I've driven across the state. I wish I would've been on my bike, but I can't exactly take Ginger back to Santa Cruz riding bitch. So, I drove my fucking car, which isn't nearly as cool as my bike. Riot, the fucker, said he'd meet me here. So, I've been left waiting.

I left straight from Kennedy's place and drove ten hours straight. My mind couldn't stop replaying our fight. Over and over, her words slashed through me. But worse, my words slashed through me, deeper than any blade ever has.

I can't stop thinking about her, regretting everything. I know she'll never forgive me, and why should she? I fucked up and I know that, but I don't know how to apologize for it.

I don't apologize.

I don't fuck up.

But this time I did.

I can't afford to let her overtake my thoughts tonight. One wrong move could get me killed.

I was worried the entire drive that I'd never be able to focus on this, on finding and taking Ginger. But now that I'm here, hiding and waiting for Riot, the night shrouding me, I feel invigorated. I'm ready to hunt him down. Every other emotion I've felt in the past few hours fades away. It's only me and my prey.

I'm standing outside the rat's house. It's more of a fucking compound, but nothing is fully secure. There's always a way in. I flick my cigarette to the ground and stomp it out with the toe of my boot.

Belfast sent me a layout of the house and pointed out where the guards didn't patrol. So, that's where I'm heading first. He doesn't have a lot of guards, so it seems his father didn't want to take the time or money out to protect his last living son.

I glance at my watch again. Two-fifteen in the morning. Riot was supposed to be here before two. We were supposed to go over a plan, but we're running out of time.

A hand lands on my shoulder, and my body reacts. Grabbing their wrist, I spin as I try to fling them over, but they twist out of my hold effortlessly. My chest heaves as I scan the darkness for them, but nothing. They're a fucking ghost.

Then it hits me.

"Fucking Riot," I say, my teeth clenched. "We don't have time for this."

"Then stop being a bitch and let's go," he says too close to my side. I spin around, finding nothing but a shadow darker than the rest of the black forest around us. "You haven't changed. Still reacting without thinking. Still unaware of your surroundings."

"I knew you were there," I say. I can't see his face in the darkness, but I know he rolled his eyes.

"Sure." His massive body shifts as he shuffles his feet, readying himself for whatever we're about to do. "Did you look at the layout?" I nod. "Follow my lead."

"No," I scoff. "This fucker infiltrated my club. He's mine. You follow my lead." There's a tense beat of silence, then he grunts his agreement.

"Fine, but if I think you're fucking around, I'm taking over." I roll my eyes and turn my back on him. Which is probably the most dangerous fucking thing to do to a mercenary.

I walk along the fence line, ignoring the presence at my back. I can't see past the solid wall, but I can see enough to know that lights are on. A few guards are stationed outside, a few inside, but it's mostly security cameras we need to avoid.

Once we're at the back of the property, I hoist myself onto the stone wall and drape my legs over the other side. My guns are strapped to my legs and hips, my machete sheathed across my back like a sword, and my other fighting knives are within easy grabbing distance.

I'm ready to kill everyone.

My blood thrums as I stalk closer. I'm alert of everything—the killing haze brings me more clarity than I've ever felt. There's nothing and no one getting past my senses, not tonight.

Pressing my back against the wall, I look through the sliding glass door. There's a hall light on. It's late, so I'm assuming the rat is asleep. Easy to get him, easy to kidnap him, easy to kill him, too. But I can't take Axel's kill.

I glance at Riot and, finally, I can see his face. His brutal, tattooed, scarred face. He gives me a small nod, then moves to the other end of the house. I glance around the corner and watch him climb up the side of the wall, seemingly effortlessly.

Turning back toward the door, I crouch and use a lock-pick to get it open. I send Belfast an alert and wait a few seconds, as instructed, for him to turn off any alarms.

My feet are silent as I enter. A blade is already in my hand as I creep closer, always on the lookout for a guard. A muffled thud sounds from upstairs, and I jerk my head up.

Fucking Riot.

He's not a team player, not that I'm much of one either. But he's fucking annoying, never letting anyone else have the glory.

I take the steps three at a time and sprint down the hallway. I push the mostly-open door further and step into the dark room.

Muffled whimpers hit me and I whip my head around, finding a gagged man on the bed, a giant figure looming over him.

"Took you long enough," Riot grumbles.

"Fuck off," I snap as I stalk toward Ginger. "Nice to see you again." I lean forward, finding fresh blood trickling down his face. My lip curls away from my teeth as I sneer at him, loving the way he flinches. "The guards?" I look up at Riot and he tilts his head to the side. I follow the direction, finding two bodies stacked on top of each other, bloody and dead.

"A gift for the others," he says darkly. "I sent them on a wild chase when I got here. We have," he looks down at his watch, "about two minutes before they're back." I take a deep breath and look back at Ginger.

Riot hogtied and gagged him, but not before knocking him around some. I can't say I'm exactly sorry for the busted lip and bloody nose. I just wish it would've been me who gave it to him.

"Let's go," Riot growls. Grumbling to myself about how much of a fucking bastard he is, I jam my shoulder too hard into Ginger's stomach and throw him over my shoulder, grunting at the weight.

We rush down the steps, and maybe I purposefully knock Ginger's head against the walls a few times. Bolting across the floor to the back door, I close it on the way out. I'm not a monster. Riot hops onto the back wall first and I pass him Ginger, then follow them over.

Riot is already stalking away with him still slung over his shoulder like he weighs nothing. And to that fucking ogre, he probably doesn't.

It annoys the shit out of me that he can walk at the same speed most people jog without getting winded at all. Fucking annoying.

Headlights shine and we duck into the tree line.

"I thought you said we had two minutes," I hiss. He throws me a look over his shoulder as he drops Ginger unceremoniously to the ground.

"They're faster than I thought," he says, almost appreciatively. I roll my eyes as I grab my knife at my side.

"We need to go," I say. "Now." He gives me another look and I give him the finger. His face stays blank, no emotion given away.

And everyone calls me a psycho.

My phone vibrates in my back pocket, but I ignore it. We silently watch the few trucks drive into the compound, and once we hear the gate close, Riot grabs Ginger by the ropes and takes off down the side road again, his footsteps sure and unhurried.

I keep pace beside him, letting my foot hit Ginger's head hanging by the ground with every step. "Throw him in my trunk," I say, and Riot gives a hard nod. We turn toward my car as a bright light shoots into the sky. "Fuck." We take off at a full sprint as a siren roars behind us. The gates slide open as we run, the trees hiding us.

Trucks soar past and men are shouting from behind us. Ginger tries to scream past the gag, but it's too muffled. I bring my foot back and kick him in the face, bone crunching at the impact.

He stops screaming.

I parked my car deep in a thicket of trees, mostly hidden from view. Riot, of course, knows exactly where I'd parked. He probably scouted the area first instead of coming straight to me. Fucker.

He gets to it before me. I pant as I rest my hand against the side of the car, glaring at him. His face is hidden in the dark shadows of his hood, but I can feel his eyes on me. Assessing.

I pop the trunk open, and he drops Ginger into it without much care or thought. Without a word, he turns on his heel.

"That's it?" I ask, standing straight. My heart is pounding and my breathing is still ragged. I really need to start running again. Fuck.

He pauses and looks at me over his shoulder. "That's all you needed me for, wasn't it?"

"Yeah." I fold my arms over my chest, my eyes narrowing. "If you sold us out, I'll fucking mutilate you." He chuckles darkly.

"I'd like to see you try, Kiwi," he says. "If you could get close to me with a blade, I'll let you do whatever the fuck you want to me." My body hums at the challenge. But then a muffled thump sounds from the trunk, and I let out a sigh.

"We'll play next time," I mutter. "Got a rat to exterminate." I knock on the trunk a few times, and before the words are fully out of my mouth, Riot is stalking away again.

I watch his retreating form for a few more seconds, then realize I'm on enemy territory and need to get the fuck out of here.

Hopping in the car, I keep the lights off as I drive through the dim forest until we reach the main road. Then I merge into traffic, and off we go back to California.

Kiwi

Somewhere down the road, my phone vibrates again. I'd forgotten to check it earlier. I lift my hips and pull it from my back pocket, the car swerving slightly. I sigh sharply through my nose when I see Kennedy's name.

It's not that I'm not excited to hear from her, it's just that I don't want to get yelled at after dealing with Riot. But if she's calling, there's a reason. Unease twists my gut as I answer.

"What's wrong?" I say. More anxiety settles when she doesn't immediately answer. I tighten my hold on the phone, trying to calm myself. "Kens, love. What's wrong?" She hiccups and I push my brows together. "Kens?" I grip the wheel with one hand, my focus not on the road, but on her.

"Why'd you leave?" Her voice is slurred, and the unease fades and gives way to irritation. I don't know why it bothers me that she's drunk—maybe it's knowing last time she was, she slept with Archer.

I try to push that thought away.

"Are you drunk?"

"Alittlebit." The words all run together, telling me just how drunk she really is. I've never heard her as anything other than

142

borderline pissed off, so this is new. Her drunk voice is soft, more feminine and sweet, and it's throwing me off.

"What's going on? Why are you drunk?" I check the time on the dash, pinching my brows together again. "You're supposed to be working tonight." She giggles—actually fucking giggles—and my heart swells, my irritation fading.

"Spencer is on bartender duty," she says. "Can you imagine him in a miniskirt?"

"I'd rather not," I say dryly. "I'm a little busy here, babe. So—"

"Why'd you leave?" she asks again. I run my hand over my head, feeling overwhelmed. I knew I shouldn't have come. I should've stayed in Santa Cruz where I could be there in case something like this happened.

Not that I ever thought this would fucking happen.

"I had to come hunt this guy down," I say.

"No, why'd you leave?" She emphasizes the word, and I know she's not talking about me leaving the state. She means why did I leave her.

"You told me to," I say, and she hiccups again. I'd give fucking anything to see her right now. I'd never describe Kennedy as cute—she's far too brutal to be cute—but right now, she's fucking adorable. "I'm gonna FaceTime you."

I don't give her a choice, I just hit the video call button and wait for her to answer. She does immediately, her eyes glassy as she stares at the phone. She's laying in bed, surrounded by her million pillows. I set the phone up on the dash, splitting my attention between her and the road.

"Hey, pretty girl," I say. Her face turns bright red and I grin at her. She looks younger when she's drunk. She's not scowling, she's smiling.

"Hi," she says shyly. It does stupid shit to my heart, her soft voice and shy smile. It falls and a sad look crosses her face.

"Hey, don't frown," I say softly. "Smile for me, baby." She bites her lip to keep from smiling, but it breaks and she gives me the biggest

143

smile I've ever seen from her. "I like your smile. Prettiest smile I've ever seen."

"Thanks." She tucks her dark hair behind her ear, looking uncomfortable for probably the first time in her life. She gets that sad look again and I want to kill myself for being the one to make her sad. "I'm sorry, Kiwi."

"Say my name," I murmur.

"But you said—"

"I know what I said," I say, interrupting her. "And I was a fucking idiot. Don't call me Kiwi again."

"Sir yes sir." She does this weird mock-salute thing that looks more like she just slapped herself in the face and I bark a laugh.

"Say it, brat." I lift my brow and she giggles again. It's fucking weird to see her like this. I wish I was with her instead of a million miles away.

"Ezra," she sighs dreamily, and I grin.

"Now, why did you get drunk tonight?" I turn back to the road, scanning the highway for a road to turn down so I can give her all my attention.

"I was sad," she admits, and my eyes snap to the phone.

"Why's that?" I want to crawl through the fucking phone and hold her as she wipes her cheek.

"I was mean to you," she says. "And I'm sorry."

"I already forgave you," I say softly. "Anything you ever do or say is already forgiven." She presses her lips together in a small frown to keep herself from crying again, and I just can't fucking help but to smile at her.

"You mean that?" I nod as she speaks.

"With my life, love," I say. "Don't make getting drunk a habit, yeah?"

"I won't," she says, scooting down in her mountain of pillows more. "Archer doesn't handle his liquor well." My body surges at his name, suspicions rising.

"You got drunk with him?" I try to keep my voice even. She nods lazily, her head flopping around.

"He had to take me to the bathroom because I felt sick, but he ended up being the one to barf." She laughs hard at that, her eyes squeezed shut and her mouth wide open. "You should've been there."

"I don't want you drinking around men when I'm not with you," I say. She blinks a few times, her eyes still dazed as she tries to focus on the camera.

"Seriously?"

"Yes," I grit out. "You're mine, Kennedy. And I don't let what's mine party with men alone." She scrunches her nose at me, scowling again.

There she is.

"I wasn't alone. Spencer was there, too."

"You're not helping your case, love," I say flatly.

"I didn't know I had a case to help." Her scowl deepens, and it takes all I have to keep my face serious.

"Do you remember what I said I'd do to you—"

"You wouldn't." My seriousness cracks at the horror in her voice, and I huff out a laugh.

"I would," I taunt. "And I will." I scan her again, frowning when I notice she's in one of her thin tank tops. I hate that she was drunk and vulnerable around men when I wasn't there to protect her. Even if Archer seems like a decent guy, he's still a guy, and I can't trust anyone to not take advantage of her.

"No," she says stubbornly.

"You don't call the shots, do you, love?" I lift my brows and she rolls her eyes.

"I think I should," she huffs.

"Eh, I like things the way they are," I say. "I'm in charge, and you follow my orders."

"I'm not a dog," she snaps.

"I know," I say. "A dog behaves a hell of a lot better than you do."

Her mouth falls open, genuine shock filling her face. She sputters for a second, but I continue grinning. Looking at her with her mouth open makes me remember her on her knees, and my dick twitches.

Finally, I pull onto a side road and shut the car off. Leaning back in the seat, I just stare at her. At her beautiful scowling face, her shiny dark hair a blanket around her tattooed shoulders.

"Let me see what you're wearing," I say, my voice deeper. She blinks a few times, shaking her head slightly.

"What?"

"Show me what you're wearing," I say again. She glances at her door, then scoots up and leans against the headboard. She tilts her phone down and I get a good look at her top and see she's not wearing any pants. "Take it off."

"My shirt?" She tilts the phone back to her face. She's flushed and panting slightly, so I think she's as turned on as I am. I move my hand to my cock, palming it over my jeans. Her gaze follows my movement, and she licks her lips.

"Yes," I say as I lower the zipper. "Your shirt and panties." She sets the phone down and I watch the ceiling as she rustles around. When she lifts the phone again, she's topless. "Do you have any toys?"

"Maybe," she says slyly.

"You need to set your phone up. You'll need both hands." She bites her lip as she stumbles out of bed, nearly falling to her knees. She catches herself at the last second, then sets the phone up on her nightstand, letting me see her full body as she twirls around a few times. "Turn around and bend over."

Slowly, she spins around. She bends at the waist, letting her fingertips brush the floor, her ass on display for me.

"Good girl," I purr, and she looks over her shoulder at the phone. "Spread your legs." She shuffles her feet apart, opening her legs until I can see her pussy. Gripping the bed with one hand to steady herself, she reaches between her legs and slides her fingers over her clit. "Did I say you can touch yourself?" I slide my hand into my jeans and wrap it around my achingly hard cock as I watch her hand drop away. She makes a frustrated sound, but I choose to ignore it. If we were in person, she'd get a punishment for that, but I'm too fucking hard to care right now.

"What now?" She twists more to look back at me, her dark hair a perfect backdrop to her pretty, pale face.

"Get a toy," I say. She bites her lip as she turns around, letting me get a perfect view of her pierced tits. She rummages around in the drawer, making the phone shake slightly before she pulls out a pink vibrator. "Lay down and tease yourself for me."

She re-angles the phone toward the bed and lays back on it, spreading her legs wide as she leans on one elbow. She slowly sticks the tip of her vibrator into her mouth, letting her tongue swirl around the head, her eyes on me the whole time.

I pump my fist over my cock, my orgasm already tightening my body. Slowly, she drags it to her breast, letting it brush over her peaked nipple, then the other.

"What now?" she breathes, her words still slightly slurred.

"Turn it on and hold it on your clit," I rasp. She drags it down her body, turning it on as she goes, and lightly presses it against her clit. She gasps softly as she spreads her legs more, and the grip on my cock tightens.

"Like this?" She rubs it in a small circle and her legs tremble.

"Fuck yourself with it," I groan. I drop my head back against the seat, pumping myself faster. She presses it inside her and her back arches. "Just like that, love. Harder."

She fucks herself harder, her muscles flexing with each stroke. Her hips roll with her movements. I'm mesmerized watching her. My orgasm tightens my lower stomach and I grunt with every pump of my hand.

"Do you wish that was my cock?" I grunt, and she nods frantically.

"Fuck me, Ez," she moans. She lets out a high-pitched whimper, her legs falling apart more.

"Come on," I groan, pressing my back harder into the seat, my hips lifting. "Be a good slut and come for me." Her head falls back as she moans again. "Fuck, I can't—"

I nearly throw my phone when Ian's name pops up. My release teeters on the edge, then disappears as my phone vibrates again. I try to calm my breathing before answering.

"Hello?" I say warily. "Everything okay?"

"It's mom," he rushes out. My heart thunders in my chest, and I drop my dick, suddenly realizing I'm still holding onto it. I shove it back in my pants but stay leaning against the seat. "She's drunk, and I think she's crying. Something's wrong."

"She's okay," I sigh. "She'll be a bit hungover in the morning, but she'll be fine."

"But I've never seen her like that—"

"Ian," I say and he stops talking. "I was just on the phone with her. I promise she's fine." He's silent for a long moment.

"You're not fighting anymore?" His voice is cautious, and I sigh again. My cock is still painfully hard, but I'm way past the point of wanting to come now.

"We're good," I say, cutting myself off before I can say, "I hope."

I don't know if she'll even remember any of this in the morning. I don't know if she'll still be pissed at me when she wakes up and is sober. Or if she'll be even more pissed at me for watching her fuck herself while she was drunk.

That doesn't make me a scumbag, does it?

"We're good," I repeat. "You good?"

"I'm good." I chuckle at his harsh tone. "When will you be back?"

"You missing me already, kid?"

"No," he rushes out. "No, I'm just wondering. So I know when to expect you." I laugh again. Kennedy's kid through and through.

"I'm on my way back now," I say. "But I have to deal with some shit. It'll probably be a few days before I see you again." He's silent again, and I check my phone to make sure he's still on the line.

148

"Alright," he finally says. "See you later."

"Call if you need anything else," I say. He clears his throat awkwardly before hanging up. When I look back at my phone, it's just my regular lock screen. She must've hung up when she saw I wasn't there anymore.

I should call her back, but I need to get this shit done. The faster I get Ginger back to Axel, the faster I can be home with my girl. And her son.

My family.

Mine.

Kennedy

My head feels like it's going to roll off my shoulders. It's throbbing, spinning, and I feel like I'm dying. I smell like I'm dying. I'm sure I look like I'm dying, too.

I'm never drinking again.

Never.

I stare up at the spinning ceiling and try to calm my breathing. Breathe through the nausea. Breathe through it.

Someone—probably Ian—knocks on the door, and I wince. There's a brief pause and I stupidly think he walked away, but he knocks again. Groaning, I slide from my bed and crawl the few feet to the door, my legs too weak to hold my body up.

One eye closes as I try to steady myself, then the other one follows. I can't puke on my carpet. It'll be a bitch to clean. Bathroom. I need the bathroom.

I blindly reach for the doorknob and pull the door open. I crack one eye open and glare up at Ian, who looks downright pissed.

"Move," I breathe, swatting at his leg. He doesn't budge. "Ian, move." I feel it. The churning in my stomach is getting worse. I scramble to my feet, but the constant movement makes me even dizzier and I nearly topple over.

"Mom!" Ian shouts, a scolding note in his voice. I brace myself on the doorframe, one hand on my rolling stomach.

"Bathroom," I push out. "Sick." His eyes widen comically. It's a sick sense of déjà vu as I'm hoisted into his arms and rushed to the bathroom. He unceremoniously drops me onto the floor, my knees crashing into the tile, then runs to the door. To his credit, he's handling my puke a lot better than Archer.

I rest my forehead on my forearm, leaning against the toilet as I try to breathe through it.

"What do you need?" Ian asks.

"Hair tie and water," I rasp. A black silk scrunchy is shoved into my hand before he hurries away, his footsteps rattling the walls. He rushes back into the room, a bottle of water already open, as he shoves it at me. I grunt my thanks as I take it.

"Is this about Kiwi?" he asks quietly, almost shyly.

It's moments like this that I remember he's still just a kid. He might be big, he might look like a man, but he's not. He's just a boy. My baby. And me coming home drunk, carried by Spencer, probably scared him half to death.

I pride myself on being his mom and I know I fuck up sometimes, but last night I really fucked up.

"No," I say as I slowly turn to face him, pressing my back against the toilet and folding my legs. Taking a small sip of water, I watch him. He's holding himself tightly against the doorframe, his eyes worried as he stares back at me. He looks exhausted, like he hadn't slept last night. And knowing him, he probably didn't. "Are you okay, bud?"

He straightens his shoulders, forcing himself to be strong. I wonder how often he does that without me realizing it.

"I'm fine." I take another sip of water, letting the coolness soothe my sore throat. "But you and Kiwi had that fight and he left, then you came home drunk..." He trails off, his face still guarded.

151

"I just had a couple drinks on an empty stomach. It hit me harder than I had expected," I say, sighing softly. "But this wasn't about Ezra. Ez and I are—" Memories of last night come flooding back and I squeeze my eyes tightly shut. "Fine." I can't believe I did that. Had phone sex with him. I've never done that, and I never thought I would. But leave it to Ezra to make me forget all my boundaries.

Ian opens his mouth to say something, but pauses when someone knocks at the front door. We stare at each other for a moment, wondering if we ignore it, they'll just go away. But they knock again and I sigh.

"I've got it," Ian says, waving at me as he turns down the hall. Staggering to my feet, I use the wall to guide me from the room to the hallway.

Bright sunlight pours in around Ian's body, blinding me from seeing who's on the other side. But then he turns and looks at me over his shoulder and I see Enzo.

My stomach twists and I forget how bad I'd just been feeling.

"Oh my God," I breathe as I hurry toward him. Ian steps to the side, grabbing Enzo's bag from him as he enters. His eyes are on the floor—his eye is on the floor. The other one is swollen shut. He barely looks like himself from how swollen and bruised his face is. "Jesus."

"I'm fine, Ms. K," he mumbles.

"You're not fine," I snap as I take another step toward him. My hands shake as I lift them to his face—his poor, ruined face. "Why was it so bad this time?" He glances up at me, his one dark eye searing my soul.

"I fought back," he says darkly, and my stomach drops. "You should see how he looks." He tries to give me that cocky grin I love, but the cut in his lip spreads and he winces. Blood pools between his lips, into his mouth, and my stomach twists further.

I glance up at Ian, finding him staring at his friend with a mix of rage and adoration. I understand. I feel the same fucking way.

He fought back.

He fucking fought back.

152

"You should've just stayed with us," I say, gently scolding him. He looks between us, then shakes his head.

"I can't stay long," he says, dropping his eyes again. "I just wanted to say goodbye."

"Goodbye?" Ian repeats.

Something thick lodges in my throat at the look on Ian's face. Enzo's black hair sways as he tilts his head back, breathing deeply. He's always so casual, so fun and loving, that seeing him like this breaks me. It also enrages me so fucking much I want to leave this house and find his father.

"I gotta get out of here," Enzo rasps, his head still back. "I can't stay in California anymore."

"You can't leave," I say. "School? And—" He lets out a humorless laugh as he looks back at me. Ian steps beside me to glare down at his friend.

"Like I was ever gonna graduate," he says bitterly. "I think my mom is in North Dakota. I'll find her—"

"If she's even alive," Ian grumbles. "She's no better than your dad."

"At least she won't beat me," he shoots back. I shuffle closer to Ian and grab his wrist, wanting him to stop talking, stop pushing.

"She won't," Ian agrees, ignoring me. "But one of her many boyfriends will." Enzo stares at him, his mouth clamped shut. Then his chin wobbles and every fucking wall I have around my heart crumbles.

"I almost didn't survive this time, man," he croaks.

He inhales sharply and pinches between his eyes. He's too fucking young to deal with this. To be scared of dying at his father's hand. He puffs his chest out, firming his face as he looks between us. But I still see it—the hurt. The fear. The need to be loved. The pain.

I don't give him a choice, I just pull him into my arms and hold him. He's stiff for a moment, then he lets out a broken-sounding sob. Then his arms are around me as he buries his face into my neck. His tears soak into my skin, and I squeeze him tighter.

"It's alright," I say, stroking his head. "I've got you. We've got you." I squeeze my eyes shut at the raw pain I hear in his voice, at the guttural sobs coming from him. Ian rests his hand on Enzo's shoulder, the only amount of comfort he can give him. "You're staying here, alright?" He nods against me, his face slick against my skin. "You're ours, okay? I'm going to figure out a way to get you away from him. I'll figure out a way for you to never see him again, alright?" He nods again and pulls back.

He doesn't look like he believes me, but I can't leave him to travel across the country to a mother who might not even remember him. I can't leave him in the custody of his father, who will kill him one day. It's not a matter of if he'll do it, just when. And I'll hate myself if something happens to him when I could've saved him.

"You can put your shit in my room," Ian says, stepping out of the way. Enzo roughly clears his throat, and swipes his hand over his face.

"Thanks." Enzo grabs his bag from the floor. He hesitates, looking like he wants to say more, but he doesn't. He just turns and heads silently down the hall, his shoulders rounded in.

"Are you okay with this?" I ask immediately after the door shuts. "Are you fine with him living here?" Ian nods, his face shifting into that same firm, bloodthirsty look he'd had when he protected me from Ezra.

"I hate his dad," he says, glancing down the hall. "I fucking hate him."

"Ian," I sigh. It's a small reprimand for cursing, but I know it doesn't matter. Not right now. His chest heaves with each angry breath, his fist shaking at his sides. "He's safe now." I put my hand on his chest as I stare up at him. He's vibrating. "Ian, he's safe."

"For now," he says. "But what happens when he has to go back?"

"We'll figure it out," I say. "I'll talk to some people and figure out how to keep that from happening, alright?" He continues staring down the hall for another long moment, then finally looks down at me.

"We don't have the room or the money," he says, and guilt pushes at my chest.

"You do not worry about that," I say, pressing my finger firmly into the center of his chest. "I'm the mom. I worry about that. You— you're the kid. Worry about kid shit." He gives me an incredulous look, and I force myself to grin back. "Can't you at least give me some credit?" I lift my brows. "I got us out of that other shithole. I can get us out of here, too." A muscle in his jaw ticks, but he finally nods. "Don't worry. I've got this all handled."

He doesn't believe me.

I don't believe me, either.

Kiwi

I readjust my grip on my knife. It's slippery from all the blood I've spilled.

All the rat blood.

Bash stands in the center of the room, his arms crossed as he stares down at a broken and bloody Ginger. Reid, Heather, and Addie stand in the back of the room, their faces just as grave.

"We really have to keep this asshole alive for Ax?" I ask, eager to kill him. Bash slides his eyes to me.

"Yes, Kiwi," he says dryly, and looks back at the rat. Ginger's head is forward, blood and sweat dripping from his face onto his clothes and floor. He's long since passed out from the pain.

Bash rears his fist back and punches Ginger in the face. I grin as the bones crunch, forcing more blood to spill from his nose. He lets out a gargled, agonized scream that makes me smile even broader. Bash grips his hair and yanks his head back, angling it so he can continue whaling on him. Any control Bash had snapped the second his fist connected with Ginger's face. It's like all the stress and aggression and rage from the last few months are boiling out of him into those punches.

I rub my hands together as blood slings from Bash's fist, coating his boots, hitting my jeans, staining the floor.

"Alright, enough," Reid barks. "Bash, that's enough!" Reid grabs Bash's arm before he can land another hit. Bash whirls on him, shoving him back so hard he nearly falls to the floor. He's all Reaper right now. There's no Bash left. "Ax's kill." Reid stares at him, his face hard and still fucked up from the brutal beating he'd received at the hands of Montgomery's men.

Bash's shoulders rise and fall with his harsh breaths. His head barely turns toward Addie, but her face gives away nothing. Whatever silent conversation they have makes him let out a hard breath, then nod.

Axel said he wanted to kill him, not that we couldn't bring him close to death first.

Bash turns his attention back to Ginger. He's passed out again from the pain Bash just inflicted. I slap his face a few times, bringing him back to consciousness. "Were you trying to buy her for yourself, or for someone else?" Bash asks, his voice cold.

"Who?" Ginger rasps. His eyes flutter open and he stares directly up at Bash. Something breaks in Bash and he grabs Ginger's bloody, ripped up shirt.

"Skye, you sick motherfucker," he snarls. "My fucking niece." He hits Ginger in the face again, and I can't say I blame him. I would've done a lot more by now, but it's not my kill.

Ginger grins through the blood and pain, his focus solely on Bash. "For myself," he rasps. "Gonna take her home with me. I'll make her mine forever." Bash rams his fist into his face again, then shoves him back as he yanks his famous black blade from his pocket.

He flicks it open and holds it in front of Ginger's face.

Nothing.

There's nothing human on Bash's face.

There's no remorse on Ginger's.

"I'm going to shred your skin from your fucking bones," Bash says, his voice a low promise. "I'm going to fucking enjoy it, too."

"Bash," Addie says warily, taking a step forward.

"I won't kill him." Bash keeps his eyes on Ginger's. "Kiwi, where's your peeler?"

I let out a hyena laugh as I rush toward my box of toys. Knives and torture devices galore. Makes my dick hard just looking at it all. I pull out my sharpest peeler and turn toward Bash, my eyes catching on Heather's.

She's staring at me like she doesn't know me. But she has no room to judge. She's killed men before, too. She pretends like she's not as bloodthirsty as the rest of us, but she is. I know she is.

"Can I do the first one, Prez?" I ask excitedly. Bash tilts his head, his sweaty hair plastered to his face as he watches me slowly approach. He gives me a small nod and steps back. "Christmas came early. Thanks Prez."

I crouch beside Ginger and grin up at him. Using my knife, I cut the leg off his sweatpants, exposing his pale thigh, and shove the fabric around his ankle. "Need a tan, mate." I tap my knife against his skin and his muscle twitches.

I run the sharp blade over him, watching goosebumps ripple. This is the part I love, the part I crave. The anticipation of the first slice, the fear in their body, the excitement in mine. There's something fucking glorious about that first cut, watching the fresh blood seep from it.

"Tell us a bit about your daddy," I say, still stroking the knife against his skin. Ginger doesn't respond, and I flick my eyes up to him. "Does he have your baby sister locked away so he can fuck her? Or has he already sold her to the highest bidder?" Ginger's jaw tenses, something like hatred flickering in his eyes. "Ah."

Looking back at Bash, I know he saw it, too. Ginger's soft spot—his sister.

"Or is he saving her for you?" I ask, looking back at him. His lips press into a hard line, like he's forcing himself to not speak. "I bet she's pretty. Does she have red hair like you?"

We just need this fucker to talk. Once he does, I know he'll sing and we'll get all kinds of information.

"What do you think, Prez?" I look back at Bash. "I say we take his sister. It's only fair. Since he tried to take our girl, we take his." Ginger jerks on his restraints and I smile. Bash's jaw tenses under his thick, dark beard.

"Don't fucking touch her," Ginger snarls, his voice hoarse. I peer up at him again, my blade still going back and forth. He's seemingly forgotten about it. Good.

"Or what?" I taunt and he jerks on the bindings again. "She's seventeen, right? Almost legal." He snaps his teeth at me, snarling. "And that barely legal pussy—" I groan and hear uncomfortable shuffling behind me.

I might be a sick fuck, but I'm not sick enough to go after barely legal girls. Ginger, if he was fucking smart, would know that. But he doesn't. Or he's too far gone in this little game I'm playing with him to remember he's never seen me with a woman under twenty-four.

"You know all about that, though, right?" I continue stroking the blade up and down his thigh. "They're different, aren't they? Feel better. Tighter." He jerks forward again. "How's your sister feel, Ging?"

"Fuck you," he spits. "Leave her out of this. She doesn't know any of this shit. She's not in the life." I narrow my eyes, but he keeps talking. "She's innocent. Don't fucking touch her."

"Innocent," I muse. "Innocent like Skye?" He freezes. "Is she more innocent than a seven-year-old?" His eyes widen as I press the tip of the blade against his thigh. "Is she more deserving of safety than Skye? Skye's not in the life either, but you were still going to take her from us."

She's our little club princess, and while kids aren't my favorite, that one is. That one I've claimed. She's under my protection—she's under the protection of every man and woman in this fucking club. We take any threat to her seriously. And this motherfucker threatened her in the worst way.

I press my blade slowly into his thigh, feeling his skin and muscle separate. He hisses through his teeth, his hateful eyes trained on mine. I take my time embedding the knife.

"You know the lengths we'll go to keep her safe," I say darkly as I look down at the blade disappearing into his leg. "You know that kid is the beating heart of this club. And yet," I look up at him, "you're stupid enough to try to take her away. Why?"

He doesn't say anything. His bloody spit flies as he tries to breathe through the pain.

"We're going to enjoy this," I say, my voice soft. "We're going to enjoy watching Ax slaughter you. You know what he can do, you've seen it." He pales at that, at the memories of Axel killing a man with his bare hands, squeezing the life from him. "He's going to make it a slow death. As much as we," I jerk my head back to Bash and Reid, "love Skye. She's his daughter, man. You fucked up."

I stop sliding the blade in when I hit bone. To his credit, he still hasn't screamed. But I'm about to make him. Pain-filled screams are my favorite songs, the thing that brings me calmness and comfort. The thing that makes me forget about the rest of the world and only focus on ridding it of the sick, twisted, evil fuck in front of me.

Grabbing the peeler, I hold it in front of his face. Ginger was a Prospect for a year and was only recently patched in. He saw some shit, but he hasn't seen all of it. And this, the peeler, he hasn't seen.

It's my favorite, but I save it for the really evil ones. Like him.

"Tell us where we can find the girls in L.A.," Bash drawls, his voice shaking with his restraint. I rest the peeler on Ginger's thigh, right in front of the blade. He stares down at it, anticipating the first slice. "Ginger!" He snaps his attention to Bash.

"They—they take them to this warehouse," he says, his chest heaving. "If you let me out, I'll show you. I can—" I snort and dig the peeler blade into his skin. "Wait. Wait." I ignore him as I drag it down slightly, watching the thick red blood pool around it. "Wait!" His body jerks, forcing his leg back. Skin begins to slide through the peeler. "My dad isn't involved in this."

"Bullshit," Bash scoffs.

"No, no." Ginger shakes his head, his eyes squeezing shut as I slowly drag the peeler down more, letting more skin slide through. He lets out an agonized scream, but I don't stop. And I won't until Bash tells me to. "He's involved, but he's not close to it! Montgomery is just a grunt. He buys and sells girls and gives my dad the money. My dad hasn't ever even met him. He has hundreds of men like Montgomery around the state."

"We know he's trying to expand," Bash says, and Ginger nods frantically, letting out another pained scream.

"He's trying to take over the entire West Coast," he pants. "He'll never stop. Even after he's dead, my brother will take over."

"You haven't heard?" I grin up at him, finally pausing my peeling. He's breathing heavily as he stares down at me.

"What?"

"Your brother is dead," I say. "Daddy killed him." He shakes his head a few times, his throat bobbing.

"No," he says. "He'd never kill Oli."

"Apparently he did," Bash says dryly, uncaring of Ginger's spiral. "How do we stop him?" Ginger's jaw flexes.

"I don't know," he breathes, then screams as I begin peeling his skin again. "He doesn't meet with people he hasn't known for years. He won't take on new grunts unless they can be vetted by the others." Bash begins pacing behind me. I feel his mind working overtime as he tries to scramble together a plan. "You can't take him down."

"Every empire falls," I promise.

"If you let me go," Ginger says again, his voice breathy and broken, "I can get information for you. I can help—"

"Why would we trust you?" Bash snarls. "Why would we ever want to work with you?"

I pause. Ginger's eyes flick between Bash's, then he looks at Reid, then down at me.

"I wasn't really going to take her," he admits quietly. "I just needed you to take this shit seriously." I glance at Bash as his eyes narrow. "I—" Ginger's throat bobs as he swallows thickly. "I've been trying to save my sister for years and I thought taking this job was an opportunity to have you help me do that." Bash's eyes stay narrowed as he takes a step forward.

"You infiltrated our club so we could help you save your sister?" he growls. Ginger nods weakly, his face pale. "Tell us everything."

So, Ginger did. He told us everything. He told us his story, his father's story. My stomach twisted with each damning word, each kernel of new information.

We are in way over our fucking heads.

Kennedy

"How are you feeling?" Spencer asks as I step behind the bar. I glance at him as he stalks toward me.

"Better," I mutter. "I'm really sorry, Spence." He waves me off casually, but his face stays its usual intensity.

"It's fine." He rests his forearms on the bar, leaning over it as his eyes narrow. "How do you keep up with everyone?" I tilt my head to the side.

"What do you mean?"

"There are a lot of guys here every night, and you keep up with their orders. I couldn't remember who ordered what. It was a mess." I smile slightly, dipping my head as I shrug.

"I've been doing this for a long time," I say. "You just...figure it out."

"Do any of the guys fuck with you?" he suddenly asks, and I rear my head back.

"Fuck with me?" I repeat, blinking at him.

"Yeah, you know. Do they—" He waves his hand, trying to say it without saying it. Do they touch me, or more?

163

"Yeah," I mutter as I look down. "Not all the guys, just some. It's usually outsiders." I glance at him, finding his face thunderous. "Milo and I had to kick out some drunk assholes the other night, but they came back and one of them tried to touch me, but Milo got him. We kicked them out again."

"What?" he says deathly low. "Why is this the first I'm hearing of it?" I shrug as I run my fingers through my hair.

"You've never asked," I say, my eyes on the bar. He's silent, his eyes boring into the top of my head. He opens his mouth to say something more, but the door swings open.

We turn our attention to it, and I groan. Ezra swaggers in, his usual cocky grin plastered on his face as he slides his sunglasses on his head. His walk is so fucking over the top it should look ridiculous, but it doesn't.

Spencer straightens to his full height and turns around, leaning against the bar as he folds his arms over his chest. Ezra jerks his chin at him as he approaches.

"What's up, Spence?" he says, resting one arm on the bar and leaning heavily on it. He doesn't look at me, not even a glance.

"What are you doing here?" Spencer sighs. He doesn't sound irritated, just tired.

And I understand why. Ezra—Kiwi, as he is now—is tiring.

"Can't I come see my second favorite Prez?" he asks, his white teeth flashing with his grin.

"I'd rather you didn't," Spencer retorts. "A phone call is just fine."

"But what's the fun in that?"

They stare at each other, then Spencer sighs again. "I'll be in my office." He glances at me, like he knows I'm the real reason Ezra is here. We silently watch Spence disappear down the short hall and listen to his office door click shut.

Ezra doesn't look at me as he says, "How are you doing, love?"

My stomach twists, but I force myself to take a steadying breath. He turns toward me, his eyes melting as they meet mine.

"Why are you here?" I ask. My voice doesn't come out as sharp as I'd wanted. It comes out small. Shy. And I hate myself for it. His expression melts even more as he turns fully to face me.

"Just wanted to check on my girl," he says. "Make sure she's doing alright. Was your hangover a bitch this morning?" He bends his arm and rests his head on his fist as he stares at me. He stares at me like I hadn't called him a freak only a few days ago. Like I hadn't hurt him. Like he hadn't hurt me.

"Ian helped out," I mumble. "I feel fine."

"And Arch?" he asks. I pinch my brows together.

"What about him?"

"Have you talked to him today?" He tries to keep his face and voice casual, but I see it in his eyes, the tightness, the possessiveness.

"Ask what you really want to ask, Ez," I say, resting my hands on the bar and leaning forward.

"I want to know if you've talked to him." He keeps his head propped on his fist, his expression never changing. But his eyes darken.

"If I have?" I challenge, and he huffs out a humorless laugh.

"Are we really doing this again?" he asks. "Are you really going to fight with me right now?"

"I'm not fighting with you." I stand at my full height and fold my arms over my chest. His eyes drop to my tits, and the look on his face makes my body irrationally heat. "Ez." I snap my fingers in front of his face and he finally lifts his gaze to mine. "I'm not fighting. I just want to know what your deal with Arch is."

"You know what my deal is, love," he says. "I don't want you around him."

"Kinda hard to avoid him. I work here, at his club's bar." I throw my arm out, vaguely gesturing around us, and he shakes his head.

"You know what I mean," he breathes. "I don't like that you got drunk together."

"Why?" I snap. "I'm a grown woman. I can do whatever the fuck

I want." He shakes his head as I speak, a stupid, humorless grin on his face.

"To my knowledge, the last time you two were drunk together, he tripped and landed his dick inside you. I'm not letting that happen again." I blink at him.

"You have no right to tell me who I can or can't fuck," I snarl. "We're not together, Ez. And even if we were, I would never allow you to treat me like this."

"Like what?" He tilts his head to the side, that irritating smirk still on his stupid face.

"Like I'm your property."

"You are," he says flatly. "You're mine, Kennedy. You belong to me."

"I am *not* your property, Ezra. You do not own me."

"I do," he says unapologetically. "I own every fucking inch of you, Kens." My lips tighten, hateful words I know will bruise him ready to burst free. "But you own me too. I gave you my heart and my soul the moment I saw you. I'll happily brand your name into my body and let everyone know I'm your property. That I belong to you."

I blink at him.

He's fucking crazy, I know that, but...fuck. He says some shit that makes my knees go weak.

"I mean, you'll have to do the same," he says. I roll my eyes, huffing out a breath. *And he's back.* "How badly do you think a brand hurts? Scale of one to ten. Worse than a tattoo?" I bark out a laugh at the absurdity of it, of him, but when I look at him again, he's serious.

"Ez," I laugh again. "That's insane. Come on."

"I'm insane, in case you haven't noticed."

"I have," I say dryly. "But you're not burning a fucking brand into your skin for me." I shake my head a few times. "I'm still annoyed with you! Don't distract me." He grins wolfishly. "You can't tell me what to do. I'm serious about that. I won't be controlled."

He shrugs as he pushes off the bar. "We'll see about that, love."

166

"No," I shake my head, "I will never be controlled. If you ever try it, I'll cut your balls off."

"Fuck, you know how to get my dick hard," he says as he adjusts himself and I take a deep breath, trying to keep calm.

"Can you fuck off for a while?" I ask, and he snorts.

"Nah."

"Ez," I growl. "I need time."

"Time for what?" He looks genuinely confused at the question, and I let out an exasperated breath.

"This." I wave my hand between us. "I need time to figure this out. Figure us out."

"What is there to figure out?"

"I have to think about Ian," I say. "I have to think—"

"He's mine, too."

"Stop." I squeeze my eyes shut. "Just stop saying shit like that."

"It's true," he says darkly. "You're both mine. Forever."

"But I'm not sure we want to be." He goes deathly still, his eyes narrowing.

"What?"

"I just—"

"No, what does that mean? You're not sure you want to be?" His jaw works to the side as he glares at me.

"It means that I'm still not sold on the idea of being with you," I say, steeling my spine and lifting my chin. "It means that I don't want to be with someone in an MC. It means I refuse to let you barrel your way into my life and take over. I'm not that type of woman, Ez. And if that's what you want, find someone else. I'll never roll over and submit to you."

"You have once," he says. "You'll do it again. You'll do it in all aspects of your life. You'll learn to trust me. You'll learn to lean on me." I shake my head as he speaks.

"I can't rely on anyone," I say.

"You can rely on me."

"And what happens when you die?" I ask, my voice rising. "What happens when you get taken away in cuffs? What happens when I find you with your dick buried in some club slut?"

He stares at me, his square jaw so tense it looks like he's about to crack his teeth. Slowly, he lets out a breath.

"One," he says, holding his finger up, "I will never die."

"You're human. Everyone—"

"*No,*" he says, shaking his head, emphasizing the word. "I will not fucking die on you. Do you understand me? You'll have to go first because there's no fucking way I'm leaving you alone in this world." My throat tightens, but I force myself to breathe through the growing emotions. "Two. I won't get fucking arrested, Kens. Come on. And three," he holds three fingers up, "I have no interest being inside anyone but you. No other woman will ever compare to you. I have no need to fuck anyone else, to want anyone else, if I have you."

I take a shaky breath. "You said you were mine from the moment you saw me," I say quietly, my eyes flicking between his, searching for an answer I'm terrified of. "Have you slept with anyone since that day?" He's silent, his expression turning guilty, and I let out a humorless laugh. "See? They're all just words, Ez. You can say whatever you want, but they don't mean shit."

"You told me to fuck off," he says, his voice rising. "You can't hold my past against me."

"Like you do to me?" I counter. "You bring Archer up every chance you get, and that was years ago. Not weeks ago. Or has it only been days? When was the last time you fucked someone else? This morning?"

"I'm not doing this," he says, shaking his head. "We're not fucking doing this." I round the bar, my eyes on his.

"No, tell me," I push. "Tell me when the last time was that you fucked someone." I step up to him, my chest brushing against his. My head is tipped almost all the way back, but I still feel like I'm glaring down at him. "Want to know my last time? Three years ago with Archer. That was the last time. When was yours?"

"A few weeks ago," he admits through gritted teeth. "It—she didn't mean anything. She's with someone else now, anyway." I let out a humorless laugh.

"So if she was single, you'd still be fucking her?" I fold my arms over my chest.

"We were fucking stressed!" he shouts, and I flinch. "We were on lockdown and there was nothing else to fucking do. It was something to make us forget this shit for a while. It didn't mean anything. I don't give a fuck about her! I don't—"

"Who was it?" I say in a low voice, interrupting him. If she was on lockdown with him, she's close to the club, close to him. His mouth hangs open, and I see the thoughts whirling in his head. He realizes he fucked up and is trying to figure a way out of this. "Who, Kiwi?" He winces like I physically hit him.

"Heather," he finally says, and it's like a blow to the fucking gut. "We fucked a few times. I hooked up with her and Reid before they were together. That was the last time I slept with anyone." My heart feels like it's about to crack. "But it meant nothing." I shake my head as he speaks.

"You have been judging me for fucking days," I hiss as I press my finger into the center of his chest. "You've gone on and on about Archer, about how upset you are that we slept together. But that was one time. We were together one fucking time. Not a *few* times." I spit the words at him, disgusted. "I never had a threesome with him and someone else. You've made me feel bad about my past, even though you did the same shit. You did worse! Heather, Kiwi? Really?"

"She was there," he says quietly, unapologetically. "That's it."

"I gave you my heart and soul the moment I saw you," I snarl, throwing his words back at him. "That was just bullshit. A pretty line to get me in bed."

"No!" His voice booms around the room as he slams his fist onto the bar, his chest heaving as he breathes through his teeth. I keep my spine stiff even though I want to cower away from him, from his outburst. "That's not fucking it!" He hits the bar again, harder, and I take a large step back. "What do you want me to say?"

"Nothing," I murmur. "There's nothing you can say." Tears burn my eyes as I watch him whirl and punch the closest wall. His body is vibrating. He's seconds away from exploding. "Get out, Kiwi. Just...leave."

His broad shoulders rise and fall with each ragged breath. He keeps his back to me as he tries to calm down.

"Is this how it'll always be?" he finally says, his voice raw. "You'll always find something wrong? Something to fight with me over? Some way to push me away?" He turns toward me, and every bit of warmth he ever had in his eyes is gone. His face is distant. Cold. "You'll never make me happy. You'll never give, just a little fucking bit, so I can be happy. So I can have you. Have Ian. Have a fucking family? You'll always push, and push, and fucking *push*, until you finally get your wish and I leave? I'm only a man, Kens. I can only take so much. And this back and forth," he shakes his head, "I can't do it. I won't do it. I'll fight to be with you tooth and nail every day for the rest of my life, but I'll only do it if I know you'll fight for me too. I won't put this effort into someone who doesn't want me. Who is disgusted by me. Who hates me."

"I don't hate you," I say, my chin wobbling.

"Could've fooled me." We stare at each other, each waiting for the other to say something, anything, to fix it. It's like that day in the bathroom all over again, but this time...this time I know it's permanent. Whatever it is, it's severed and gone.

Forever.

I remind myself that it's fine. That it's better this way. That everything this man is and represents is something I don't want. It's something I've never wanted. I remind myself that his dick is barely dry from where he'd had it buried in Heather only a few weeks ago. I remind myself that no matter what he says, he'll eventually stop following through on his words, like everyone else.

And I remind myself that if I'm too much work for him, too diffi-cult, then he's not the man for me.

So I take a step back, my arms wrapped tightly around myself as I tilt my chin up.

"Goodbye, Kiwi," I say.

He stares back at me, his face giving nothing away.

"Goodbye, Kennedy."

Kennedy

It's too fucking late—or is it too early? It's nearly five in the morning and I'm just getting home from the bar. I want to curl up and die, but I have to be at the café at seven.

I slide my jacket off as I head toward the kitchen, ready to stuff my face with something, then take a power nap before work. Opening the fridge, I find it still mostly empty, but at least Ian was nice enough to leave me a slice of pizza.

Cold pizza and a beer for dinner it is, then. Or is it breakfast?

I don't think I really care.

After Kiwi left, there was something in my gut screaming at me to go get him. That I'd made the biggest mistake of my life. And I think whatever intuition I had was right.

I can't keep the negative thoughts at bay. I keep replaying his words over and over and over.

"You'll never make me happy. You'll never give, just a little fucking bit, so I can be happy."

Those words cut deep. They shredded my soul. And the look on his face, in his eyes, gutted me. His expression was burned into my mind and it's all I see when I close my eyes. It's him, so devastated behind a mask of indifference, a mask of anger, that made me realize my feelings for him go a lot deeper than I ever realized.

I'm hurt that he made me feel bad for sleeping with Archer when he slept with Heather. But she has a man now; she doesn't need mine. And knowing her, and honestly, knowing Ezra, I believe him when he says it was casual, that it meant nothing.

But I've been single for so long. I've been on my own for so fucking long I think I've forgotten what it's like to have someone, another adult, to rely on. It sounds too good to be true—*he* sounds too good to be true.

He says all the right things, even if he gives them a crazy spin. But he cares about Ian, and that's the most important thing to me, that the man I'm falling for loves my son, too. Ian has to be a priority, not just to me, but to him, too. And I think we would be Ezra's entire life.

A part of me is terrified to lower my guard and let him in. I know when I do, there's no going back. Once I'm in, I'll be all the way in. I know it's me who has pushed him away every time. And I know he was right when he said I'd push until he cracked and proved me right by leaving. But that would be all on me. That would be my fault, to have broken a seemingly unbreakable man like him.

Footsteps sound from the living room, and I lift my head as Ian walks into the dark kitchen. I feel like it's been years since I've seen him, since I've held him. Tears sting my eyes and I sniff hard, wanting to push them back. But they don't. They spill down my cheeks and I cover my face with my hands.

"Mom?" Ian says, his voice groggy from sleep. "What's wrong?" I cry harder at the question.

I've ruined so many lives. My own, Ian's, my parents, Ian's father's...now Ezra's.

I can't take the weight of it anymore. The weight of knowing I'm responsible for fucking everything up, all the time. Ian deserves a better mother, one who should've given him a father when he was a baby. One that should've fought his biological father harder so he could know him. One that wouldn't turn away the first good man to ever enter her life.

But I've ruined it all. Everything.

I know I've fucked him up and he'll need therapy for the rest of his life. I'll be fucking lucky if he ever talks to me after he moves out.

His arms wrap around me, unsure and wary, and I cry harder at his touch. This isn't his job. Taking care of me, comforting me—*this isn't his job.* I try to pull myself together, but with every hyperventilating breath, I sob harder.

He holds me tighter, and I let him. I break and press my face harder against him. He's silent. He doesn't push me for answers, or try to reassure me. He just gives me his presence, and that's all I need.

"I'm sorry," I say against his shirt, now damp from tears. "I'm so, so sorry, Ian."

"For what?" His voice is soft, one I haven't heard before, and it breaks my heart even more. He doesn't sound like my baby. He sounds like a man. Not a boy growing into a man—a man.

"For being such a shitty mom," I say. "I don't know how I've fucked it up so bad, but I have. You deserve so much, baby. You deserve to live in a house, not a rundown apartment. I want to give you the world. I want to give you a father. I want to give you more, and I can't. I fuck it all up and I'm sorry you've had to deal with it. That you've had to deal with me."

His arms tighten, and he rests his chin on the top of my head. "You give me everything, Mom. I don't need a dad, not when I have you. You haven't fucked anything up." His words just make me cry harder. "What happened?"

I let out another broken sob, and he pulls away to look down at me. His face is mostly shadowed, the growing sunrise illuminating the side of his face.

"I ruined everything with Ezra," I say. "I—I shouldn't even be talking to you about this."

"Mom," he says, squeezing my shoulders.

"I think I like him," I admit. There's a pause, then he snorts.

"Yeah, no shit." I blink at him. "I've never seen you look at anyone the way you look at him. Even when you look like you want to kill him, there's...*something*. Something in your eyes." I just stare at him, unable to say anything. "He came by the other day before he went to Oregon. I called him when you came home drunk because I was worried."

"You did?" I don't know how to feel about that.

"He cares about you. I thought he'd know what to do."

"So if I brought him around," I say slowly, "it wouldn't be weird for you to see me with him? You'd be fine with it? With us?" He shrugs again. "Ian, you always come first. And if you tell me you don't like him, then everything ends."

"Does he make you happy?" he asks, and I take a deep breath.

"When he's not being an insufferable ass, yes." He cracks a small smile.

"And you make him happy?"

"He says I do," I say, trying to ignore his earlier words.

"He'll protect you and treat you right?"

"I didn't know this would turn into an interrogation," I say, laughing awkwardly. But he doesn't laugh. His face doesn't shift.

"Will he?" he asks again, and I sigh.

"Yes," I say. "He'll protect me and you. I think he'd jump in front of a bullet for us." He shakes his head, his brows furrowing.

"Not us," he says, "*you*. Will he do that for you?"

I don't know why it's so hard to admit that yes, Ezra would burn the world for me. I know he would. His intensity, everything about him screams at me that he would.

Every reason I gave him why I needed to think about this, about us, was bullshit. I knew it as the words left my mouth, and I know it now. They were convenient excuses to give him because I'm scared. Scared of giving him my heart. He could easily crush it if he wanted, and that terrifies me.

But being alone, being without him, never seeing him again, terrifies me even more.

"Yes," I finally say. "He'll protect me and treat me right."

"Then I'm fine with it," Ian says simply. "I think he's the only man who isn't terrified of you." I laugh softly, agreeing with him. "I think I like him, too."

"Yeah?" I ask, smiling at the red creeping into his cheeks.

"He's cool," he says, taking a step back. "He said he'll teach me how to surf." I laugh softly again.

"You're easy to win over," I say, and he shrugs.

"Surfing and him treating you right, that's all I need from him." My heart squeezes.

"Ian, if he's in my life, he'll be in yours too." His words flow through my head again. He called us his family. "I think he'd really love to spend time with you. I think he wants to build a relationship with you, without me in it." He scrunches his nose.

"Don't say it like that," he says. "It sounds weird." I bark out a laugh, then slam my hand over my mouth, remembering Ezno is still asleep. Ian waves his hand toward his bedroom. "He could sleep through a freight train." I tip my head back, a small smile on my face.

"I'll talk to Ezra tomorrow," I say, feeling determined to make this work. I won't let my insecurities and unsurities ruin this. I want him.

Kiwi

I 'm done.

I'm done with Kennedy. I can't handle this back and forth shit she has going. She doesn't want me? Fine. She's made it perfectly clear what she thinks of me and my club. I'm not giving up a part of myself because she's scared. Because she doesn't understand it.

I'm not leaving my family behind.

These men are the only people who have ever, *fucking ever*, made me feel normal. They've never once made me feel like a freak, even though I am. They know I'm crazy, they know I love the thrill of the kill, but they use it to their advantage. They don't try to change me.

Maybe I should've told Kennedy about Heather sooner. Maybe I should've been more understanding about her and Archer. But there's something about knowing your girl has slept with another man that just does something to your soul, as her man. She might be jealous or upset about Heather, but she isn't murderous over it. Not like I am.

I have to reign it in every time I think about it. I have to force myself not to hunt the bastard down and slaughter him for thinking he had any right to touch my fucking woman. Even though I didn't know she even existed at the time, she was still mine. She was mine the second she was conceived.

The fact I have to share her with Ian pisses me off, but that boy is fifty percent Kennedy, which makes him mine, too.

It *made* him mine.

Not anymore.

Neither of them are mine anymore.

I stalk down the steps to the kill room in the basement, my hands tightening into fists at my sides as I kick the door open. Ginger's head snaps up, his face pale under the dried blood.

"Hey, motherfucker," I say, jerking my chin at him. "Ready for some more fun?"

"I thought—" His voice is raw from his screams, his lack of water. Piss surrounds his chair and I snarl at it, at him, at the fucking world. "I thought after I gave you that information, you'd leave me alone."

"Yeah, you thought fucking wrong," I say, stalking to the table in the back. I pull my box to me and sift through it, trying to find something fun to play with. Something that'll make him squeal like a little piggy.

I never said I was a good man, or a sane one.

Pulling the pliers from the box, I turn toward him, a smile spreading across my face. He barely lets me take a step forward before he starts begging, his voice rising with each word as he stares at the pliers.

"P-p-pl-please," he says, his body trembling. "What else do you want to know?"

"There's more you can tell me?" I ask, tilting the pliers back and forth, taunting him. His eyes widen as he realizes his mistake. "You really are a fucking rat. Ratting on us, ratting on Daddy." I shake my head as I push off the table. "Do you have any honor?" I clutch my fist to my chest as I stalk toward him. "Do you have any morals or loyalty? Don't you care about anyone but yourself?"

His eyes stay locked on the pliers, but I move behind him, crouching to get closer to his hands. They're too red and swollen in the tight bindings, but I don't really give a fuck.

Twisting his hand, I pick which finger I want to fuck with first. I press the pliers onto one of his nails and gently tug, just enough to make him scream in fear, not pain.

"Please, man," he says, his voice breaking. He's close to sobbing. "Please—"

"Please, what?" I ask, tugging harder on his nail. "Did you really think we'd just...let you go? After you threatened our girl?"

"It wasn't real," he cried. "It was just—" I don't let him finish speaking. I yank hard and rip his nail off.

His scream echoes around the room, full of agony.

I move around him and hold his nail in his face. "Look," I say, tilting it back and forth.

"You're fucking psychotic!" he screams. "What the fuck! You fucking—" His eyes finally focus on the nail, and he freezes. He leans to the side and retches, and I roll my eyes.

Why is it all men have a weak stomach when it comes to torture? Whether they're the ones torturing or the ones being tortured.

Just be a fucking man and get over it, you know?

I drop the nail to the floor and move behind him again, ready to pull off the rest of his nails, mostly because I'm annoyed now. I grip a nail and begin to tug tauntingly on it when the door opens.

"Kiwi!" Bash barks, and I roll my eyes as I push to my feet, staring at him over Ginger's head. He's still sobbing and gagging, and just generally freaking out. It's annoying as shit and fucking with me. This was supposed to be my peaceful time, but he's fucking it all up. "What the fuck are you doing in here?"

"Playing," I say with a small shrug. "Needed to do something to take the edge off."

"So go take a few shots or fuck someone, go for a fucking ride, I don't care. But don't fuck with our captives without my permission."

He glares at me from the doorway, his face furious. "Get the fuck out. Right now."

"But—"

"No!" he shouts. "Out. Now." I huff out an irritated breath. That one nail didn't relax me enough to sleep through my misery.

Ride it is, I guess.

I toss the pliers back into the box and head for the door, ignoring Ginger's slumped body. He must've passed out. Pussy.

Bash is still standing in the doorway, his eyes hard as he glares at me. He steps out of the way, letting me storm past. He grabs my arm before I can ascend the stairs.

"What the fuck is going on with you?" he snarls.

"Nothing." I keep my back turned, not wanting to look at him. "I'm good, Prez."

"No, you're not," he says, shaking me slightly. "If you can't get your shit under control, you're fucking out."

That makes me go deathly still.

Slowly, I turn to face him. Whatever he sees on my face makes him drop his hand and straighten to his full height, his chin tipping back in challenge.

"You're kicking me out of the club?" I ask quietly, my voice low and hard.

"No," he says. "But I'm taking you out of this shit. If it's getting to you, then we'll find something else for you to do. Something that's not so involved." I clench my jaw.

"Are you saying I'm incapable?" I ask, and he lets out a hard breath.

"No, and you know I'm not," he says. "I'm saying if you're about to go off the deep end, I need to know that now. I can't worry about you while I'm trying to fix this shit. So, are you good, Kiwi? Or do I need to find something else for you to do?"

I stare at him, my body vibrating.

"I'm good, Prez," I say darkly. "I'm fucking great."

"That didn't look like you were great," he says, tipping his head toward the door. "That looked like you're riding the edge."

"I'm fine," I say again. He shakes his head as he lets out a breath.

"One more time," he says, holding his finger up. "If you fuck around one more time, you're on Prospect duty. You understand?"

Babysitting duty, he means.

"I understand," I say.

"Don't make me do it, Kiwi," he says tiredly. "Please just take a fucking breath and think before you do shit. I need to know I can trust you to not fucking lose it right now. I need you to hold it together. Just until this shit with Montgomery is over. Can you please, *please* fucking do that for me? I'm in over my fucking head here, man."

It's the first time I've ever heard him say that. It's the first time he's ever been anything other than the best. My Prez. It's the first time he's ever been human in my eyes.

"I can do that, Bash," I say. "I've got your back. You know I'll take a bullet for you and kill the fucker from the other side. I've got you and I've got the club." His jaw tenses as he nods.

"I'm relying on you right now," he says. "With everyone gone, it's just you, me, and Reid. I need you here. I need you all here." He taps the side of his head. "Stay with me, man. Just a bit longer."

"I'm here," I say firmly as I square my shoulders. "I'm right here. Not going anywhere, Prez."

Kennedy

I t's been a whirlwind of a day and I haven't had a chance to call
Ezra. I want to tell him I fucked up and that I'm ready for *us*.
To try, at least. See where this can go.

He's absolutely insane and I don't know why I even like him, but
I do and I'm done trying to fight it. Ian likes him, I like him, even
Rasputin likes him—but to be fair, that dog likes everyone. It's time to
put my fear aside and try, for his sake and mine. And for Ian's, too.

Ian has never had a man in his life. It's always just been me. He
was too young to remember my dad, and even if he wasn't, we didn't
see him or my stepmother often enough for them to have a relationship. He only knows the struggles and strength of a single mother. He
doesn't know how people are supposed to love each other in a relationship, and if I can show him that with Ezra, I will.

I finish wiping down the bar and grab my purse. Milo headed
home half an hour ago since I thought I only had a few things left to
do, but I'd forgotten about cleaning the bathrooms and ended up
staying later than I'd wanted. Again.

It's nearly four. Since Milo left, I have no way to get home except
to walk. Which is fine. I live only a few blocks from The Crossroads.

182

I guess I could call Ezra, but I don't want to. Not yet. I want to talk to him when my back isn't aching, and I'm not cranky. I want to be well rested and preferably caffeinated before talking to him about everything.

Especially because I have a feeling like he's going to gloat and tease me about liking him like we're middle schoolers. But for him, I'll endure it. *I guess.*

Stepping out into the dark balmy night, I quickly lock the door. I shouldn't have let Milo leave. The parking lot is too dark, and it always makes me uneasy to walk through it alone at night. I've asked Spencer to put a few security lights in the back for years, but he's never gotten around to it.

Something crunches behind me—boots on gravel. Multiple boots on gravel. My spine stiffens, but I try to force myself to stay calm. I'm probably just paranoid. The guys come and go from the bar at all hours, it could be one of The Berserkers.

But something in my gut is screaming at me to run back inside.

I rummage in my purse, pretending like I'm looking for something. I huff out an irritated breath, like I can't find what I'm looking for. I'm aware of every shift of gravel, of every movement in the shadows, of everything. The hair on my arms stands on end at the threat lingering around me.

I turn back to the door and, with shaky hands, try to push the key back into the lock. My hands tremble too badly to get it on the first few tries, but as I hear someone clear their throat, it finally slides in. Closer and closer I hear them come, their boots crunching, their presence mocking.

They're not in a hurry. They know they can overpower me, attack me, rape me, kill me. Why would they try to hurry?

I wrench the door open and haul ass inside. Slamming the door, I flip the lock and press my hand to my chest, feeling my heart thunder beneath it. A part of me doesn't feel any safer inside the bar than I did outside. But at least there's a door separating me from them now.

The door knob jiggles, and a scream lodges in my throat, choking me. I clamp my hand over my mouth, forcing myself to keep quiet. My breathing is harsh, my eyes wide.

Sweat trickles down my back, across my forehead, as my mind races. Did I lock both entrances? I always do, but I'm second guessing myself.

Turning on my heel, I run down the hall and across the floor to the front door. I nearly sob when I see the two deadbolts locked. Then actually start sobbing when that doorknob turns.

"Fuck," I whimper. Tears and sweat sting my eyes.

I can't cry.

Not right now.

Not yet.

Think.

I need to think.

There's a shotgun behind the bar. I've never shot a fucking gun in my life, though. I have no idea how to use it, but it's the only thing I have. And a shotgun will scare someone a lot more than a fucking baseball bat.

Sprinting across the room, I stumble and fall behind the bar, scrambling to rip the gun off the mount on the underside of the wood. The door shakes again, voices growing louder, as it finally comes free. I sink onto the floor and hold the gun on my lap as I press my back against the wall.

I need to get out of here.

I can't sit and wait for them to get inside.

But I can't make myself move. I can't feel my fingers, or my toes. I'm barely able to fucking breathe. My hands fumble at my pocket until I manage to slide my phone free.

I call the only person I can think of, the only person I want right now. The only person I know will save me.

Pressing the phone to my ear, I wait as it rings.

And rings.

And rings.

Another sob tries to work its way up my throat, but I force myself to swallow it.

Then I hear his voice, and the tears finally overflow from my eyes.

"Calling to grovel?" He sounds like his usual arrogant self and in other circumstances, I probably would've told him to fuck off. But right now, his voice only makes me cry harder.

"Ez," I whisper, my voice barely audible. There's a beat of silence as the tension fills the dead air between us.

"What?" His voice is a low growl. "What's going on?"

"I'm at the bar," I try to say but I'm nearly hyperventilating. Is this what a panic attack is? Koda has them all the time, and I've never known how to help her. "People are trying to get in."

"I'm on my way."

Just like that. No other questions, no reassurances. Nothing.

Just a promise.

A threat.

"Ez, I'm scared."

"Fuck, baby. Don't say that." His bike engine turns on, a loud comforting rumble. "You don't get scared." I choke on a sobbing laugh.

"I'm scared now. Please—" I choke off the word, barely able to stop myself from begging him to hurry. "I need you."

"I'm on my way, Kens. I'm coming. I was at your place waiting for you. I'm close."

The door shakes again, harder this time. Then someone knocks against it and I let out a small yelp.

"They're trying to get in," I whisper. I bring my knees to my chest, sandwiching the barrel of the gun between my thighs and stomach. "What if you don't make it in time?"

"I'll make it," he says, his voice dark. "Whoever is there is fucking dead."

"I have a will," I say quietly. "It's in a small safe under my bed."

"Kennedy," he growls.

"The combination is Ian's birthday." I wipe roughly at my face, and jump when something hard thumps against the door, like someone rammed their shoulder into it. They do it again and the wood splinters. "Tell him—" My voice breaks again.

"Stop, Kennedy."

"Tell him I love him, please. Will you?" My nose burns as tears stream down my cheeks. "Tell him I'm so proud of him and the man he's becoming. Tell him he's the best thing to ever happen to me."

"You'll tell him yourself!" he roars, but I'm not listening to him anymore. I'm too focused on the door, on the people trying to get in.

"And, I'm so sorry, Ez," I force myself to say. "I should've never treated you like I did. I should've never called you what I have. I should've—I should've let you in sooner. And if you can't forgive me, I under—"

"Kennedy!" he shouts, but I'm sobbing harder now.

"I was starting to fall for you," I admit. "I think I could've loved you."

"I'm fucking coming, baby. I'm almost there."

Wood breaks, and a broken whimper leaves me. "I was going to call you today and tell you I was ready. I was going to tell you that I'm ready for you. For us."

"Kennedy, please." He sounds hysterical, like he's riding on the edge of fury and pain.

More wood breaks and I bite my tongue to hold in my scream. Men's voices are loud now, filling the silent bar. The door, my only protection, is being ripped apart.

"They broke the door," I whisper.

"Fucking shit," he shouts. "Don't hang up. I'm almost there, Kens. I'm so fucking close. When I get there, I'm killing everyone in that building and taking you home. I swear to God, you're never leaving my sight again."

The door finally breaks fully and they thunder inside. It's impossible for me to know how many there are based on their footsteps alone. It could be two, or it could be ten. But even one is too many.

"Where is she?" a man asks, his voice harsh. My chin wobbles as fear overrides my body.

"I'm almost there, love," Ezra says, his voice muffled as I pull my phone from my ear. It trembles in my hand as I slide it onto the shelf in front of me, leaving the line connected like he said.

"Check the back, I'll check the office," another orders. There are only two speaking, so I hope that means there are only two and not ten like I feared.

They walk across the room, the old wood floors creaking under them. I shift onto my knees and bring the gun up, aiming it at the entrance of the bar, ready to shoot.

The room is dark and apart from my too loud breathing and the men walking around, it's silent. Eerily silent.

The gun shakes, the metal silently clacking together. A shadow rounds the bar and stops only a few feet away. Instead of immediately pulling the trigger, I freeze. I stare up at the faceless man, completely helpless.

"Found her," he calls, his voice mocking.

He's not jumping or attacking me. Maybe I overreacted. Maybe it was just a misunderstanding.

But then he steps closer and grabs the end of the gun. He easily yanks it from my trembling hands and tosses it onto the bar.

"You were gonna use that?" He jerks his chin at the discarded gun. I stare up at him, my vision blurry. In the faint light, I can make out some of his features, but I don't recognize him.

Reaching down, he grips my shoulder and tries to haul me to my feet. Instead of helping him by standing, I throw myself back to the floor. He lets out an irritated breath as he reaches for me again.

"If you want to play like that, we can," he says. "Wasn't gonna hurt you."

I don't believe him.

Blindly, I kick out. The bottom of my boot connects with his hand and he jerks it back, hissing as he shakes it out a few times. It breaks me out of my daze enough to not feel totally frozen. I scramble back until my back connects with the wall.

As soon as I'm forced to stop, I realize I should've run past him.

I'm cornered.

I can't go anywhere.

"Bitch," he snarls. His voice is faintly familiar, but I still can't place him. He steps closer and I kick out again, my boot connecting with his shin. Instead of jumping back like I expected, he grabs my ankle and drags me forward.

I hit the floor at the sudden movement, my head knocking painfully into the wood. I twist and claw at the floor, splinters embedding under my nails. I try to kick with my other foot, but he grabs that ankle before it can connect with anything.

He drags me from behind the bar, my body scratching along the floor. I grip the end of the bar and hold on with all my strength.

Ezra said he was close. I just need to stay alive until he gets here.

He yanks on my ankles harder, and something pops. I grunt at the pain and try to hold onto the wood tighter. Suddenly, he drops me, my breath leaving me as I slam into the floor.

His hand slides into my hair and he wrenches my head painfully back, forcing me to look up at him. His hold tightens and I claw at his wrist, slicing his skin with my nails.

"Fuck." He slams my head into the side of the bar and I cry out. Stars dance in my vision and my head immediately starts throbbing. He hits my head again, harder than before. "You gonna stop? Or do I need to knock you the fuck out?" I scream as he hits my head again.

Hot blood pours from my head, dripping down my face and neck, staining my skin. I press my hands flat against the wood before he can fling my head against it again.

"Stop!" I scream, my throat raw. He throws me back onto the floor, and before I can right myself, his heavy, booted foot lands a kick to my stomach. I grunt out a breath as I turn onto my side. He kicks again.

I can't breathe. I can't think past the pain.

He rears his foot back again, and when he brings it forward, it connects with my face, sending me flying onto my back. Blood clogs my throat, choking me as I cough.

I stare up at him, my breath gargled in my chest as I try to breathe. He bends and grips my hair, shaking my head as he brings me to my knees.

"I told you I didn't want to have to hurt you," he snarls. "This is your fucking fault." He shakes my head again, but I'm too dazed to say or feel anything.

"Got her?" the other man asks as he hurries in. "Fuck. What did you do to her?"

"Bitch tried to shoot me." He uses his head to point at the bar.

"We were just supposed to take the money, not fuck with her," the other says warily. The one holding my head laughs humorlessly.

"And let this stuck up bitch get away with what she said?" I blink a few times, trying to see through the blurry vision. What I said? What did I say?

Then it dawns on me.

The drunk fuck from the other night.

He's doing this because I kicked him out of the bar?

"Yeah, but you didn't have to beat her," the other says. The one holding me tightens his fist in my hair and I weakly try to lift my hands to his wrist.

"Should do a lot fucking worse," he sneers. His shadowed face peers down at me, his fist in my hair ripping strands out.

"I wouldn't."

That voice.

I sob. I sob harder than I ever have in my life at the sound of Kiwi's low, gravelly voice, his accent thicker than I've ever heard.

Both men whirl toward him, and the one holding me shoves me back down. I land on the ground with a hard thud, the pain in my body momentarily forgotten as I watch Kiwi stalk forward, a predator going after his prey.

Kiwi

I've never felt so much fear in my life, followed by indescribable rage. The way Kennedy sounded so fucking terrified, gutted me.

I prowl forward, flicking my eyes between the men who dared touch my woman. The one who had a fistful of her hair is watching me with a nasty sneer on his face.

I think I'll take my time with him.

I pause when I get to them, shifting on my feet, anticipating their first move. When neither of them lunges for me, I swing. My fist connects with one of their faces, bone crunching at the impact. Blood pours from his nose as he brings his hands up to cup it, an agonized scream ripping from his throat.

I can't linger on this fucker, not with his friend at my back. I punch him again, and again. His body goes stiff, then he falls back onto the floor with a heavy thud. I don't think I killed him, just knocked him out.

I should have enough time to slaughter his friend before he wakes up.

"Your turn," I say as I turn around, glaring at the man who's still hovering over Kennedy. "You touched my girl." He stammers something that I don't listen to. I stalk toward him, trying to ignore Kennedy lying on the floor, her face bloody. "I'm going to take my time killing you."

He steps back, his foot landing on her. She lets out a small, pained whimper and I see black.

"You mother*fucker*," I snarl.

He trips over her body, landing on his ass. He tries scrambling back as I continue stalking toward him, my head low and eyes locked on him. I pause when I get to Kennedy. She stares up at the ceiling, her chest barely rising and falling.

I crouch down, sweeping her dark hair away from her bloody forehead, my gaze still on him.

"I'll be with you in a second, love," I murmur. Her eyes shift to me and a small breath leaves her parted mouth. I stop stroking her hair and stand.

I didn't have time to grab my usual weapons. I have a knife on me, but my gun is on my bike, and the rest are at the clubhouse. I was waiting at her apartment for her.

I was going to fucking demand that she be with me. I wasn't going to give her a choice anymore, and if I had to kidnap her and keep her locked up until she agreed, then I was fully prepared to do it.

After peeling Ginger's nails off, I realized that she's the only person I'll ever want, the only one I'll ever need, and I won't let her go. A woman like her, a connection with someone, only comes around once in a lifetime, and I can't give her up. I couldn't calm down torturing him like I usually do because she's the only one who can bring me comfort. Even if she is the most infuriatingly difficult and stubborn person I've ever met, I need her.

I love her.

I step over Kennedy's body as I slide my knife from my pocket, flicking it open as I move toward the scurrying man. He flicks his eyes between me and my blade.

"Not so tough now, huh?" I ask. "It was real easy for you to fuck her up, but me?" I want a fight. I don't want him to roll over and let me have this kill easily.

I want to fucking obliterate him.

"You're a pussy, aren't you? Only a fucking bitch would attack a poor, helpless woman." His eyes flash and I know I'm getting to him.

"I'm not the bitch," he says, his voice too low. My brows flick up.

"No?" I continue stalking toward him. "Then who is?" His eyes lower to Kennedy, and I lunge.

I tackle him to the floor and fling my blade across the room, letting it skitter along the floor. This is a bare hands kind of fight, a bare hands death. Gripping his throat with one hand, pinning him to the floor, I bring my fist down on his face over and over.

He blocks one of my punches and shoves me off him, making me land on the floor. He scrambles to his feet, staying crouched like an animal on the verge of attack. I wipe my lip with my thumb, laughing at the blood I see.

He's not dumb enough to take his eyes off me again.

I jump to my feet, making him stumble back a small step. I laugh again, high pitched and piercing in the silent bar. I leap forward, making him move backward.

"Fucking pussy," I say, laughing again. "This will be so fucking fun."

When I jump forward this time, he forces himself to stay put, but I see the fear in his wide eyes. He lands a blow to my jaw, snapping my head to the side. I rub it as I look back at him, nodding slightly.

His eyes widen more, aware that he just royally fucked up.

Another small whimper comes from Kennedy and it just pisses me off all over again.

I failed her. I should've come straight to the bar instead of waiting for her at home. I should've been here to protect her, and I wasn't.

I decide I don't care about taking my time anymore. I snap my fist out, hitting him hard and fast. As he tries to recover, I move behind him, kicking the backs of his knees and forcing him to kneel on the floor. I lock my elbow around his throat, my other arm around his head, and squeeze.

His body flails and he claws at my arms, but I squeeze harder. My eyes roll back, my nostrils flaring, as I feel the life drain from him. He tries to get his feet under him again, but he can't.

He starts going limp. He tries fighting it, but it's only a matter of moments before he's gone. His breath turns gargled as he tries to inhale, but he can't, not with me crushing his throat. I follow him to the floor as I squeeze tighter, his body finally relaxing. I hold on for another minute, just to make sure the fuck is really dead.

I let go and check his pulse—or lack of one. He's gone. Fucker got off a lot easier than he should've.

But I need to take care of my girl.

I half run, half crawl to Kennedy. I slam to my knees, skidding to her, my hands already outstretched. I stroke her face, trying to wipe the drying blood from her pretty skin.

"I'm here, baby," I say softly. "You still with me?" She tries to nod, but her face crumples in pain. "Where does it hurt, love?" She tries to lift her hand, but it limply falls back to her side. "Don't move. Just tell me."

"Head," she rasps. "Belly." Her hand slides onto her stomach and she cries out.

My hands shake as I lift her shirt, then curse so violently she winces. Bruises are already blooming across her abdomen, some of the skin torn open.

"What did he do?" I ask darkly, my jaw clenching.

"Kick," she whimpers. "Hurts, Ez."

I squeeze my eyes shut.

Suddenly, I'm on a New Zealand beach, those same words pouring from Elaine's lips.

I tell her I know.

I promise her I'll help.

I swear everything will be fine.

I failed her, too.

193

"It's gonna be okay," I choke out, the words of my past haunting me in this moment. When I open my eyes, it's a bloody blonde head I see instead of Kennedy's dark one. It's *her* bruised blue eyes instead of Kennedy's hazel ones.

I slam the heel of my palm into the side of my head, trying to get rid of the haunting images.

Out.

Out.

Out.

I need them out.

I hit myself harder, screaming at the pain slashing through my chest. This can't be happening, not right now. I don't get flashbacks anymore. I thought these were behind me.

But seeing Kennedy broken, seeing her bloody, it's like Elaine all over again.

I was almost too late again.

"Ez," Kennedy says, her voice far away. "Ezra." A cool, sticky hand slides into mine and I open my eyes.

I stare down at her, my chest heaving. Tears track through the dried blood on her face as she stares back at me.

"I'm sorry," I say, choking on the same words. "I'm here, okay? I'm here." She nods. She nods just like Elaine had, and I wince, squeezing my eyes shut again.

Is she about to die in my arms too? Am I about to lose her?

My shame chokes me. I failed them, the two people I should've never failed.

"You came," she rasps. Some of the haze in my mind dissipates.

Different words. Different people. Different night.

The Crossroads fade in around me, reminding me that I'm here, in California, not New Zealand. I'm with Kennedy, the love of my life, not my sister.

"Of course," I say, wiping my eyes with the back of my hand. "I'll always come for you."

"I'm sorry," she says, but I shake my head.

"Don't," I whisper as I stroke her hair. "Don't apologize for anything. We both said and did shit we shouldn't have. But I'm here now, okay? I'm not going anywhere. I have you." Her chin wobbles. "Can I pick you up?" She tries to nod again, and winces. "Did he hit your head?"

"Yes," she breathes, the word slurred.

It takes all I have not to spiral again. But with her hand still around mine, I force myself to stay here with her.

"Can you hold on to me while we're on my bike?" I ask, my thumb smoothing over her forehead. She closes her eyes as she takes a deep breath, then nods.

My heart breaks for her.

She's strong, even now, even broken and bruised and bloody, she's pushing through it. She's stronger than I am, than I ever will be.

I press a soft kiss to her forehead, letting it linger before I pull away and slide my arms under her. She hisses through her teeth as I lift her, cradling her to my chest.

This wasn't the way I saw my night going. I never thought I'd be holding her like this.

Her head rests against my chest, her body limp in my arms, as I leave the bar, not caring enough to clean up. I'll call Otis or Spence on the way home and let them know what happened, and that I'm going to fucking kill them for ever leaving her there alone.

Then I'm hunting Milo down. That fucker should've been there with her. This should've never happened.

When I get to my bike, I pause. There's no way she can hold on to me while we ride.

"I need to move you," I murmur. She barely nods, her face scrunching in pain. "Can you wrap your arms around my neck?" She takes another deep breath like she's readying herself, and slides her arms around me. I shift her body to my front, putting her chest against mine and her legs around my waist. She lets out a whimper of pain, her face pressing into my neck, and it breaks me. Tears burn the back of my nose as I listen to her small whimpers and heavy breathing. "I know, baby. I'm sorry. I've got you. I'm so sorry."

She doesn't say anything—there's nothing for her to say. She just tightens her hold on me, squeezing my waist with her legs. That's all I'll get from her, and it'll have to do.

I slide onto my bike, still holding her in front of me, one arm wrapped around her waist as I grip the handlebar with my other. I shift the bike, kick the stand up, and press a kiss to her bloody cheek.

"Hold on to me, love," I say against her ear. She nods and tightens her hold around me again.

This is probably the most dangerous way to ride, but I don't know what else to do. I can't leave her here while I get a car, and I'm not waiting around for one of the guys.

"Ready?" I ask. She lets out a soft moan of confirmation, and I kiss her cheek again.

My chest hurts. I just want to take her pain away because I can endure it.

I can endure anything, I've proven that to myself, but seeing Kennedy like this, it makes me realize maybe I can't.

I can't handle her hurting.

So I kiss her again, and slowly take off down the road.

Kennedy

My body aches as Ezra carries me up the steps to my apartment. I don't know what time it is, but I'm hoping it's still early enough that Ian and Enzo are asleep. I cling to Ezra, never wanting to leave his arms.

He somehow manages to open the door with one hand, kicking it closed with his foot.

"Shh," I hiss, and his arm tightens around me. "The boys are asleep."

"Sorry, love," he whispers as he moves through the small apartment, his footsteps impossibly silent. We get to the bathroom and he sets me on the counter, but I keep my arms wrapped around him. "I need to fill the bath." He tries to pull away again, but I tighten my hold, whimpering.

I don't know why, but I feel like if I stop touching him, I'll be back there. I won't be safe anymore.

He pulls back enough to look at me. Smoothing his hand over my head, I wince as he grazes the lump on my temple. His eyes darken, but he tries to stay calm.

"I need to fill the bath, Kens," he says again, softly. "I'll be right here." His eyes bore into mine. "I'm here. You're safe."

Safe.

I'm safe.

But why do I feel like I'll never truly be safe again?

I force my arms to drop away as I lean against the mirror. He stares at me, not moving away. His kiss startles me. It's soft—softer than anything I've ever felt from him before. Not demanding or intense. Just...soft.

He steps back, dipping his head to hide his burning face as he hurries to the tub. After turning the water on and checking the temperature, he turns back to me.

"I called Blade to come check you out," he says quietly, but not unapologetically. My insides tighten at the thought. I don't want to be checked out. I just want to sleep.

"I'm okay," I croak. He ignores my words as he moves back to me.

"Arms up," he says. I stare at him. "Arms up, love. You can't take a bath in your clothes." I sigh and lift my arms.

I expect his hands to roam, to linger, his eyes to burn me up with *that* look. But they don't. His face stays soft as he undresses me, like he's done it a million times before. I move to cover myself with my arm, but he catches my wrist.

"Don't hide from me, Kens. You've never done it before, don't start now."

My arm falls back to my side, my lips parting with a breath. He barely gives me a chance to let the words sink in before he's gently lifting me and setting me in the tub. The water is warm, and I sigh at the feeling. All other thoughts leave me as I lean back, my eyes closing.

His calloused hands glide over my bare skin, washing away the blood. I keep my eyes closed, whether because I don't want to see the blood, or because I'm too tired to keep them open, I don't know. But he lets me. He doesn't ask what happened. He doesn't expect me to talk.

He just washes me; washes away the feel of that man touching me. Washes away the blood caking my skin and hair. He washes away the night.

I must've dozed off at some point, because warm water being poured over my head wakes me. My eyes snap open, but he continues pouring the water over me. I try not to look, I try to keep my gaze on his, but it slowly slides to the water.

There's so much blood.

I choke out a sob.

"It's okay," he murmurs. But it's not.

It's not okay.

I always thought I'd fight back. I always thought I'd be the person to never freeze in the face of danger, to always fight as hard as I could until the very end. But in those moments, my body stopped. My mind stopped. *I* stopped.

If Ezra hadn't showed up when he did, what else would've happened? What else would I have *let* happen?

If I would've just shot him, I wouldn't have needed Ez. If I would've just pulled that trigger, I could've been safe. I could've saved myself. I wouldn't be like *this*.

Another sob leaves me, the tears hot against my skin. I thought I was stronger than this, better than this.

But I'm not.

Ezra's lips press to my shoulder, one of the only places not bruised. "It's okay," he murmurs against my skin, his breath warm. I wipe my face as I nod, not trusting myself to speak. "I'm not going anywhere, okay? Even if you tell me to, I'm not leaving you."

My chin wobbles as more tears fill my eyes. I look up at him, at his gentle expression.

"Why?" I breathe, my eyes searching his. "I've been nothing but horrible to you, and—and you still want to be with me." I try to clutch my knees to my chest, but the soreness of my stomach stops me. I hiss at the pain, my hands gripping my shins as I breathe through it.

"Don't move," he scolds. His fingers firmly grip my chin, tipping my head back to look at him. "I'm here because I'm in love with you. I have been since the first moment I saw you. I don't know what it was, but there was just something about you. Something that screamed mine. I was always told that I would know when I found her, the one. And you're the one, Kens. So no matter what you throw at me, I can take it. No matter what words you use to try to slash through me, I can take it. And I *will* take it. For you. I'm not going anywhere, love."

Tears stream down my face as I stare up at him, his face uncharacteristically blank. He's not letting any of his crazy bubble to the surface, and somehow, that makes it all the more real, it makes his words more real. He's not saying them during some manic episode, or because he's still riding the high of killing those men.

He means it—*he* does. Ezra. Not Kiwi. Not the crazy biker with a taste for blood. Not the man who threatens to cut a man's hands off for looking at me. That's not Ezra. That's Kiwi.

Ezra is soft and sweet and...mine. He's mine. All of him. Crazy, soft, loving, killing biker. Ezra and Kiwi, Kiwi and Ezra. They're one and the same, and mine. All mine.

More tears drip from my eyes, but not from the pain anymore, not from his words, but with the realization that he's right—he's the one. I was stupid to think that he wasn't. I was stupid to think that anyone else would be able to handle me and my bullshit.

It's only him.

He's the man who can handle me without changing me, without dampening me. He's strong enough to throw back whatever I give him.

He's mine.

"You don't have to say it back yet," he says. "But one day..." His blue eyes search mine, longing clear in them. "One day, you'll tell me that you're mine, that you belong to me, and it'll be the best day of my life." He lowers his mouth to mine and brushes his lips across mine in a fleeting kiss.

He looks like he wants more, like he wants to kiss me harder, longer, like he wants to claim me, but he holds back. And that makes more tears flow. Our gazes stay locked for a few heartbeats, nothing but the sound of our breathing and water dripping.

Then his phone rings and breaks the spell. Not completely, just enough to get him to move. He kisses my forehead as he pulls his phone from his back pocket, not caring about his wet, soapy hands as he presses it to his ear.

"Hey, yeah. She's awake." He rests his hand on my cheek, lightly cupping my face as he strokes his thumb along my cheek. "Door's unlocked. Come in."

I press my face into his palm, needing the warmth and safety of his touch. I turn my head enough to kiss his wrist and he inhales sharply. Lifting my eyes to his again, he's staring at me like he's never seen me. Like he really is in love with me.

Kennedy

Blade checked me out, and apart from a few cuts and bruises and suspected concussion, I'm mostly fine. After the blood had been washed away, the lump on my head wasn't as bad as we'd initially thought. Ezra was worried that the man had broken my ribs, but luckily, Blade didn't think so. They both made me promise to see my doctor tomorrow to get checked out, and I reluctantly agreed.

"Let's get you in bed," Ezra says as he locks the door behind Blade. He leans his shoulder on it as he folds his arms, his eyes on me. He looks exhausted. I nod, and wince at the light headache pounding at the back of my head.

Ian's door opens, and my body stiffens. I clutch the blanket tighter around my shoulders, my eyes shifting to the hall. Anxiety swirls with each step, and then he's there, pausing as he rubs his eye.

His gaze meets Ezra's first, then slowly slides to me. He drops his hand to his side when he sees my face and lurches forward a step, before stopping himself.

"Mom?" he whispers, his eyes widening.

202

"Hey, bud," I say softly, forcing myself to smile. His throat bobs as he turns to Ezra.

"You—"

"He didn't do anything," I say, interrupting him before he can spiral and blame Ez for anything. He's blaming himself for enough.

"You were supposed to protect her, not hurt her." I sigh as I rub my forehead.

"Let me get your mother to bed, then we can discuss what happened," Ezra says in a voice I've never heard from him before. An authoritative voice. *A father's voice.* It's enough to make Ian stiffen and throw his shoulders back.

"Some men broke into the bar," I blurt, and both of them turn their attention to me. "I called Ez and he saved me. That's all that happened." Ian turns back to Ezra, but his face doesn't shift at all. They have a silent conversation, one I'm too tired to try to decipher.

"We'll talk later," Ez says in that same low, calm voice. Ian's throat bobs as he swallows whatever retort was about to fall from his lips. He looks back at me, his face softening.

"I can stay home from school today," he says. "I can help take care of you." My heart warms and I smile softly at him.

"You just want an excuse to miss school," I snort, and he rolls his eyes. "Nice try, bud. But I'm fine." I force my face to stay blank as I push to my feet. Ezra's hands shoot out as he lurches forward, ready to catch me. "See?" I hold my hand out, the other still clutching the blanket around my shoulders. "Fine." Ian doesn't look convinced, but with another glance at Ezra, he must see that I'm in good hands.

Good, crazy hands.

"Will you call me if she needs help?" he asks Ezra, and he nods, a serious expression on his face. "I'll come straight home." He looks back at me and I wave my hand again, dismissively.

"You have—what club do you have today?" His face turns red as he glances at Ezra.

"It's D&D, and it's not a club," he mumbles. I glance at Ezra, finding him grinning at my son.

"I like D&D," he says. Whether or not it's true, I don't know. But I want to kiss him for making Ian not feel bad about his hobbies. "I used to play with—" His face falls, his eyes going unfocused. Then he blinks and that sad, faraway look is gone. "With some friends when I was your age." I narrow my eyes slightly. I want to pry, but not right now.

Later.

Later when I'm not tired and when my body isn't trembling from the amount of energy it takes to keep me upright. Ezra must see whatever strain I'm trying to hide from Ian, because he moves forward and wraps his arm around my waist, taking most of my weight.

"I'm going to bed," I say with a yawn. Ian's eyes flick between us, and I wait for it. For the accusations, the blow up, the anger.

But nothing comes.

Instead, he just nods. "You'll be with her all day?" Ian asks, and Ezra nods again. "You'll take care of her?"

"With my life," Ezra vows, putting his fist to his chest.

"I am capable—" I cut myself off.

Am I capable of taking care of myself? After tonight...

I didn't fight back. Why didn't I fight back?

"You're more than capable, love," Ezra agrees, and I rest my too-heavy head on his shoulder. He kisses the top of it, and my eyes lock with Ian's. But again, there's nothing.

I don't know why I expected something, but he looks fine. Fine with whatever is going on with Ezra and me.

"You're together now?" he asks quietly, and Ez's arm barely tightens around me. A lump forms in my throat, and when I open my mouth, I hesitate. The room gets thick with tension as they both wait for my answer.

I glance up at Ezra, his eyes guarded in a way that makes my heart ache. I smile softly at him, then turn and rest my head against his shoulder again as I look at Ian.

"Yeah," I murmur. "We're together." Ezra lets out a long, relieved breath. Ian's face stays blank, like he's carefully hiding what he's really thinking and feeling beneath a perfect mask. "Is that okay with you?" He lifts his chin, ever the mature man he wants to so badly be.

"Yes," he says, then looks at Ezra, his face hardening. "If you hurt her, I *will* kill you." I fold my lips between my teeth.

He has no idea who he's just threatened. But Ezra nods, his face still gravely serious.

"I'd kill myself for you," he says. "I won't hurt her." They have another silent conversation, one between a man and a boy—a boy that's becoming a man. I wait with bated breath, then let it out when Ian nods his approval.

"You still have another hour before you have to be up for school," I say tiredly. "Go back to bed."

"I can't sleep with Enzo snoring," he groans. I wince with guilt. I forgot Enzo was still here.

"Tell him to sleep on the couch from now on," I say, ignoring Ezra's gaze. "You'll both sleep better if he's in here." Ian nods, a thankful look on his face, then turns and heads back down the hall, stopping at the bathroom before heading to his room.

"I'm still staying here, Kens," Ezra says as soon as Ian's door shuts. "I'm not leaving you alone."

"I know," I say. "Can we go to bed now, please?" I tip my head back to look at him. His brows are pushed together in confusion and I huff out a breath. "You can sleep with me." My stomach twists with the anticipation of his rejection.

"Yeah?" His smile is slow to curve his mouth, but when it does, it's full and bright, and blinds me.

"Yeah," I laugh. "Bed. Now."

He snorts a laugh, and scoops me into his arms, cradling me to his chest as he carries me down the hall.

He'd pulled the blankets back and got the bed ready when Blade was here. Now, he rounds the bed and lays me down so gently tears sting my eyes. He handles me like I'm precious, or fragile. Breakable. Special.

No one has ever handled me like that. I've always had to be

strong enough to withstand whatever is thrown at me. No one has ever looked at me and thought I was soft, or that I needed gentleness. And I never thought I did, either. But with Ezra, he brings out the softness in me, even when I don't want him to. He brings it out because I know he can handle it. He can take the brunt of the shit I'm carrying, and he'll do it willingly.

I force the tears back as he covers me with the blankets, tucking them in tightly around me.

"I sleep on that side," I say, using my chin to point at the other side.

"I'll sleep on that side from now on." He brushes a kiss to my forehead. "I'm going to check the locks and make sure the boys are okay. You need anything?" More tears choke me as I stare up at him.

"I'm okay," I rasp.

He smiles sadly as he strokes my hair, then kisses me again before he leaves the room. I strain to hear his light footsteps as he walks through my apartment, like he's done this a million times before, like this is our nightly routine and not the first time he's ever done it.

He shuts my door after he walks back in and hesitates at the side of the bed. I roll onto my side to watch him, trying to hide my wince. Our eyes lock, but neither of us say anything. He strips to his boxers, his abs flexing as he turns the lamp off, bathing the room in complete darkness, and slides into bed beside me.

I can't remember the last time I slept beside someone that wasn't Ian. I can't remember the last time I was in bed with a man that wasn't intent on fucking me.

"Thank you for coming tonight," I whisper. He rolls onto his side, his breath tickling my arms.

"I'll always come for you," he replies, his voice just as quiet. I clear my throat, forcing the emotions away. His hand slides across the cool sheets until he finds mine and laces our fingers together.

"Why do you get that side now?" I ask, and he gives my hand a slight squeeze as he laughs.

"It's between you and the door," he says. "It's easier to protect you."

My heart stops.

No one—literally no one in my entire life has ever, *fucking ever*, thought about protecting me. Not like this. Not so casually. He lifts my hand and presses a kiss to the back of it.

"You're—" I choke off the word, my attempt at reigning in my emotions failing. "You're special, Ez." His breath brushes along my skin.

"You are too, Kens."

We go silent again. We don't speak for so long that I think he's gone to sleep, but he squeezes my hand again, letting me know he's there. He's still with me.

Finally, the tears leak from my eyes. I can't stop them. A sob wracks my body, shaking the bed as I cry. He slides closer and carefully wraps his arms around me, pulling me into his chest. He holds me as I cry, as I soak his chest with my tears. His chin rests on the top of my head as he idly strokes my back.

"I was so scared," I admit. I wrap my arm around him, needing to be closer. "I was terrified, and I thought you weren't going to answer." His arms tighten as he listens to me. He doesn't say anything, nothing to reassure me, he just lets the words and tears fall. "I thought I'd never see you again, or Ian. And I thought I was going to die. I thought they were going to—" I choke on my sob. "I thought they—"

"You don't have to say it," he murmurs. "Don't think about what you thought they were going to do, okay? Nothing happened. I got there in time. You're safe, Kennedy."

He pulls me closer to him, and I slide my leg between his, tangling our bodies together. And for the first time in my life, I break. I break so wholeheartedly that I fear I'll never be put together again.

But I will be.

I will be because of him. Because Ezra will hold me through it, making sure my pieces don't shatter completely. He'll put me together again, and even though it terrifies me to give him that much power over me, over my heart, I decide I don't care.

I decide to trust him.

Kiwi

Something flutters along my jaw, featherlight. Goosebumps ripple across my body and slowly, my eyes open. The sun blinds me, but it's the woman next to me—the woman kissing my jaw, that has all my attention.

"Good morning," I say, rolling onto my side to face her. She smiles lazily at me, her eyes softer than I've ever seen before. The side of her forehead is red and bruised, and the lump on it reminds me I can't do what I want to do to her right now.

She slides her hand over my arm, her fingers tracing the lines of the tattoo on my shoulder, following them to my chest. I inhale sharply as she lightly circles my nipple with the tip of her finger.

Her eyes drop to my chest as she goes around and around, making me groan. My hand slides over hers, pinning it to my chest.

"You need to stop," I growl. Her smile turns wicked, but when she winces slightly, my boner goes away. "You need to be asleep."

"I'm fine," she says, and I lift my brow. "Okay, I feel like I got hit by six buses. But I'll be fine."

"Of course you will be," I say, gently brushing her hair behind her ear. "You always are." Her eyes flick between mine, her expression

209

unreadable. "I'll make us some food. You just sit here and look pretty. Shouldn't be too hard for you." I wink, and she rolls her eyes.

"You need to brush your teeth," she says, shoving my shoulder. I laugh as I lean forward, making kissing sounds before peppering her face with kisses. She groans and shoves me again, and when I pull away, she roughly wipes her cheek with the palm of her hand, scowling at me. "Why are your kisses so wet?"

"What?" I bark out a laugh, my hand on her hip tightening slightly. "I don't have wet kisses."

"Yeah," she nods, scrunching her nose. "You have grandma kisses." I huff out another laugh.

"You really know how to make a guy feel good, love," I say as I slide out of bed. I press a quick kiss to her forehead, making sure to make it extra slobbery, and jump back before she can smack me.

Scratching my bare stomach, I walk through the apartment, fully expecting it to be empty. I abruptly stop when I meet Ian, a sandwich halfway to his open mouth.

"What are you doing home?" I ask, folding my arms and leaning against the wall. He lowers the sandwich and glances down the hall. "She's still in bed." His shoulders slump in relief.

"I didn't want to leave her alone," he says quietly.

"I'm here, kid," I say, and he shrugs.

"I didn't know." He shifts on his feet, looking down the hall again. "I thought you'd leave this morning." I shake my head as he speaks, then run my hand through my hair, yanking on the tangled curls.

"I'm not going anywhere," I say, and he nods. "We told you last night—"

"I know," he blurts. "I just didn't believe it." My brows raise, and he shakes his head. "No, I *did* believe it. I just assumed she would wake up and kick you out again." I snort a laugh as I push off the wall.

"The day's not over yet, kid." I clap him on the shoulder as I pass him on the way to the kitchen.

"Hey, Kiwi?" he says hesitantly, and I pause, my hand still on his shoulder.

"What's up?" Our eyes meet, and a pit opens in my stomach.

He chews his lip as he glances down the hall again, then turns toward me. My hand falls to my side as I watch him struggle to find the words.

"Do you know how to fight?" he suddenly asks, and I blink at him.

"Uh." I rub the back of my neck. How the fuck do I navigate this without Kennedy killing me? "Yeah. I do." His eyes stay on mine, and honestly, it surprises me. He hasn't found his confidence yet. "Why?" He looks over his shoulder again, and when he looks back at me, he takes a small step forward.

"Can you teach me?" His voice is low, almost inaudible. I narrow my eyes at him.

"Why?" I ask. I won't tell him no. Fighting is a skill every man should know—it's a skill every person should know. So if Ian wants to learn, I'll teach him. Fuck, I'll get Heather to teach him. "Is someone fucking with you?"

"No," he says, shaking his head. "It's Enzo's dad." My brows flick up again.

"Enzo's dad," I repeat and he nods, then scrubs his hand over his face. "You want to fight his dad?"

"He just—" He lets out a sharp sigh. "When Enzo was changing, I saw—" He lets out another breath, red creeping up his neck and face. "I saw burn marks. Like, cigarette burns." He rests his hand on his ribs, indicating the spot he saw the burns, and I clench my jaw at the words. "I didn't know things were that bad, and I just want his dad to pay. I just—he hurt my best friend, you know? I want to hurt his dad for hurting him."

"I get that," I say, chewing on my lip. "Enzo's staying here for a while, yeah?" Ian's face falls.

"He's still talking about leaving," he mumbles.

"And you think fighting his dad will make him stay?" I ask gently, and he shrugs.

211

"If you won't help, I'll figure something else out." His voice comes out too sharp, too much like his mother's, and I nearly laugh.

"I didn't say I won't help." I grin at him, then lift my eyes behind him, finding Kennedy shuffling down the hall, her hand on the wall, the other wrapped around her middle. "I'll help you, okay? Later, though." I rush past him, grabbing her hips to stop her. She glares up at me, and I've never been so turned on before. "What do you think you're doing?"

"I'm going to the kitchen," she says.

"I told you to stay in bed."

"And you're not the boss of me," she hisses. I smirk, my hands tightening on her hips in warning.

"Are you sure?" I ask, lowering my voice. "I remember you enjoyed obeying me." She growls, and shoves at my chest. I step to the side, but keep my arm wrapped around her waist as I help her shuffle toward the couch.

"Why are you home?" she asks Ian.

"Leave the kid alone," I say, gently pushing her onto the couch. "He was worried about you." Her face softens as she looks at her son.

"I told you I'm fine," she says, and I snort.

"You're not fine," I retort. "Now," I put my hand in her face, "stay." She snaps her teeth at me, and I quickly run away, her and Ian's laughter following me into the kitchen.

Kennedy

"He said I was fine, Ez. I can walk."

Ezra is carrying me from the doctor's office to his car, which is fucking embarrassing. I know not to wiggle around now, not after he popped my ass while we were in the waiting room and a few people saw. I nearly killed him, but didn't want witnesses.

"He said you have a concussion," he grumbles. "Said you're lucky to be fucking breathing. Your bruises are fucking awful today—" I huff out a harsh breath and glare up at him. He's being a bit over-dramatic.

"This is ridiculous," I say. "Nothing happened to my legs. I can walk."

"You could barely hold yourself up to take a shower this morning," he says, still not looking at me. The muscle in his jaw feathers, his eyes hard as he walks across the parking lot.

As my doctor had listed my injuries, Ez's face grew darker and darker. I was proud of him for keeping his shit under control, but I could feel it boiling—his crazy was moments from overflowing.

"Should've taken my fucking time killing that bastard," he

mutters as he slides me into the car. I keep my arms folded over my chest as he buckles my seatbelt, something else I learned not to do, otherwise he pouts.

He slams the door shut and roughly puts his sunglasses on, his blond curls bouncing as he swaggers around the car. His walk is fucking ridiculous, the sway of his shoulders and hips, so over the top it should be funny...but it's not. It's so fucking hot.

What is wrong with me?

He starts the car, but doesn't immediately pull out of the spot. He just grips the wheel and stares straight ahead, his jaw tense.

"You could've died and it would've been my fault," he says, his voice low. I blink at him.

"No, it would've been their fault, not yours." He shakes his head as I speak, his eyes trained on the car in front of us. "Ez."

"It would've been my fault," he says again, his knuckles white on the steering wheel. He inhales slowly, then lets it out, his face contemplative. Finally, he turns his head and I stare at myself in the reflection of his glasses. "I let my sister die."

My heart lurches into my throat as I stare at him. I don't know what to say to a confession like that, and judging by his expression, I know this is shaky ground. One wrong word will fuck everything up —it might make him spiral.

"How?" I ask, still unsure if that's the right thing. His throat bobs as he swallows, then he turns forward again.

"She was my twin," he sighs, and drops his forehead to the wheel. "We were seventeen, and these guys invited her to the beach. They always fucked with me and when I told her they were no good, she ignored me. She said that I was too possessive of her and I needed to let her have fun." He laughs humorlessly, then looks at me again. "She was right. I was possessive of her." He takes his glasses off and pinches his eyes. "She was too sweet and soft for this world. People always took advantage of her, our mother took advantage of her. I felt like I needed to protect her, you know? But I guess I smothered her instead."

214

He takes a shaky breath as he leans back in the seat, his eyes slowly closing. I stay silent, barely breathing as I wait for the rest of the story. His brows push together in pain, and I reach for him, wrapping my hand around his.

"I told her not to go," he rasps. "I told her they were going to just be mean to her, but she didn't believe me. One of them, he flirted with her and she thought he liked her." He tries to run his fingers through his hair, but they get caught on the curls. "She went with the group of them after school one day. I was late—I can't even remember why I hadn't walked her home. I was probably flirting with some girl. I just wasn't with her, so Elaine went with them."

My chest tightens. The pain in his voice makes me want to cry.

"She called me, and her voice was the same as yours last night." He looks at me, his blue eyes red-rimmed. "She said she was hiding from them, that they convinced her to get in the water, and they stole her clothes. She was naked, and hiding, and scared. It was getting dark, and—and I was so fucking mad at her, Kens. I was fucking furious. I said things I shouldn't have said." His voice breaks on the last word and I unbuckle my seatbelt, uncaring that the metal hits the window as I let it fly back.

Climbing over the console, I settle myself on his lap, wincing at the pain in my stomach, and wrap my arms around him. He buries his face in my neck and lets out a broken sob. I squeeze him tighter, tears burning the back of my nose.

"What happened, baby?" I murmur. I play with his hair, twirling a curl around my finger.

"I said whatever happened to her was her fault. That she deserved whatever they did to her because she didn't listen to me." His arms wrap around me and he clutches me to him, his body vibrating as he struggles not to cry. "I thought they just took her clothes as a prank. I didn't think—" He takes a deep, shuddering breath. "I didn't think anything would happen, you know? I was just —I was mad at her. She always told me I let my emotions speak for me, that I never thought before I spoke." I pull away from him and

215

wipe his tears with my thumbs, his stubble scratching against my palms.

"You were just a kid," I say softly. "Kids make mistakes." He shakes his head, his eyes scrunching closed. "What happened?" I keep my palm on his cheek, and he presses into my touch, sighing softly.

"I got to the beach and found her—" His face scrunches again, and a tear leaks from his eye. I gently wipe it away, wanting to wipe the pain away. "She was bloody, and her body had cuts and bruises all over it. There was so much blood—blood on her thighs, and I knew what happened. But she was barely breathing, and—I was scared." He uses the back of his wrist to wipe his eyes. "She died in my arms, and I didn't know what to do, so I called my mom. She accused me of killing Elaine. She said she always knew I was sick—she always knew I was a *freak*." His eyes lift to mine, the blue burning brightly, and my stomach drops. "I carved the word into my stomach the day of Elaine's funeral. It's all my mother called me, so I branded myself with it."

I feel sick.

Truly fucking sick.

But there's so much shame and rage mixed with it. Rage at his mother for ever treating him like that, for not realizing the amazing man he is. Rage at myself for ever being cruel to him. Shame for spewing the same insult at him as *she* did.

"I'm so sorry, Ezra," I murmur, and truly mean it. I would've never called him that if I knew the weight of the word. "I didn't know —I'm sorry. You're not a freak, you know that, don't you? You're not, Ez." His dimpled chin trembles, but the rest of his face stays blank. "Tell me you know I don't think you're a freak." He barely dips his chin in a nod.

"When the cops came and told my mom what happened, that I wasn't involved, she still blamed me. She said it was my fault for letting her go with them. And she was right. It *was* my fault. I should've done more. I should've walked home with her. I should've

216

fought those fucking guys for ever even looking at her." His body shakes violently, not from the pain and grief, but from anger, the pure, undiluted rage in his soul.

"It wasn't your fault," I say again, stroking my thumb along his cheek. He tries to pull away, but I put my other hand on his face, forcing him to look at me. The look in his eyes is one that could kill. "It was not your fault, Ezra." His eyes search mine, but he doesn't lighten.

"I killed them," he rasps. "There were three of them, and I killed them. They said it was an accident, but—but I didn't believe them. Then I left New Zealand and came to The States. I've never been back, and I never want to go back."

I force myself to keep my breathing steady, my heart steady, my voice steady, as I say again, "It wasn't your fault."

I press gently on his face, wanting him to feel my words. My heart aches for him, for all the pain he's had to endure alone over the years. His throat bobs as he swallows, and finally, I feel like I'm getting to him.

"I know you don't like what my club is involved in," he says quietly. "I know you think it's wrong. But I vowed to myself that I would kill every bad man on this fucking planet when I saw my sister's dead body. That's why I'm doing this, Kennedy. Not because I want to be anywhere near these sick fucks, but because I have to kill them. I have to protect everyone from them." A giant lump forms in my throat, and I try to swallow past it, but I can't. Not with the fierce look in his eyes, one that promises death. But, somehow, it promises safety, too.

I understand now. I understand him. Why he's so intense about everything, why he came into my home and never left, why he's so protective of not only me, but Ian, too.

He lost someone he loved, and he doesn't want to lose anyone else.

"I know," I breathe. "I know you do, Ez." I wrap my arms around his neck again and rest my head on his shoulder, nuzzling against

217

him. "Will you tell me about her?" His arms tighten as he clutches me to his chest.

"One day," he whispers, his voice tight. "But not right now." I nod against him, and he rests his cheek against my head as he rubs his hand up my back. "I'll tell you one thing, though. She would've loved you. Absolutely fucking adored you." I squeeze my eyes shut at his words. I don't deserve them, not after everything I've said to him, how I've treated him. He's done nothing but protect Ian and me, but love us.

"Thank you, Ez," I whisper. He stills, his body tensing.

"What?"

"Thank you." I pull away, finding his eyes wide as he stares at me. I brush a fallen curl from his forehead, and press a gentle kiss to it. "Thank you for everything." When I pull away, he's still staring at me in shock. "What?"

"No one has thanked me—" His voice breaks, and he roughly clears his throat before speaking again. "No one's thanked me before." I search his eyes, but there's nothing there. Nothing but that sad, lonely, lost boy.

"You're a good man, Ezra King." He closes his eyes at my words, his lips tightening as he lets them soak in. "Thank you for coming for me last night. Thank you for putting up with my bitchy attitude. Thank you for looking out for Ian." His eyes flutter open, his lashes damp. "And thank you for choosing me."

His hand wraps around the back of neck and he roughly pulls me to him, crushing his lips against mine. "Never thank me for that," he rasps against my lips. "It's my honor to be your man." My throat tightens again, but I push the tears back and kiss him.

I can't handle any more words, not right now. I don't think he can either. We need to touch, and kiss, and fuck. We need each other.

"Let's go home," I say, pulling away. He pulls me back to his mouth, and I let his tongue slide against mine. His kiss is hungry, and demanding, and claiming. I feel him hard under me, and I rock my hips, hissing through my teeth at the soreness that radiates through

218

my body. "Home." I rest my hands on his shoulders and move away again.

His hooded eyes are lustful as he stares back at me, his pupils blown so wide the blue is almost gone. Slowly, his hands glide down my body and he gropes my ass through my jeans.

"I'm taking my time with you when we get home," he says darkly, and goosebumps ripple over my skin. "I'm going to make you come so many times we lose track. Then I'm going to fuck you." His grin is wicked, and desire shoots through my body.

"Okay," I breathe, and he grins wider.

"Are you speechless?" he asks, his eyes twinkling. "All I have to do is promise to fuck you and you'll forget how to speak? That's good to know when you annoy me in the future."

"Fuck off," I laugh and swat at his shoulder. "Such a dick." He lifts his hips, grinding against me in emphasis. "Idiot."

I keep a stupid smile on my face as he helps me slide back to my seat. His hand wraps too high around my thigh as he pulls from the parking space and drives us home.

Kiwi

I hadn't meant to tell Kennedy about Elaine like that. I honestly didn't know if I ever wanted to tell her about my past, but everything that had happened to her reminded me too much of what happened to Elaine for me to ignore. I sat with Kens and listened to her doctor list her injuries, and for the second time in my life, I felt totally helpless.

I couldn't do anything to take the pain away. I couldn't change what happened last night. I didn't protect her, just like I hadn't protected Elaine, and it made every emotion I've pushed down over the years bubble to the surface.

Kennedy doesn't blame me for what happened, but I blame myself. *I* was the one she called for help. *I* was who she needed when she was in danger, when she thought she was going to die. *I* was the one she was counting on to save her, to protect her, and I didn't.

Last night, I felt everything I do now, but the relief that she was still alive overpowered every other emotion. But today, while we went over everything that had been done to her, it finally hit me. It ran over me like a fucking semi, and I had no one else to blame but myself for what happened. I should've done more. I should've been better.

My hackles rise as we walk into the dimly lit apartment. Shouting fills the small space, and I immediately push Kennedy behind me as I pull my gun from my waistband. She tries to move past me, but I hold my arm out, giving her a firm look that she chooses to ignore.

"Ian—"

"Hush," I hiss. Her mouth snaps shut and her eyes go wide. I try to take a deep breath to calm down, but I can't, not when she's still fucking hurt and something might be happening to Ian. "Stay right here. I mean it, Kennedy." She barely nods, but it's enough for me.

I slowly move down the hall, scanning the bathroom and her room as I pass them. Ian's door is cracked open, so I peer inside, readying myself to burst through and grab him before killing the threat.

But I pause.

"You can't leave," Ian says, his voice rising with each word.

"I can't stay here!" Enzo shouts. "I won't stay here. If I do, he'll fucking kill me. I *know* he will." I squint, trying to see them better. Ian paces the room, his hands on his head.

"Just live with us. My mom doesn't care." Enzo lets out a long breath.

"I can't live here, man," he says gently. "She's dating that guy now. This place is getting too crowded."

"So we'll move," Ian says, his voice breaking. "We can find a new place." Enzo sighs. I force myself to stop breathing, to just listen. "I can get more hours at the store, and—and I'll help pay for a new place. Just don't leave."

Tension builds between them, and I hold my breath, waiting.

"I have to go," Enzo finally breathes. "There's nothing for me here. No reason for me to stay."

"What about *me*?" Ian says, his voice sharp but thick with emotion. Enzo sighs again, but Ian pushes. He takes a step forward, his hands balling into fists at his sides. "You know how much I hate school, how much I hate it here. Just wait until we graduate and I'll

221

go with you. I'll go anywhere with you." My heart breaks for the kid. "Please don't leave me, E."

"We'll still be friends," Enzo says quietly. "You know we'll still talk all the time. And we can still play with the guys online."

"I don't want to lose you," Ian says so softly I barely hear him. But his next words are like a bomb. "I love you—I'm *in* love with you."

My breath catches in my throat at the confession. I wait for Enzo's reply, but it never comes. Instead, the door suddenly swings open and I'm met with Enzo's angry face.

"Great," he mutters as he pushes past me. "Fucking great." My gaze meets Ian's, and he roughly wipes at his face. I glance behind me, finding Kennedy trying to talk to Enzo. When I look back at Ian, his face is red, and he wipes at it again.

"You heard?" he asks. I'm still frozen, still trying to figure out exactly what I heard.

"Yeah," I say, keeping my voice light. His chin shakes as he steps toward the door.

"Figured." He looks past my shoulder, and I wince when the front door slams shut. The look on his face guts me, and I open my mouth to reassure him, to tell him that maybe Enzo just needs time, that it'll be alright. But before I can say a word, he shuts the door in my face.

Something crashes, and he lets out a choked sob, then Kennedy's at my side, reaching for the doorknob, but I catch her wrist.

"He needs a minute," I murmur. Her eyes flash as she yanks her hand from mine.

"He needs *me*," she hisses, and reaches for it again. But, again, I stop her.

"Give him a minute," I say again, firmer. Her jaw clenches as she glares at me, but she can give me that look all she wants. He needs time to himself, not his mother demanding answers from him. Not right now.

Her throat bobs as she stands at her full height, her eyes narrowing. "What happened? Enzo wouldn't tell me." I shake my head. I won't tell her this. I won't out Ian, not before he's ready. I shouldn't have been listening to him, but I was, and I heard what he'd said, but that doesn't mean it's my place to tell anyone about it, not even Kens. I'll take this to my grave if that's what he wants.

"He'll tell you when he's ready," I say with a small shrug.

"Ezra," she growls. "What the fuck is going on?" The door opens and we both stiffen as we look toward Ian. "Hey, bud," she coos, but his eyes are on me.

"Can I talk to you?" he says, his voice flat. I glance at Kennedy, finding her brows lifted.

"Me?" I put my hand to my chest, and he nods as he takes a step back. Kens and I glance at each other again, then I clear my throat. "Yeah, of course." Stepping inside, I try to ignore the look on her face as I shut the door.

Leaning against it, I fold my arms over my chest and watch him. He sits on the edge of his bed, his head hanging and eyes closed.

"I don't know if I'm ready to tell Mom," he finally says, and I swallow hard.

"Alright," I say. "We'll tell her whenever you're ready." His eyes lift to mine, and I push off the door. "It'll be alright, Ian." I sink onto the bed beside him, resting my shoulder against his.

"I wasn't ready to tell anyone," he says, dropping his eyes again. "It just came out." I nudge him with my shoulder, and he looks at me again.

"It's okay," I say, and his face finally breaks. Tears fill his eyes as he shakes his head.

"It's not okay," he cries. He covers his face with his hands, and I wrap my arm around him, my thumb stroking his back. "I lost my best friend. Why couldn't I just shut up?" He hits the side of his head, and I grab his wrist before he can do it again.

"He'll come around," I say gently. "And if he doesn't, he's not a friend you would want, anyway." He cries harder at that, and I wince.

This parenting shit is hard. I have no idea what the fuck to say.

I tighten my arm around him, holding him against my side. He rests his head on my shoulder as he cries, and my heart aches even more for him. His tears soak into my shirt, but I let him soak it. I let him get it all out, and when he finally pulls away, he uses the bottom of his shirt to wipe his face.

"I'm not gay," he says.

"Wouldn't matter if you were," I say, shrugging. "Your mom will love you either way. I'll—I'll care about you no matter who you like." I can't drop the L word on him. Not until Kennedy drops it on me first. He shakes his head, wiping his eyes with his shirt again.

"I—I like both," he mumbles. "Girls and guys." I nod in under-standing, then clear my throat.

"I've hooked up with a few guys," I admit, and he snaps his head to me.

"Really?" he breathes, sounding shocked. I shrug as I rub the back of my neck. I don't know if talking about my sex life is the best parenting tactic, but it's the only one I have.

"Yeah," I say, shrugging again, nonchalantly. "There was one guy that I had a—" I try to find the right word. "If we couldn't find anyone else to sleep with, we'd just fu—hook up together. Sometimes we had threesomes, but it was usually just us."

"He was your boyfriend?" he asks, sounding slightly amazed.

"God no," I snort. "He was a fucking loser. But he was hot." Ian's mouth falls open, and I let out a laugh.

"You're bi, too?" he asks quietly, and I shake my head.

"I just like who I like, and fuck who I want. Gender doesn't matter to me, the person does." Ian's eyes search mine, and some of the weight lifts from him. "It's okay to love who you love, kid. Don't let anyone make you feel bad for being who you are." Fresh tears well in his eyes, and I nudge him with my shoulder again. "But stop crying, yeah? You're gonna make me cry, and I don't think your mom will let me live it down." He laughs softly, wiping his face as he nods. Slowly, his smile falls.

"I don't think Enzo will speak to me ever again," he says, looking down at his hands in his lap.

"You don't know that," I say. "Give him time, Ian. He'll come around." *I hope.* He nods a few times, but doesn't look like he believes me. "Hey, how about we go surfing? Your mom can go with us so she can see it's not that dangerous, and I can teach you—"

"Not today," he sighs, his shoulders slumping.

"Then let's do something else." He slides his eyes to me. "I'm not letting up. You need to get out of the house." He chews his lip, his eyes searching mine again.

"You've really slept with men?" he asks, and I nod.

"I have."

"And the guys in the club don't make fun of you?" His voice is quiet, and I wrap my arm around him again.

"Nah," I say, hoping he can't see through the lie. Years ago, before Bash ever became Prez, some of the Old-Timer's gave me hell. But after breaking a few noses and stabbing one, they stopped. "My Brothers are my family. I'd die for them, for their Old Ladies, and their kids. I know they'd do the same for me and mine. When you have that kind of bond, who you're attracted to doesn't really matter anymore. You'll find your people, kid."

He lets out a long breath, and it feels like a cleansing one. Finally, he nods and gets to his feet. My arm drops to my side as I watch him move to his dresser and yank a drawer open.

"What do I wear to surf?" he asks, his back to me. His question startles me, and I blink a few times before standing.

"Whatever you have is fine. We'll get you a suit soon," I say as I move toward the door. I'll call Reid and ask him to bring me our boards. "Everything is going to be okay, Ian. I promise." His gaze meets mine again, and he holds it for a beat before he nods.

"Thanks, Kiwi."

"Ezra," I say softly. "You can call me Ezra." His lips tip up in a small smile, then he nods again.

"Ezra," he whispers. "Thanks."

Kennedy

"**I** fucking hate the beach," I grumble. "I get sandy and gross. I hate it."

"Kind of hard to avoid the sand, love," Ezra mindlessly says as he throws his arm around my shoulder. I wince and shoot him a look. "Sorry." He presses a kiss to my cheek, then leans against the car.

I still don't know what the fuck they talked about. Ian won't even look at me, and I feel like I've done something wrong. But I don't know what I've done.

"There they are," Ezra announces, and my stomach tightens. He pushes off the car, a bright smile on his face. Ugly, angry jealousy shoots through me, and I try to stomp it down.

Turning, I force a smile as Reid and Heather pull into the spot beside us. She gets out of the car first, looking ridiculously gorgeous as usual.

"Kiwi-Boy!" she shouts, throwing her arms above her head.

"Heather-Babes," he laughs, and I snap my head toward him, my fake smile falling.

Reid slides from the car and ignores us as he unstraps the boards from the car. Heather prances around the car and stops in front of us. Ian is instantly at Ezra's shoulder, and I grit my teeth. Him too? *Really?*

"Hey, Kennedy," she says brightly. Her eyes quickly scan my face, taking in the bruises I covered with makeup, and meets my gaze again.

"Hey." I try to sound pleasant, but I know she can see it on my face, hear it in my voice, read it in my body language—I don't like her.

I've never had an issue with Heather before. Apart from being too loud and a little bitchy, I thought she was fine. She's a good friend to Addie and Koda, and that's what matters to me. Those girls have been through Hell, so knowing they have a girl like Heather at their back always made me feel better.

Now, however, I want to fucking cut her for looking at Ezra. If I wasn't such an idiot and demanded to know who he was fucking at the clubhouse, I wouldn't have a problem with her. So call me jealous, or insecure, I don't care. He's mine, and right now, all I can think about is his dick inside her.

I feel Ezra's stare on me, his body tensing as if he's just remembered he told me about their hookup. He clears his throat and tries to wrap his arm around my waist, but I subtly shift my body away from him.

"You know Kens," he says. "This is her son, Ian."

"Hey," Heather says, jerking her chin at him. I slide my eyes to Ian, finding his face bright red. I let out a sharp breath, and she looks back at me. "I haven't seen you in forever." Reid leans the boards against Ezra's car and takes his place beside her.

"Yeah," I mumble. "Been a while." Tension fills our little group, and the look she gives Ezra makes me want to pop her fucking eyeballs out.

"I didn't know your son was so..." She turns her attention to him, and I grit my teeth, my hands balling into fists at my sides. "Old. I thought he was a toddler or something." She laughs, showing everyone her perfect teeth, and Ian chokes out a laugh.

227

"I'm sixteen," he says, his voice deeper than usual. It takes all I have not to fucking laugh.

"In five months," I say, and he shoots me a look that tells me to shut up, but I just lift my brow, waiting for him to argue. Wisely, he doesn't.

"You're letting him teach you to surf?" Reid asks, jerking his chin at Ezra. He leans against his car, his arms folded over his chest. Ian shrugs and tries to mimic his pose by leaning against Ezra's car.

"I know a little bit." I roll my eyes and look toward the water. "Are you going to surf with us?" There's too much fucking hope in his tone, and I clench my jaw. I don't need to look at him to know he's asking *her*.

"I was planning on it," Heather laughs. I keep my eyes on the water, not wanting to see her and Ezra look at each other anymore. "But I need to tan." I press my lips together as I look back at her, finding her holding her arms out. "He won't let me do it at the house." She rolls her eyes as she points at Reid with her head.

"I don't want everyone in the neighborhood watching you sunbathe," he says unapologetically.

"I thought only Bash was a possessive caveman, but it seems to run in your blood," she says, and the corner of his mouth curves. The look he gives her scorches even me, and I shift uncomfortably.

I've never felt so inadequate next to someone. I know I'm not ugly, but I'm not Victoria's Secret level hot like she is.

"You're welcome to hang out," Ezra says, and I glance up at him. His shoulders are back and his face is tight, but his eyes...they're soft.

"Can we get in the water now?" Ian asks, looking at Ezra too. Ezra laughs as he throws his arm around his shoulders, pulling Ian to his side like he's done it a million times before. And the way Ian's looking at him, like Ez hung the fucking moon, makes my chest tighten.

I feel like an outsider looking in. Like Ian isn't mine anymore, like Ezra isn't mine. I feel like the stray tagging along, like I'm not totally welcome.

"Sure thing, kid," he says. "Are you getting in the water, too?" It takes me a moment to realize he's talking to me and I straighten.

"Probably not," I say, and try to ignore the way Ian's face falls. "I'll stay in the car. I can read—"

"Oh, don't be silly," Heather says, putting her hand on my arm. I snap my eyes to her, but she's smiling. "You can't sit in the car alone."

"I don't mind," I say tightly.

"Come on," she grins, "we can talk shit about Ezra."

I run my tongue along my teeth as I slowly look up at him. He looks like he's moments away from a panic attack, or bolting. Maybe both. Her hand slides off my arm as she laughs awkwardly.

"Or not," she says.

Ezra and I stare at each other for a too-long moment, then I smile tightly.

"You know, that would be great," I say. "I'd love to learn all of his secrets."

"Will you get him set up?" Ezra rushes out as he looks at Reid. His brows flick up, but he pushes off the car and grabs a board.

"Come on," he says, jerking his chin at the other board. Ian grabs it and holds it under his arm like Reid, then they make their way across the sand to the water. Heather lingers for a moment, her hands wringing together. I don't try to hide my glare.

"If I did anything—"

"Can you give us a second?" Ezra says, his voice gentle. My teeth nearly crack. She glances at me again, then hurries after the boys. As soon as she's out of earshot, I whirl.

"Are you fucking kidding me?" I hiss.

"What?" He throws his arm up. "I didn't know they were staying."

"It's not about that and you know it." My eyes narrow into slits as he searches my face. "She calls you Ezra, too?" His brows bunch together.

"She snooped through my shit and found my ID," he says slowly. "She calls me Ezra because she knows it annoys the fuck out of me."

"So, you *are* Ezra to someone," I say, and he inhales sharply.

"Love," he says, his lips twitching. "All the guys know my name. She knows it. Fuck, I think Addie knows it."

"You made me think it meant something," I say.

"It does." He tries to grab my hand, but I pull it out of reach, and he sighs. "It does mean something, Kens. I don't let anyone else call me that, only you and Ian. It's—it's important to me." He drops his eyes to his feet. "Elaine always told me I'd know when I found the one. And somewhere along the way, it got into my head that I would know the one when she said Ezra. I'd feel it just...click. And when you said my name for the first time, everything clicked into place. Everything solidified in my head, even more than before, that you were meant to be mine." I flick my eyes between his, my throat growing thick with emotion. "Would you even care if we hadn't slept together?"

Just like that, all the words he'd just said are washed away.

"It doesn't matter," I say. "You—" I clench my hands, forcing my tears to stay back. "The way you look at her—you like her." He rests his hand on the car as he glares down at me.

"No," he says. "I don't. She's a friend—"

"Do you fuck all of your friends?" I snap, and he lets out a humorless laugh, shaking his head.

"Actually, yeah," he says sarcastically. "I've fucked a lot of my friends. I've fucked multiple of them at one time. Is that what you want to hear? You want me to tell you about every partner I've ever had? You wanna hear about every dirty thing I've ever done with anyone?" I press my lips together to keep them from wobbling. "I've been in more threesomes than I can count. That one with Heather and Reid? It wasn't the first time Reid and I fucked someone together. I don't remember the names of some of the people I've slept with. I've stuck my dick through glory holes and—"

"Okay." I hold my hand up as I squeeze my eyes shut. "Enough."

"No, you want to know," he snarls as he steps toward me. "So I'll tell you. Everything will be out in the open so you can't get mad at me for this shit again."

"I don't want to know," I grit out, opening my eyes to glare at him. "I'm not mad that you've slept with her." I take a deep breath, trying to process my emotions. "I care that you still look at her like—"

"I don't want to fuck her," he says, then takes a deep breath, his face softening. "I would never cheat on you. Of all the things I've done, I've never cheated on someone." He reaches for me, and I let him. He gently cups my face and wipes a falling tear with his thumb. "You're mine, Kens, and that means I'm yours, too. What do I need to do to prove that to you? I'll stop talking to her if that's what you want. I'll cut her out of my life completely." I close my eyes as I lean into his touch.

"You're really just friends?" I ask.

"We're just friends," he says, his thumb still gently stroking. "I told you, we only slept together because we were bored and wanted a distraction. It meant nothing to either of us. Look at me, baby." His voice breaks, and I force my eyes open. "I don't care who or what it is, I'll never let anything come between us. You own me, Kennedy. And, when you're ready to give yourself fully to me, I will cherish your trust for the rest of my life. I won't do anything to ever break it. You mean too much to me to ever fuck this up. Ian—Ian means too much to me, too. You're—" He lets out a breath as he steps toward me. "You're my family, even if you're not ready to say it, you and that boy are mine." His eyes lift above my head, and I know he's looking at Ian. "I love you both, with all of my fucked up heart." His gaze meets mine again, and I can't help the tears that leak from my eyes.

"You mean that?" I croak, and he nods before resting his forehead against mine.

"I'm going to marry you one day," he whispers. "I'm going to adopt him, and give you both my last name. Then I'm going to get you pregnant again." I close my eyes, letting myself picture this life with him. "When I say I love you, Kennedy, it's because there aren't enough words to convey how much I feel for you. When I say I need you, it's because I fucking *need* you to survive." He presses his lips to mine, a tear dripping onto my cheek from his eye.

"I'm trusting you, Ez. If I ever find out you've even thought about fucking someone else, I will chop your dick into tiny pieces and feed it to you. Understand me?" I glare up at him, ignoring the stray tear that slips from my eye. "I won't hesitate."

"You have no idea what you do to me," he sighs, his face dreamy. "That was the hottest thing you've ever said." I roll my eyes, and he quickly presses his lips to mine. "I swear on my life, I will never even look at another person." I flick my eyes between his, and decide to believe him. I let out a long sigh, my body relaxing against his.

"I'm sorry." I wrap my arms around his neck, wincing as my sore muscles stretch. "I'm not usually jealous, but—"

"I understand," he breathes. "I still want to murder Archer. If I'm being totally honest, I want to kill every man who has ever even kissed you. And, I know it's fucked up, but I want to kill Ian's father for getting you pregnant before I could."

I pause, and pull my head away. His eyes twinkle with amusement and I throw my head back, laughing. His lips land on my neck, gently kissing and sucking toward my jaw, then my chin before settling on my lips. His tongue slides into my mouth, and I moan against him. He lets his hands roam over my body, stopping when he gets to my ass.

"I need to fuck you," he breathes between kisses.

"Tonight," I promise. He kisses me harder, his hands groping my ass, my thighs, my waist. "Fuck, maybe we can do it in the backseat now." He laughs against my mouth as he cups my breast. My head falls back and he kisses down my neck again.

"If we were alone, I'd bend you over the hood of this car," he growls, and I moan again. "I'd eat your cunt from behind until you came all over my tongue." His other hand slides between my legs, and my eyes roll back. "Then I'd stretch you with my cock."

"Ez," I groan, my fingers digging into his back.

"Get a room!" Someone—Reid, I think—calls from behind us. I

pull away, but Ez holds me tighter, kissing me longer, probably in spite. I give him one last long kiss, and pull away. He steadies me until I don't feel dizzy with lust, then grabs my hand.

"Are we good?" he murmurs, tucking my hair behind my ear. I kiss his palm and he sighs.

"We're good," I say. He steals another kiss, then stands at his full height.

"You're not sitting in the car alone," he says. "You're going to sit your pretty little ass on a towel and watch Reid and I teach your boy how to stand on a fucking board." I roll my eyes at the authority he puts into his voice. "And if she bothers you, just tell her to fuck off."

"I've always liked her," I admit as we turn toward the small group. Heather is rubbing oil on her skin and I nearly groan. I need to get my crazy under control. If Ezra can do it, so can I. "I just don't like that you two have—" I wave my hand dismissively. "Whatever. It is what it is. I'll play nice."

"I like when your claws come out," he says, dipping his head toward me. His lips brush against my ear, and goosebumps ripple over my body. "It's hot when you get jealous."

"I wasn't jealous," I say. He kisses my cheek before we start walking toward them.

"You were totally jealous."

"Not even."

"Possessive," he says. "Possessive and jealous."

"Ez," I warn. He suddenly stops, his mouth open as he stares down at me.

"You're just as fucking crazy as I am, aren't you?"

"Fuck off." I shove his shoulder, making him laugh. He starts walking again, but I grip his shirt and haul him toward me. "I'm crazier, Kiwi. Don't forget that." His eyes spark as he slowly grins.

Kennedy

I groan as I recline on the pillows. Ezra winces for me, his hand a steady pressure on my back as he helps me slowly lower myself.

"Sore?" he asks, and I nod. I'm not hurting as much as I thought I would be after a beating like that, but my muscles ache. He strokes my hair away from my forehead, his eyes soft. "Sorry, love."

"It's okay." I sigh at his gentle touch, my eyes slowly shutting.

"Let me check the locks and Ian, then I'll come to bed, okay?" I nod, my eyes still closed. His lips brush against my forehead and I listen to his steady footsteps as he makes his way through the apartment.

With a small sigh, I roll onto my side and stare at the door, anticipating him. I try to push the panic that builds in my chest away and remind myself that I am safe. But being alone makes me spiral.

"Goodnight, kid," Ezra's deep, accented voice slices through my haze, and I open my eyes.

I'm home.

I'm with Ezra.

I'm safe.

He kicks the door shut as he slips his shirt off over his head. The few hours we were at the beach gave him a tan that seems to be getting darker by the minute. His hair is somehow more blond, and his smile...it's more genuine. Like a weight has been lifted from his shoulders. I don't know if it's from being in the ocean, or if it's because we're in a good place, or if it's something else entirely. But he looks happy. His eyes are happy.

He flicks the lamp off as he slides into bed beside me, still smelling like the salty ocean water and sunscreen. He showered when we got home, but it seems like that scent is embedded into his soul.

"What are you thinking about?" he whispers into the dark room.

This is becoming my favorite thing, our nighttime talks in the dark. It's somehow easier to open up to him, to be more vulnerable when he can't see me.

"I was thinking that you still smell like the beach," I say softly, and he huffs out a laugh.

"Hopefully that's not a nice way of telling me I smell," he teases. I slide my hand across the sheets, searching for him. He immediately finds me and laces our fingers together.

"No," I sigh. "It's just you. I like it." I hear him smile, and I can't help mimicking him. "What are you thinking about?" His thumb mindlessly strokes the back of my hand.

"I never thought I'd find you," he whispers. My throat tightens painfully and I squeeze my eyes shut. "I didn't think my person was out there. But you were."

"Ez," I breathe, a plea to stop talking. He brings my hand to his mouth and gently kisses the back of it before putting it to his chest, letting me feel the steady rhythm of his heartbeat.

"Come here," he rasps, holding his arms out. I slide across the bed and he immediately wraps me up, anchoring me to him. My leg finds its place between his, and we sigh contentedly at the rightness of it all.

I nuzzle against him, his chest hair tickling my face. We lay together in silence, his hand rubbing up and down my back as he rests his chin on the top of my head. My eyes drift shut, basking in him.

"If this is how every night for the rest of my life will end, I'll die a happy man," he murmurs, his voice vibrating through his chest. I pull my head back to look up at him, finding the faint light reflecting in his blue eyes.

"Me too," I breathe. His mouth tucks up at the corner as he tucks my hair behind my ear.

"You'll die a happy man, too?" he asks, and I shove his shoulder.

"You know what I meant, asshole," I laugh. He smiles as he presses his lips against mine. Slowly, he slides his hand up my side and grips my waist. I lean into him as his kiss becomes harder and more urgent.

"You made me a promise," he growls into my mouth.

"Yeah? What was it?" I breathe between kisses. His hand moves to my ass and roughly gropes it, his calloused fingers digging into my flesh.

"You said I could fuck you tonight." He kisses down my jaw and I tip my head back, giving him more access to my throat.

"Mm," I groan. "I don't remember promising that." He nips at my neck, the stinging bite of his teeth making my eyes roll back. "Lock the door." He leaps out of bed, his legs tangling in the blankets, making him nearly fall to the floor.

"You didn't see that," he says, breathing heavily as he bounds toward the door. I laugh as he locks it and prowls back toward me, flipping the lamp back on.

"I didn't realize you were so clumsy," I say, wiping my eyes.

"I'm not clumsy," he growls. He climbs on the bed and I roll onto my back, letting him hover above me.

"So clumsy," I breathe as I trail my fingers along his stubbled jaw, lightly tracing the hard edge until I get to his mouth. He bites the tips of my fingers before kissing them. He grabs my hand, holding it to him as he kisses along it, down my arm, to my shoulder, the curve of my neck. "Ez." My eyes flutter shut as he trails his lips along my skin, branding me.

He says nothing as he gently tugs my shirt off and tosses it to the floor. Then his mouth is on me again, kissing down to my breasts. He groans as he sucks my nipple into his mouth, his tongue playing with the piercing before he moves to the other. He takes his time, trailing his tongue along my sternum tattoo.

"I told you when we had more time I was going to worship your body," he says, his voice vibrating against me. The soft golden glow of the light reflects off his hair, making it look like spun gold.

"Please," I breathe, arching my back into him. He sucks roughly on my nipple and I groan.

"Quiet." He clamps his hand over my mouth, and the dominance in it, the control he has over me, makes me wetter. He moves down my stomach, gently kissing the bruises. "I'm sorry I couldn't make it before they hurt you." My throat tightens as I stare down at him. I pull his hand off my mouth and run my fingers through his hair, tugging on the knotted curls.

"It's okay," I whisper. "You still came. You still saved me." He shakes his head as he kisses my stomach again.

"Not soon enough," he says, his voice full of self-loathing. "It will never happen again." I grip his hair tightly in my fist and his eyes snap to mine.

"It's okay, Ezra. I'm okay. I'm alive."

"You're hurt." His eyes drop back to my stomach and I yank on his hair again. His eyes flash and his lip barely curls.

"If you keep this up, I'm going to smack the fuck out of you," I say, and he blinks at me. A slow grin spreads across his face, and he snakes his way back up my body.

"You're going to smack me, love?" he purrs, his face an inch above mine. My mouth goes dry and I try to swallow past it as I nod. "I don't think so." He dips and bites my neck hard enough to hurt. "If you do that, I'll do something a lot worse than just edge you. Understand?" He pulls back enough to look down at me. "Don't lift your hand to me, Kennedy. You've done it before, and if you do it again, I'll tie your hands behind your back until you've learned your lesson." My eyes widen, and I nod frantically.

"I'm sorry," I blurt, but he shakes his head as he moves back down my body. "I shouldn't—"

"Keep your mouth shut," he says as he pushes my legs apart and settles between them. "I don't want to hear you anymore. Unless you're screaming my name." He winks at me before he tugs my panties down my legs.

He throws my legs over his shoulders as he slides his arm across my hips, pinning me to the bed. He kisses and bites along my inner thighs, his fingers roughly massaging me. Finally, he slowly drags his tongue over my clit and my eyes roll back.

"I won't ever get tired of this," he mumbles, then licks my piercing, flicking it back and forth. "Maybe I'll get my cock pierced, too. Would you like that?" I glance down at him, and the image of him between my legs, his mouth on my cunt, his devilish eyes burning into my soul, is one that I will never forget.

"If you want to," I breathe. He roughly sucks on my clit and my hand moves to his head. "Fine. Yes. Pierce your cock." He gently laps at my clit again, rolling his tongue in a circle. "Fuck."

"Just the head?" he asks between licks. "Or the whole thing?"

"I don't care," I groan as I roll my hips against his face. "The whole thing." I feel him smile against me before he starts eating me like crazy. My fist tightens in his hair as I grind against his face, helping him drive me toward my orgasm. "Ez, please. Fuck. Please." I grip the sheets, my nails digging into my palm.

He doesn't stop. If anything, my begging only encourages him. He growls and pulls me tighter to him, his fingers digging into my thighs. My back arches off the bed as I edge closer to release, my soreness secondary to everything I'm feeling.

I put my hand over my mouth, forcing myself to be quiet when it's the last thing I want to do. Ezra's hand slides between my legs and he slips two fingers inside me, curling them as he fucks me with them, hard.

My orgasm teeters on the edge, and when he roughly sucks my clit, I moan into my hand. I clamp around his fingers, and he groans, the vibration shooting through me and forcing me into oblivion.

He gently laps at me as I come down, his fingers slowly sliding in and out. I finally collapse back to the bed and he pulls his mouth away from my pussy to kiss my thigh, to my hip, and up my body.

"I love the way you sound," he says before kissing me deeply, his tongue exploring my mouth. I groan into his mouth as I wrap my arms around him, holding him to me.

"Please fuck me," I breathe. He rocks his hips against me, letting me feel how hard he is.

"I'm recording it," he says as he pulls away. I blink at him. He reaches for his phone on the nightstand and I grab his arm.

"What?"

"I'm recording it," he repeats as he taps on his phone a few times. "I want to remember our first time forever."

"Ez," I choke out a laugh. "You can't record—" His eyes lift to mine and I pause.

"Yes, I can," he says. "And I'm going to. I want to watch my cock sliding into your sloppy cunt for the first time for the rest of my life." I just stare at him. He sighs, tilting his head to the side. "You really don't want to watch me fucking you?" I bite my lip as I think, and he laughs. "That's what I thought. Open your legs."

Hesitantly, I spread my legs wider, and he unceremoniously slides his boxers off, leaving him naked. I've never once described a dick as beautiful, but Ezra's is. Somehow, it's perfect.

Which shouldn't be fucking surprising. This man is a walking ego, of course he has a pretty dick.

He aims his phone down, and the little beep as he presses record makes me hold my breath. My heart hammers in my chest as I watch him stroke himself for the camera, his groans throaty and so fucking hot.

"Ready for my cock, love?" he breathes. He rubs the head of his cock against my clit, and I whimper. Slowly, he pans the camera over my body to my face. I quickly slap my hands over it, hiding. "Don't hide. Let me see how beautiful you are." I spread my fingers and glare at him through them. He grins as he lowers the camera back between my legs. "Look at this fucking pussy." His words are barely audible as he zooms in, using his other hand to push my legs wider.

I force myself to take a deep breath and calm down. It's not like he'll show anyone the video. He's far too possessive to do that. It's still fucking terrifying giving someone this much power over me.

He rubs his thumb against my clit, and my worries start to fade. He works it back and forth, making me moan into my hands. Finally, I drop them away and stare down at where his cock bobs in front of my pussy.

"Fuck me," I breathe. "I need you."

"What was that?" He points the camera back at me, a stupid grin on his face. I flip him off, and he laughs.

"I *said*," I say, drawing the word out. "I need you to fuck me. I need your cock, Ez."

"Fuck," he breathes. He doesn't waste anymore time as he aims the camera back at his cock. He strokes himself as he presses against my entrance. "Such a tight little cunt." I grip the sheets as he slides into me at an achingly slow pace. "Feel me stretching you, baby?"

"Yes," I moan. "Please, don't fucking stop."

"Not if my life depended on it." He slams the rest of the way in, making me yelp and slap my hand over my mouth. He gives me a slow mocking grin, like he knew what my reaction would be and did it on purpose.

He pulls out then roughly slams back in, his soft grunts filling the room. I brace my hands flat on the headboard above my head, holding myself in place as he fucks me. My tits bounce with each thrust, and I squeeze my eyes shut to focus on not screaming.

His hand drops to my waist, holding me in place, the other still pointing his phone at where we're joined. My nails dig into the fabric headboard and I wrap my legs tighter around his waist.

"Fuck," he grunts. "Roll over." He suddenly pulls out and my eyes snap open.

"What?" I pant. My gaze drops to his hand and I watch him roughly stroke himself, his head red and angry, the rest of his cock painfully hard.

"Roll over," he repeats. "Ass up." I roll my eyes as I slowly turn around, lifting myself to my knees as I press my shoulders into the bed. "That's it, love. That's what I love to see." He roughly gropes my ass, his fingers digging into me. I twist and look over my shoulder, finding the camera way too fucking close to my pussy.

"Ezra," I hiss, and he lifts his head, his eyes innocently wide.

"What?"

"Turn the fucking camera off," I snap. "Just fuck me. Come on." He grins again, wicked and crazy. He tosses his phone to the bed beside us, but I know he didn't stop recording. Whatever. I'm too fucking turned on to care at the moment.

He straightens and aims his cock to my entrance again. "You want me to fuck you, love?" I nod, my neck straining to look back at him. He slides his hand up my back, tracing the tattoo up my spine, before he rests his hand on my head, pinning me down.

Without warning, he slams into me, and I scream into the bed. He doesn't hold back as he fucks me, the headboard banging against the wall with each hard thrust.

"Is this what you wanted?" he snarls. I reach blindly back and he grabs my arm with his other hand, pinning it behind my back. I try to catch my breath, but I can't. Not when he's so thoroughly fucking me. "You wanted me to fuck you like a whore?"

He adjusts his hold on my wrist, and I arch back into him, letting him hit deeper. I press my face into the bed to muffle my screams. Each thrust hits a new spot, a deeper spot. I wave my hand around, looking for him, and he slides his fingers between mine.

I tighten around him, feeling another orgasm shooting toward me. My body coils tighter as heat courses through me.

"Fucking come on my cock," he grunts. He lets go of my hand and moves his hands back to my hips, readjusting his grip as he fucks me wildly. "Beg me to let you come, you little slut."

"Please," I cry. "Please let me come. Fuck, I'm so close." I claw at the sheets by my head. He barely stops, and I glance over my shoulder at him, finding him grabbing his phone again.

I don't have time to say anything before he starts fucking me again. He rests his hand on my lower back, and I push my hips into him, meeting each thrust. Slowly, he slides his thumb down and when I feel a pressure on my ass, I stiffen.

"Ez," I breathe warily.

"You'll like it," he says as he slowly presses his thumb inside me. "Relax." Easy for him to fucking say. He's not the one with a thumb in his ass.

"Ezra," I say again, but he ignores me as he presses deeper.

"So fucking tight," he groans. "Have you had a cock here?" He wiggles his thumb for emphasis and I gasp at the feeling.

"No," I say. "And I never will."

"We'll see." I open my mouth to argue, but he slams into me harder, hitting a spot so deep it hurts. "Play with your pussy. Rub your little clit." I slide my hand between my legs and find my swollen clit. My fingers brush against his thick cock, and I slide my hand lower, wrapping around his base, then lower, cupping his balls. "Oh, fucking hell."

My hand tightens, and he hisses, whether in pleasure or pain, I don't know. I slide my other hand between my legs to my clit again. I'm close to the edge, and with every thrust, every stroke of my fingers, I'm closer.

"I'm so fucking close," he says. "God, keep your grip tight, baby. Fuck, that feels so good. Your whore cunt feels so fucking good." I tighten my hand more and he groans louder. "I'm going to come inside you, so fucking deep."

"No," I breathe, panic filling my chest. Even though I'm on the pill, it's never one-hundred-percent. "Pull out." He grumbles something I can't understand, and I squeeze his balls tighter in warning.

"I don't think I will," he says. "I'm going to fill your fucking pussy with my cum every single day until you're pregnant with my baby."

"Ezra," I groan. My orgasm is almost there—so close my body begins vibrating.

"Fuck, yeah. Ready for my cum, whore?"

"No," I cry again. "Don't."

It's a sick game of me begging him not to come in me, and him ignoring it. It's fucking sick because the begging, the fear of him actually doing it, turns me on so much more than it should. My eyes roll back as I clamp around his cock until he can't move. I press my face into the bed and scream my release. Before it's over, he forces his cock to move, fucking me fervently.

"Coming," he grunts before he pulls out. My body twitches with aftershocks as he spills his hot cum over my ass. He slips his cock back inside me, barely thrusting as it softens. He leaves it there as we catch our breath.

He roughly wipes his cum off me before plopping onto the bed beside me, his face sweaty and flushed. "Wash your hands," I say, and he huffs out a laugh. I'm still on my knees, my ass still high in the air. I'm too tired to move. My body feels like it's permanently in this position.

He presses a quick kiss to my cheek and slides out of bed. Before he moves, he slaps my ass like I'm his fucking teammate. "That was great. You did good." I flip him off as I slowly lower to my side, not bothering to look for my discarded clothes.

"Put something on before you walk out there," I sigh as he reaches for the door. He pauses and looks around, finding his jeans and slipping them on.

"Good thinking, babe." He taps the side of his head and winks at me before slipping into the hall.

I try to stay awake as I stare at the door, but my eyelids are too heavy. I don't hear him come back to bed, but when I wake in the morning, I'm wrapped in his arms.

Ian

It's weird being in class and not sitting beside Enzo. It's been a week of this. Every time he glances at me, he quickly looks away again. Every time I tried to talk to him, he hurried away. I hoped Ezra was right and Enzo would come around and at least talk to me again, but he hasn't.

I lost my best friend. I don't entirely regret telling him the truth, but I regret the way I did it.

My phone vibrates, and I sigh before glancing at it. "Hey, Mom."

"Hey, we're going to the clubhouse. One of the guys just got married and they're celebrating," she says. I scrub my hand over my face as I lean back in my chair.

"Cool," I mutter, unsure of why she's telling me.

"Do you want to go?" I push my brows together.

"Why would I go?" I ask, and she huffs out a laugh.

"So you can meet everyone."

"Everyone wants to meet you!" Ezra shouts in the background.

"I'm not really in the mood to talk to anyone," I say quietly. The line goes quiet, then I hear her hiss something to Ezra.

"That's fine," she says. "Do you want to talk about it?" My heart lurches at the thought.

It's not that I think Mom would care about my sexuality. I know she would be supportive, but...

I don't know why I can't tell her yet. I can't reveal this part of me yet. Ezra knows because he overheard it, but if he hadn't, I wouldn't tell anyone. And I probably wouldn't tell anyone for a long time. If ever.

"I'm just tired," I lie. I can practically see her eyes narrow, assessing my words.

"Sure." The word is tight, and I know she knows it was a lie. My phone beeps and I pull it away to look at the new caller. My stomach drops to my feet at the name.

"Mom, I gotta go."

"Wait—" I hang up before she can say anything else.

"Hey," I answer breathlessly.

"Hey." Ezno's voice is tight, unsure. "I—I left my clothes at your place."

"Right," I breathe. "I can bring them—"

"I'm already here," he grumbles. "Answer the door. I've been knocking for like five minutes."

"No, you haven't," I say as I push to my feet.

"Long enough," he mumbles. I hang up as I walk down the hall, my hands shaking from the anxiety building in my body. When I get to the door, I pause, my hand hovering over the doorknob. Rasputin lifts his head from his spot on the couch, a patch of sunlight warming his little body.

"What do you think?" I whisper, but he just blinks at me. With a final breath, I pull the door open. Our eyes meet and I nearly crumble, but I force myself to stay on my feet, to look him in the eye. "Your bag is still in my room. I can get it—"

"I'll grab it," he says as he walks past me, his shoulder brushing my chest. He quickly averts his eyes as he hurries away. Raspy jumps off the couch and follows him, me on his heels.

When I get to my room, I stand in the doorway. He shoves clothes into his bag, his eyes on what he's doing. The tension rippling off him smothers me, and I force myself to take a breath.

Enzo is my best friend. It doesn't need to be like this.

"Hey, E," I say, and his shoulders stiffen. "I'm sorry about what I said. I—" I swallow hard, the words tasting bitter before I say them. "I didn't mean it. It was just a heat of the moment—"

He turns toward me, his thick black brows low over his dark eyes. "You didn't mean it?" My throat is too dry to swallow anything, and my body is wound too tight to speak. So I hesitantly nod. We stare at each other for a moment, then he turns back to his clothes.

"Did you want me to mean it?" I whisper, taking a small step forward. He pauses again, his hand halfway to a discarded shirt on the floor. I hold my breath as I wait for him to answer, but when half a minute goes by, I let it out and retreat back to the doorway.

Finally, he stands, his body tense. He turns toward me, his eyes shadowed as he stares at me.

"I don't know," he breathes. "I—it confused me." My heart gallops, and my hands shake harder.

"Sorry," I say again, but he shakes his head.

"I've always thought of you like a brother," he says, and I nod in agreement. That's what we'd always been, but somewhere along the way, my love for him shifted from platonic to something more. Something I couldn't explain. "But when you said that—" He squeezes his eyes shut and takes a deep breath. "I've thought a lot about it. I like girls." I nod a few times, blinking the tears back. He opens his eyes, and they look as damp as mine. "But I like you, too."

We stare at each other. The words I've wanted to say to him are totally lost to me. He looks terrified, like he's scared of my reaction. I try to play it cool, like what he's just admitted hasn't shaken me to my core.

"Cool," I say, then wince. His lips twitch, then a slow smile cracks his face, then he barks out a laugh. I can't help the shy smile that spreads at the sound of that laugh.

"No wonder you've never dated anyone," he laughs. "You're shit at this."

"I dated Amanda," I say defensively, and he rolls his eyes.

"She sucked your dick twice. That's not dating."

"Yeah, but she did it while we were on dates. That's dating." He huffs out another laugh as he shakes his head.

"You have so much to learn, man," he says. Slowly, his smile falls, and he clears his throat. "You never liked her, did you?"

"I did," I say. "I, um, I like guys and girls." I rub the back of my neck awkwardly. He nods a few times, his eyes flitting around the room as he thinks.

"So, what does that mean?" he asks, and I push my brows together in silent question. "I mean—what does that mean for me? I know I like girls—I like girls a lot—but I like you, too. I don't know—" His voice sounds frantic, and I take a few steps toward him, anticipating him moving away from me, but he doesn't.

"I think I'm bi," I say honestly, the words still foreign to me. "You could be, too. Or maybe you just like who you like, regardless of gender." I think about Ezra, and wonder if I could ask him to talk to Enzo about this. He'd know what to say more than me. "But you don't have to label yourself, you know?" He nods a few times, looking unconvinced.

"Where do we go from here?" he asks, and I shrug.

"I don't want to lose you as my friend," I say quietly. His hands ball into fists at his sides. "If you're unsure about your feelings, we can forget I said anything. We can just go back to how we were—"

"I'm not unsure about my feelings," he says. "I'm—I'm scared of how people will react." He says *people*, but I know he means his father.

"We don't have to tell your dad," I murmur, risking another step toward him. "And if he finds out, I'll protect you from him, E." He nods a few times, his eyes wide as he stares up at me. "I'm here, you know that. I'm not going anywhere."

"I know," he breathes, then squeezes his eyes shut. "What if—what if we figure out that we don't work together? What—"

"We've been best friends since we were six," I say. "I think if we weren't going to work out, we would've already ditched each other."

"But being friends is different from—from being more." I take the last step to him. This is closer than I've ever stood beside him, but things are different now. Or I'm hoping they will be soon.

"If we decide we don't work like that, then we'll go back to being friends," I say softly. "I need you in my life, even if we stay just friends forever. That's okay. Don't try to force yourself to feel anything you don't because you're scared you'll lose me. You won't. I'll still be here." His throat bobs as he swallows, then barely nods.

"Can we keep this a secret?" he whispers. "Just for a while. Until I'm ready—"

"Mom doesn't know," I blurt. "Only Kiwi. I'm not ready to tell anyone yet, either." He lets out a relieved breath, his shoulders falling slightly. "We can take our time."

He lowers his eyes to my hands, his jaw working as he thinks. I don't back away, and I won't until he tells me to.

"Can I touch you?" he whispers.

I swallow my excitement down as I rasp, "Yes."

Slowly, he reaches out and grabs my hand. His hand is rough and calloused from his time in shop class and working on cars at his uncle's garage. Mine are too smooth in comparison.

I lace our fingers together, my heart hammering in my chest. I wait for him to pull away, to wipe my touch from his hand on his jeans, but he doesn't. He just stares at our hands.

Finally, he looks up at me. He's only a few inches shorter, but I feel like I tower over him. I squeeze his hand gently, reassuringly, and he squeezes it back.

"We can get through anything together," I say. "Friends, or more. It doesn't matter. We'll figure this out. Together."

"Together," he agrees. We stare at each other for a beat too long, the tension threatening to snap us. I let out a breath as he shuffles closer, brushing his chest against mine.

"Can I kiss you?" I breathe, my eyes searching his for any hint of disgust or uneasiness. "It's okay—"

"Yes," he says. The room grows thicker with tension, with the need rippling off us.

I lower my head toward his, giving him plenty of time to react, to pull away, but he doesn't. "Are you sure?" I whisper, just a breath away from his lips. His breathing is shallow as he nods. My eyes flutter shut as I brush my lips against his, getting my first taste of him.

He pulls back suddenly, and my eyes snap open. He stares at me wide-eyed and I brace myself for him to slap me, or call me names, or run away. But he doesn't. He pushes onto his toes and crushes his mouth to mine, his tongue sliding along my lips.

We're shaking as we unclasp our hands and grip each other. I let my hands roam over him, feeling the hard planes of his body. He bunches the back of my shirt in his fists as he pulls me tighter to him. I feel him hard against me, but I force my hips back. We're not there. We might never be there. And that's okay, because if all I ever get from him is this kiss, it'll be enough. It'll be more than enough.

It feels different, kissing a guy and not a girl. I don't have a lot of experience with girls, but I know that I've never felt like this. Like I'm burning from the inside out. Like I'll die if my lips don't stay on his.

One of his hands slides into my hair and he yanks my head back. I groan at the feeling as it awakens something in me I didn't know was dormant. He sucks along my neck, biting and licking his way down to my collarbones.

"E," I groan before pressing my lips to his again. Breathlessly, we pull away. His eyes are as hooded as mine, as lustful and eager for more. "I—I'm not ready for more." He nods, his mouth parted as he pants.

"Me either," he admits as he drops his eyes to my mouth. "But— but I liked that." I let out a shaky laugh as I step away enough to take a full breath.

"Me too," I say. "Does this mean we're..." I narrow my eyes slightly, watching him think through it.

"Together?" he breathes, and I nod, impatiently waiting for his answer. He grabs my hand again, staring at the contrast of his darker and my paler skin beside each other. "Let's not label it." I swallow hard. "Let's just...have fun."

"Fun," I repeat, and he nods. It's not commitment, and it's not what I want, but it's what he's willing to give. "One condition." He lifts his eyes to mine, a silent question in them. "We're exclusive. You don't date or fuck anyone else. I won't either. To the outside world, we're still just friends, but behind closed doors, you're mine."

His brows lift, a small, cocky grin curving his lips. "I didn't realize you were so possessive," he smirks.

"I didn't realize it either," I admit, my voice low. "But with you, I am." He grins broader at that.

"Good to know." His smile slowly falls as he nods. "I can agree to that. At least for now." I roll my eyes.

"For now?" I say, and he shrugs.

"If a better offer comes along, I have to take it." I shove his shoulder, laughing softly.

"Whatever," I say. "There is no one better than me."

"Yeah," he sighs. "There's really not."

Kiwi

I had to leave Kennedy with the girls while Bash, Ryder, Reid, and I talked to Ginger. He's a lot less talkative today than he has been in the past, which is disappointing. And fucking annoying.

Bash leans against the wall, his arms folded over his chest. Ryder stands by the door, watching everything. As our Enforcer, you'd think he was the one to get his hands dirty the most, but he's not. It's usually Bash, Axel, and me. He's the one we call when things are really fucking bad. We've all silently agreed to not make him kill anyone unless he has to. It eats away at him a lot more than the rest of us.

Don't get me wrong, though. He will fuck someone up without hesitation. He'll just dwell on it for the rest of his fucking life.

I wrap a chain tightly around Ginger's ankles as Reid fills a giant bin with water in the corner. Ginger keeps his mouth clamped tightly shut, his one good eye frantically flicking between the four of us.

"You can start talking at any time," I say as I secure a lock through the chain. I jerk on it a few times, testing it. "You know what you need to say."

I shrug when he doesn't speak and push to my feet. Grabbing his chained hands, I pull him to his feet. He sways, his body off center from the beatings he's taken and the chain around his ankles.

Ryder jams his shoulder into Ginger's gut and hauls him easily over his shoulder. Ginger grunts out a breath, but no one really gives a shit. I take my time as I grab a hook, pulling it from the ceiling and attaching it to the chain around his ankles.

Running to the wall, I crank the lever and watch the hook slowly retract back into the ceiling. It's not until Bash and Reid slide the barrel full of water toward him that he begins to panic.

"Oh, now you have something to say." I lean against the wall, folding arms over my chest. His feet press flat against the ceiling, his eyes wide as he stares down at the water below him.

"We learned a few things," Bash says, crouching so they can be face to face. "One, we learned you lied to us." He tilts his head to the side, grinning as Ginger's eyes go wide. "You said your father wasn't involved, but one of our guys just saw him meet with Montgomery."

"I don't know," Ginger says frantically. "The last I spoke to him, he wasn't involved—" Bash slams his fist into Ginger's ruined face. He groans as blood drips from his face into the water.

"One of our guys says Montgomery gave him a girl," Bash says darkly. Taz called us earlier to let us know what he saw. He's close, so we're planning on going to L.A. soon to finish this. "Now, why don't you tell us the truth?"

I press the lever, letting Ginger lower a notch toward the water. He screams and thrashes as he realizes what's about to happen.

"Okay! Okay," he screams. "Wait!" Bash pushes to his feet with a small groan and rests his hands on his hips as he glares down at him. "Where did they meet?" I let out an irritated breath.

"Does it matter?" I ask. His face is a disgusting shade of red, and Ryder shifts on his feet.

"We need to hurry before he passes out," he mutters, his arms folded tightly over his chest.

"Was it downtown?" Ginger asks, his voice nasally and slurred.

"If it was, then it's legit. Dad bought the girl. If it was at any of the other warehouses, it was a test."

"A test?" Reid asks, taking a step forward.

"Of loyalty," Ginger explains. We glance at each other. It wasn't downtown.

"Why would he need to test him?" Ryder asks. "I thought he was vetted?"

"He was," Ginger says. I let out another impatient breath and lower him another notch.

"Can you hurry the fuck up?" I snarl. He sounds like he's about to hyperventilate and it gives me a sick amount of satisfaction.

"Dad said something about thinking some of his guys were going to turn on him," he says quickly. "He thought they were going to bring the whole thing down so he's probably testing everyone who works for him and getting rid of the ones who aren't loyal." We glance at each other again. "Can I get down now, please?" He looks at the water, but we ignore him.

"Do you think Montgomery is playing him?" Ryder asks. Bash's brows are furrowed tightly together, his lips pursed into a thin line as he thinks.

"I don't know," he breathes. "How can we get close to him?" Ginger shakes his head.

"You can't," he says. "No one gets close unless he knows you personally."

"He doesn't work with anyone he's never met? Maybe a buyer in a different country?" Reid asks. Ginger's eyes flit around the room, and I lower him another notch for encouragement. The top of his head touches the water and he squeezes his eyes shut.

They snap open, wild, as he searches the room. "Australia!" he shouts. "He has a partner in Australia. I don't know if they've met yet, but they've traded girls for years." Bash nods a few times.

"Someone can pretend to be him," Reid says quietly. I nod, a plan already forming.

"He'll know!" Ginger says frantically. I lower him another notch, making him scream out a sob, and Bash shoots me a look. I give a small, unapologetic shrug. "Fuck! I—I don't know! You have to know everything they've done. My father will know if you're faking it."

"Good thing we have you to tell us everything we need to know, right?" I ask, and he shakes his head.

"I don't know everything!" he shouts, and I shrug again.

"Give us enough information to get close," I say. Bash nods a few times and takes a step back toward the door.

"That could work," he mutters. "If we cut the head off, the rest will die." I nod in agreement. "We could save a lot more girls like that. Instead of going for his grunts, we go for him."

"Yep," I say. Ginger's body swings with his violent sobs and I roll my eyes.

"Chapel," Bash grunts, turning toward the door. "We need to plan."

Kiwi

"**A**re you sure you're ready to go back? It's only been a few days." I chew on my thumb as I watch Kennedy put her makeup on. She sighs and finds my gaze in the mirror.

"I'm sure," she says. "I can't take this much time off. If I don't work, I don't get paid and I need money."

"I'll pay your bills," I say and her body stiffens. Slowly, she sets her brush down and turns toward me, leaning against the counter.

"You're not paying for anything."

"Why not? I'm living here now, so I should help," I say. She shakes her head as I speak, and runs her hand through her silky hair.

"You're not paying for anything," she says again. "You have your own bills—"

"I've been living at the clubhouse for a while," I admit. "I have enough money saved so we could get a bigger place." She blinks at me. "We could get a room for Enzo—"

"We're not talking about this right now." She turns back toward the mirror. "I feel like I've barely seen Ian lately, and I still don't know what the fuck is going on with him. It's like he's avoiding me. The last thing he needs is to be uprooted from his home and—"

256

"He won't feel like he's being uprooted," I say as I move behind her, lightly wrapping my arms around her. "He'd love the extra space. And Raspy would love a yard to play in." She chews her lip as she stares at my reflection.

"I don't want you paying any of my bills," she says again, and I open my mouth, but she continues. "Let me think about moving, okay? I'll need to talk to Ian about it before I agree to anything." I kiss the curve of her neck.

"Alright," I murmur against her skin. "I've already been looking at places anyway." She rolls her eyes as she looks back at herself. I slide my hands onto her hips, pressing her ass against me as I watch her put on her lipstick. "He'll be fine. In fact, I think he'll love a bigger place if it means Enzo will live there." Her eyes drift to mine.

"Are they even talking?" she asks, and I shrug.

"They'll figure it out." I kiss her neck again, at the spot I know drives her wild.

"Ez," she says, and I lift my gaze. "What happened?"

"Nothing for you to worry about," I say. It's been the same answer I've given her for days, and I know it's not going to hold much longer. But I'll figure it out when I get there. I kiss the back of her head and take a step back. "If I think you're getting too tired tonight, I'm taking you home. Spence can just fuck himself. I'm not letting you run yourself into the ground." Her shoulders fall as she turns her attention back to herself.

"I'll be fine," she mutters, but she has a death grip on the counter and her hand trembles as she finishes applying her makeup.

She can lie to herself all she wants, but she can't lie to me. I see right through her bullshit. She's scared to go back, and I understand why. She'll never feel safe there again, and I hate the world for it. I want to kill Spencer and Milo for leaving her alone. Then I want to kill myself for not protecting her.

"I'm going to take Raspy for a walk," I say, and she nods.

"Take Ian with you?" Her eyes are guarded, and her voice is tight, but I nod as I knock on the doorframe.

"Sure thing."

"And get him to talk, please? Just make sure he's alright." My heart softens at the worry in her voice.

"I'll take care of him, love," I say gently. "I'll take care of you, too."

"I know," she breathes. "Just—could you tell him I want to know he's okay? I know he's not ready to talk about what happened, but can you just let him know I'm here when he's ready? He's still first on my list."

"Of course," I murmur. "He's okay." Her lips press into a thin line as she nods. She stares at herself in the mirror, and I wait for her to say something else, but when she doesn't, I decide to leave her alone. She's still processing everything, I know that, but he's not alone.

I hesitate before knocking on Ian's door. There's some shuffling, and it sounds like he trips over something before landing heavily against the door, and I smile to myself. It barely opens, and he shifts himself in front of the opening, blocking the rest of his room. My smile slowly falls as I narrow my eyes.

"You okay?" I ask, trying to peek over his shoulder. He moves with me, blocking my view.

"Yep," he says. "All good."

"Can I come in? I want to talk to you about something." His throat bobs as he swallows hard.

"Um, I'll just come out. Give me a sec—" He tries to shut the door, but I rest my hand flat against it.

"What's going on?"

"Nothing," he says quickly. He glances over his shoulder, and I see a hickey on the side of his next. I bite back my laugh.

"So, why won't you let me into your room?" I push on the door, but he pushes back, keeping it mostly closed.

"It's a total mess in here," he says, laughing awkwardly.

"It's always a mess." I lift my brows at him. "Open the door, kid."

"I—I—" His eyes dart between mine.

"Just open the freaking door, man," someone calls, sounding half asleep. I grin as he lets out a sharp sigh.

258

"You're not fighting anymore, then?" I ask, and he shrugs. "Does your mom know he's here?" He shakes his head.

"Please don't tell her," he says, and I hold my hands up.

"I'm not getting in the middle of this," I say, and his shoulders slump. "Just talk to her. You know she won't care."

"There's nothing to talk about," Ian says.

"Yes, there is," Enzo calls from the room, and Ian rolls his eyes.

"I'm going to walk the dog. Talk to her while I'm out." He rubs the back of his neck, looking scared and unsure.

"Ez—" Kennedy calls as she leaves the bathroom, then abruptly stops. "Hey, bud. You going to walk Raspy?" I glance over my shoulder, finding her looking worried but trying to hide it.

"Um." I look back at him, finding red creeping up his neck into his face. He shoves his hand through his messy hair, and leans against the doorframe with a sigh. "Can I talk to you, Mom?" I step out of the way, letting them talk without me interfering.

"Of course," she says, shooting me a look. I just shrug and press my back against her closed bedroom door, my eyes flicking between them. "Everything okay?"

"Yeah," he says, waving dismissively. He glances at me, then back to Kens. "It's about the fight with Enzo. He's—we're good now."

"In here, Ms. K!" he calls, his voice still groggy. A smile ghosts her lips as she nods.

"You're not fighting anymore?" she asks, and Ian shakes his head. "Okay, yeah. Um." She looks at me again, and I guess that's my cue. I tap my neck, telling him I see the hickey, and he smacks his hand over it.

"Have fun," I chuckle, giving them both a cocky grin and heading down the hall. I glance over my shoulder a last time before heading out with Rasputin.

They're still standing a few feet from each other, and Ian looks like he's about to have a panic attack. Kennedy's shoulders are tense, but after this conversation, they'll be back to normal. Everything will be fine.

Kennedy

Ian and I stare at each other until we hear the front door quietly shut. He gives me a lopsided smile as he rubs the back of his neck.

"So," I say, huffing out a laugh. "What's up?" His chest rises as he takes a deep breath and looks back into his room.

I impatiently wait for his answer, for him to acknowledge me, for something. I don't know why he's acting so weird. He had a fight with Enzo—so what? They've had a million fights but have always worked it out.

"Yeah," Ian sighs. "Stay here." Enzo grumbles something, and Ian's shoulders relax. I wring my hands together, my heart in my throat, as Ian turns back toward me. "Your room?" He sounds scared, and it breaks me.

I can't find my voice, so I nod and enter the room, letting him follow and shut the door. I sit on the bed and pat the spot next to me, eyeing him warily. He hesitates before sitting, but he doesn't face me, or lay back on the pillows like he usually does.

"Is this about Ezra?" I blurt. "Do you not like him here?" He looks shocked at the question, but I can't keep myself quiet. Every-

260

thing I've been worried about overflows from my mouth. "Do you not like us together? I can break things off—"

"Mom, no," he says, shaking his head. "I like Ezra. I—it's a little weird that he's always here, but I'm getting used to it. I like that he's here. I like that you have someone. That you're not alone anymore." Emotion tightens my throat as I flick my eyes between his, searching for any hint of a lie. But there isn't one.

"Then what's this about?" I murmur. My hands are twisted tightly together in my lap as I wait. He lowers his eyes to the floor as he leans forward, resting his elbows on his knees. "You know you can tell me anything, bud. What's going on?" I rest my hand on his back and he tenses, but I keep it there and stroke my thumb back and forth.

"Enzo and I had a fight the other day," he finally says.

"It seems you've made up," I say hesitantly, and he scrubs his hand over his face.

"Yeah," he breathes. "Kind of. Things are still weird." His fingers dive into his hair as he continues staring at the floor.

"What was the fight about?" I murmur. He takes a shaky breath, and I scoot closer to him.

"I told him I loved him," he whispers. My heart hammers in my chest as I stare at the side of his head. "I'm in love with him." He doesn't look at me, and somehow, that makes it worse. My mind reels as I try to scramble and search for the right words.

"And...he doesn't feel the same way?"

"Did you hear what I said?" he asks, finally turning to face me. His eyes are wet and red, but no tears fall. "I said I'm in love with him. *Him.*"

"I heard what you said, Ian," I say softly. "And I'm asking if he feels the same way?" His eyes search mine, and I let him.

"He didn't at first," he says, dropping his head again and looking at the floor. "That's why he left. But he came back the other day, and —things were just so weird between us and I hated myself for it. I still do. I—I might've ruined things with my only friend, and if I would've just kept my mouth shut—"

"Baby, it's okay," I whisper as I wrap my arm around him. I try to pull him to me, but the stubborn kid holds his ground, so I drape myself against him, forcing him to let me hold him. "It's okay."

"Ezra overheard everything," he says, and understanding hits me. He didn't want to out Ian. Every time I start to worry if Ezra is the right choice, shit like this hits me in the face. He's a good man. A really good man, and one I don't deserve.

"And he helped you?" I ask, and he nods slightly.

"Kind of," he says. "He helped me see things differently, you know?" He turns to look at me and I smile softly as I brush his hair away from his forehead.

"He has a way of doing that," I say, and he snorts. "Enzo is in your room..." I trail off, leaving the questions open-ended. His face turns red and I fold my lips between my teeth.

"He came over the other day and we worked it out," he says quickly. I press my fingers into him, lifting my brow, silently demanding more of an explanation. "It's nothing serious. We're just seeing where things go."

"Wait." I hold my hand up, my brows scrunching tightly together. "You're dating now?" He clears his throat as he sits up, and I let my hand fall away. "I didn't know Enzo was gay. I saw him with girls—"

"We're not gay," he says, and my brows flick up. "I'm—I like both." He mumbles the words and my lips twitch. We've never talked about girls, or boys, or crushes. It's new territory for us. "Enzo—I don't even know. I think he just likes who he likes, and I guess he likes me." He laughs awkwardly as he rubs the back of his neck.

"What's not to like?" I tease, and he rolls his eyes. "So, you're dating." He shrugs again.

"We're not labeling it," he mutters.

"That's never a good idea," I say, and he pushes his brows together. "A friends with benefits thing—"

"Mom!" he groans. "I don't want to talk about this."

"Well, we're going to," I say, giving him a hard look. "Friends with benefits never works. One of you always falls for the other, and it'll break your heart. If you want to be together but aren't ready to take the next step, put some boundaries in place."

"I know," he says, his hands covering his face. "We're exclusive to each other, but we're keeping it a secret. We don't want anyone to know that we're—" He drops his hands, his face falling. "We're not ready to come out yet."

"Thank you for telling me," I say, and he blinks. "What?"

"It's just—you're handling this really well." He eyes me warily. "Ezra didn't tell you?"

"I'm your mom," I say with a shrug. "I don't care who you like as long as they treat you right and make you happy. You were worried about telling me?"

"A little bit," he admits, wincing slightly. "I didn't know how you would react, and I didn't want you to be mad." I wrap my arms around him again, and this time he lets me tug him toward me. I press a kiss to his temple, and a bit of his tension leaves his body.

"I'd never be mad about this," I murmur against his temple. "I love you, Ian. You can tell me anything and that won't change." His shoulders shake, and I hold him tighter. "I hate that you were scared to tell me this."

"I just didn't want to lose you," he says, his voice thick with emotion. My heart breaks at the words and tears fill my eyes.

"You'll never lose me," I say. "No matter what, you will *never* lose me." It might take a second to get used to Ian and Enzo dating, but Ian is still my son. I'll get used to it. With that thought, I pull away from him and he looks up at me. "We need to talk about rules." Slowly, his brows push together. "Get Enzo." I jerk my chin toward the door and he slowly rises.

"Why?"

"Now that you're together, things have changed a bit." His eyes widen and I sigh. "We need to figure out sleeping arrangements."

"But—"

"I wouldn't allow you to have your girlfriend sleep in your room with you. Why would you think I'd allow your boyfriend to sleep with you?" I lift my brows and his face heats. "Please." I jerk my head toward the door again, and he hurries to his room.

I sigh as I comb my fingers through my hair. Of all the things I thought were wrong, this was not it. The only thing that bothers me is that he was scared to tell me. Have I done something to make him think he couldn't trust me? Did I make him believe that I wouldn't love him over something like this?

The front door opens and Raspy's excited breathing and jingling collar fill the apartment. I smile to myself and move across the room before poking my head into the hallway. Ezra's eyes meet mine as he slides his cut off, tossing it on the couch.

Ian's door suddenly opens and the boys stop, their eyes wide as they stare at me.

"Do you want Ezra in here for this?" I ask, flicking my eyes between them. Enzo looks up at Ian, and there's something in his eyes, something I've never seen that makes my heart swell.

"Um, yeah. Sure." Ian tries to play it off like he's not freaking out, but I know my son and this is him freaking out.

"You sure?" I ask, narrowing my eyes. He nods a few times and looks around me, his tension leaving him at whatever he sees on Ezra's face. "Living room, then."

I head down the hall, stopping when I get to Ezra, and he wraps his arm around my waist. He lowers his mouth to me, kissing the top of my head. "How did it go?"

"It's not over yet," I say. "Back me up, please. I don't need you trying to make light of anything." His brows bunch.

"You're—"

"Not upset," I say. "But if they're together, I don't exactly want them in the same room together all night." His face relaxes and his lips twitch.

"Right," he breathes. "You know they'll still—"

"I know," I say, holding my hand up. "I know."

Ian and Enzo sit on the couch beside each other and Raspy jumps between them. He paws at Ian's arm until he rests his hand on Raspy's back. Enzo looks terrified, and Ian looks...well, he looks terrified too.

"Okay," I breathe, looking between them. "I don't even know where to start." I run my fingers through my hair as I pace in front of them. "Do you have condoms?"

Every man in the room chokes.

"What?" Ian croaks, his face red.

"You should be safe, no matter who you're sleeping with," I say.

"Oh my God," he groans. "Can we not—"

"Your mom is right," Ezra says as he steps beside me. "You can still catch something, so condoms—"

"We're clean," Enzo says, glancing at Ian. Ezra shrugs as he slides his hands into his pockets.

"And if you ever decide to sleep with someone other than each other, you need to know to be safe," he says. Ian's face is buried in his hands, not looking at anyone.

"So," I say hesitantly. I didn't think this was how I was going to have the sex talk with my kid, but here we are. "Do you have—"

"Yes, Mom," Ian groans. "God, please stop talking about my sex life."

"A few more things," I say, wincing. Finally, he lifts his head and gives me a pleading look. "Sorry, kid."

"What else?" Enzo asks.

"You can't sleep in the same room together anymore," I say.

"Why not?" Ian asks as he sits up. I glance up at Ezra, and he subtly nods. I'll let him take this one.

"Well, we'd be shit parents if we let you two fuck while we're home," he says, and I blink at him.

"That's not it," I hiss, and he shrugs. "Well, that's kind of it." I pinch between my eyes. "I know you're going to find ways to mess around behind our backs, and that's fine. It's part of being a teenager. But—" I look at Ian, then shift my eyes to Enzo. "You're not going to do it here, at least not while I'm home. I wouldn't let a girl sleep in your room, and I'm not going to let a boy. Understand?" They both nod, their eyes still wide. "The door stays open when you're in his room." I point to Ian and Enzo nods. "One more thing. Enzo, you know I love you like you're my own, but if you break my baby's heart, I *will* fucking end you." His eyes widen comically.

"Right," he says, nodding. "Yeah. Right. Okay. I'm not going to do that." I slide my hands in my back pockets as I lift my brows. "I won't hurt him."

"Mom," Ian says, and I grin.

"Just messing with you," I say, and Enzo's shoulders slump. "But I'm serious. Don't hurt him." He nods and takes a deep breath, glancing at Ian.

"Can we go—"

"No, actually, I need to ask you something," Ezra says, and I turn toward him. He's staring at the boys, totally ignoring me. He crouches, resting his forearms on his knees as he flicks his eyes between Ian's. "What do you think about finding a new place? Something that will fit us all?"

"Us?" Ian asks, glancing at me. I clench my jaw and tighten my hands into fists in my pockets. This was not what I meant when I said we'd discuss it.

"Well, I'd like to live with you," Ezra says, eyeing him. "But this place is kind of small, so what if I found a new place? A house or a bigger apartment?" Ian glances at Enzo, and Ezra follows his stare. "We'll find a place with an extra room for you."

"Really?" Enzo breathes, his eyes widening. He looks shocked. "You'd–really?" He looks up at me, and the look on his face guts me. I sit on the edge of the couch and rest my hand on his shoulder.

"Of course," I say softly. "Our home will always be your home." Tears line his eyes, but he quickly blinks them away.

"Thanks, Ms. K," he whispers, and I squeeze his shoulder. He pinches his eyes before looking at Ezra. "Thanks—Kiwi." He hesitates on his road name and Ezra smiles.

"You can call me Ezra, if you want," he says.

"That's your real name?" Enzo asks, and Ez huffs out a laugh as he stands. "I was expecting something—"

"Cooler?" Ezra finishes for him and Enzo shrugs. "Sorry to disappoint, kid." Enzo stammers, but Ez just laughs.

"He's kidding," I say, glaring at him, and he winks. "We have to go to the bar tonight. Are you two going to be fine here alone?"

"You're going back to work already?" Ian asks, eyeing me.

"I need money." I stand and move next to Ezra. He wraps his arm around me again, pulling me tightly to his side. "I don't have time to cook anything, but I'll leave you money for pizza or something." The boys nod as they stand, and Rasputin jumps off the couch. "Remember what I said," I point at them, "wrap it."

"Oh my God!" Ian shouts. I laugh as he races past me toward his room. After the boys disappear down the hall—leaving the door open, like I said—I turn toward Ezra.

"You're so mean to that poor kid," he laughs, wrapping both arms around me. I rest my hands on his chest as I smile up at him.

"I'm his mom, I'm supposed to embarrass him."

"If my mom would've ever told me to wrap it, I would've jumped off the nearest cliff." I throw my head back and laugh. His lips meet mine in a gentle but firm kiss, and I slide my hands up his chest and around his neck.

"Maybe if she had, you wouldn't be such a man-whore," I tease.

"I doubt it," he says, kissing me again. "It's in my blood to be a whore." He presses his lips to mine again, and the kiss quickly turns into something hot, and I pull away.

"Later," I breathe. "We can have fun later." He kisses me again and drifts his hands down my back to my ass. "Ez."

"Fine," he sighs, nipping at my lips. "Later." He slaps my ass as I turn from him, and I glare at him over my shoulder. "If you keep giving me that look, I'm going to bend you over right now." I grin and hurry down the hallway.

Kennedy

It's been a few days since the sex talk with Ian and Enzo, and surprisingly, they've been following these new rules to a T. I never thought about what it would be like to watch my son fall in love, but it has made my heart happy to see him with his person.

His person isn't currently with us, and he's being a fucking grump.

"Why am I here?" Ian groans. I nudge him in the ribs with my elbow, giving him a look that makes him roll his eyes and shut up.

"Because Kiwi wanted us to meet everyone," I say for the millionth time today.

"Yeah, but why am *I* here? You're his girlfriend." He throws his hand toward me.

"And he's claimed you as his," I sigh, pinching between my eyes. "I don't know, Ian. He asked for you to come, so you're here. Talk to him about it."

"Ready?" Ezra jogs to us, a giant smile lighting his face. The club-house door bangs shut behind him, the sound making me wince. I nod and try to stomp my growing anxiety down. He taps Ian's head, then wraps his arm around my waist, yanking me to his side. "Everyone is already inside."

I glance at Ian and give him a reassuring smile as Ezra ushers us into The Brotherhood's clubhouse. I blink a few times, letting my eyes adjust to the sudden dimness, and look around. It's not what I was expecting.

There's exposed brick, beautiful dark hardwood floors, industrial lighting, and a little old bar against the back wall. A pool table sits in front of it, and a few tables and booths are scattered around the room.

Addie and Heather are standing together, and I reign my jealousy back at the sight of her. Ezra and I talked about this—they were just a fling. An emotionless fling.

There's a blond man standing beside Addie, and he looks completely enamored by her. I grin to myself thinking about Bash beating the shit out of him if he caught him staring at his girl like that. But she's always had that effect on people.

At the café, she took no one's shit, but all the customers still loved her. They loved Koda, too, but that's because no one can hate her. She's way too sweet to be hated.

Ezra guides us to the small group, and they stop talking. Addie's face lights up when she sees me, then her mouth falls open when she looks at Ian.

"Holy shit," she breathes. "I just saw you. How are you this tall already?" I glance at him, finding his face bright red as he rubs the back of his neck.

"Hey, Addie," he says with a lopsided smile.

"Oh my God!" she says, looking at me. I shrug, unable to hide the smile on my face. "Your voice! You sound like—"

"A man?" I ask, and she nods. "Yeah, it's fucking with my head, too." She laughs, but still looks in complete shock. I don't blame her. Ian shot up practically overnight.

"Hey, Heather," he says, trying to drop his voice more. His face reddens when she winks at him, and I pointedly clear my throat. She slides her eyes to me, a wicked grin curving her full mouth.

"We'll talk when mama bear isn't around," she teases.

"Try it and you'll find mama bears are harmless compared to me." Her brows raise, but she gives me an appreciative smile.

"I knew I liked you, Kennedy," she says. I don't smile back, and Ezra pinches my side. I snap my head toward him, barely refraining from flashing my teeth. I calm down when I realize he's staring at me the same way that guy was staring at Addie. It makes something in my heart swell, but I can't show that so I roll my eyes and look back at the group.

"This is August," Ezra says, clapping the other blond man on the shoulder. I scan him from head to toe and back, and have to admit he's pretty. He's an inch or two taller than Ezra, and his hair is a darker blond, but his eyes are just as blue. They could be brothers. "He's one of my oldest friends in The States. We met when I was eighteen and he was sixteen."

"Let me guess," I say dryly. "You met surfing?" August throws his head back and laughs.

"Fuck no, I don't surf," he says, his white teeth blinding in the dim lighting. "I beat the fuck out of him for hitting on my mom."

"He has a thing for moms apparently," Ian grumbles, and my head swivels to him, my eyes wide. His eyes are just as wide, like he hadn't meant to say it. There's a brief pause before everyone, including myself, erupts in laughter.

"What can I say?" Ezra says, wiping his eyes. "MILFs are my weakness." I slap his shoulder, but he stays grinning.

"Fuck off," I laugh, and his arm tightens around my waist as he kisses my temple.

"Wait. This is your kid?" August points to Ian and I proudly nod. "How old are you?" He scans me again, and I laugh.

"Thirty," I say. "He's fifteen." His brows lift.

"Shit," he breathes, scrubbing his hand over his mouth, eyeing me again. "You were just a baby yourself."

"Yep." I glance up at Ian, finding him staring down at his feet. He's always felt weird about me being a teen mom. He feels like he ruined my life, or took my youth from me, but I don't see it that way. Since I had him so young, I get more time with him. "I'd do it again," I gently nudge him with my elbow and he looks at me, "in a heartbeat." The corner of his mouth barely tucks up, and I nudge him again, hiding my own smile.

The front door flies open, and an excited squeal fills the room. We turn toward the sound and find a young blonde girl barreling straight toward us. There's a giant smile on her face, her two front teeth missing. She has a remote controlled car clutched in one hand, and a candy bar in the other.

"Addie!" I step out of her way as she launches herself into Addie's arms. Addie picks her up and spins her in a circle, laughing as the girl gives her cheek a sloppy, sticky kiss. "I got you this." She holds the candy bar out, and Addie gently takes it.

"Thanks," she says, hugging her tighter.

"Your surprise is in the car, Heather," the girl says, and Heather smiles brightly at her.

"Skye!" a man barks, and I snap my head in that direction. I ignore the giant tattooed man stomping across the room and zero in on the tiny woman beside him.

I rush toward Koda and wrap her in a tight hug. I squeeze my eyes shut as she hugs me back. I hadn't realized how worried I truly was about her until this moment. After the shit she's been through, I just want to wrap her in bubble wrap so she won't ever get hurt again.

"Hi, Kenny," she laughs as she pulls back. She looks up at me, then slides her eyes to the side and her mouth falls open. "Ian?"

"Hey," he laughs.

"You're huge, oh my God!" She steps out of my grasp and gawks up at Ian.

She's tiny, but looks even smaller beside him. She looks ridiculously small beside Axel, her giant husband. I glance over Ian's shoulder, finding him crouching in front of the girl, gently scolding her. She rolls her eyes, and I bite my lip to hold in my laugh.

"She's Axel's kid?" I ask, throwing my thumb over my shoulder. Koda nods proudly, then sees him talking to her and lets out a long breath.

"I'll be right back," she sighs. "I need to play referee or she'll walk all over him."

"I didn't know she had a kid," Ian says, and I shrug.

"Stepkid," I clarify. We watch her run her fingers through Axel's mop of hair, and his broad shoulders slump, as if her touch grounded him. He lets go of Skye's arm, and she bounces on the balls of her feet.

"I need to see Uncle Bashy!" She turns back toward Addie, her father completely forgotten. "I have a present for him. And for Uncle Reid. Where are they?"

"Chapel," Heather says, grinning down at her. Axel lets out a soft groan as he gets to his feet and wraps his arm around Koda. Ian and I step beside Ezra and he slips his arm around my waist, holding me proudly to his side.

"Shit," Axel says, staring at Ezra's arm around me. "This is a thing?" He waves his fingers between us and I shrug.

"Damn right it is," Ezra says. He taps Ian with the back of his hand and winks at him, making Ian's face turn bright red. "They're mine."

"You sure you know what you're getting yourself into?" Axel asks me, and I shrug again.

"Crazy calls to crazy, and apparently, I'm fucking nuts." He throws his head back and laughs, his stubbled throat bobbing.

"Well," he says as he looks down at Koda. He smiles before he looks back at me, and fuck, are all the guys in this club this hot? "Welcome to the family."

Kennedy

"So, this is your room?" I look around, taking in the cluttered, messy space. It smells like him, like salt air and coconuts, and something else, something entirely him—entirely Kiwi.

"Yep," he says proudly. "Nice place, huh?" He flops down on his unmade bed and laces his fingers behind his head. I press my lips into a smile as I nod, still taking everything in.

He keeps a cocky smile on his face as I stalk around the room, my hands clasped in front of me. I glance at him, a grin curving my lips as I open the top drawer of his dresser. Mostly clothes fill it, but before I close it a small box in the back corner catches my eye. I know I probably shouldn't snoop, but I can't help myself.

I grab it and hold it up, my brows raising in silent question. He shrugs, his eyes on me as I sit on the edge of his bed. Slowly, I open the wooden box and peer inside.

One blink.

Another.

Then I laugh.

"Seriously?" I pull out the little jar of weed and wave it around.

273

"Are you fifteen? Why are you hiding it?" He snorts a laugh as he slides to the edge beside me.

"I don't want anyone stealing my shit." He grabs the little glass pipe from the box and holds his hand out for the jar. I set it in his palm and watch him pack the bowl of the pipe, then grab the lighter. "Want the first hit?" He holds them out, and I hesitate before grabbing them.

"It's been years since I've smoked," I admit as I hold the pipe to my lips.

"Oh, it's like riding a bike." He grins as I inhale a deep lungful of smoke, my eyes immediately watering as I try to hold in my cough. I try to hold it for a second, but release it as I cough, the smoke billowing from my mouth in a giant cloud.

I cover my mouth with my fist as I shove the pipe and lighter at him, still having a coughing fit. Tears leak down my cheeks and my chest aches, my head feels light and floaty, but I feel good.

He laughs before taking a hit, much larger and more impressive than mine, then releases the smoke without coughing. He stares at me as I try to recover, that stupid smile still on his face.

"Fuck," I hiccup, then laugh. I wipe the tears from my face as he takes another hit and holds the pipe out to me again. "Ian's going to kill me." I grab it and take a deep breath before inhaling more smoke.

"Should I get him to smoke with us? Then he can't get mad," he says, and I shove his shoulder.

"I'm not smoking with my kid, asshole," I say, rolling my eyes.

"Be a lot cooler if you did," he says, trying to adopt a different accent.

"Fuck off, Matthew McConaughey," I laugh. "Was that you trying to sound like him?" He nods as he grabs the pipe from me again. "That was God-awful."

"I can't be great at everything," he says with a small shrug.

"I didn't realize you were good at anything." His head snaps toward me, his eyes sparking as he takes in my sarcastic grin.

"You better watch it," he says, putting the pipe and lighter back in the box and setting it aside.

"Yeah?" I shift toward him, my eyelids feeling too heavy. "Or what?" His jaw tenses as he flicks his eyes between mine, then drops them to my chest and back up. "Make it more obvious." I roll my eyes, but he tackles me to the bed mid-roll.

"How's this? Obvious enough?" he breathes as he straddles my hips and yanks the neck of my tank top down to expose my bra.

I nod as I fumble with his shirt, trying to pull it over his head. He whips it off before dropping over me, catching himself on his forearms by my head before pressing his lips to mine in a bruising kiss. I wrap my legs around his waist, holding him tightly to me as he kisses down my jaw, to my neck.

"Let me tie you up," he says against my skin, his voice vibrating through me. "I've wanted to tie you to the bed and have my way with you for days." I catch his lips with mine and drag my fingers through his hair, tugging lightly on the ends.

"No," I breathe, and he starts to pull away, but I hold onto his hair tighter, keeping his face near mine. "I want to tie you up instead." He pauses, then smiles against my mouth. He kisses me again, harder than before, then flips onto his back and kicks his boots off as he shimmies out of his jeans.

I roll off the bed, stumbling and catching myself on the edge as I remove my clothes, leaving my bra and panties on. He fumbles in the drawer beside his bed, then rolls onto his back, a thick black rope in his hands. I'm not even going to ask why he had a rope in his bedside drawer.

His eyes are wild and his smile is wicked as he watches me crawl onto the bed and straddle his hips. He settles onto his pillow, making himself comfortable, before dropping the rope on his chest and lifting his arms above his head.

My hands tremble as I grab the rope. I've never done this before. I scoot up his body and wrap the rope around his wrists, then around a post on his headboard. He tugs on it experimentally, then shifts his eyes to mine.

"How do you feel?" I ask, and he nods, his smile widening.

"Helpless," he breathes. "I like it. Do your worst, love."

A slow grin spreads as I lower my mouth to his, dodging his lips at the last second to kiss his jaw. He huffs out a laugh as I trail my tongue down his neck, gently nipping at the base of his throat. I move lower, sliding my body over his as I kiss along his chest.

His hips lift off the bed, his breathing ragged and shallow as he stares down at me. I bite down on his pec, my eyes on his, and he hisses through his teeth, jerking on the restraints. I move to his nipple and trail my tongue around it, making him groan.

"Fuck, Kens," he breathes.

His face, chest, and neck are flushed, his breathing still harsh. I move to his other nipple and roughly bite it, making his back arch and press against my mouth. I tug it away from his body, the skin stretching painfully. He jerks on the rope again, his muscles flexing and veins popping as he tries to alleviate the sting of my bite.

I bite my way down his body, loving the sounds he makes. He widens his legs, his feet at each corner of the bed as I settle between them. I run my hands over his hard thighs, feeling them flex under my touch. He presses his head back into the pillow, his eyes squeezed shut as I lightly trail my palm over his cock in his boxers.

"You're torturing me," he groans, bucking his hips.

"Not yet," I purr. His eyes open wide, his chest heaving and teeth bared as I lay my tongue flat against him, the thin fabric separating us. "I want you to beg for it, Ez."

His hips lift again, demanding more, but I won't give it to him. Not yet. My fingers slip under his waistband, teasing him as I lick the ridged outline of his cock again.

"Fuck," he hisses. "Please. Kennedy. Fucking *please*." I smile up at him, my eyes lifting to the straining fists above his head.

Achingly slow, I lower his boxers until his cock comes free and slide them down his legs, tossing them to the floor. He moans as I wrap my hand lightly around him, my palm teasing him. He bucks his hips again, fucking my hand, needing the friction. I kiss his thigh and it trembles under my lips. Moving higher, I kiss the hard planes of his lower stomach before finally pressing a gentle kiss to his head.

"I didn't think you'd tease me this fucking badly," he says. Sweat beads along his brow, his eyes wild and dark. "Just suck my cock, Kens. *Please.*" He emphasizes the word, the sound near guttural, and I finally give him what he wants. My lips wrap around him and I lap at his head, swirling my tongue around him until his eyes roll back. "More."

I push myself lower, taking more of his cock into my mouth. I lift my eyes to him again and push his cock into my throat. I swallow around him, making him choke. His hips lift again, and I open my mouth wider, letting him fuck my throat the way he wants.

His biceps strain as he pulls against the rope, his fists shaking as he bucks his hips. I brace my hand on his thigh and wrap the other around his base, squeezing as I stroke him with my mouth. My hand twists with each movement, making him groan low in his throat.

I smile around his cock as I slide my hand between his thighs. His body trembles, his eyes going wide as I press my finger against his asshole.

"Oh fuck," he shouts. "Kens, love. Fuck." I don't push inside, just tease him. He spreads his legs more, planting his feet flat on the bed, silently begging for more.

I lick down his cock and suck one ball into my mouth, twirling my tongue around it. His back arches off the bed as he pants through his bared teeth. I move my mouth lower, replacing my finger with my tongue.

"Oh my God!" His hips buck as I stroke his cock with my fist, my tongue lapping at him. He pulls his legs back more, giving me more access. I squeeze him, twisting my hand around his head before stroking him to his base. My tongue presses against his ass, harder until it slips inside.

His eyes go wide, his hands jerking on the bindings. His thighs tremble as he holds back his release. I move back to his balls, sucking and stroking them with my tongue. His body is red, sweat coating his abs and chest.

"Kens," he groans my name, and the sound goes straight to my needy pussy.

I lick up the underside of his cock, and take him deep into my mouth again. I take as much of him as I can before gagging, then pull back to focus on his tip. I do it over and over until his body is wound so tightly he looks like he's about to explode. I've never felt a cock this hard before, and I know it's because he's holding himself back, holding in his release until he can come with me.

"Stop," he pants. "I'm close. Stop." I hollow my cheeks, sucking him hard, and the wooden headboard groans as he pulls on it. "Please." He says it again, and again, I smile.

I never thought he'd beg. I never thought he'd give up control. I never thought I'd want it. But now that I have it, I think I want more.

His salty precum coats my tongue and I finally pull off him in a loud pop. He pants, his chest rising and falling exaggeratedly. I slide my panties off and kick them to the floor before lifting up on my knees. His eyes drop to my body as I unhook my bra, tossing it to the floor with the rest of our clothes.

"How badly do you want it, Ez?" I breathe as I slide my hand between my thighs. My head falls back as I slide my fingers over my swollen clit, my other hand cupping my breast roughly.

"So fucking bad," he rasps. "Sit on my face first. I need to taste you. I can see how fucking wet you are." My fingers slide over my clit again, faster and I let out a loud moan. I clamp my hand over my mouth, trying to stifle the sound. "Be as loud as you want. No one will hear anything."

My hips grind against my fingers and I moan louder, my pleasure rising. The wood groans again, and I finally open my eyes, my hand falling from my breast to his thigh to steady myself. I rub my clit faster and my mouth falls open. He mimics me, his brows rising as if he can feel my pleasure too.

"Come for me, love," he whispers. A small whimper leaves my throat. My orgasm teeters on the edge, and my thighs tremble as I force my fingers to move faster. "That's it. Let me see you come."

My nails dig into his thigh as I come, my moan loud. It echoes around the room as my body shudders, my orgasm threatening to make me fall. My hips grind faster, chasing more pleasure as my fingers rub the last of it out of me.

"Fuck," he breathes when I finally collapse, letting my hand fall away. I barely have enough energy to crawl up his body. I press my fingers against his mouth and he happily opens and sucks on them, his eyes on mine as he swallows everything. "On my face."

I hesitate before moving up further. I've never done this before—I never knew people actually fucking did this. I thought it was just a thing in books or porn. But I should've known he'd want this.

I straddle his head and immediately, his lips suction around my clit. My hands grip the top of the headboard as I lift my hips, not wanting to suffocate him.

"Sit," he growls, the vibration against my pussy making me gasp. "All the way down. Ride my face and don't stop until I tell you to."

Somehow, he's taken over again. All my power and dominance has disappeared. He's in control—he's always in control.

Slowly, I lower myself down more, and he lifts his head, pressing his mouth harder against my pussy. My hips roll against his mouth and he growls his approval. His tongue slides against me, my body still riding the aftershocks of my orgasm.

He doesn't slow down or start gently—he eats me like he's starving, like he needs me to survive. My knuckles turn white on the headboard, and my stomach tightens with the promise of another release.

I ride his face like he told me to, using his mouth, his tongue, his nose for my pleasure, not caring about anything but getting off again. My hand falls to his hair and I tangle my fingers in it, roughly pulling it, making him groan. My hand tightens into a fist, and he groans again, the sound of it sending me closer to the edge.

"Almost," I breathe. I press harder against his mouth and his

279

tongue slides inside me. I yelp at the feeling and move my hips back, grinding my clit along his tongue. "Fuck, like that." He holds his tongue still and lets me move my hips back and forth, my clit gliding along his stiff tongue until my release tightens my core.

I cry out, my hands tightening in his hair and around the head-board again. I don't stop riding his tongue, not until my release has passed. I sit back on his chest, my chest heaving as I try to catch my breath.

"We're doing that every fucking day," he says, his mouth and chin glistening. "I need you to ride my face like that until I fucking die." I huff out a laugh and grasp his face between my hands. I press my lips to his, trailing my tongue along them and tasting myself. "Ride my cock now. I'm about to fucking explode."

I kiss him again, then slide down his body. My body still aches, and the bruises have turned an ugly yellow color, but he still stares at me like I'm beautiful. Like he sees past the tattoos, past my basic good looks, and sees me. Really sees *me*.

I hover my pussy above him, gently teasing his tip. He lifts his hips again, barely pressing against my entrance. I rest my hands on his chest and slowly guide him in, letting him stretch and fill me like no one ever has before. I slide down his cock until he's fully inside me, and rock back and forth a few times, letting myself get used to his size.

"So close," he rasps. "So fucking close."

"I'm on the pill," I say as I lift my hips and roughly slam back down. I moan at the hard thrust, and do it again, fucking myself harder on his cock. "Do you want to come inside me, Ez?"

"Fuck yes, I do," he says, nodding frantically. My pussy contracts around him and he grits his teeth together, his jaw flexing under his light stubble. "Do that again." I tighten around him again, and his eyes roll back.

My nails dig into his chest as I ride him, slamming myself down every time, knowing how hard he likes it—how hard I like it.

"Call me your whore," I pant. His eyes are wild as he stares up at me, his body coiling tighter.

"You're my fucking whore," he sneers, baring his teeth. "My dirty fucking slut." My eyes close as another orgasm crests. "Filthy bitch, riding my cock like that. It's all you're good for, isn't it? A warm little cocksleeve for me to fill with my cum?"

"God, yes," I groan, fucking him faster. "More. Don't stop, Ez."

"Just a little fuckhole," he says, panting through his teeth. "My little fucktoy. My needy whore." I cry out as my orgasm hits me and I clamp around him. He fucks me from below, slamming his cock faster into me. "My fucking girl. Say it. Say I own you. Say you're my property."

My mouth opens, but all that comes out is a needy whine. My fingers dig into his pecs more, my orgasm still barreling through my body. Finally, he slams into me and stills.

"Fuck, *Kennedy*," he groans my name, his eyes squeezed shut as he holds himself deep. His biceps bulge as he holds his coiled body up, keeping himself buried as he comes inside me.

Finally, he drops back to the bed, breathless. His eyes flutter open, and we stare at each other for a long moment, then I let out a breathy laugh.

"That was fun," I say as I untie his wrists. He grunts his agreement and rolls his wrists a few times. I lay beside him and rest my head on his chest, sighing as he trails his fingertips lightly down my bare back.

"Why won't you say it?" he whispers, his fingers never stopping. "You're mine. You know you are. So why won't you just say it?"

"Can we not talk about this right now?" I sigh. His hand flattens against my back when I try to pull away from him. He holds me tighter against his side, and I give in, relaxing back against him.

"Just tell me why," he murmurs.

"I'm not ready," I say honestly, and squeeze my eyes shut. "I really like you, Ez. And Ian—Ian thinks you walk on water. But I'm

281

just not ready for that. Not yet." His hand begins moving again, gently stroking in long soothing movements.

"Alright," he says, and I pull back enough to look at him.

"Alright? That's it?" I push my brows together, and he shrugs.

"You're not ready," he says. "It's not off the table. But I know you'll say it one day." I search his eyes and find nothing mocking or insincere in his words.

"That's very mature of you," I say slowly, narrowing my eyes. He laughs again, his body shaking with it. His face softens as he tucks my hair behind my ear.

"I'll wait," he says softly. "For however long it takes for you to say it, I'll wait, Kennedy." He lifts my hand to his lips and gently kisses my palm, then closes my fingers over it, sealing the kiss in. "I'll wait."

Kennedy

A hand slides into my hair, roughly fisting it. I grip the man's wrist, my eyes pleading with him to stop, to let go.

He doesn't.

The crunch echoes in my head, too loud and sickening. He slams my face into the wood again, his mocking laugh sending panic rushing through my chest.

"Ezra!" I scream his name like a prayer, my throat clogged with the gushing blood from my nose. "Kiwi!"

I need him. I need Ezra.

Kiwi.

Him.

I can't survive this without him.

I scream his name again, louder.

I claw at the faceless man's arm again, begging him to stop.

Something crashes and we turn our attention to it.

It's him. On some instinctive level, I know it's him. His body is nothing but a dark form, a silhouette against a fiery sunset backdrop, like Hades rising from the Underworld.

"Ezra!" His name is a broken sound, and his head shifts to the side.

283

There's nothing remotely human about him. Nothing but a monster, a beast, ready to strike, ready to kill his prey.

The man's hand tightens, his snarl ripping from his throat as he bashes my face into the wood again.

Kiwi doesn't do anything.

He just stands there, his body vibrating with his fury. He tries to move, but an invisible force stops him.

I scream for him again, beg for him to save me, to help me.

He tries to take another step, but that wall keeps us separated.

The man suddenly falls, his face lifeless and featureless. A monster.

A true monster.

I try to crawl toward Ezra. He's roaring as he bangs against the invisible shield between us, his body still nothing but a shadow. I claw at the wooden floor, splinters embedding under my nails as I try to move toward him—toward my savior.

A hand slides into my hair, roughly fisting it.

I turn toward Ezra again, but he's disappeared. I scream for him again, my voice not thick with blood anymore.

Then the man slams my head into the wood, and I draw in another breath to scream.

A crash.

We look.

It's a shadowed form—Ezra.

Everything starts over. A constant loop, forcing me to relive my terror over and over and over and—

"Kennedy!"

My eyes snap open with a loud gasp. Hands grip my shoulders, keeping me pinned. Sweat coats my skin as I frantically look around, my breath coming in harsh gasps.

I thrash against the damp sheets, trying to free myself of his hold.

"Mom." I blindly turn toward Ian's voice, feeling a different kind of panic fill my chest. My baby is here. The man is here, too. I have to protect Ian. "Mom, are you okay?" I search the dark room, trying to find him. Where is he? Why can't I see? Why can't I find him?

Then his large, cool hand slides into mine, and I look down, finding him kneeling beside my bed, his eyes so wide and terrified—like a little boy. A broken sob leaves me, and, finally, the hands on my shoulders drop away.

I'm home.

I'm in bed.

I'm safe.

We're safe.

"Ezra," I say, my voice hoarse and panicked. "Where is he? Ezra. Where's—" I drop Ian's hand as I try to scramble from the bed, trying to find him. "Ezra!" Tears pour down my face as hands move back to my shoulders, pinning me to the bed again.

His face comes into focus above mine, his eyes wild and frantic. "I'm right here, love," he says, his voice low. "I'm here. You're safe. I'm right here." He grabs my hand and puts it on his chest, and the steady beat of his heart finally gives me enough peace to take a full breath.

"Ian?" I look down, finding him even more terrified. I swallow the thickness in my throat as I reach for him again. "I'm sorry." My voice is too raspy, too raw. Everything is too raw.

"Are you okay?" he asks again, softly.

"Fine," I breathe. I move my hand from Ezra's chest and wipe my sweaty forehead with my palm. "Sorry."

"Don't," Ezra growls, his voice dark. "Don't apologize."

In a fluid, animalistic motion, he leaps from the bed, a snarl ripping from him as he paces the bedroom. He punches his fist into his hand, muttering to himself. Sweat glistens across his bare chest and abs, his hair a mess of tangled, knotty curls on his head.

"Ez," I whimper. I sit up, and Ian jumps to his feet, putting his hand on my back, helping me. I lean against him and he takes all my weight, his hand a steady pressure on my back. We silently watch Ezra turn into Kiwi, his rage rippling off him in heavy waves.

285

"I need to dig that motherfucker up and shred his fucking body," he snarls. He abruptly turns toward the closet and yanks it open. A hanger snaps as he pulls a shirt from it and slides it over his head. "Gonna dig him up. Gonna kill him again." He's muttering to himself, like he's in a trance. "Gonna desecrate that fucker."

I can't tell if it's Ian or me trembling, or if we both are. We continue watching him spiral into a person we don't recognize. Even the night he saved me, he wasn't like...*this*.

"Ezra," I whisper again. "What are you doing?" His head snaps toward me, his eyes highlighted by the moonlight pouring through the window. They look black.

"I'll be back," he says as he shoves his boots on.

"Don't leave." Ian and I say it at the same time and he stiffens. Slowly, he turns toward us, blinking rapidly.

"What?" he says, tilting his head to the side. Goosebumps ripple over my arms and down my legs. He's a shadow like he was in my nightmare, and I try to breathe through the lingering terror.

"Don't leave us," I repeat, my voice soft. I hear him swallow, and he stumbles back a small step, like the words were a physical blow. "Ez?" I pull the blankets back and hesitate before moving to my knees. "What happened?"

I glance over my shoulder at Ian, finding his head lowered and eyes on the floor. I look back at Ezra, and find his body vibrating. "What happened?" I ask again.

"You were screaming," Ian rasps. "You were screaming for help, and kept saying stop. I've never heard anyone sound like that." I turn back toward him in time to see him roughly wipe his cheek. "Was it—you were dreaming about what happened?" I nod, reaching my hand toward him. He takes it and holds tightly to me.

"You called for me," Ezra says, and I look back at him. Words are lost to me; even as I try to think of something to say, nothing comes. "You were thrashing around and screaming for me, for help, for it to stop." His eyes bore into mine from across the room. He doesn't move forward, like he's scared.

And that's when it hits me.

He *is* scared. He's fucking terrified. They both are. I scared them, my guys.

I did this to them. *I* scared them.

Tears fall freely from my eyes as I double over, clutching my stomach as I sob. No one moves to me. No one touches me. I feel them staring at me. I feel the unsurety flowing from them both. But they don't move.

"I'm sorry," I cry. "I didn't mean to—"

Their weight dents the bed on both sides, then their hands are on me. Ian's on my shoulder, Ezra's on my thigh, their touches bringing me comfort in their own way.

"I didn't—"

"It's okay," Ezra says softly. I shake my head. It's not okay.

I'm not okay.

Is this what I have to look forward to for the rest of my life? Nightmares that wake everyone up and terrify them? Will I always have to look over my shoulder now? Will I always be scared of men that aren't mine?

The little bravado I've found in the last few days is fake. It was all fake before, but now that I know I'm weak, that I can't save myself, that I can't save anyone, it all feels like a sham. I don't know who I am anymore.

If I'm not the bitch, the strong, single mother, the unapologetic woman who takes no one's shit, who am I? Under all the layers of bullshit, who the fuck am I?

"Ian, go to your room," Ezra says, his voice soft. Ian makes a sound of protest, his hand tightening on my shoulder. "I'll come get you if I need help. But please," he emphasizes the word in a way that tells me it's not a request, "go to your room." I feel the hesitation as the seconds pass.

Glancing at the door, I find Enzo hovering in the doorway, looking scared. I smile weakly at him, but he doesn't relax. I nudge Ian with my elbow, and subtly point at Enzo with my chin. Ian follows my gaze, and takes a deep breath.

"Go to your room," I murmur, wanting him to comfort his friend. I scared everyone tonight even though I hadn't meant to.

Finally, Ian kisses my head and rises. It's the first time he's ever done that and it makes more tears burn my eyes. Ezra stays silent until the door quietly clicks shut, then he grabs me and pulls me to his lap. I wrap my arms around his neck as he wraps me up, clutching me to his chest.

"Talk to me," he murmurs as he strokes my back.

"Nightmare," I say, as if that wasn't already obvious.

"Kennedy." It's a reprimand, and for some stupid reason, I feel the disapproval to my core.

"I tried to get to you," I rasp. "In the dream. You were there, but you couldn't get to me. And every time I tried to crawl to you, he would hit me again. You couldn't save me, and I was too weak to save myself."

"I did get to you, though," he says softly. "That was just a dream, love. I saved you. You protected yourself—" I huff out a breath and his body stiffens. "You protected yourself." He says it again, more firmly, and I shake my head.

"I froze," I say. "I was scared, and I froze—"

"Do you think I wasn't scared shitless?" I pull my head away from his chest and peer into his grave face. "Every time I go up against someone, I'm scared. I was scared the first time I got into a fight, and the night you called me—I've never been so fucking terrified, Kennedy. We all get scared. That's okay."

"But you still fought," I say. "I didn't."

"You think you didn't fight?" he says, dropping his voice. "If you didn't fight, you'd be dead right now." I shake my head. "You're the strongest person I know, Kens. I'm not just saying that because I love you, I'm saying it because it's true."

I fold my lips between my teeth, my eyes searching his face for any hint of a lie. But I don't find anything but brutal sincerity.

"Just because you didn't kill him, doesn't mean you're weak," he says, tucking my hair behind my ear. "Just because you called for help doesn't mean you're weak. You used the best weapon in your arsenal —me. I wasn't fighting for myself that night. I was fighting for you."

"I could've shot him," I say, and he shakes his head.

"Have you ever killed someone before, Kens?" I push my brows together, and shake my head. "I never want you to know what it's like. For me, I know I'm going somewhere worse than Hell. You let me do the killing and protecting—you stick to keeping yourself alive until I can get to you. That doesn't make you weak—" He interrupts me before I can say anything. "Say it. Say you're not weak for needing me." I swallow thickly as fresh tears fill my eyes.

"I'm not weak for needing you," I whisper. He gives a hard nod.

"Say you fought back," he demands. "Tell me you're strong."

"I fought back." The words break, but I force myself to push the rest out. "I'm strong."

"Damn fucking right you are," he growls. "Say it again. Say you're strong." I wipe my cheek as a tear falls.

"I'm strong," I say again, my voice thick.

"I'm going to make you say that for the rest of your fucking life," he promises. "I'll never let you forget who you are, understand me? I will never let you fall into self-pity. It's not you. You're strong, and unapologetic, and—and perfect. You're fucking perfect."

I let out a long breath, feeling some of the weight lift from my shoulders.

"I'll get back to myself," I whisper, and he cups my face with his hand, his thumb stroking my cheek.

"You didn't go anywhere," he murmurs. "You just forgot. I'll remind you." I smile weakly, and he brushes his lips over mine, then lets out a harsh breath through his nose. "We need to talk about that fucking boy." My eyes widen.

"Ian? Why?" I ask, alarmed.

"He ran in here when he heard you screaming," he says, shaking his head. "I told him to stay back, and he told me to fuck off." I choke out a laugh, then cover my mouth with my hand. He gives me a firm look, but I see his lips tip up in a mischievous grin.

"So, what did he do wrong?" I ask.

"He ran toward danger—"

"There was no danger," I point out, and he shakes his head.

"There could've been," he says. "He didn't think twice about it and that's not gonna happen again. He needs to listen to me when I tell him to stay put, even if it involves you. It could be life or death. Same goes for you." My smile falls as I nod. He's right. He's not being a dick—he's trying to keep us safe. "It's admirable he wanted to protect you, but—"

"But he's just a kid," I finish, and he nods. "I'll talk to him."

"We," he says, lifting his brows in challenge. "*We* will talk to him." I roll my eyes and nod. "I'm glad he's protective of you. You've done a good job raising him, but—him running toward possible danger fucking terrifies me. I'd fucking die if anything happened to him."

"Me too," I sigh as I scrub my hand across my forehead. He kisses my temple and pulls me back to his chest.

"He's a good kid," he says. "Reminds me a little too much of myself at his age." I snort.

"I doubt that," I say. "You were a heathen."

"How do you know that?" he asks, sounding offended.

"You're a heathen now," I say, tipping my head back to look at him. He looks thoughtful for a moment, then nods.

"Yeah, you're right," he says. "Okay, he's better than me. But still reminds me of myself." I roll my eyes as he presses his lips to mine. "Let's go back to bed, yeah? I'll fight off any nightmares." I smile softly and feel something in my chest shift into place.

This is what love feels like.

Kiwi

I snuck out before Kennedy or the boys woke up this morning. I needed more clothes since I've been living here instead of the clubhouse. So, I grabbed as much as I could fit in a backpack and rode back here.

I hated leaving them, especially after Kennedy's nightmare last night, but I felt something shift between us, something I can't explain. Whatever it was, I think it's a good sign, like we're another day closer to her fully giving herself to me and accepting that I'm here forever.

Slowly, I push the front door open. I try to stay quiet in case they're all still asleep, especially Kens. She needs the rest more than anyone else. Today is her first full day back working both jobs. I want to tell her to quit one and let me take up the slack, but I know she won't go for it. Not yet.

As I step into the little apartment, I sigh when I hear Amy Winehouse blaring from the kitchen. It's the voice accompanying it that makes me pause.

On silent feet, I move through the living room and lean against the wall leading into the kitchen. She's in her silky black robe and one of my shirts. The tattoos on her legs are on full display, and I take them all in slowly. I haven't had the chance to inspect every single one like I desperately want to. Her dark hair is twisted in a clip at the back of her head, some of it falling around her face. Her hips swing in time with the song as she waves the spatula around.

"Ian! Enzo!" she shouts, her head still bobbing to the music. "You're gonna be late!"

Somewhere in the apartment, a door opens and closes, but I'm too enthralled by Kennedy's voice, her body moving, her ignorance to me standing here to look. I couldn't tear my eyes away even if my life depended on it.

She sings louder, belting out the chorus with a voice that causes goosebumps to ripple down my arms. She's amazing. She's amazing at everything she does, but this, singing and dancing and being carefree —this is what she was meant to do.

The boy's footsteps shake the floor as they approach, murmuring and laughing together. They abruptly stop and I slide my eyes to them, putting my finger to my lips, telling them to be quiet. I jerk my head at Kens, and they follow my gaze.

They watch her with me, a small smile on Ian's face. I stare at him watching her and wonder if he realizes how lucky he is. I wonder if he knows how incredible his mother truly is.

"Ian!" she shouts again, sounding slightly annoyed. Carefully, she lifts the pan off the stove and slides scrambled eggs onto two paper plates, then whirls and grabs waffles from the toaster, tossing them on the plate, too. She never falters, her movements fluid and voice solid.

She turns toward the fridge, yanking the door open, then screams. Her wide eyes meet mine as she presses her hand to her heaving chest. We stare back at her, probably looking like a pack of lost puppies. Her face and neck flush crimson, and she tries to shake it off.

"Boys," she breathes, flicking her eyes to them. "Breakfast." She grabs the plates and holds them out. Enzo doesn't hesitate to take it and make his way to the little table, but Ian hesitates.

"You okay?" he asks, and she waves him off.

"I'm great," she says, a little breathlessly. He nods but looks like he doesn't believe her, and takes the offered plate from her.

He sits beside Enzo, closer than I've seen them sit beside each other, and I smile at the sight. They're getting more comfortable navigating the new direction their relationship is going, but more than that, they're getting more comfortable around us.

"Orange or apple juice?" she asks as she dips her head down to look at the fridge. "We have milk, too." She gives me a grateful look, and I wink at her. She's been low on groceries every day I've been here, so I did a quick shop yesterday afternoon, much to her annoyance and appreciation.

"I can get it," Ian says, and she pokes her head above the fridge door, her dark brows furrowed.

"Since when can you get it?" she asks, laughing softly. "Sit. Eat." She glances at me, and I push off the wall to stand closer to her. She's magnetic. "There are eggs on the stove. Help yourself." Her voice is quiet, almost embarrassed, and I flick my brows up. But she doesn't say anything else as she grabs the milk. "Chocolate or regular?" She doesn't look at anyone as she opens a cabinet, pulling out a bottle of chocolate sauce.

"Mom," Ian groans. Finally, I glance at him, finding his face bright red and Enzo snickering beside him.

He's embarrassed she's getting milk for him?

"I'll have chocolate," I say as I step around her, my hand gliding along her waist and lower back. She glares at me over her shoulder, but her lips twitch in a small smile. "Extra chocolatey, love." I press a quick kiss to her temple, and she swats at me.

"Chocolate," Ian mumbles. "I can do it—"

"You never make your own—is it because he's here?" She jerks her thumb at me, and I pause, the eggs sliding haphazardly onto my plate. "Jesus, you're going to make a mess. Get out of the way."

"I got this," I say, shooing her. "Just make our drinks." When her brows lift again, I smile sweetly and add, "Please." The boys laugh under their breath and I smile wider, feeling triumphant.

"Can I have orange juice?" Enzo asks, and it finally breaks her of whatever spell she was under.

"Of course," she says mindlessly.

This morning feels natural. Normal. Like we've done this a million times before.

It's a morning I always dreamed of having when I was a kid. I wish I could've woken up to my mother singing in the kitchen while she made Elaine and I breakfast before school. I wish I could've gotten embarrassed that she was still making chocolate milk for me when I was fifteen.

I wish I could've had *this*.

But I didn't have it, and the next best thing is giving it to Ian. I want to wrap my arms around Kens, move my hips with hers as she sways to the music still playing. I want to kiss her neck and make her sigh as she makes our drinks. I wish I could rest my hands flat against her stomach and hold her to me, breathe her in.

She's still weird about PDA in front of Ian, which I get, but fuck, it drives me insane not touching her. I drop a few more eggs onto my plate, frowning when I notice I've taken most of them. So I put them back into the pan, grab another plate and serve her the larger portion.

"The waffles," I say mindlessly as I slide around her, my hand pressed against her back again.

"I can make them if you give me a second," she mumbles as she stirs the milk.

"They're in the freezer?" I continue, ignoring her. "How many for you? Two?" Her eyes snap to me, her lips parting.

"I—what? No, I'm fine." She waves her hand dismissively. "I had coffee, I'm good."

"Coffee is a drink, not food," I say as I pull the freezer open. "Oh, we have choices. Goody. You want chocolate chip, blueberry, or regular?"

"Mom's are the blueberry," Ian calls, his mouth full of food. I grin wider when she rolls her eyes.

"You're teaming up on me and I don't like it," she says, glaring at the three of us.

"Get used to it, Ms. K," Enzo says, making Ian laugh. I smile to myself as they joke with each other, her eyes on mine, a hidden smile on her brutally beautiful face.

I step around her again, this time purposefully grinding my hips against her ass. She swats at me, and I barely dodge her as I open the box of waffles. She takes the boys their drinks, and they give their thanks as she turns back toward me. I lean on the counter, my arms folded over my chest as we stare at each other.

"Here you are, my love," I say, holding her plate out. She stares at it, looking confused. Slowly, she lifts her eyes to mine, and I push it further toward her. "You made food. Eat."

"There's not enough left for you," she says, glancing at my plate. "You'll be hungry in ten minutes."

"Kens, just eat the damn eggs," I say. "I'm a grown man. If I get hungry in ten minutes, I'll cook something else."

"Ez," she sighs, her shoulders slumping. As she opens her mouth again, the toaster pops and our waffles are ready. I drop them on our plates, and when I look up, I find her still standing in front of me, looking unsure.

Sighing, I grab my plate and side-step her, making my way to the table and setting the plates beside each other. By the time she makes her way over, the boys are done with their food and on their feet, aiming for the front door.

"Tell your mother bye," I call over my shoulder. Everyone pauses, but I ignore them as I slide on to my chair. "And tell her you love her." Again, I'm met with silence. I take a sip of my milk and sigh happily. Extra chocolatey.

"Bye, Mom," Ian says hesitantly. "Love you."

"Love you, too, bud," she laughs. "You have everything you need? Both of you?"

"Yes," he groans, and she laughs again.

"Just gotta check, you know?" I can hear the smile, the love and warmth in her voice, and it goes straight to my chest. "Have a good day. Ez can pick you both up this afternoon, if you want." I glance over my shoulder at her and she gives me a questioning look.

"I don't wanna ride bitch," Ian says and I bark out a laugh.

"I'll have my car," I say around a bite of eggs. "I'll even let one of you drive home." Their faces light up as they glance at each other, then me.

"It's the Camero, right?" Enzo asks, and I nod, grinning.

"Yeah," I say. "Goes zero-to-sixty in five seconds—"

"Dear God," Kens breathes as she drops her head back. "Please keep my kid safe."

"With my life," I vow, putting my hand to my chest. Enzo nudges Ian with his elbow and they have a silent conversation, then Ian nods.

"I forgot," he says. "We need to go to Enzo's place and grab the last of his stuff." Kennedy and I look at each other, and I wipe my mouth with a napkin before turning fully toward them.

"I'll take you by there," I say, and Enzo shakes his head.

"We can go," Ian says. "We'll just walk home."

"Will your dad be home?" Kennedy asks warily.

"No," Enzo says. "He had to work out of town this week." Her throat bobs as she swallows. She glances at me again, and I subtly shrug.

"Call one of us if you need anything," I say seriously, and they both nod. Kennedy's chest rises as she takes a deep breath, then slowly releases it.

"Go," she says after a tense moment of silence. "You're going to be late." She gives each of them a quick peck on the cheek before sending them on their way.

She stares out the window for a moment, her hand on her chest as she watches them. I move behind her, finally wrapping my arms around her and resting my chin on her shoulder. Her hand rests on my forearms as we watch the boys get on the bus, laughing.

"You're a good mom," I whisper. She blinks a few times and shakes her head as she turns toward me. "He's lucky to have you.

They both are." She laughs breathily as she looks at the window again as the bus drives off.

"He's a good kid," she says. "He makes it easy."

"He's a good kid because you're a good mom," I say, and she shakes her head again. "Stop doubting yourself." Her eyes close as she takes a deep breath and nods.

"You really think so?" she asks in such a small voice it breaks my heart. I step back enough to spin her around, planting my hands on her hips as she stares up at me.

"You're an incredible mother," I say seriously. Tears line her eyes and she quickly blinks them away. "He would do anything for you because he knows you'll do anything for him. You love him, and it's a beautiful, real love that a lot of kids never get to feel from their mothers. Don't ever doubt yourself, Kens. Truly good kids don't come around often, but good mothers? They're even rarer."

"Ez," she breathes, understanding blooming on her face. I shake my head as I squeeze her hips, then drop my hands away.

"Let's eat," I say, turning toward the table. She catches my hand, forcing me to stop and look back at her.

"You can talk to me about it," she says quietly, her eyes searching mine. "About anything. I'm here."

"I know," I say, my throat tight. She stares at me for another moment, then takes a deep breath, slowly releasing it.

"Let's eat." She keeps her hand wrapped around mine as she leads me back to the table. In a daze, I sit beside her and stare at the plate of food.

I don't know why right now of all moments it's hitting me that I hate my mother. I don't know why I haven't thought those words before, or ever muttered them. Even after she did all that she did, I made excuses for her in my head but now, watching Kennedy with Ian, I realize that no excuse is a good enough one.

I was a kid who had just lost his twin sister. She should've taken care of me, she should've protected me. She should've protected us both long before the day Elaine died. But she didn't. She was selfish and only ever thought about herself. She's nothing like Kennedy—there's nothing good or redeeming about her.

I stab an egg with my fork and try to ignore the way my hand trembles as I bring it to my mouth. I risk a glance at Kennedy, finding her watching me intently, her face soft. When our gazes meet and linger, whatever senses you get when you become a mother must kick in, because she immediately wraps her arm around my shoulders.

Her arm is too short and my shoulders are too broad—I'm too big and she's too small, but she still holds me. She clutches me tightly, the way only a mother can. And it's not that I even want her to be my mother. It's not that I have mommy issues—well, I do, but who doesn't? It's not that I want a mother's love from her. I feel like I'm not only grieving my sister, but the boy I was then, too. He died right beside her.

Then she whispers three gentle words, and they fill me up in ways I've never felt before and will probably never feel again. Tears line my eyes as she says them again.

"*I have you.*"

I wrap both arms around her as I push my chair back, hauling her into my lap. She sits sideways across my thighs, my head still buried in her neck. My arms tighten until I'm sure I'm crushing her, but she never pulls away. She lightly runs her fingers up and down my back, then up my neck and into my hair, gently finger-combing my waves.

"Thank you," I finally breathe. She nods, her cheek rubbing against mine. "I promise I'm not broken." I pull away from her so she can see my eyes. I need her to know this—I am *not* a broken man. I'm not someone she needs to heal, someone she needs to fix. She gently pushes a curl from my forehead and rubs her thumb under my eye, wiping the wetness I didn't know was there away.

"We're all broken, Ez," she whispers, her eyes flicking between mine. "We just have to find someone who's broken pieces fit with ours."

I press a gentle kiss to her lips, and she rubs her hand down my back. It's a soothing, comforting gesture. She pulls away to study me, and I slide her plate closer, stabbing an egg, then bringing it to her mouth.

She looks startled, but hesitantly opens and lets me feed her. It feels right, taking care of her like this. She's taken care of me, of my unhinged emotions in a way no one ever has. The least I can do is take care of her in a way she's never had either.

"Tell me something," I say. She grabs her coffee and takes a small sip.

"What?"

"I don't know. Something about you." I shrug as I cut her waffle and hold the piece to her lips. She doesn't look as uncomfortable accepting this bite of food. She thinks as she chews, her eyes on the table.

"I was Ian's age when I got pregnant with him," she says.

Alright, that's not what I expected.

"I turned sixteen when I was five months pregnant." She chews on her bottom lip, looking uncomfortable. "I don't really talk about this." I don't say anything. I just let her navigate her thoughts and what she wants to say. "His dad was a few years older. Now that I'm an adult I realize how fucked our relationship was and how much of a fucking predator he was. But at the time, I thought I was cool because an older guy was showing me attention."

"How much older?" I ask, unsure if I want to know the answer.

"He was nineteen, almost twenty." She shrugs, looking uncomfortable. "When I told him I was pregnant, he said I was lying so I could trap him." She laughs humorlessly, shaking her head as she lifts her eyes to the wall behind me.

Memories shadow her face, her sardonic smile falling as she relives her past.

"He worked with my dad at The Berserkers bike shop. When I got pregnant, he was a Prospect. My dad nearly fucking killed him when he found out." Her gaze drops back to mine.

"Is he in Ian's life?" I ask, already knowing the answer.

"No." It's a harsh word. Final. "He's never met him. He never got patched into the club, and left a few years after Ian was born." My mouth opens and closes a few times. I hadn't expected that answer. "After I gave birth, he tried to poke around, but I told him to fuck off. Then a year later, when Dad died, he tried to reach out again, but again, I told him to fuck off. He's not on Ian's birth certificate. He was nothing more than a sperm donor."

"Fuck," I breathe. My arm tightens around her waist. "And you've never dated? You never thought of finding a guy to be Ian's father?"

She glares at me. I don't fully know why she looks so pissed or why that question seemed to hit a nerve, but I wince all the same.

"No," she says tightly. "I've dated over the years, but nothing serious. Ian has been, and always will be, my number one priority. The second a guy showed me he wasn't worthy of my son, I dumped him." She gives me a look, and I swallow hard, reading between the lines.

That kid holds my future in his hands. One word about not liking me, and everything could get ripped away. It's a scary thought, knowing a teenager has that much power, but I understand.

I decide to change the subject, not realizing it might be an even more sensitive topic than his father.

"So, your dad passed when Ian was a baby. What about your mom?" Her jaw clenches, then she clears her throat and takes another sip of her drink.

"My parents divorced when I was a kid. I lived with my mom until I was fourteen, then she decided she was tired of being a mom. I moved in with my dad and stepmother after that. When I got pregnant, she blamed my dad and the club. Then, after he died, she said some awful things and I haven't seen or spoken to her since. She tried to reach out a few years ago, said she's found Jesus, but the damage was done and I hold grudges." She flashes me a grin, but it doesn't meet her eyes.

"Seems we both have shitty mothers," I say, and she nods her agreement. I study her for another moment. "Do you want more kids?" She bites her lip as she shoves her eggs around her plate.

"I've thought about it." She glances at me before quickly dropping her eyes back to her food. "But I've never been with anyone long enough for that to even be a consideration."

"Would you have a kid with me?" I whisper. Her throat bobs before she glances at me again.

"One day," she says just as quietly. "If that's what you wanted."

"I've never wanted kids," I blurt. Her spine stiffens.

"Oh. Yeah. That's fine."

"Wait, no." I let out a breath. "Fuck, I'm not good at this shit. Sometimes I start talking without thinking about what I'm saying. I meant I never wanted kids until I met Ian. Then I realized I was fine being a dad. The more time I've spent with him, with you, the more I've realized it's something I want to share with you. I want a mini-me running around."

"God save us all," she mutters before laughing. "No, the universe will punish you with a girl."

"Punish me?"

"Yeah, for being such a man whore. We'll definitely have a little girl who will be just as crazy as her dad."

"And as beautiful as her mom." I tuck a piece of fallen hair behind her ear as I smile. I can almost hear our future daughter running around, squealing for Kennedy to play with her, for me to pick her up and swing her around.

I can see our future, and, fuck, it's a future I want.

Ian

Enzo's house is exactly as I remember, down to the old pizza boxes stacked in the corner, to the pile of dishes in the sink. His father, thankfully, is nowhere to be found. His worn recliner is still angled in front of the old television, his ashtray full of discarded, half-smoked cigarettes.

"Why are we here again?" I mumble behind Enzo. I follow him down the short hallway to his room. It's like a breath of fresh air when he opens the door.

As much of a wreck as the rest of the house is, his room is spotless. But that's mostly because he barely has anything in his room. All of his important things can fit in his backpack. It makes my heart ache for him, knowing he's had to go without his entire life so his father can have everything.

"I just need the last of my stuff," he says as he moves to his dresser. He opens it and rummages around the mostly empty drawer. "My mom's necklace is in here, and my sketchbook is under the mattress." I lift his thin twin mattress and gently pull his old, worn sketchbook out.

"You need a new one," I say, and he lets out a sharp breath.

"With what money?" he mumbles. My throat tightens, but I force myself to swallow past it.

"I can get you one," I say, and he turns toward me, a small cardboard box clutched in his hand.

"I don't need you buying me shit." His voice comes out harder than I expected, and I push my brows together.

"Why are you like this?" I say, throwing my arm at him. "If I want to buy you a sketchbook, I will, and you'll accept it."

"I'm not a fucking charity case, Ian," he snaps. "I can get it myself, and if I can't afford it, I don't need it. You've already taken me in as a fucking stray. I don't need you buying me anything else."

I take a small step toward him, and he shifts his angry eyes to me. They're lined with tears, and his chin wobbles. He presses his lips together to stop it, but it doesn't. It just makes it worse.

"I'm not a charity case," he says again, his voice thick.

"I know," I murmur. "I never thought you were." His face stays angry. I grab his hand and stroke my thumb over his knuckles.

We're still trying to get used to this new dynamic. We've been friends forever, and sometimes I forget I can touch him like this. I risk another step toward him, anticipating him to retreat. Instead, he drops his head forward, resting it on my chest. I wrap my other arm around him and rub my hand over his back. I've seen Ezra comfort Mom like this, and it seems to help her.

He tries to breathe through his emotions, and I silently let him. There's nothing I can say, nothing I can promise him that will make things better. He'll still be unwanted by his father, and abandoned by his mother. She left when he was ten—plenty old enough for him to remember her, and remember her leaving. His father was a dick before that, but after she left, he got worse.

So much fucking worse.

"I just want to graduate so I can fucking move on," he says. I rest my chin on the top of his head, and he steps closer, wrapping both of his arms around my waist.

"We'll go somewhere when we graduate," I promise, my voice soft. "I'll take you wherever you want to go."

"You'll never leave your mom," he says, and I tighten my hold on him.

"She'll have Ezra. She won't need me. Not as much as you." Finally, a small sob breaks from him, and I press my lips to the top of his head. "It's okay." I don't know what else to say. "It'll be okay."

He bunches my shirt in his fists as he forces himself to calm down. His body shakes as he breathes through his emotions, and I let him.

"You can cry," I whisper, and he shakes his head. He takes another breath, deeper than before, the sound gasping, shuddering, and broken. "Cry."

He tightens his hold, and I feel it—the moment before he lets it out. The moment right before he takes that last breath, the final breath that's holding him together, and just...breaks.

His sob is hard and guttural and breaks my fucking heart. Tears soak into my shirt, and I squeeze my eyes shut, trying to take the pain in his heart away. But I can't. I *know* I can't. And that somehow makes everything worse.

Before this thing between us grew, before we turned it into something real, the fury and hatred I felt for his parents, his father knew no bounds, but now? Now, I want to burn the world down and watch Enzo rise from the ashes.

Rage, searing hot, builds in my chest. I can't stand this, the sounds he's making. I can't fucking stand the pain that's radiating from him, the loneliness I can do nothing to fill, the abandonment, and the million other issues he has because of *them*.

I've known him my entire life, and this is the most vulnerable I've ever seen him. It shreds me apart to know that I could've been there for him like this for years. That if I would've admitted to myself that I was in love with him years ago, maybe things would've been different. Maybe I could've protected him more. Maybe he would've let me protect him.

"I hate him," he cries. "I fucking hate him." He says it with so much conviction I feel it to my core. His sob is violent, and tears burn the backs of my own eyes. I squeeze them shut, trying to stay strong, but it's hard when he's like this. "Why would he do this? What did I do to deserve it?"

"Nothing," I say firmly. "None of this was your fault."

"But—"

"No," I interrupt. He pulls his head away from my chest and stares up at me. "It was not your fault. This is all on him." His face is red and splotchy, and a shadow of stubble coats his jaw. But it's his eyes that hold me captive. They're beautiful, and full of all the colors I love.

He nods, but I know he doesn't believe me. Not really. He might never believe me.

I grip his shoulder, squeezing reassuringly. He gives me a weak smile, his eyes sad. Just so fucking sad. I hesitate for only a moment before moving my hand to his chin and gently gripping it between my thumb and forefinger.

His breath hitches as he flicks his eyes between mine. I give him time to stop me, but he doesn't. He meets me halfway, our lips crashing together in a hard kiss. It's not awkward like it was with Amanda. This doesn't feel forced, it never has with Enzo.

His mouth is frantic, his movements jerky as he reaches for the hem of my shirt. I hesitate, my stomach tightening with anxiety. But I let him drag my shirt off over my head. He pushes me back toward his too-small bed. My legs hit it and I roughly fall to my ass and stare up at him, both of us panting hard.

He gives me a slow grin as he slides his shirt off over his head, tossing it to the floor beside mine. His chest flushes red, and I grip my hands into tight fists to stop myself from touching him. I can see the hard outline of him through his jeans, and a part of me wants to take him out, but another part is terrified. Not only of his reaction, but mine.

What if I hate it? What if he does? What if we take that next step and it breaks whatever *this* is?

But then he presses on my shoulder, and I lie back, my eyes still like saucers as he lies beside me. We turn onto our sides and stare at each other, our breath mixing in the small space between us.

"We don't have to do anything more," I say softly. His hand hovers over me before he lets his fingertips trail down my arm, making goosebumps ripple over my body.

"I think—" He cuts himself off when his hand gets to mine. "I think I want to try something more." I swallow hard, and he smirks at the sound.

"What?" I rasp. His hand slides from my hand onto my hip, his fingers teasing the hem of my jeans.

"I've never done it," he says, then laughs softly. "Obviously. But I've had it done to me a lot. I think I'll know what to do."

"E," I say, drawing the word out, unsure. "It's okay—"

"I know," he says.

His eyes lift to mine again, and I press another kiss to his mouth. He presses his bare chest against mine, and I slide my hand onto his waist, unsure of where to touch him. All I know is that I need to touch him, to feel him, but I don't know where, or how.

I'm still a virgin. He's very much not.

I kiss along his jaw, and nip at his neck. He groans, and the sound nearly makes me come undone. My hand slides down, and I grip his hip. He moves his hips forward, pressing himself against me.

"Ian," he says, and my eyes roll back. He's never said my name like that—*no one* has ever said my name like that.

The front door slams, rattling the walls, and our eyes snap open. He shoots off the bed, tripping and falling to the floor. He throws my shirt at me as he picks his up.

"Lorenzo!" his father calls, and my heart lurches into my throat. "You home?"

"Ah, just a sec, Pop!" he hollers back. "Hurry the fuck up." His voice is a barely audible hiss. The doorknob turns, but I'm still fumbling with my shirt, trying to turn it rightside out again. "Wait. I'm changing."

Enzo launches himself at the door, putting all his weight into it. His eyes are wide as he stares at me, his chest heaving.

"Open the fucking door," his dad snaps. He shoves it, making Enzo lurch forward. He pushes back, slamming it shut again.

"Get in the closet." He points at this closet, and I scramble to it. I slide the door closed as his father pushes the door harder, forcing Enzo to trip and fall forward.

"Who the fuck is in here?" I stare at his father through the slats of the door, trying to calm my breathing. Carefully, I pull my phone from my pocket and call Ezra. I don't know why I call instead of text.

"No one," Enzo says as he straightens. He subtly shifts his body between his father and me. "I was just changing clothes." His father's eyes narrow into thin slits.

"You think I'm stupid?" He scans the room again, his eyes lingering on the rumpled bed.

My hand fumbles with the phone as I pull it from my ear. Ezra didn't answer. Fuck. I type a quick text to him, telling him only three words—*I need you.*

My hands are shaking so badly the phone slides from them to the floor. I swear under my breath as I stoop to grab it.

"Who the fuck is in here?" Enzo's father shouts. I stop moving, half crouched, half standing. His footsteps thud on the carpet and I hold my breath, hoping he doesn't look in the closet. This was a stupid idea. I didn't need to hide. I've been in Enzo's room a million times.

"Wait, Dad," Enzo says, his voice shaky. "It's—no one's here."

But it's too late.

The closet door flies open and I stare into Enzo's father's black eyes. He blinks at me, a moment of confusion on his face. Then understanding filters in and fury like I've never seen fills his eyes.

Enzo tries to push himself between us, but his father shoves him away as he grabs my shirt. I step on my phone, hearing it crunch under my sneaker. He hauls me roughly from the closet, and Enzo rushes to my side, trying to get in front of me.

I block him with my arm, forcing him behind me. His father laughs humorlessly before spitting something so vulgar and vile at us, it makes me wince.

"Really, Lorenzo?" his father says, throwing his arm at me. "Couldn't've had a girl in here like every other boy your age? You had to have—" His lip curls in disgust as he stares at me. "A *boy*?"

"It's not what it looks like," Enzo rushes out. His body trembles violently, and I want nothing more than to comfort him, but I can't right now. I sway back and forth on my feet as I track his father.

Ezra's words from the first day I met him come floating into my head.

Can you back your shit up, kid?

I never thought I could, not really. I knew I'd go down swinging protecting Mom, but this feeling of wanting to protect Enzo is the strongest thing I've ever felt before. At this moment, I come to terms with my fate.

I will die to protect Enzo.

If that's what it takes, I will do it so he can get away, so he can be safe.

Fear doesn't take root in my chest like I expect it to. Instead, a calm sort of rage settles there. I stand taller, squaring my shoulders as I glare down at his father.

My arm is still out, blocking Enzo from moving forward at all. His father slowly shifts his eyes to me, and I lift my chin higher, a clear challenge. A cruel smile curves his lips, and I feel my own mouth curl, surprising him as much as myself.

"So, it *is* what it looks like," his father says. I shuffle forward a small step, shifting my body between Enzo and him more.

I don't know if Ezra got my text or not, or if he even knows where I am. He knows I was coming here after school, but he doesn't know where Enzo lives. And even if he did, it doesn't matter. It'll be too late by the time he gets here.

"You should leave, E," I say, keeping my eyes on his father. His brow lifts.

"*E?*" he asks mockingly. An ugly sneer contorts his face before spitting out more vile shit. I inhale sharply, my rage threatening to boil over.

"Dad, calm down," Enzo says placatingly. "It's not what you think. We're—we were just—"

"Spare me the details." He holds his hand up, his eyes still on me. His other hand tightens into a fist and I let mine tighten, too. His eyes drop to my fist at my side, and he smiles again.

"You've known Ian forever," Enzo says, his voice shaking. "It's not like that. We're just friends." It's like a knife to the heart hearing those words come from him, but I know it's the safest thing to say right now.

"Then why was he in your closet?" He lifts his brows. "I'm not dumb, son. I've been your age. Where do you think I hid?" I swallow hard, still tracking him, anticipating his next move.

"It's not—he was helping—" He's floundering, and there's no way for me to save him.

It's exactly as it looks. I was hiding in his closet. It looks...like a boyfriend hiding from his partner's parent.

"This is what you do at his house?" His eyes return to me, disgust burning bright. "I don't give a shit what his mother lets you do over there, but under my roof? I don't allow shit like this." He waves his finger between us. "You wanna play bitch to him, fine. But find somewhere else to do it."

"That was the plan," I say, and his father's eyes snap to mine.

"Ian," Enzo hisses, but I ignore him.

"We're packing his shit. He's never coming back," I say, unable to keep the smile from my lips.

"You were trying to run away, son?" he asks Enzo, and I snort, drawing his attention to me again.

"It's hardly running away," I say. "It's more like running from you, and finding protection." His father's eyes turn hard.

"What's that supposed to mean?" he asks.

We've never brought this up. All the times I've been here and ignored the fighting in the other room, the way I always had to pretend like I didn't notice the bloodstains on Enzo's upper lip from his father breaking his nose. This was always the dirty secret no one brought up.

But now I don't give a fuck.

I'm too far gone to care anymore. I'm too pissed off that he's been hurting my friend to care.

"You know what it means," I sneer.

He steps toward me, and I mimic his movement, moving closer to him. I'm a few inches taller than him, so I look down my nose at him, wanting him to feel small. My chest inflates, and I feel like I'm on top of the fucking world, like nothing could take me down.

Without warning, his fist connects with my jaw. Pain shoots through my head as it snaps back. Enzo lets out a scream, and it echoes in my head. I blink a few times, trying to right myself. No sooner than I'm steady on my feet does he land another punch.

I cry out this time, bringing my hand to cover my face as blood gushes from my nose. He jams his fist into my stomach, and I double over, grabbing it. Faintly, I hear Enzo talking, *begging*, but I don't know what he's saying.

"You wanna come into my house and disrespect me like this?" his father snarls.

I shoot my fist up, catching him on the underside of his jaw, making his head snap back. He grunts out a breath as he grabs his jaw. It's the first time I've ever punched anyone, and it hurt way more than I expected.

He tries to punch me again, and I barely dodge it. I punch his face, and one of his teeth slices through my knuckle. I hiss at the pain and shake my hand out. That was a mistake.

He hits my face, and this time, something crunches. I blindly push him away, but he brings his knee up, hitting me between my legs. My eyes cross at the pain, and I fall to my knees, dropping my hands from my face to cup myself.

He spits more words at me, but I can't hear past the roaring in my head. Another punch lands on my face, and my jaw snaps to the side. Another, and I fall back, landing on the floor.

My vision is hazy as I try to stay alert, stay awake.

Enzo.

I can't pass out, not when he needs me. I croak his name, blindly reaching for him. But I can't feel him, I can't see or hear him.

"Enzo," I rasp. But it sounds like I'm in a wind tunnel.

A shadow looms over me, and my eyes droop before I snap them open. The form is blurry, but I know who it is. I anticipate the next blow, but it never comes. Instead, another figure tackles the shadow to the side and a loud crash drowns out the roar.

I try to sit up, but I can't. Blackness invades the edges of my vision, but I push it away as I try to sit up again. Crashing and banging surrounds me, and a scream, one like I've never heard before, one full of anger and rage and hate, fills the room.

It's the last thing I hear before I pass out.

Kiwi

Axel washes the blood from his hands, letting the red water flow toward the drain. I stare at it, a sick sense of pride swelling inside me. I've never seen anyone kill someone the way Ax killed Ginger. He was ruthless and brutal in a way I can only aspire to be. It was beautiful, like watching a ballet.

But it's the grim satisfaction on his face that has me pausing.

Is that how I look after I kill?

I've never thought about it before—I've never really cared. But something has changed. Maybe it's Kennedy. Maybe it's Ian. Maybe it's because I have a family now I don't feel the need as strongly anymore. At least when it comes to killing strangers. If it came down to killing someone trying to hurt my family, that's a different story.

But that's still not normal, is it? I can't expect Kennedy to trust me, to ever love me, if I'm still unhinged. If I still want to kill.

Maybe I do need therapy.

I clear my throat, and Axel shifts his eyes to me. We're still in the kill room, Bash and Reid in a hushed argument on the other side of the room. Ryder and Gage, one of the Nomads, are taking care of Ginger's body.

"How do you feel?" I ask, and he blinks at me.

"What?" he says, then shakes his head. "I mean, I—I'm fine, I guess. The threat to my baby is gone." I analyze his words.

"So, it's fine to kill someone who's threatening your family?" I ask, and he shrugs as he dries his hands on a towel. He tosses it in the steel sink and turns toward me, leaning his hip against it as he folds his arms over his chest.

"I don't think it's fine," he says slowly. "But I don't give a shit. I'll go to prison, or Hell, wherever, if it means I protected Koda and Skye." I nod, my eyes narrowing.

"And what does Koda think?" I ask. He tilts his head to the side, his messy waves falling across his forehead.

"She's protective of Skye, too," he says. "What are you asking?" I twist my lips to the side.

What *am* I asking?

"I don't know," I admit. "She doesn't care about this?" I jerk my head to the bloody floor. Axel glances at it, grimacing slightly.

"I don't think she loves it," he says. "But she'd rather know Skye is safe, even if I don't have clean hands."

"But—" I let out a sharp sigh. "Does it make you a bad person? To kill someone?" His head rears back.

"That's a new one," he says, laughing awkwardly. "You find Jesus or something?"

"No," I say, shaking my head. "I found Kennedy." His face softens and understanding fills it.

"Oh," he says, smiling softly. "I think if you're killing just to kill, you're probably a psychopath. If you're killing for a reason, then no. I don't think it makes you a bad person to protect your family."

"What if Skye finds out?" I ask, and he takes a deep breath.

"Well," he runs his hand through his hair, "I'd hope she'd understand that anything I've ever done was to protect her."

I nod a few times. "I think I'm over killing and torturing people," I say, and he chokes on a laugh.

"Just like that?" he asks, amusement filling his face. I shrug as I slide my hands into my pockets.

"Yeah," I say. "Unless I'm protecting my girl or our boy, I don't think I need to kill anyone again." He nods a few times, his smile spreading.

"That's probably the most sane thing you've ever said," he laughs. My phone vibrates against my palm and I pull it out, finding a number I don't know calling me.

"Gotta take this," I say, and Axel jerks his chin at me as he turns toward Bash and Reid. I walk to the door and slip into the hall before answering.

"Kiwi?"

"Yeah? Who's this?" I ask, my voice hard.

"Enzo," he says. His voice is frantic and dread pools in my stomach. "It's—Ian—my dad."

"Where are you?" I ask as I take the stairs up three at a time. I grab my keys on the way out the door.

"My house," he says. "My dad came—" There's shouting, and I grit my teeth. "Stop!" My blood turns to ice at the terror in his voice. The line goes dead as I fling my leg over my bike. I turn the engine on as I call Kennedy. She answers on the first ring.

"Hey," she says, sounding soft and light.

"Where does Enzo live?" I ask as I take off out of the parking lot.

"What?"

"Enzo, baby. Where does he live?" I try keeping my voice light, but I can't. Not when I'm not even sure what I'm riding in to.

She rattles off an address, and I mentally look at a map of the city. It's not far from the clubhouse. "Why? What's going on?" I'm reluctant to tell her. A part of me wants to lie and say I'm just picking them up, but I can't lie to her. Not about this.

"Enzo called me and said something's going on with his dad and Ian." She makes a choking sound, and it makes my heart squeeze.

"Ian?" she repeats. "He's hurt?"

"I don't know," I say. "I'm heading there now."

"Come get me," she says hurriedly.

"It'll take too long. I need to get to him." There's silence, and I hold my breath. I'll argue with her on this one. I'm not leaving him alone longer than necessary, even if it's to get her. I'd love to see what she'd do to Ezno's father, but another time, when our boys aren't in danger.

"Fine," she breathes. "I'm at The Crossroads."

"Alright," I say. "Don't worry, love. You trust me, right?"

"Yes," she says, and shock ripples through me at the lack of hesitation.

"Then trust that I'll protect him," I say.

"I do," she says, her voice thick. "Please, Ez—"

"I know, baby," I say as I turn onto Enzo's street. My stomach coils tighter as I scan the house numbers. "I'll protect him."

"I know," she says. "Ez—I—"

"I'm here," I say as I stop in front of the house. "I gotta go."

I hang up before she can say anything else, and turn the bike off before sliding off it.

I stalk up the driveway, my eyes lingering on the beaten up truck parked there. I don't bother knocking, I just kick the front door open. The wood splinters and flies everywhere as I stride inside. Immediately, I hear a fight from the back of the house.

I've never moved so fast in my fucking life.

I rush down the hall, and the sight in front of me makes me stop in the doorway, my heart stuck in my throat.

Ian, face bloody and eyes closed as he lays on the floor, but it's Enzo that has my blood turning cold.

The hatred in his face is something of nightmares.

He's straddling his father, his hands wrapped around the man's throat. His face is red, and his eyes are bulging, tears dripping from them. Enzo's hands and arms shake as he strangles his father.

"I hate you," he cries, his voice choked. He lifts his father's head, then slams it back onto the floor. "Hate you!"

His voice makes me move. I'm at his side in an instant. I wrap my arms around him and pull him off his father. He inhales a huge breath, but doesn't move.

Enzo thrashes in my arms, screaming and clawing at me to get back to his father. I drag him away, hissing as his nails break my skin.

"Enzo," I say, but he's too far gone.

"I'm going to fucking kill you!" He screams the words with his whole body, and chills ripple over my body.

I fling him into the hallway and step in front of him when he scrambles forward. His eyes lift to mine and whatever he sees in my face makes him pause.

"Ian," I say, and his eyes flash.

"My dad," he rasps. "He—we were—"

"I need to get him out of here," I say, and he nods. It doesn't matter what they were doing, why his father was here. I just need to get them out of here. I glance around. "You have a car or something? I can't take you both on my bike." He shakes his head.

"I don't have my license." I sigh as I nod.

"Stay here," I say.

Turning back toward the room, that same dread pools in my stomach when I see Ian lying motionless on the floor. The only reason I haven't torn Enzo's father apart yet is because Ian's breathing is steady.

He's alive.

And that's the only thing keeping me from going on a killing spree.

I kneel beside him, ignoring Enzo's father's gurgling as he tries to find his breath again. I wince at the blood on Ian's face, at the weird directions his nose is going, at the busted lip, the bruise already forming on his jaw.

"Hey, buddy," I say gently.

I don't know if it's best to wake him up or not, or if I even can wake him up. I stroke his bloody hair away from his forehead, but he doesn't stir. I don't know if I can pick him up. I glance over my shoulder at Enzo, finding him chewing his thumb as he stares at us, his eyes flicking between Ian and his father.

Pulling my phone from my pocket, I hesitate before calling Bash. This is what I have my Brother's for—to help when my fucking kid almost gets himself killed.

"Yeah?" he answers gruffly, and I roll my eyes.

"I need your help." That's it. That's all I need to say for him to round up the guys and head for me. "It's Ian. I don't have time to get into it. But I need you, Reid, and Ax." I give him the address, and he promises they'll be here in a few minutes.

After I hang up, I notice the missed call and text from Ian, and my stomach bottoms out.

I need you.

That's all the text said.

This is the third time I've let my family down.

First Elaine.

Then Kennedy.

Now Ian.

When will I protect the people I love instead of getting to them after they've already been hurt?

I go back to stroking Ian's head. Enzo kneels beside me, his hands trembling as he grabs Ian's hand. I stare at the contact, shocked he's touching him in front of me.

"This wasn't supposed to happen," Enzo whispers. I stare back at Ian, gently coaxing him awake. "He wasn't supposed to do this."

"What?" I ask. When he doesn't immediately answer, I look at him. Tears stream down his face as he stares at Ian, and my initial rage settles at the sight. "What happened?"

"We came to pack my stuff," he says, wiping his nose with the back of his hand. "Things got—we—" He gives me a pleading look, and I nod in understanding. "Dad got home and found Ian in the closet. He said things—" He lifts his gaze to his father, and that hatred comes back to his face. "Then he started hitting Ian. When Ian fell, I tackled my dad and— and you saw the rest."

Ian's chest rises and falls in steady breaths, and I rest my hand on it, trying to bring comfort to myself. Enzo's father groans, and my head snaps up. I zero in on him as I climb to my feet.

I step over Ian and move toward the man. He pushes himself up and leans against the wall. His eyes are closed until he senses me, then he opens them.

"Who are you?" he spits, his voice hoarse.

"You hurt my son," I snarl. His eyes widen, but surprisingly, he stays silent. "You're fucking dead."

I bring my foot up and kick him square in the center of the face. He cries out at the pain, but I don't care. I'm going to kill him with my bare hands.

I brace my hand on the wood paneled wall as I bring my foot up again. I don't bother waiting for him to lower his hands before I stomp him again. And again. And again.

He slumps to the floor, and I keep bringing my foot down on him. I don't stop until he's unrecognizable. Faintly, I hear someone curse from the doorway. It's too deep of a voice to be one of the boys.

"Kiwi," Bash says, but I ignore him as I continue stomping on Enzo's father's face. Again and again, I stomp on him until I'm positive he's dead.

With a final blow, blood and bone and tissue fly in different directions, splattering on the wall and my jeans. I lean against the wall, breathing heavily. I let myself calm down before I turn toward the guys.

Enzo is staring up at me with wide eyes, his mouth slightly open. His hand is still clutching Ian's, his hold so tight his knuckles are white.

Maybe I got carried away. Maybe I shouldn't have killed him in front of Enzo, but he's mine now, too. I don't want his father to ever hurt him again.

And now he can't.

"You're welcome," I say, giving a shallow bow.

"Fuck," Reid chokes. I glance up at him, grim amusement on his face. He can pretend he's not as fucked in the head as me, but he is.

He totally is.

"We need to get the boys out of here," I say. Bash takes in the scene around us. "And we need to clean this shit up."

"Nothing leaves this room," Axel says. Enzo tilts his head back to look at the giant man looming over him. "Do you understand me? Nothing. Leaves. This. Room." Enzo nods frantically, his mouth opening and closing.

"Nothing," he repeats. "Never. No." He looks around at us towering him and I know we're giving the kid a complex, so I kneel beside him. "I promise I won't tell anyone. I—I didn't even see what happened. I—"

"It's okay, kid," I say. His shoulders slump, and I rest my hand on his back. "Sorry about that. I get carried away sometimes." His eyes stay like saucers as he stares at me.

"Understatement of the fucking year," Reid mutters, and I flip him off.

I stare down at Ian, relief flooding me when he barely stirs. Relief seems to flood Enzo, too. His face relaxes as he clutches Ian's hand to his chest. I glance up at the guys, but no one says anything. Bash lifts his brows in silent question, and I dip my chin. He nods in understanding, then sighs.

"This is such a fucking mess," he says as he runs his fingers through his hair. "I'll call the Nomads. Fuck, Ry is gonna kill us for this."

"He'll get over it," I snort.

"He'll hold this grudge to the grave," Axel says. "We already took him away from Madi and Izzy all day. Now this? He's going to kill us." I shrug.

"Don't give a shit. I need to take my boys home." I look between them, and Reid tosses me his keys.

"Don't get blood on the seats," he says. "It's a bitch to get out."

Kennedy

I stare at my phone as I pace behind the bar, my thumb between my teeth. I've already chewed the nail as short as it'll go. The waiting and not knowing is killing me.

Finally, it lights up and I let out a frantic sound as I reach for it. I fumble it before answering and pressing the phone to my ear.

"Is he okay?" I rush out.

"I need you to listen, okay?" Ezra says.

My stomach drops.

"What?" My hands shake. "How bad is it?"

"He's alive, okay?" he says. I clutch the counter as my world tips. "He's alive."

"He's—Ian." I let out a choked sob, drawing Otis' attention.

"I got there too late, but he's alive. He's—"

I throw my phone against the wall. A pained sound leaves me as I clutch my rolling stomach. I crouch, bringing my knees to my chest. Tears stream down my face as a hole opens in my chest. I dig my fist into my stomach, trying to staunch the ache.

He's alive, I tell myself. But Ez was too late. He was too late. He —Ian's alive. But he was too late.

"Kennedy!" Otis rushes to me. "What the fuck—"

"Ian!" I cry, my eyes squeezed shut. I can't open them. Everything is spinning, toppling out of control.

Arms wrap around me, and I don't know or care who it is. I press my face against their chest as I sob.

"What happened?" Otis asks, his voice too gentle for such a giant, scary man. "What the hell happened?" I shake my head. I can't say it. If the words leave my mouth, everything will be real.

"Are you fucking kidding me?" Archer's voice slices through the air. "Fuck. Fuck, yeah I'll take her."

My body feels boneless as I slump forward, folding in on myself.

"Shit, Kens," Otis says, gritting his teeth. "Come on. Get up."

My baby. Ian. He's hurt—or worse.

No.

Ezra said he's alive.

But for how long?

How could I let this happen?

How could *he* let this happen?

A hand lands on my back, and it rubs small circles. Another sob rips from me at their touch. Gently, they push my hair to the side, exposing my face.

"Kens, babe. Kiwi has him at home," Archer says softly. "Come on."

His words barely register.

"He's home?" I rasp as I turn my head, finally opening my eyes.

"He's alive," he says, just like Ezra had. "He's going to be okay."

ARCHER HALF CARRIES ME, half drags me up the stairs. My knees are too weak to carry myself, and I'm terrified at what I'm about to see. On the ride over, I calmed down enough to stop crying hysterically. But now that I'm home, everything is about to hit me again.

"I can't," I breathe. Archer's arm tightens around me.

"Your man has your boy," he says sternly. "You know Kiwi killed the fucker who touched his son."

"Ian—" I choke on his name. "He's not his—"

"Yeah," Arch says. "He is."

We get to the porch and I stare at the door. I notice every chip in the paint, every scratch and dent for the first time. When did it get so bad?

Suddenly, it swings open, and blood is the only thing I see. Ezra's covered in it. On his face, his clothes, his boots. Everywhere.

"Ez," I croak. He reaches for me as I fall into him. His arms feel better than Archer's. They feel right. Safe. "Where is he?"

"In bed," he says against my hair. "Axel and Blade are working on him." I nod against his chest, trying to ignore the blood I know isn't his. "Baby, I need you to listen to me." He pulls away and smooths my hair from my face. "He's real fucked up. His face—" His eyes lift above my head, then Archer's hand lands on my back. "Enzo's dad fucked him up, but it looks worse than it is, okay? His nose is broken, and he has bruises, his lip is busted—"

"What the fuck happened?" I cry as I step back. Archer's chest holds me up, but doesn't bring any comfort.

"I was late," he says. "I—he called me, but I didn't hear my phone. But I got to him, and he's okay. He's alive—"

"You keep saying that like it matters!" I shout, and he winces. "I don't care that he's alive! He shouldn't have been hurt in the first place."

"You're right," he says, dropping his head forward. "I'm sorry."

"He's my fucking baby, Ez," I say, my voice breaking.

"I'm sorry," he says again.

He stays staring at his feet, and I wait for him to say something else, something to fix this, but he doesn't. I step around him, and he lets me.

That breaks me more than anything. He doesn't reach for me, or try to stop me. He just lets me walk alone to Ian's room.

"You shouldn't be seeing this," Axel says. For a moment, I think he's speaking to me, but then I realize he can't see me. And I can't see Ian. Everyone is surrounding him, blocking him from me. A territorial rage fills me, one only a mother can have, and I step forward.

"I'm fine, Ax," Koda says, and I stop. Her eyes are trained on the bed—on Ian. Axel lets out an irritated breath but doesn't argue. Blade is by his face, crouched over him, his hands moving quickly. Koda hands him items I don't know the name for.

"Is he okay?" I ask, my voice smaller than I'd ever heard. Koda's head snaps up and when her eyes meet mine, tears fill them.

"He will be," she says.

"Why did Kiwi let you in here?" Axel grumbles. "Kiwi! Come get your—"

"I need to see my son," I say. His gaze drops to mine, his lips tight. "You're lucky I'm not ripping you away from him. And the only reason I'm not is because, for whatever reason, you're helping him."

"For whatever reason?" He tilts his head to the side. "You're one of ours. He's one of ours. We take care of our own, Kennedy."

I don't try to correct him. We're not one of them.

"Baby," Ezra says as his hand lands on my back. "Blade is cleaning him up."

"I can see that," I say. I shift my glare at him. His eyes look... broken. For once, they're not full of humor, mischief, self-loathing, bloodlust. He's just broken. And it shatters the rest of my sanity. "Ez."

"I know," he says.

But he doesn't know. He doesn't know because I don't know. I don't know what the fuck I'm feeling or thinking or what I want to say.

"Ms. K." I whirl around, finding Enzo shoved in the corner. Rage fills me, but Ezra's hand tightens.

"He won't move from that spot," he says in my ear. I take a deep breath.

"Hey, kid," I say as softly as I can.

323

"I'm sorry," he blurts. Tears fill his raw eyes, and I shake my head as I step toward him. "I should've—I'm so sorry, Kennedy."

It's the first time he's ever said my name, and it's like a punch to the gut.

"Baby, stop," I say. "Come here." I hold my arms out, but he shakes his head.

"I—I ruined everything. I'm sorry. I'll leave when I know Ian's okay. I won't come back—"

"Lorenzo," I snap, and his mouth shuts. "You are a part of this family. You're not going anywhere." From the corner of my eye, I see Ezra give a firm nod of agreement.

"You're stuck with us, kid," Ezra says.

Enzo wraps his arms tighter around himself as he pushes into the corner more. Tears drip freely from his eyes, and it's like no matter how hard he tries, they won't stop.

He looks so young, so scared and lost. It's that moment I remember he's still a baby—they both are. They're just boys, no matter how deep their voice gets, or how much they play like grown ups.

They're just kids.

Ian groans from the bed, and immediately I move toward him. Axel steps back and holds his hand out for Koda. She takes it as she carefully walks across the bed. He grabs her and lifts her off the bed like she weighs nothing. She gives him a look, but he doesn't look apologetic for manhandling her.

A sob lodges in my throat when I see Ian.

Blood soaks his sheets, and his shirt is ripped open. Bruises have already formed on his arms, chest, and face, but it's the way his nose juts in different directions, and his bottom lip busted in half, that has me crumpling.

Someone's arm wraps around my waist before I can fall to the floor. I look up, finding Axel's golden eyes boring into mine. Something passes between us, an understanding that no one else can fully understand. It's a pain, a fear, only another parent can understand and sympathize with.

"He's going to make it," he says firmly. "He fought back." Reluctantly, I look toward Ian's hand. He's right. His knuckles are busted open and red.

"Of course he did," I choke. Another arm around my waist and Axel immediately lets go. I don't have to look to know it's Ezra.

"He's a strong kid, baby," Ez says.

"He needs to be in the hospital," I say, wiping my face. Everyone glances at each other. "What?"

"We can't take him to the hospital," Axel says, and I blink at him.

"Why not?"

Again, silence fills the room. Ezra clears his throat and I turn my gaze to him.

"I killed him," he says. My mouth opens and closes a few times, my words completely lost. "I killed Enzo's father. I should've kept him alive so I could torture him for the rest of my life." When he looks at Ian, his face morphs into a bloodthirsty expression I've only seen once—at the bar when he was saving me.

"What does that have to do with going to the hospital?" I ask.

"They'll ask questions," Axel says. "Questions we won't have an answer for. Since he's a minor, they'll want the cops involved, and—"

"And Ez could go to jail." I run my hand over my head as I let out a breath.

"I'm sorry," Ezra says, and I shake my head.

"Why did he do this?" I ask. Silence fills the room again, then Enzo speaks.

"My dad caught us together," he says quietly. I turn toward him, finding him looking even more terrified than before. His wide eyes frantically flick around the room, taking in the massive men around us.

"He caught you together?" I repeat, and he nods.

"We weren't doing anything like that," he says quickly, and I almost smile. "But I made him hide in the closet when my dad got home. It was my fault. I shouldn't have taken him home with me—I didn't know he'd be back today. I thought he was leaving—"

"It's not your fucking fault," Ezra growls. "This is all on your father." Enzo's chin trembles, but he nods. I can tell he doesn't believe the words. He'll never believe the words.

I take a deep breath and turn back toward Ian. He groans again, and I grab his hand.

"I'm here, bud," I say softly. His eyes barely flutter open, and I choke out a sob. I force myself to smile through it. "Hey, baby."

"Mom," he breathes. Blade moves out of the way, letting me get closer. I kneel beside the bed and gently brush his black hair from his forehead, trying to ignore the way his pale skin is stained with his blood.

"I'm here," I say. "I'm right here. I'm not going anywhere." He barely nods, his face scrunching in pain, before he relaxes into sleep again. I press a gentle kiss to his forehead, letting my lips linger.

It's not until Ezra kneels beside me, his hand covering mine and Ian's, that I realize everyone except Enzo has cleared from the room. My eyes meet Ezra's, and he gives me a grim smile.

"He's going to be okay," he says, and I nod. "Axel says he'll have a few scars, but he'll be okay." I stare back at Ian, taking in his swollen face.

"He'll love the scars," I say. "He'll be just like you, Ez."

There's a beat of silence before he tightens his hand around us.

"God help the kid."

Kennedy

I listen to Ezra's hard footsteps as he walks through the dark apartment. Ian's door opens, then Ezra's deep rumble fills the silent space, telling him goodnight. I stare up at the ceiling, my hands resting on my belly.

It's been a week since it happened. Ian is healing quickly, and he wasn't as injured as I'd initially thought, but even a paper cut is too much.

"Night!" Ezra calls as he shuts Ian's door. Enzo grunts from the living room and my lips twitch into a small smile. The boys are still grumpy we won't let them sleep in the same room anymore.

He walks into the bedroom and kicks the door shut before he leans against it, folding his arms over his chest. I turn my head to stare at him, and he stares back. His eyes search mine, and mine search his.

We're on shaky ground. I still haven't told him I love him, and we've barely had time to do anything except kiss. I know it's weighing on him—it's weighing on me, too. But I just don't have the mental or emotional energy to go down that path with him right now.

But there's a nagging voice in the back of my head telling me I'm using this as an excuse to not take that last step with him. It's telling me I'm trying to protect myself from getting hurt. But if I never take the chance, if I never just say it, I'll still get hurt. I'll lose him if he doesn't think he has me. Losing Ezra would be the nail in my coffin. I don't think I could survive it.

"Hey," he says softly.

"Hi," I say. "The boys okay?"

"All good." He stays leaning against the door, and it makes me uneasy. He scans my face again, and I hold my breath, waiting to hear what he has to say. "Are *we* okay?"

"Yes," I blurt without thinking, then close my eyes. Taking a deep breath, I open them and sit up. I pat the bed beside me and his eyes narrow before he sits beside me. "No. I think—" My eyes flick between his. "I don't think we're okay."

He lets out a breath, his shoulders slumping forward, defeated. I rest my hand on his knee, and he covers it with his own. I lean against him, pressing and holding my lips against his shoulder.

"I'm so sorry," he says, his voice thick. "I am so fucking sorry, Kennedy. I know I fucked up. I should've had my phone on loud. I should've been there to protect him, and I wasn't." He pinches between his eyes, and looks at me. His thick lashes are damp, and his eyes red.

Suddenly, he slides from the bed to his knees and I blink, startled. "Ez," I say, reaching for him, but he moves out of my reach. "Come here." He roughly shakes his head, then clears his throat.

"Let me—" He rests his hands on the bed as he stares up at me. "I'm on my knees begging forgiveness, Kennedy."

My throat closes completely.

"I don't deserve it. After everything I've said and done to you, I don't deserve you. I should've never called you a bitch when we were fighting. I should've never left that night. I—I should've been at the bar. I should've been with Ian. I should've protected you both, and I couldn't. I didn't." His words are falling from his mouth quickly, and his breathing is ragged and uneven.

"Ez, baby," I say as I crawl toward him. He pushes away again, not letting me touch him. I kneel at the edge of the bed and stare down at him.

"I should've protected you and our boy," he says as he wipes his face. A small, choked sound leaves me at the words—*our boy*. I don't think it's until this moment that I realize, yeah, Ian is his. Maybe not by blood, but he's Ezra's son in all the ways that matter.

"It's okay," I say, and he shakes his head again.

"It's not." He wipes his face again, and it shatters me. "It's really not. I've given you no reason to ever trust or love me. I'm nothing but a—a—"

"Don't," I breathe, but he ignores me.

"*Freak*," he says. "But I'm trying. I'm trying to change. I'm trying to be better. I'm trying to figure out the right way to be your man and his father. I'm trying, Kennedy."

"I know," I whisper. "You're already perfect, Ez. You don't need to change for us. Just be you. Just be there for us."

"I've let this family down twice." He holds up two fingers. "I can't ever let it happen again."

I slide from the bed and kneel in front of him. He doesn't retreat from me this time. Instead, he slumps forward, but doesn't touch me. I rest my hand on his knees and lean my forehead against his, my eyes closing. His breath is warm and minty against my mouth, and it brings me a weird comfort.

"I love you," I whisper. His body goes rigid. "I'm in love with you, Ezra King."

He doesn't say anything for a moment, and I pull away to look at him. He lifts his head and stares into my soul, his eyes blazing and teary.

"You mean it?" he breathes, and I nod. "You—you love me?"

"Yes," I say. "I—I've been awful to you, too." He shakes his head as I speak.

"You've never been awful," he says. "You're incapable of being

329

anything other than perfect." I huff out a small laugh. "This means you're mine?"

"I'm yours," I say, looking up at him again. His shoulders fall, not in defeat, but in relief. His face softens, his entire body softens. *Almost* his entire body. "And you're mine."

"I'm all yours, love," he rasps. His eyes flick between mine, and I know there's more he wants to say. But he hesitates.

"What?" I ask, and a small smile curves his lips. He stays silent as he gets to his feet, then holds his hand out for me. I give him a worried look as I slide my hand into his.

"If you're mine," he says, moving to the chair in the back of the room. His jeans are flung haphazardly on it, and he grabs them. "Then you need to claim me." I blink at his back.

Claim him?

"Ezra," I say warily. "What are you talking about?" He turns around, a large pocket knife in his hand. He tilts it back and forth and I retreat a step. "Ez. What are you doing? Put the knife down." He shakes his head as he stalks forward.

"Claim me," he says. I press my back against the wall, and he cages me in. My breath is ragged, and my heart is racing.

"With that?" I use my chin to point at the knife he's holding out to me. He gives me a hard nod. "I'm not stabbing you." One side of his mouth curves in a grin.

"Not asking you to stab me," he says, laughing slightly. "Carve your name into me. Brand me. Make me yours."

"I—what?"

He takes a step back and shoves his boxers down, letting his hard cock free. I clamp my hand over my mouth, from shock, or amusement, or a weird mixture of both.

"What the fuck?" I say behind my hand. "Put your pants on!"

He ignores me as he sits on the edge of the bed, spreading his legs and planting his feet firmly on the floor. He opens the knife and slaps the blade against his palm a few times.

"Come here," he says, pointing at the space between his legs. I don't move. Of course, I'm not going to fucking move. He's sitting on my bed naked with a fucking knife! "You look terrified."

"You have a fucking *knife*," I hiss, throwing my hand at him. He shrugs. "I'm not cutting you."

"Yeah," he says, looking down at the blade. "You are." I let out a manic laugh, pressing my back harder against the wall.

"You're not cutting me," I say, and he grins.

"Maybe not tonight," he says, "but I will."

I drop my head against the wall, silently praying for strength.

"You really want me to carve my name into you?" I ask, looking at him again. He nods eagerly.

"Anyone can get married. Anyone can make promises. But this—" He waves his knife around. "This is truly forever. Tattoos can be removed, scars can't."

"You're insane," I breathe. "Truly fucking insane."

"I've never pretended to be anything else," he says, grinning wickedly. "Your name, right here." He pats the inside of his thigh, and I take a deep breath.

"You really want this?" I ask again, and he nods. I push off the wall, and walk toward him. My knees are shaky, and by the time I get to him, I collapse to the floor between his legs.

His cock stands up, resting against his lower stomach. I try not to look at it, but fuck, it's right in my face and leaking precum. He's *genuinely* excited for this.

He holds the knife out to me, handle first. I hesitate before grabbing it, our eyes locking.

"Your name," he says, rubbing his thigh again. "Make it deep."

My heart is in my throat as I spin the blade around, trying to figure out the best way to hold it to do this.

I can't fucking believe I'm doing this.

I let out a long breath as I press the tip of the blade against his thigh. He lets out a muted grunt, and I glance up at him, finding him with wild eyes.

"Do it," he breathes.

With a final breath, I drag the blade down. Blood immediately wells, then begins to drip down his thigh. Instincts kick in, and I press my hand against the wound.

"Oh my God. Oh my God!" I panic. "I can't believe I did that. Does it hurt?"

"No," he groans. He grips his cock in his fist, the head turning an angry shade of reddish purple. "Keep going." He pumps himself as I watch, mesmerized.

I pull my bloodied hand away and make the next cut. He groans and slams his fist down, gripping the base of his cock tighter. I quickly make the last slash in the **K** and let out a breath.

"Lick it," he grunts and I snap my head to him. "Taste me, Kens."

"No one said anything about licking your blood," I say. He swipes his finger through his blood and brings it to his mouth. I watch with a strange mix of curiosity, horror, and arousal as he sucks it off his finger, groaning at the taste.

My mouth waters. It's the first time in my life I've been truly worried about my mental state.

This can't be normal.

Then again, Kiwi isn't normal.

I hesitate as I move toward his leg. His eyes open, locking on mine as I trace the cuts with the tip of my tongue.

"Fuck," he groans, drawing the word out. "Suck on it." I wrap my mouth around the cut and flick my tongue over it before sucking gently. His arm holding him up goes weak, and he nearly falls back on the bed. "Fuck. *Fuck.*"

The warm coppery tang fills my mouth, and surprisingly, it's not unpleasant. It's not as gross as I thought it would be. It's not great either. Tolerable.

I pull my mouth away, breathing heavy. It's still bleeding, and the sight of the crimson contrasting his pale inner thigh is turning me on more than anything else ever has.

Fuck.

I need to go to therapy.

"Keep going," he growls.

I don't waste anymore time as I drag the blade across his skin.

I make it to the final **E** before I stop. Blood is flowing freely from his thigh, and he's pumping his fist harder over his cock. His thighs are trembling, and I know he's about to come. I glance up at him.

"I can stop here," I say, and he shakes his head.

"I'm so fucking close," he groans. "Keep going." He rests his hand on the back of my head, and I continue spelling my name. It's a few inches long, and smeared with sweat and blood, but there it is. My name is carved into his flesh forever. "Suck my cock." He grips my hair in his fist and pulls my face toward him.

My mouth opens as he bucks his hips, shoving into my throat. I gag around him and rest my hands on his thighs, but he doesn't stop. He thrusts into my mouth with feral abandon.

"Fuck," he groans as he slides his other hand into my hair. He grips my hair in both hands, holding my head still as he fucks my mouth with brutal thrusts. "Fucking slut."

I moan around him, and he groans again.

"I can't believe you like being called my slut," he says, almost to himself. I drop my hand from him and slide it between my legs. My hips roll against my fingers as I find my clit through my panties. "Fuck, that's it. Play with that cunt."

My eyes lift to his. Veins pop from his neck as he stares down at me, his hands tightening in my hair. I keep my gaze on him as he uses my mouth the way he wants, spitting degrading names at me the entire time. It heightens my orgasm, and when I come, I cry out around him.

"I'm coming," he grunts. "Down your throat." I suck on him, and he slams his hips up a final time before stopping. "Take it all. That's it. Swallow. Good girl." He wraps his hand around my throat to feel me swallow his cum. He pumps into my mouth a few more times, then drops his hands away.

I suck in a huge breath. He stares down at the bloody mess on his thigh, then lightly runs his fingers over it.

"Now I'll have you with me wherever I go forever," he mutters. Once my breathing turns normal, I press a gentle kiss to his knee. He glances at me, that same dark excitement still lighting his eyes. "Your turn."

"Ez," I say, shaking my head.

"To come," he says, grinning wickedly. "Or—" He picks the knife up in question. I stare at it, then drop my eyes to my name.

"Fine," I say, and his smile broadens.

"That's my girl." Warmth spreads through my body at the words. He holds his hand out and helps me stand. His gaze scorches me as I undress, his eyes lingering on my breasts, then dropping to my pussy. Without warning, he reaches out and cups me. "So wet. What was it? Carving me up, or sucking my cock?"

His finger easily slides inside me, and he pumps it a few times. I grip his forearm as he presses a second finger inside. My head drops back as he finger fucks me.

"Mmm," he groans as he drops his mouth to my neck. His teeth dig into my skin before he sucks, hard. I know I'll have a giant mark there in the morning, but at the moment, I don't care. "Lay down."

I lay on the edge of the bed, and Déjà vu comes rushing back to me when he towers above me. I think he's thinking the same thing, because he pauses and just stares at me. He dips and presses his mouth to mine, sliding his tongue against mine roughly before he pulls away.

"Legs nice and wide," he says as he kneels. "It'll hurt, but don't pull away. Understand? If it's too much, tell me to stop." I nod and hold my breath as he holds the knife against my thigh. He pauses and looks up at me. "Which name do you want?"

"What?"

"Ezra or Kiwi?" He looks like he's afraid to hear the answer. I rest my hand over his, squeezing gently.

"Ezra," I whisper. His jaw clenches, then he nods and looks down at my thigh again.

"Rub your clit while I do this," he says. "I can't do both." He flashes me a grin and watches as I slide my hand over my body. When my fingers connect to my clit, he makes the first slice.

I'm thankful his name is shorter than mine.

I clutch the blanket in my fist as he carves his name. My fingers move faster, and at some point, the pleasure overrides the pain, and my back arches.

"Quiet," he hisses, gently slapping my thigh. "You're going to wake the whole neighborhood."

"It hurts," I groan. "Oh, fuck." My back arches until my shoulders and head lift off the bed. I convulse as I come, my entire body tensing and shaking.

I rub my fingers faster, drawing out all the pleasure I can. Suddenly, he shoves my hand out of the way, and his mouth connects with my pussy. He draws my orgasm out with his mouth, flicking his tongue against my sensitive clit until I fall back to the bed. He slides his tongue inside me, and I rest my hand against his head. I almost push him away. It's almost too much. But fuck, it feels so good. Everything feels heightened.

Finally, he pulls away. My eyes open and I stare up at the ceiling, trying to catch my breath.

"Look," he says. I lift my head and stare down at the sharp, bloody letters.

EZRA

He's marked me, in more ways than one.

Tears fill my eyes, and I don't fully understand why. All I know is that he's mine, truly mine now.

"I love it," I whisper, and lift my eyes to him. "I love you."

He drapes his body over mine, gently pushing my hair from my forehead, and kisses me deeply. He grinds his hard cock against my hip and I grin against his mouth.

"Insatiable," he says. He pulls away to look at me, his eyes softer than I've ever seen. "Mine."

"Yours," I breathe.

Kiwi

"**S**tay here," I say, giving Kennedy and the boys a firm look. "This shouldn't take long."

"We'll be right here," Kennedy says, sounding exasperated. She glances at Ian, her eyes still holding that same haunted look they've had since she saw him bloody on his bed.

"Keep them in line," I say to Ian. He blinks at me, then straightens his spine.

"Me?" He presses his hand to his chest as he looks between his mother and Enzo.

"You're the only responsible one in the family, kid," I say.

"I resent that." Kennedy folds her arms over her chest as she glares at me. I grin and press a wet kiss to her cheek, making her groan.

A piercing scream echoes through the clubhouse common room, and Ian winces. I spin in time to see Skye running toward us, an electric car and the remote in her hands.

"Ian! Look!" She waves it around when she gets to our group. "I told you I'd bring my car to show you." She takes in a huge breath, but her smile falls when she notices Ian's cuts and bruises on his face.

336

"You're hurt." She presses her little fingers against her cheek, her smile disappearing completely.

"He's alright," I say, but she doesn't look at me. "You're alright, aren't you?" I glance at him, and nearly laugh. I've never seen anyone more terrified.

"Daddy!" Skye screeches. "Daddy, Daddy, Daddy!" She whirls around, forgetting about her toy car as she rushes back across the floor to the door. It swings open, and Axel comes in, his hair windblown and wild.

"What? What's wrong?" He frantically looks around, and I snort a laugh. He always looks on the brink of a heart attack.

"Ian's hurt!" She points an accusatory finger his way, and I step back.

"I'll let you deal with this," I mutter in Kennedy's ear. She grins before nudging me away with her elbow.

"Hurry," she whispers. "Our reservation is in an hour." I salute her, and she flips me off.

"Not in front of my kid," Axel groans, scrubbing his hand over his face. Koda laughs at his side, covering her mouth with her hand.

"Come on, you big fuck." I clap him on the shoulder, and he closes his eyes as he takes a deep breath. "Time for Church."

"I have bandaids," Skye says, and Axel lets out another breath.

"He doesn't need bandaids, Skye-Girl," Koda says softly. I direct Axel away from the group and toward the Chapel door.

"I feel your pain," I say, and he slides his eyes toward me. "You know, since I'm a dad now, too." I throw my thumb over my shoulder. "Kids, am I right?" He blinks at me, then shakes his head.

"Yeah," he breathes as he pulls the door open. He pauses, pulling my arm until I stop. I stare up at him, confused. "So, it's real then? They're yours?" I nod, and can't help the wide smile that spreads across my face.

"All mine," I say proudly. Axel smirks as he claps my shoulder.

"Congrats, man. I mean it."

I stay smiling as I find my seat, ignoring everyone's shocked expressions. Ryder and Gage, one of the Nomads, exchange a look. August, another Nomad, sinks on to the chair beside me.

"Did you just get laid or something?" he asks, leaning toward me. "I'd be smiling if I got to sleep with that girl, too." My smile falls and I snap my head toward him.

"Maybe don't say that about his girl," Axel says from the other end of the table. August blinks a few times and looks around, confused. Finally, he meets my eye again, and whatever he sees makes him blanch.

"Shit. My bad," he says, holding his hands up. "Didn't mean it like that. I just meant, if I had a girl—"

"Stop talking, Auggie," Ryder says, his voice a deep rumble. August clamps his mouth shut and turns his attention toward Bash, but keeps one eye on me.

A part of me is proud I didn't just bash his face into the table, but another part of me thinks I'm going soft. But that's what happens when you have a family, right? You're not as bloodthirsty as before.

My smile returns as I focus on Bash. Everyone looks uncomfortable, which I don't totally understand. I'm not a grumpy asshole like the rest of them. I always smile.

"Taz said he needs our help," Bash says, drawing my attention. "We're going to head to LA in a few days." I glance around, my smile gone again.

"I can't leave Kens and the boys," I say. Everyone exchanges a look, and it pisses me off this time. "Bash, we all have families. We can't just leave."

"Yeah," he says, resting his arms on the table as he leans forward. "We can. And we are. This is what we signed up for when we got patched in. The club and our Brother's come first. Taz needs us, and we'll be there."

"But—"

"The girls will still be here," he says, cutting his eyes to me. "Addie and Heather will keep them safe."

"Judging by how that kid beat his friend's old man, I think he can hold his own," Ryder says.

"You're fine leaving Madi and Izzy?" I ask, and he takes a deep breath.

"It's not ideal," he admits, glancing at Bash. "But we follow our Prez. That's how it is."

"But—"

"Kiwi," Bash snaps. "Drop it. We're going to L.A. in a few days. End of discussion."

I cross my arms over my chest and slouch back in my chair. I don't want to leave them. Every time I'm not around, something happens and I can't keep letting them down. Twice is two too many times, but three times? That's unforgivable. That's punishable by death.

"We can leave our families here at the clubhouse," Bash sighs. "If that'll make everyone feel better, we can leave them here. We know it's secure and I'll leave a few of the Brother's behind to guard them." He looks around the table at everyone.

"Yeah, let's do that," Axel says, glancing at me. "It's better than them being home without us."

It's a compromise. Not one I love, but it'll have to do.

Now, trying to convince Kennedy and the boys to stay here. That'll be a different challenge.

Bash gives us another moment to argue, but when no one does, he nods and bangs his fist on the table, finalizing the decision.

"Cyrus left this morning," Reid says, and Bash nods. "He's taking Ava home." Ava was one of the girls we saved when we got Madi back. And I feel fucking awful she'll be stuck with grumpy-ass Cyrus. He's a Nomad, and while the others like their solitude, that fucker takes it to another level.

"What's going on with Taz?" I ask. Bash scrubs his hand over his face and leans back in his chair.

"He's really fucking close to finishing this bullshit. He said he thinks he found the place where the girls are being held. He just needs help getting them out."

We all look at each other, a strange mix of relief and dread coiling in my stomach. We've been working at ending this for months—we've lived and breathed this, and now we're so close to finishing, I can taste it.

What happens when it's all done? Where do I go from there?

Bash's words grate on me, too similar to Kennedy's for it to be a coincidence. I can't ignore it when a sign like that is blaring at me.

"This is what we signed up for when we got patched in. The club and our Brother's come first."

"The club comes first," she said. *"It'll always come first."*

THAT NIGHT, their words still haunt me. I stare up at the dark ceiling, my fingers absently tapping on my stomach.

Do I leave the club, or do I stay? Which comes first? My family, or my other family?

"Ez," Kennedy says, her voice low.

I never thought I'd understand women when they said their parental instincts just kicked in one day, but today, I felt whatever that thing is inside me shift. Kennedy was chasing Skye, playing with her, making her laugh, and it was beautiful. Ian's my son in all the ways that matter, but it wasn't until I saw Kennedy sweep Skye into her arms that I realized I wanted another one. I want one that shares my blood. I don't want to wait anymore. I want one now.

But can I do that? Can I ask Kennedy to give me a child when I'm still so tied to the club?

She rolls on top of me, straddling my hips as she stares down at me. "I was talking to you, and you weren't listening," she says.

"Sorry, love," I mutter, and rest my hands on her hips. "What's wrong?"

"I'm fine," she says, resting her hands on my stomach. "What's wrong with you? You've been in a weird mood all night." I push her hips back, then drag them forward, letting the warm, firm press of her cunt against my soft cock stir it to life.

"I just had some stuff on my mind," I say, lifting my hips. "Nothing for you to worry about." She slides her shirt off over her head and tosses it to the floor. I slide my hands up the length of her body to cup her breasts.

"It's my job to worry," she sighs, rocking her hips. "Talk to me." I slide my hand down and rest it on her stomach. She pauses, her eyes dropping to my hand.

"I want one," I whisper. "I want a baby with you. Right now." She rests her hand over mine, our fingers twining together.

"Me too," she says. My eyes snap to hers, but she's still staring at our hands on her stomach. "Maybe when we have a bigger place."

"And you have my last name," I add. "When both of you do." Finally, she looks at me. Her lips tip up in a small smile.

"Alright," she says softly. "We'll talk about it again soon." I nod, but don't tell her I'm ready now. I want to get her pregnant tonight. My throat is tight as she leans forward to press her lips against mine. I press my lips harder against hers, feeling tears pool in the corners of my eyes. When she pulls away, her smile falls and her eyes widen. "What's wrong?"

She pushes my hair away from my face, then gently strokes her fingers down my cheek to my jaw. Her touch brings me comfort, and I lean into it.

"I'm going to leave the club once we're done with this shit," I manage to choke out. She stares down at me in shock.

"What?"

"I can't let anything come before you or Ian," I rasp. "Or this baby when we have it." My fingers flex on her stomach, and her hand tightens around mine.

"You can't leave," she says. "You—you love it. It's who you are."

"You've wanted me to leave since we first met," I say, and she shakes her head.

341

"I was wrong." I flick my eyes between hers. "I think it's need-lessly dangerous, but if you left, you wouldn't be you anymore. I fell in love with you, Ez. I fell in love with Kiwi. If you leave, you're leaving him behind and I'm selfish and want all of you. They're your family. You'll be miserable working a regular job, and you'll hate not seeing them all the time. You need them as much as they need you." Her words are frantic as she speaks, and it stabs me in the gut.

"Bash said the club and Brother's come first," I say, and she nods.

"I knew what I was signing up for when I got involved with you," she says. "I don't want you to give up a part of yourself for me. You'll resent me for it one day."

"That's impossible," I scoff. "That would never happen." She rests her fingers against my lips as she nods.

"It could, and it will if you leave. If you want to leave because it's something *you* want, then I'll support you." Her eyes search mine, willing me to understand and agree with her. "But if you're leaving for me—" She shakes her head. "Don't leave for me, Ez."

I stare up at her, my mind and heart warring.

I know the club will always have to be my top priority. I've never thought about it before, but now that I have people relying on me, a family relying on me, can I really put anything before them?

"It doesn't have to be all or nothing," she says. "The club welcomed Ian and me with open arms. They welcomed Enzo, too. I was worried someone would say something about their relationship, but everyone has been great." She takes a deep breath. "I want to be in your family too, Ez."

"You want to be a part of The Brotherhood?" I ask quietly, and she nods.

"Addie told me a bit about it today." She shrugs a shoulder as she drops her eyes. "I can help. I can't fight or shoot or do anything Addie and Heather can. But I can bartend for the club. I can help with the kids. I can clean. I can—"

"You're not doing any of that," I say, cupping her face. She lifts her eyes to mine. "But you'd really do that for me?" She nods, her eyes filling with tears. "You know," I smile at her, "everything you just described sounded an awful lot like being my Old Lady." She rolls her eyes, but she can't hide the smile on her face. "Is that what you want?"

She sucks her bottom lip between her teeth as she searches my eyes. A few moments pass, and I'm not sure either of us are breathing. This feels big—bigger than us carving our names into each other. This feels bigger than a wedding. This feels like *the* moment.

"Yes," she finally breathes. "I want that." I beam up at her, and my heart feels so warm and heavy, it feels like it'll overflow. "I just want you."

"I want you, too," I say, stroking her cheek with my thumb. She leans into me, her eyes closing as if she's soaking in my touch. "If it becomes too much, I'll leave. The club is important, but I can't let it take you and the boys from me. So one word, and I'm gone."

"I love you," she whispers, lowering her mouth to mine again.

"I love you."

Her hand slides between us and under the waistband of my boxers. Everything is gentle and languid, something neither of us have had with each other. When I'm achingly hard, she pulls my boxers down just enough for my cock to come free.

She tugs her panties to the side and slowly lowers herself, breathing deeply as I impale her. Her pussy squeezes me, massaging my cock as she slowly rides me. Our lips never break, even when her body trembles as she barrels closer to her release.

She whimpers into my mouth, her body tensing as she comes. I hold and kiss her through it, groaning at the tight feel of her around me. Finally, her body relaxes and I roll her onto her back, never letting my cock slide from her.

I hook her leg around my waist as I stroke my cock with her pussy. She rests her hands on the headboard, letting me slam into her harder. Her back arches deeply, and I lower my mouth to her nipple. I play with the piercing until she cries out.

Another orgasm shoots through her, and I press all the way inside her as I groan into her mouth. I fill her up with my cum, silently hoping she gets pregnant this time. I thrust a few more times, pushing my cum deeper.

Our breathing is ragged as we kiss, our bodies still tight with our releases. It wasn't enough. It'll never be enough.

I slip from her and roll onto my side, facing her. She nestles into me, my arms tight around her. I listen to her breathing until it evens out, then kiss the top of her head.

When I met her months ago, I never thought she'd want me back. I thought she would be the woman I'd have to chase for the rest of my life. But here we are, tangled together with our boys in the other room.

My family.

Epilogue
Kennedy

One Year Later

Amy Winehouse blares through the speakers Ezra installed throughout the house when we first moved in. It's my favorite thing, even if I won't tell him. Having music follow me from room to room has been the best thing.

After everything, Ezra kept his promise and found us a bigger place to live. Each of the boys have their own rooms, which I couldn't be happier about. Ez and I have the entire upstairs to ourselves, and the boys, Ez included, have shifted the basement into some kind of game room.

I'd be lying if I said I didn't spend most of my time down there with them.

I'm not working at the café or bar anymore. Since Ian and Enzo are doing online classes and on track to graduate early, I've been working at one of the Salvatore's garages. When Bash learned I had a good memory and was decent with numbers, he hired me almost immediately.

Is it a dream job? Well, no. But it's better than working two jobs and never sleeping. I was running myself into the ground and it wasn't until Ez came into my life that I really realized it, or even really cared.

I groan as I stoop to grab a sock off the floor. Living with three guys has its downfalls—like them never picking up after themselves. Seriously, what is it with guys?

The music suddenly shuts off and I glance up at the ceiling, like looking at one of the speakers will magically make the music turn back on.

"Love, I'm home!"

I can't stop the stupid smile that spreads across my face at his voice. I poke my head from the bathroom as he rounds the corner. When our eyes meet, he smiles brightly.

"How's my favorite girl?" he asks as he walks toward me, his arms outstretched.

"She's good." I pat my growing belly before he wraps me in a tight hug.

"I meant you," he laughs against my hair. "How are you, mama?"

I shrug and he pulls away. I let out a small, whiny groan.

"I've been craving carrots and mustard all day," I say, and he grimaces.

"Mustard is so fucking gross," he breathes as he runs his hand through his hair. "I brought you some more."

"I knew there was a reason I loved you." I pat his chest and step around him. He catches my wrist, and I look back, finding him with his brow raised. "Among another million reasons."

He huffs out a breath before kissing the back of my hand. We walk hand in hand to the kitchen, and when I see the table, I pause. My eyes slide to him, but his face is blank.

"I know I said I'd give you my last name first, but she had other plans," he says, resting his hand on my swollen stomach.

"You're not proposing to me like this, Ezra." I throw my hand at the ring box sitting on the table.

"You seriously want me down on a knee and all that shit?" he says, and I blink at him. His shoulders stiffen at whatever he sees on my face, his throat bobbing as he swallows exaggeratedly. "Okay, fine. I'll get down—"

"Not now!" I say as he begins to kneel. He stares back at me. "Do it another way, without me having to tell you to kneel. Make it more romantic than just putting the box on the table. Ezra, come on."

My chin wobbles and he immediately wraps his arms around me. He peppers my face with kisses until I laugh and shove him away. If I wasn't pregnant, this would've been a fine proposal. I honestly don't care. But hormones have me all fucked up.

Hormones and the romance books Arden has been lending me. They've raised my standards too fucking high.

"Okay, I'll do it tomorrow," he says, and I roll my eyes.

"You're not supposed to tell me—whatever." I wave my hand at him and move toward the fridge. Yanking it open, I grab my carrots and mustard and turn back around.

He's kneeling, the box in his hand.

"Like this?" he asks. My hands shake as I drop the food on the counter and stare at him.

"I didn't mean now," I choke out.

"I know," he says. "But I'm impatient and can't wait." He takes a deep breath, his eyes flicking between mine, and opens his mouth. He hesitates, like he's trying to find the right words.

I shuffle a step closer to him, reaching my hand out. He grabs it, kissing my knuckles again.

"Mom!" Ian walks into the kitchen and abruptly stops. Enzo runs into his back and nearly falls to the floor. "What's going on?"

"No way!" Enzo rounds Ian to peer over Ezra's shoulder. "That's the ring?" He smacks his shoulder. "I told you to get the other one."

"You knew?" I ask, and he nods.

"We both did," he says, using his thumb to point at Ian. We stare at each other over Ezra's head. Red blooms on his cheeks as he rubs the back of his neck.

We're a long way away from that shitty little apartment. I think the same thought passes through his head, because he drops his hand and gives me a lopsided smile that says it all.

"Did you say yes?" he asks, jerking his chin at Ezra.

"I didn't get to ask yet," he grumbles.

"If you would've done it like this in the first place, you would've already asked," I say, and he rolls his eyes.

"Can I just do this?" he asks, looking at the boys over his shoulder.

"We're staying for this," Enzo says, leaning against the wall. I fold my lips between my teeth when Ezra looks back at me, looking grumpy as shit.

"Kens," he says, and I grin.

"Come on," Enzo groans as he pushes off the wall. "At least use her full name."

"Don't you have *anywhere* else to be?" Ezra snaps, and I barely bite back a laugh. Ian and I glance at each other again.

We had no idea Ezra and Enzo were so much alike until things settled down and we moved into this place. After Enzo began to feel safe here, the real him began to shine through. He's still recovering from everything he's been through, but he's good. He'll be good.

"Come on." Ian taps his chest and jerks his head over his shoulder.

"Don't you want to make sure his proposal is good enough for your mom?" he asks, and Ian slides his eyes to me. I huff out a quiet laugh and drop Ezra's hand.

Grabbing my carrots and mustard, I walk around them. "Try again tomorrow," I call over my shoulder. Ezra groans as he gets to his feet, his knees popping. "Maybe when the boys are busy with school."

I laugh as I plop on the couch. Rasputin jumps onto the couch and curls beside me, breathing hard. He stares at me until I give him a piece of carrot, then he jumps down and takes off down the hall.

Listening to the boys talk and laugh in the kitchen makes a smile spread across my face as I eat my weird pregnancy craving. Ezra sits beside me, his shoulders slumped.

"Yes," I whisper. He glances at me, the box still clutched in his hand. "I'll marry you, Ez."

When he gives me that slow grin of his, all I see is Kiwi. All I see is Ezra.

All I see is my future, and the love of my life.

THE END

About Haley Tyler

Haley Tyler is a dark romance author who writes your favorite book boyfriends.

She lives in Texas with her boyfriend of seven years and their dog, Maverick.

When she's not writing, you can find her reading a romance novel, scrolling TikTok, listening to her obnoxiously long playlists, or obsessing over her next book.

www.haleytyler.com
Facebook Reader Group

Also By Haley Tyler

The Salvatore Brotherhood MC Series

Killing Calm

Little Bear

Lost and Found

Safe House

Man Possessed

A Salvatore Brotherhood MC Short Story

At First Sight

Say I Do

Just One Night

Standalone

Queen of Demons

Secret Santa

The Reapers

Calling on the Reaper

Kindle Vella

Never Have I Ever

Coming Soon

For the Love of Villains Anthology

Made in the USA
Las Vegas, NV
16 March 2023

69192158R00215